TRIUMPH IN EXILE

TRIUMPH IN EXILE

by

Victoria D. Schmidt

To Lois,
A sister Douglass Alumna

Victoria

Victoria D. Schmidt
January 21, 2005

Chaucer Press

New York

TRIUMPH IN EXILE. Copyright© 2002 by Victoria D. Schmidt. All rights reserved. For information, contact the publisher, Richard Altschuler & Associates, Inc. at 100 West 57th Street, New York, NY 10019.

The author can be reached at Tel: 703-753-2933 or at OttoMisti@AOL.com.

Library of Congress Control Number: 2002109260

ISBN 1-884092-05-5

Chaucer Press is an imprint of Richard Altschuler & Associates, Inc.

Cover Design: Josh Garfield
Distributed by Syracuse University Press

Printed in the United States of America
First printing: November 2002
Second Printing: December 2003

Dedication

To my husband Ralph, my daughter Lisa and
my son-in-law Wayne Rooks

*When we resist our passions it is more on account of their
weakness than our strength.*
François, Duc de la Rochefoucauld

Acknowledgments

T here are many to whom I owe appreciation and gratitude for helping me turn a dream into a reality . . . the publication *Triumph in Exile*. I regret I can include only a few of a long list who deserve to be recognized.

First, I acknowledge Janet Henry, my high school Latin teacher, who introduced me to the joys of languages and the mysteries of foreign cultures. My French professor, Madame Alice W. de Visme at Douglass College, opened wide the gates of France and inspired me to pursue the philosophy and writings of Germaine de Staël. I am thrilled that I can make known the powerful influence they have had on my life and work.

The writers about this brilliant woman and her contemporaries as well as Germaine de Staël herself, a prolific writer in her own right, have provided invaluable data about her and the people who touched her life. The major, singular resource to which I am indebted is Christopher Herrold's *Mistress to an Age*.

Many have been generous in time spent discussing Madame de Staël with me. Her descendants . . . the Comtesses Hélène d'Andlau and Jean de Pange . . .both were gracious offering information and encouragement. This has also been true of the members of the Société Staëlienne, particularly its late president, Simone Balayé, and Madelyn Gutwirth, a founder of the United States Chapter of the Société, who read the final draft and rendered her appraisal.

In the early stages of my manuscript, Jerry Krupnick, a competent writer and meticulous editor, saw me through my first draft and gave me the confidence to go on.

As my manuscript neared publication, a filmmaker, Jane Altschuler, who has become a dear friend over the years as we shared our admiration for Madame de Staël, offered much of herself as she reviewed and commented on my penultimate draft. She has written a film script that may soon be produced based on my version of our idol's life. Nor can I neglect Jane's husband Richard, my helpful, patient publisher.

Then, my friend, Bob Snitzer. Without his computer skills my manuscript would not have reached Richard.

I am especially grateful to my husband Ralph, who supported my efforts and encouraged me to continue. He wanted to assure that, for me, *Triumph in Exile* would be published. And my daughter Lisa, now a grown young woman, who reminds me of the nights when she was a child that I would kiss her goodnight to work on my manuscript about the woman who challenged Napoleon.

I owe them all a great debt.

Table of Contents

List of Illustrations

Chronology

1766 Anne Louise Germaine Necker is born to Jacques and Suzanne Curchod Necker in Paris on April 22.

1769 Napoleon Bonaparte is born, second son of Carlo and Letizia Ramoline Bonaparte in Corsica on August 15.

1777 Jacques Necker is appointed Minister of Finance to Louis XVI.

1778 Joseph and Napoleon Bonaparte enroll at the college d'Autun in France. Napoleon enters the Brienne Military Academy.

1781 Necker is dismissed as Minister of Finance.

1783 Germaine accompanies her parents to Switzerland. She rejects their plans for her marriage to William Pitt.

1784 Napoleon attends the Royal Military School in Paris. Necker buys the barony and Chateau de Coppet in Switzerland.

1785 Napoleon is made second lieutenant in the artillery in the regiment of La Fère and is garrisoned in Valence.

1786 Germaine Necker is married in Paris to Baron Eric Magnus de Staël-Holstein, Ambassador to France and is presented at court. As Baroness de Staël she establishes her salon.

1787 Necker is exiled. Germaine gives birth to her first child, Gustavine. She publishes *Jane Grey* and *Sophie.*

1788 Necker is reappointed to his Finance post. Madame de Staël begins her liaison with Louis, Count de Narbonne-Lara.

1789 Gustavine de Staël dies. Madame de Staël attends the convening exercises of the Estates General at Versailles. Necker is dismissed and immediately reinstated Director General of Finance. The fall of the Bastille on July 14. Madame de Staël is with her parents at Versailles when rioters force their way into the palace.

1790 Madame de Staël gives birth to her first son, Auguste. Necker resigns and returns to Coppet. Madame de Staël visits her parents at Coppet.

1791 She reopens her salon in Paris, a meeting place for moderates. With her assistance, Narbonne is named Minister of war.

1792 Narbonne is dismissed. The downfall of the monarchy. Madame de
Staël escapes to Coppet. Her second son Albert is born.

1793 Louis XVI is guillotined on January 21. The Reign of Terror begins.
Madame de Staël departs for England where she harbors émigré friends.
Narbonne begins to lose interest in her. She returns to Coppet and
takes up residence in nearby Nyon.
Napoleon, who has returned to Corsica, has a falling out with
political leader Paoli. He is forced to escape to Toulon where he is
named Brigadier General and gains prominence in his defeat of the British.

1794 Madame Necker dies.
The fall and execution of Robespierre and the end of the Reign of Terror.
Madame de Staël meets Benjamin Constant. She publishes *Zulma.*

1795 Constant and Madame de Staël commence a long political and
intimate relationship. They return to Paris together. She moves
in, again, with her husband who has been reappointed Ambassador,
and reopens her salon. At the end of the year, the Directory that now
rules France exiles her. She moves to Switzerland with Constant.
Bonaparte is named Commander-in-Chief of the Army of the Interior.

1796 Madame de Staël publishes *De l'influence des passions.* In
defiance of her exile she moves to France with Constant.
Napoleon marries Josephine. He is named Commander-in-Chief
of the Army in Italy where he wins several battles.

1797 Madame de Staël returns once more to Paris as Ambassadress
and gives birth to her daughter Albertine. She meets Bonaparte
for the first time.

1798 Bonaparte departs for Egypt where he has many successes but the
French fleet is destroyed by Lord Nelson of England.
Madame de Staël meets Juliette Récamier.

1799 Madame de Staël returns to Coppet.
Bonaparte leaves Egypt for Paris. With the coup d'état of 18 Brumaire
he is named one of three Consuls.
Madame de Staël journeys to Paris.
By year's end Bonaparte names himself First Consul. He appoints
Constant to the Tribunate.

1800 Bonaparte leaves for Italy via the St. Bernard Pass and is victorious
at Marengo. When he returns to Paris at the end of the year an
unsuccessful assassination attempt is made on his life in rue St. Nicaise.
Madame de Staël publishes *De la littérature.*

1801 She obtains a legal separation from the Baron de Staël

1802 Bonaparte expels Constant and nineteen others from the Tribunate.
Baron de Staël dies. Madame de Staël publishes *Delphine.*
The Treaty of Amiens is signed with the British. Bonaparte becomes
First Consul for life.

1803 The war with England resumes.
Bonaparte exiles Madame de Staël from France. She departs for Germany.

1804 Madame de Staël visits Weimar and Berlin. She employs August Wilhelm Schlegel as advisor on German culture and as tutor for her children.
Bonaparte orders the execution of Duc d'Enghien.
Jacques Necker dies.
Napoleon is declared Emperor of France.
Madame de Staël returns to Coppet, then she visits Italy.
Benjamin Constant renews a liaison with Charlotte de Hardenberg whom he knew years earlier.

1805 Madame de Staël continues her travels in Italy through the middle of June when she returns to Coppet. Her salon becomes the intellectual center of Europe. She turns down Constant's proposal of marriage and begins a relationship with Prosper Barante who is her intermediary with Napoleon.
Bonaparte is crowned King of Italy. Lord Nelson overwhelms the French fleet at Trafalgar. The Emperor is victorious over the Austrians and Russians at Austerlitz.

1806 Madame de Staël sojourns at Auxerre, Rouen and Meulen. Constant's affection for Charlotte de Hardenberg continues.
Bonaparte is victorious at Jena and Auerstadt and enters Berlin.

1807 Bonaparte exiles Madame de Staël to Coppet. She leaves for Vienna. Her novel *Corinne* is published.
The Treaty of Tilsit is signed after Napoleon meets with Alexander I. Bonaparte abolishes the Tribunate. Auguste de Staël, now eighteen, is unsuccessful in a meeting with Bonaparte in his request for permission for his mother to return to Paris.

1808 Madame de Staël meets with Baron Friederich Gentz in Toeplitz. She visits Dresden, Weimar and Munich then returns to Coppet where she begins her treatise, *De l'Allemagne*. Constant secretly marries Charlotte de Hardenberg.
Napoleon is victorious in Spain and names his brother Joseph, King.

1809 Napoleon has victories at Eckmül, Essing, and Wagram. The treaty of Shönbrunn follows. He meets with Alexander I at Erfurt.
His marriage to Josephine is dissolved by the Senate.
Madame de Staël resides at Coppet.

1810 Bonaparte marries Marie-Louise of Austria. Rome and Holland are annexed to France. Bernadotte is elected Crown Prince of Sweden.
Madame de Staël resides at Chaumont in France and finalizes her manuscript of *De l'Allemagne*. She moves to Fossé. Bonaparte has her manuscript and all printed copies seized and destroyed. She manages to escape to Coppet with three copies. In Geneva she meets John Rocca who falls in love with her.

1811 Madame de Staël commences a liaison with Rocca. Juliette Récamier visits her in Coppet and is also exiled from France as a result. Bonaparte's son, Napoleon-François, Herzog von Reichstadt, Napoleon II, King of Rome, is born.

1812 Napoleon mobilizes his troops in Poland, declares war on Russia and launches his march toward Moscow. Madame de Staël gives birth in secret to her third son, Louis Alphonse Rocca. Leaving her newborn with a pastor, she clandestinely leaves Coppet for England traveling via Russia at the request of Alexander I. She confers with the Czar then departs Moscow for St. Petersburg. Bonaparte is victorious at Borodino and advances toward the city. He enters Moscow as Madame de Staël reaches Abo to embark for Stockholm. She arrives in the Swedish capital and confers with Bernadotte, now Crown Prince Jean-Charles. Napoleon retreats from Moscow. He abandons his troops and returns to Paris.

1813 Madame de Staël reaches London and is acclaimed for her contributions in the war against Napoleon. Her son Albert is killed in a duel. She publishes *De l'Allemagne* and *Réflections sur le suicide* in London.

1814 France is invaded by the Allies. Napoleon abdicates. Madame de Staël returns to Paris and reopens her salon, which again is the meeting place of heads of state, ministers and generals. She spends the summer at Coppet and continues entertaining.

1815 In March, Bonaparte escapes from Elba. She condemns Constant for supporting Bonaparte. In September, after the One Hundred Days and Napoleon's defeat at Waterloo, she reluctantly supports the Bourbon Restoration. Bonaparte is exiled to the island of St. Helena.

1816 Madame de Staël spends the Spring in Italy caring for John Rocca who is very ill. Daughter Albertine marries Victor the Duke of Broglie in Italy. Madame de Staël secretly weds John Rocca. She returns to Paris and reopens her salon. Often too weak to carry on, she calls on Albertine to be hostess.

1817 At the age of 51, after a cerebral stroke Madame de Staël dies in Paris. on July 14, the anniversary of the storming of the Bastille.

1818 John Rocca dies. Madame de Staël's book, *Considerations of the French Revolution* is published.

1821 Napoleon dies, also at the age of 51. Madame de Staël's book, *Dix années d'exil,* and her *Complete Works,* a stunning collection of a prolific writer, are published.

Introduction

Two hundred years ago, a megalomaniac scourged the continent of Europe taking more lives and laying waste to more villages, towns and cities than the terrorists of the twenty-first century.

The man was Napoleon Bonaparte.

Triumph in Exile is about the extraordinary woman who challenged the Corsican despot. The book is based on facts of history . . . a fictional interpretation of her life and Napoleon's powerful, inexplicable obsession for her. He hounded her, he directed his minions to stalk her and he exiled her from France. The only explanation for his implausible fixation, that I perceive, is that he feared her.

The woman was the Baroness Germaine Necker de Staël Holstein who was born to wealth and position in 1766 when France was wallowing in extravagant decadence. She evolved into a redoubtable political figure during the bloody, turbulent years of the French Revolution. Its famous tyrants and noble leaders . . . Tallien, Talleyrand, Siéyès, Robespierre, Lafayette and others . . . were among her friends, lovers, enemies, mentors and models. She was a best-selling author and an ideologue who contributed largely to the rise of Napoleon. Early in his reign, she recognized his ruthless lust for power and dared to criticize his autocratic methods and his insatiable appetite for war.

During their ensuing clash, which lasted more than ten years, her opposition earned her the label, "Conscience of Europe." While Bonaparte ruled as Emperor, she was called Empress. Her influence, which contributed to his downfall, gave credence to the banter in the courts that the "Three Great Powers of Europe are Russia, England and Madame de Staël."

Today, she is extolled by literati and historians. There is a group of ardent admirers, the Société Staëlienne, an international cult of about three hundred men and women, most of them scholars, who are so well informed about the Baroness de Staël that they are unchallengeable on all facets of her philosophy and her works.

The members meet regularly to review and savor every detail, every nuance in the life of their idol. They deliver esoteric papers and publish an erudite quarterly on her letters, essays and books. They gather at the chateaux where she lived, tread the paths she trod. Often, a devotee claims to be the reincarnation of one of her lovers or another in her intimate circle or even the Lady of Coppet herself.

I cannot disdain these savants. During my research, I, too, experienced strange sensations when confronted with eerie coincidences that linked their lives and hers with events in mine.

Yet, Madame de Staël is more obscure than lesser notables in history. She is no longer read, unlike Jane Austen, who lived during the same period, or George Sand, her successor as champion of women's rights.

Why? Germaine de Staël was a woman of her times. She wrote to please and influence her contemporaries and in this regard she succeeded. Her topics were timely. Her style was effusive and her novels, particularly, appealed to the emotional expectations and passionate curiosity of readers of her era. Therefore, her writing appears stylistically dated.

Madame de Staël is, nonetheless, a modern woman and merits a pedestal in the permanent gallery of greats. Though she was an aristocrat, an intimate of France's royal family and its court, she fought tirelessly for political equality for all classes. She lived her life on her own terms, espousing sexual and intellectual independence for women. Unquestionably feminine, she tried to act out her convictions with discretion and hoped to keep gossip of her overlapping love affairs confined to her opulently decorated boudoirs. Not always successful in this, she was often maligned in the press and in public for her guileless defiance of convention as well as for her brash political intrigue.

I learned of this remarkable woman when I minored in French in college and I, also, became intellectually obsessed with her. So much so, that I was compelled to search for and acquire all the works by and about her that I could find. I spent twenty years retracing the steps of both Madame de Staël and Napoleon, attending colloquia of the Société Staëlienne in Europe and in America, and interviewing many of her descendants. The result is *Triumph in Exile*.

Germaine de Staël was formidable. She was brilliant, generous, passionate, courageous, sometimes willful and self-indulgent but she never compromised her principles. She faced the terror, oppression and hypocrisy of her age with the naked tenacity of a Don Quixote . . . and survived.

Victoria D. Schmidt
Haymarket, Virginia
June, 2002

Madame de Staël as a young woman before the bust of her father, Jacques Necker

Prelude

The blasts of cannon fire shattered the afternoon calm of October 12, 1799.

The rumblings spread swiftly in all directions from Geneva, like violent electric thunderbolts. Ten miles to the northeast, a hillside chateau overlooking the hamlet of Coppet vibrated to the continuing volleys. To the south, high above the clear blue waters of Lac Léman, the majestic snowy peak of Mount Blanc glistened in the sun.

In the spacious, sunfilled library of the chateau, the Baroness Anne Louise Germaine Necker de Staël Holstein was jarred by the detonations as she sat at her writing desk. She stood up abruptly, drew a bright fringed shawl over her shoulders and pushed against the heavy doors that opened onto the parapet. Raising her skirts above her ankles, she dashed across the length of the building, joyous in hopeful anticipation.

Germaine de Staël, drawn along by the cannon fire was finally stopped by a stone balustrade. A cool breeze brushed soft black ringlets back over the band of her turban. Her large dark eyes flashed fire, magically transforming her uneven features into those of a stunning, attractive woman. She was breathless, her heart thumped rapidly. Slowly, as she gained her composure, her face glowed with the expectation of triumph.

"Good luck," she murmured to her faraway hero.

The Genevese were saluting the man she was counting on to lead France out of chaos and corruption and open the way for her return from exile to the city she loved . . . Paris.

The man was the promising young general, Napoleon Bonaparte.

Geneva was a short stop on his route from Egypt to the French capital, where the diminutive Corsican hoped to join Germaine's friends in a plot to overthrow the venal Directorate government.

Long before Bonaparte attracted the attention of French political leaders, the Baroness and her famous, wealthy father, Jacques Necker, had recognized his genius. Necker, the former Director General to the guillotined King Louis XVI, and his daughter Germaine had closely followed Napoleon's brilliant exploits which began with the siege of Toulon. From the beginning they predicted an illustrious future for this brash soldier—they had watched him climb the army hierarchy to the rank of general at the age of twenty-four with the ease of a seasoned warrior. He went on to capture the imagination of the populace with spectacular victories and deft personal publicity so that now, at thirty, he was the darling of France.

Germaine was kept informed of the conspiracy's progress in Paris by her former lover, Charles Talleyrand, Bishop d'Autun, one of the coup's perpetrators. She had urged Talleyrand, still a close friend and political ally, to retain Bonaparte for the critical military support. Early in October, she learned from the Bishop that the strike for the takeover was imminent and since they could not wait for Napoleon, who was thousands of kilometers away conducting the Egyptian campaign, another general would be substituted.

Germaine was outraged. How dare they recruit anyone else!

When the news reached Bonaparte through his elaborate courier system, he was irate and roared like a raging sea. This was to be his dramatic bid for political validation and an opportunity to move close to the seat of power and authority. Refusing to acknowledge the rebuff, Napoleon abandoned his floundering troops on the banks of the Nile like a shepherd deserting his sheep at a waterhole and defiantly set off for France.

The Baroness de Staël was thrilled with his resolve, for without him she saw France growing more corrupt and degenerate. She was determined to participate in the intrigue and regain her former position of power.

Madame de Staël had learned much from her own experience about the pressures of social conventions on women in politics. She often told her friends that "a woman could not exert political influence or achieve fame unless she linked her fate to that of a great man." At the outbreak of the French Revolution, seven years earlier, she had watched the mobs hail the father she adored as their hero. They stormed the Bastille to protest his dismissal and force his reinstatement. Germaine envied her mother who stood at Necker's side at the Hôtel de Ville basking in reflected glory.

At that moment, Germaine de Staël vowed she herself would settle for nothing less.

From the time she was a child, Germaine had mingled with the men of boundless power and intellect who held forth at her beautiful mother's salon. Both her parents encouraged her precociousness and sought to stimulate her insatiable mind. In early womanhood, she began her quest as Diogenes who sought an honest man with a lantern in daylight, she looked tirelessly for a man through whom she could project her burning ambition. Neither her husband nor her lovers were able to satisfy her intense appetites. She had found no man to equal her father's courage, brilliance and passion . . . until Bonaparte.

At thirty-three, Germaine was ready to risk everything to share this man's destiny. She would be the sensitive woman of intelligence and drive he needed at his side. She would replace Josephine, the shallow, depraved courtesan whom Bonaparte married after she was discarded as the mistress of Vicomte Paul Barras, the most powerful man in the Directory, France's current government.

The Baroness was exuberant. She could now put her plan into motion.

The cannons of Geneva ceased firing as bluntly as they had begun. An eerie hush, solemn as a grave, encompassed Coppet. The setting sun cast a luminous pink radiance around the chateau and a mist descended on its majestic towers.

Germaine walked briskly back through the broad French doors into the library and drew the bell pull to summon servants. Her Rubenesque figure, of medium height and overabundant for a young woman, was taut. She leaned against her desk and waited, her lips curled in a Sphinxlike smile. Picking up a letter opener, she caressed the carved ivory handle remembering the day Charles Talleyrand had given her this adulatory gift.

Within minutes, two footmen, in elegant green livery trimmed with gold braid appeared at the wide doorway.

"Please tell my father that I shall join him and my children in the family drawing room shortly," Madame de Staël's voice was mellow, gentle but authoritative. "And ask Eugene Uginet to come to the library immediately."

Uginet was the Baroness's loyal and principal factotum. With his wife, Olive, he managed the chateau's day-to-day activities with a staff of more than fifty servants. He oversaw the extensive grounds, maintained several carriages and a stable of horses. Occasionally, he represented his mistress in financial matters, and when she traveled through Europe he accompanied her. Her father's wealth and Uginet's competence permitted the Baroness to pursue her political aspirations like a head of state.

Germaine sat down at her desk as earnest as a military strategist to write instructions to Paris and pave the way for her first important move. If Bonaparte could hazard a journey, she speculated, and leave his armies without official sanction, she herself could defy exile and also return to Paris. The general was responsible to the five Directors who controlled France. With his unauthorized action, Napoleon was placing his career on the line. He could be stripped of his command and imprisoned. Germaine's decision to leave Coppet could jeopardize *her* freedom.

The Baroness was optimistic but pragmatic.

Bonaparte's uncanny run of good luck could continue, she pondered. She knew he could buttress the conspiracy and guarantee its success. But the coup could also fail. Other attempts to unseat the Directors had been thwarted. Germaine knew the risks she would be taking. She had survived the Reign of Terror that had brought death to Louis XVI and thousands of other Frenchmen. With the skill of a subversive agent, she had singlehandedly rescued scores of her aristocratic friends, barely escaping with her own life. During subsequent regimes, all ineffective, she had returned to Paris only to be exiled again to Switzerland for interference and intrigue. This time, when she approached the city gates, the Jacobins might decree to have her escorted back to Coppet or to a French prison. If she were in Paris and the conspirators lost, she could be given the ultimate sentence . . . death.

"You wanted to see me, Madame la Baronne?"

"Yes, Eugene," she replied, looking up from her desk. Uginet was a stocky, rugged man whose deep-furrowed face reflected years of strain and hard work like that of a provincial farmer.

Germaine de Staël sealed her letter and handed it to her most trusted servant.

She had written to Benjamin Constant, her political collaborator and current lover, announcing her plans to leave Coppet for France. She requested the mood of the authorities and asked him to map out a way for her to slip into Paris without arousing suspicion.

Under Germaine's tutelage, Constant, a liberal activist and writer, had become a staunch supporter of republican ideologies. He was close to the conspirators but had yet to be assigned an active role.

"Place this letter in a sealed pouch and entrust it only to our most reliable courier. It must be delivered to Monsieur Constant in Paris as soon as possible. Instruct our man that he must not return without a reply. Wait

. . ." the Baroness called out as Uginet turned to carry out his instructions. "As soon as you have put the messenger on his horse, begin preparation for my trip to Paris."

Uginet's eyes danced with surprise and excitement.

"We will not depart until I have confirmation from Monsieur Constant," Germaine added quickly. "You will have more than enough time to prepare. Olive can start immediately to pack my trunks, but make certain the rest of the servants know nothing of my plans."

Uginet was caught up in the contagious exhilaration that Bonaparte awakened in all Frenchmen. But, a dutiful servant, he suppressed his emotions. He was as eager as his mistress to witness the revolt that was being rumored would erupt in Paris. He was accustomed to Madame de Staël's sudden urges to travel. In view of her exile, her decision to return to France was reckless, but he marvelled at her audacity, agreed with her decisions and readily complied with her demands.

The first word the Baroness received was not encouraging news.

Bonaparte, who had been given a rousing reception by the people on his arrival in the capital, had created an impasse between himself and Abbé Emmanuel Siéyès, the architect of the conspiracy. Equally obstinate, neither would make the opening gesture toward the other.

The Abbé, a longtime friend of the Necker family, was a diffident but brilliant man. He had held several government posts, had drafted many constitutions (one with Germaine's help) and was currently president of the Ancients, the upper house of the legislature. A gnome-like man with a high bald head and a long, hooked nose, Siéyès was a dedicated public servant who deserved respect due a statesman.

The stubborn resistance of these two principal players acting like headstrong youths was undermining the efforts of the rest of the zealous conspirators. The delay was hindering the impetus and could detract from the element of surprise. Already some of the Jacobins were beginning to suspect betrayal.

The Baroness de Staël agonized. Would she lose the chance she had prayed for? The tranquility of the Vaud region around Lake Geneva and the bucolic beauty of Coppet, which had always bored her, began to cloy. Were she in Paris, the undercurrent and the tensions would be stimulating. She would be involved directly in the decisions and confer with the plotters. In Switzerland, she felt helpless as a pampered mistress. Her father added to her aggravation by reminding her of her responsibility to two young sons and infant daughter. Necker repeatedly tried to persuade her to remain at Coppet. His arguments provoked her.

"You know as well as I that my duty as a Necker is to help restore stability to France," she said indignantly. Still, she sympathized with this man who had given years of his life to French causes. "My sons must return to their country to prepare to carry on in your tradition. Your granddaughter must soon be exposed to the intellectual sensibilities of the Paris salons!"

Jacques Necker was growing old, and was content in the serenity and security of Coppet. It was becoming increasingly difficult to defend himself against his strong-willed daughter. As October ended, the tension between them increased like a Vesuvius about to erupt.

Finally, the atmosphere cleared.

On a bright day early in November, a message arrived from Benjamin revealing that the stalemate between Bonaparte and Siéyès had been broken. Charles Talleyrand, the consummate arbitrator, had persuaded Bonaparte to make the first move and the men met on neutral ground. Resolving their differences, they set the time of the coup for the following week. If Germaine insisted, Constant wrote, and he did not advise it, she could meet him at Charenton, the last relay post before the city gates where they could arrange her furtive entry into the city and open her townhouse.

The Baroness de Staël was relieved. Her face flushed with anticipation as she flew into action with the agility of a fencer.

Within an hour, a courier had been dispatched to Constant and her luxurious yellow berline, loaded with luggage and crowded with footmen and maids, awaited her in the courtyard.

A strong November wind swirled dry dust between the spokes of the carriage wheels and around the legs of the restless six-horse team. A sudden current whipped through the portico of the chateau where Germaine's family gathered. The Baroness kissed her father and sons. As she picked up her daughter and pressed her close, her demeanor turned enigmatic, Madonna-like, as though she changed her mind about leaving. She didn't. Giving the child back to her governess, Germaine turned away quickly and walked down the steps holding her burgundy velvet bonnet and her matching travel coat against the bitter gusts.

The levelheaded Uginet helped his mistress board the coach and climbed up on the perch next to the driver.

Madame de Staël was jubilant . . . at last she was returning to Paris.

PART I

THE TRAINING GROUND

Chapter 1
The Ideal Family

For three days and three nights she screamed in terror and agony. Why had no one prepared her for this profaning of her body? No human being should be subjected to such torment! How could women go to the altar and swear to be broken on the wheel like this every nine months!

At last, Madame Suzanne Curchod Necker's suffering was over. At six o'clock on the evening of April 22, 1766, in a mansion in the Marais district of Paris, she delivered a daughter, Anne Louise Germaine. Physically weak and subject to violent attacks of nervous prostration, Suzanne Necker had a will of steel. She determined never again to go through childbirth—and, she never did. Anne Louise Germaine remained the Neckers' only child.

The union of Germaine's parents, Suzanne Curchod and Jacques Necker, was a love match worthy of a romance novel. From the first day of their marriage, they were regarded as a model of conjugal domesticity. They shunned the easy morals of French society as aristocrats sloughed off last year's fashions. With the arrival of their child, they were admired and respected as the ideal family.

But behind the public facade was a dynamic triangle of competition, dissension and tension that tore at the fiber of the household.

Madame Necker began, even before Germaine could talk, to shape and mold this daughter, remembering that it was she who had caused her excruciating pain and deprived her briefly of the Puritan dignity she cherished. Suzanne approached her child-rearing rigidly and without humor like a callous schoolmaster.

Germaine was the perfect child, intelligent, uniquely gifted and as quick to respond as an affectionate puppy. Her mother swiftly and efficiently muffled the girl's outbursts of emotion which Germaine learned early to suppress. Had she been allowed to erupt, she might have destroyed herself, her mother or both of them. She had inherited Madame Necker's obstinate nature and her father's reserved genius. Along with these traits, however, was the unquenchable passion of a fine artist.

Only the profound love and devotion of mother and daughter for Jacques Necker bound the triad and preserved the semblance of family bliss for the years it managed to survive.

Anne Louise Germaine came from solid stock on both sides of her family.

Jacques Necker descended from a long line of Lutheran pastors in Pomerania and Brandenburg, Germany. His father, Charles Frédèric Necker, taught German princelings and later was granted the prestigious chair of professor of public law at the Academy of Geneva. He performed his duties with such distinction that he was permitted to become a "burgher" without paying the fee of 21,000 florins usually charged foreigners. He was soon recognized as one of the elite citizens of the city.

Charles Frédèric had two sons, Louis and Jacques. Louis, the older of the boys, was a brilliant mathematician and, like his father, was appointed a professor at the Academy. When his wife died he found solace in the arms of the wife of his pastor's brother. The cuckolded husband discovered the two in bed together and shot the adulterous Louis. He recovered, but the incident brought him notoriety and forced him out of his job. He fled to Marseilles where he made a fortune in financial speculation.

As a youth, the second son, Jacques, was a humorless plodder. For years he hid his burning ambition behind a good-natured, complacent smile. Jacques was vain as a *comédie française* headliner. More than anything else in the world, he coveted fame and glory. He recognized his limitations and knew he would have to work hard to achieve his goals. Refusing to pursue an academic career, he left school at fifteen and apprenticed himself to the bank of Isaac Vernet, one of the foremost financial houses in Europe.

He set about the necessary lackluster tasks with boundless patience and diligence. When he turned eighteen, his industry was rewarded. His employer doubled his salary and transferred him to the bank's rapidly expanding Paris branch.

Jacques was tall and large boned like a French farmhand. Despite a long nose, a forehead that receded at a forty-five degree angle and the strange tilt at which he held his head, some considered him good-looking. He showed none of the unrestrained need for sex that almost killed his brother nor any interest in marriage. The gaming houses, the seductive actresses and the Palais-Royal prostitutes held no allure for him.

His proper Calvinist training did not, however, prevent Jacques from following the political intrigue and observing the lavish life-style of the depraved French court for which he had a quenchless thirst. He said very little, but he listened. He was attuned to the gossip about Madame de Pompadour, King Louis XV's mistress particularly the tales of how she controlled the king and influenced affairs of government. He observed that however decadent Versailles was, France was becoming a world force and merchants and bankers were getting as obscenely rich as the maharajahs of India. This was Jacques Necker's world. He wanted to share that wealth and power. It was in this milieu he was certain he could realize his dreams.

He crammed his days with work, absorbing the intricacies of his trade, honing skills and making friends in high places. At night, he studied with the fervor of a monk the international manipulations of credit and securities, a subject which fascinated him.

In 1762, when Jacques turned thirty, his perseverance paid off. Appointed co-director of Pierre Thélusson's French bank (Thélusson succeeded his uncle Isaac Vernet), he made his first millions by buying and selling treasury bonds on an inside tip from an official in the foreign office. Jacques Necker acquired a Midas touch and became one of the most adept traders in France.

Two years later, during a wheat famine, he turned his millions over several times accumulating a fortune that was among the largest in Europe. The next year he became sole director of his company's French operations.

At thirty-two, Jacques Necker was ready for glory. He knew he needed more than money. He needed public support and social acceptance. Since women influenced political decisions through exclusive, fashionable salons, Jacques set out to find a wife as assiduously as he had to make his fortune.

Through his partner Thélusson, he met the beautiful widow of a Swiss military officer. Madame Germaine de Vermenoux was precisely what Jacques was looking for. She was charming, had a lively wit and impeccable social connections. Jacques courted her briefly with the precision of a dealmaker and proposed. Though impressed, the attractive widow, wealthy in her own right, was not eager to lose her independence, but promised an answer when she returned from a visit to Switzerland.

In Geneva, Madame de Vermenoux stayed in the home of Pastor Moultou where Suzanne Curchod, a twenty-seven-year-old spinster, was governess and tutor to the Moultou children.

Like Jacques Necker, Suzanne Curchod came from a family of ministers. She descended from a line of Huguenots who were related distantly to minor royalty. She was born and grew up in the environs of Lake Geneva.

By the time she turned sixteen, Suzanne was exquisitely beautiful, knowledgeable and intelligent. And she knew it. Her father, the pastor of the village of Crassier, was enough ahead of his time to believe in the education of women. He himself gave his daughter lessons in the arts, sciences, languages and music.

Proud and headstrong, Suzanne Curchod concealed a passionate nature behind a starchly stiff manner (which brought on hypertension as she grew older). Her father's divinity students found her charm and fragile beauty irresistible. She humored them and held them at arms length, hoping something more interesting might turn up.

Something did turn up when she was twenty. Edward Gibbon, the brilliant but homely English historian who later wrote *The Rise and Fall of the Roman Empire*, fell in love with Suzanne like a besotted school boy the first time they met. She happily returned his affection.

Edward's father got wind of the romance and recalled his son to England. The elder Gibbon refused to support the young man beyond a meager allowance if he insisted on marrying this "foreigner." Edward broke off the engagement, writing that he sighed as a lover but obeyed as a son.

It was a stinging blow to Suzanne, who wrote him a bitter, disjointed and impassioned reply. Concealing her rejection, she rejoined the lively social scene of Lausanne.

Six years later Edward returned to Switzerland, still unmarried.

In his absence, Suzanne's parents had both died and left her without property or income. As a temporary measure, she had accepted the kind gesture of Peter Moultou, one of her father's former students, to live with his family and teach his children.

On his return, Gibbon offered Suzanne friendship and she accepted.

They met almost daily at dinner, parties, theatricals and concerts. While they talked and laughed indifferently about their past attachment as though they had been casual acquaintances, Suzanne hid her true feelings. She still felt deeply for this intelligent scholar and hoped they would marry. She expressed her anguish and expectations in writing and sent him the letters. When they were together at gatherings she was gay as a coquette and flirted openly with other men. Edward accused her of impudence and insincerity. "She plays at sensibility," he surmised, and left her to continue his studies in Geneva.

The truth was that Suzanne had been severely wounded. In a short period of time, she had been discarded by her lover, she had lost her parents and had been forced to make her own way in a world that ostracized women of good family who hired out as governesses. Pastor Moultou became her friend and protector. He encouraged her to mingle with philosophers and enjoy the intellectual climate of Switzerland. He introduced her to the salons of aristocratic families where she soon became a welcome guest. But her wounds were deep and healed slowly.

During Madame de Vermenoux's stay with the Moultous she found Suzanne bright, attractive and engaging. When the Frenchwoman asked her to come to Paris as her companion and as tutor to her eight-year old son, Suzanne accepted with delight.

Back in the French capital, Jacques Necker had a surprise on his next visit to the home of Madame de Vermenoux. When he was introduced to Suzanne Curchod, it was love at first sight for them both. They were married in December of 1764, but waited till after the ceremony to tell Madame de Vermenoux. The French widow was initially chagrined, but later forgave the newlyweds. When their daughter was born a year and a half later she consented to be the godmother. In return, Madame and Monsieur Necker named their child Germaine after the woman who had brought them together.

"If you persist, Madame, your baby will die of malnutrition."

Madame Necker was shocked. Her doctor was telling her to discontinue breast feeding her four-month-old infant. She resisted because she wanted to follow the natural child-rearing methods advanced by her friend, the philosopher Jean Jacques Rousseau, in his book *Emile*. Breast feeding was fundamental. But the doctor was adamant, so Suzanne consented and turned Anne Louise over to a plump Flemish girl. She was dismayed by her failure to produce enough milk but relieved to be free of an untidy inconvenience.

By her first birthday, Germaine chattered as incessantly as a primed parrot and showed an insatiable interest in everything about her. It was clear to Suzanne that her daughter had a mind like a fertile garden . . . but she saw no evidence that she had inherited any of the Curchod beauty.

Though Madame Necker might entrust her child's physical needs to a wet nurse, its mind belonged to her. When Germaine was barely two-and-a-half, Suzanne launched her on a rigorous regimen of the classics, languages, the arts and music. Nothing was too good or too difficult for a Necker, and no one but a Necker could teach a Necker.

By the time she was four, Germaine was introduced to the laboratory in which she had to observe intellectuals and statesmen practice what her mother was teaching her. The child became a regular fixture at Madame Necker's Friday night salons, where she sat like a pet poodle on a small cushioned, wooden stool beside her mother.

Suzanne Necker loved her child with passion. Suppressed passion. She was determined to smother Germaine's emotions and train her to be a cerebral human being. She would eliminate in her any disturbing undercurrents to which she had been subjected during the years before she met Jacques Necker.

Through Germaine's childhood, the wife of the great Necker ruled her household and Paris society with the supreme grace and self-confidence of a monarch while her husband served the people and the king of France. But she pushed her daughter to the brink of the same abyss which she herself barely escaped.

Chapter 2
The Ugly Duckling

The young girl stood so close to the oversized, ornately framed mirror that her breath clouded its surface. She wished she could see beyond her reflection, beyond her physical appearance. She backed away and critically appraised her image. She did not move. She was as still as any of the marble statues that adorned the corners of the great chamber.

Germaine Necker shook her head slowly. No, she concluded ruefully, I am not a pretty girl.

She knew her mother was exquisite with beauty that could challenge Helen of Troy. Everyone said so. And she could see it herself. As the years went by the child wished that some of that loveliness would appear in her own features. But it was yet to happen, if ever.

Now that she was almost twelve, she was old enough to accept the truth. She closed her eyes, covered her face with her hands and slipped down in a limp heap on the Aubusson rug like a rag doll. She was an insignificant creature among the desks, the carved chairs, the bronze busts, the tall shelves of books against the walls and the other organized clutter of learning in this library that was her classroom.

But if she were so unattractive, why would a handsome nobleman in Marie Antoinette's court want to marry her? Though he had never seen her, Germaine was certain he must have asked what she looked like. She could still hear the voices of her mother and Count de Creutz, Swedish Ambassador to France, which she had overheard by chance the night before.

"My friend and protégé has asked me again to arrange a meeting with you and Monsieur Necker to discuss a marriage contract," the Count said.

"Germaine is very young. It will be some time before we consider taking such a step."

"My dear Madame Necker, I understand your position. But the Queen was only fourteen and Louis just fifteen when they married. Preparations were made far in advance."

Madame Necker replied graciously. "The royal family has an obligation to the people to assure the continuity of the Bourbon line."

De Creutz was not to be put off. "The daughter of France's Director General is as much a member of the aristocracy as any royal princess," he went on with the persistence of a lobbyist. "Besides, Baron de Staël is a proper candidate for your daughter's hand. He has a promising career in diplomacy."

Madame Necker's perception matched her beauty. She knew of the Baron's agility in boudoirs and his addiction to gaming tables. There were rumors that he was heavily in debt. She sensed he had a greater interest in the Necker fortune than in her child.

"He is one of the most charming men who surround the queen," she said. "Many stunning women in the court would consider him a catch. I can't understand," she said, controlling sarcasm, "just what it is the Baron sees in a plain, awkward child seventeen years younger than he."

Germaine had cringed and skulked off to a corner. Then, and again today she felt the sting of the remark, like a sword through her heart—her own mother considered her unattractive.

Yet, this nobleman wanted to marry her. His interest braced her. What, she wondered, was expected of a wife? She might be too young, but she would be free of her mother's discipline. Her lessons, once the exciting center of her life, were becoming drudgery.

Germaine's face clouded with defiance. She wanted to break the bonds with which her mother held her so securely. Germaine always studied. She rarely was permitted to play. She had no friends . . . at least none her own age. Playing alone, her one joy was to make paper dolls of kings, queens and their satellites and have them act out scenes she wrote herself. Never before had she wanted to neglect her studies. Today, she didn't care. She got up from the floor and threw a disparaging glance at the open books on her desk like a truant, defiant schoolboy. She turned toward the mirror, unable to resist the temptation of looking at herself again.

She spoke aloud. "How ugly *am* I?"

She examined her reflection sharply. This was a new experience. Strangely, a delicious pleasure. With her fingers, she tasted each of her features. Her hair . . . her generous nose . . . her full lips . . . her sallow complexion. She devoured them all with large black eyes that enlivened her face with fire. Her hands traveled down to her neck . . . it was soft and well shaped. Over her chest, the mounds that pressed against her drab dress were growing full and tender. She smiled with the joy of discovery. Her hands slipped slowly over the rest of the developing curves of her body.

Germaine was growing up and she was thrilled.

It was true that she wasn't pretty, perhaps this Baron de Staël knew that her eyes were beautiful. And that she was becoming a woman. And that she was intelligent, exceptionally so. "In fact," she breathed, "I'm brilliant." The erudite guests who attended her mother's salon could attest to that.

But what did all this matter? For there was one man who loved Germaine deeply for herself without qualification, the only man in all the world whom she could love—the only man who deserved her love in return. Germaine was in love with her father. She loved him profoundly, exclusively, tenaciously.

She respected her mother, loving her with the reserve and adoration due a goddess. The affection she had for her father was unrestrained, unqualified. Germaine herself was spontaneous and impulsive, filled with gaiety and abandon of a sprite. Necker understood his daughter and permitted her to express her free spirit.

One evening while the Neckers entertained a friend at dinner, Madame Necker had to leave the room. Germaine, who had been conducting herself in the reserved manner her mother demanded, suddenly raised her napkin and threw it across the table at her father. Necker was stunned by the unexpected bunt. Before he could reprimand her, Germaine had raced around the table, flung her arms around his neck and covered his face with kisses. She pulled him off his chair and together they frolicked about the room like a pair of children playing tag. It was such a beautiful display of affection that the guest was charmed rather than offended or embarrassed. Hearing Madame Necker approach, father and daughter quickly sat down and slipped back into their expected pattern of formality.

Another time, when Germaine was much younger, she startled a visitor who was walking in the Necker garden. Feeling the swift slash of a switch across his back, he turned to see Germaine emerging from behind a tree, laughing and wielding a long stick. "Mama wants me to learn to use my left hand," she said brightly, "and you can see how well I practice."

Germaine was an enchanting, charming and captivating child, but only when her mother was out of sight. Because her father permitted her outbursts, she loved him extravagantly. But she saw him rarely.

All of the girl's days were regulated, mechanical, restrained. Practice was the priority—there were facts, names, dates, places, to be memorized. Madame Necker crammed her daughter full of information, but she did not educate her. She knew Germaine had an exceptional mind but she did not understand the extraordinary genius and the boundless vitality that were at conflict within her. Madame Necker instructed her daughter but did not talk with her. She never tried to get to know her. She was raising her child out of duty and ambition—not with the instincts of a mother.

That Jacques Necker adored his daughter and encouraged her to unleash her exuberance was reason enough for Germaine's devotion. But he also had become a celebrity, the most popular and important man in France. Germaine gloried in that fame.

When he married Suzanne Curchod, Jacques Necker acquired a dedicated, indefatigable partner. A shrewd, subtle huckster without peer.

Suzanne knew immediately that Jacques was the "something" she had been waiting to have turn up. She saw his potential, approved his goals and was as ambitious as he and at times, more so. As soon as they were married she began inviting political and social leaders to receptions at their home. Though those who came were the intelligent young men with brilliant futures, not the decision makers, Suzanne had broken the ice. After Germaine was born, the Neckers took the next step and moved to an elegant manor house on the rue de Cléry in one of the most fashionable districts of Paris. Madame Necker's reputation for encouraging stimulating conversation and her talent for lavish, yet unpretentious entertaining was the talk of the best circles in Paris. Shrewdly, she expanded her salon and began to attract the most influential and powerful men in France. Journalists, historians, literati and statesmen flocked to admire the beautiful Madame Necker and to meet her quiet, unassuming, cordial—and wealthy—husband. Slowly, Suzanne cultivated her guests as a private stable of publicists for her husband.

When Germaine was five, Madame Necker deftly maneuvered a plan that made her the most sought after hostess in the capital. She gathered together seventeen revered philosophers and proposed that a statue be erected to honor the great Voltaire. Dazzled as though by diamonds, they agreed. She coordinated the project, raised the money and worked with the sculptor. When Voltaire succumbed to the adulation and became one of Suzanne's ardent admirers, Parisian society, also dazzled, followed suit.

Jacques was not idle. In 1768 he had made a short visit to Switzerland and returned with the post of minister of the Republic of Geneva to the court of Versailles. A minor appointment but recognition in the public sector. The next year he was made a director of the French India Company, which allowed him to grant patronage and demonstrate his financial genius on a broader scale. By 1772, Necker, sensing he had attained a grasp of public life, sold his interest in his bank and concentrated on economics, writing technical papers on finance and politics.

By the time she was ten, Germaine began to relate to her father's drive, tenets and goals. She thrilled with daughterly pride as she watched him gain public acceptance. In 1776 her parents took her to England to closely observe the English parliamentary system for which Necker had great respect. Later as a grown woman, she espoused the system and was grateful to her father for the pains he took to instruct her in this democratic form of government.

When the Neckers returned home, Jacques undertook a deliberate campaign to gain a position in France's government. He supplied facts and figures to a new English newspaper that flooded France with denouncements of Jacques-Robert Turgot, the Controller General. When the beleaguered man was forced to resign, King Louis XVI named Necker head of France's financial administration with the title of Director General of Finance. Though all ministers worked through the cabinet, Necker had the privilege of direct access to the King.

Suzanne went on promoting Necker's image at her regular Friday night salons—now held in the sumptuous Controller General's grand residence.

There was another side of the Neckers' life which endeared them to the French populace. They did not spend all their time with the rich, the elegant and the powerful in splendid surroundings. By instinct, desire, background and design, Suzanne and Jacques were philanthropists. They gave time and money to help the poor and the deprived. Suzanne paid visits to the sick in hospitals and often took Germaine with her. Necker's popularity grew steadily.

The elaborate doré clock struck the hour.
Startled, Germaine turned toward the marble mantle on which the

clock rested. Eleven. A whole hour before her mother would return and quiz her on her reading.

She sighed deeply. If she applied herself she could easily answer any question her mother would pose. But today, Germaine had no interest in books. She felt a deep need to talk . . . to someone . . . someone who would understand . . . anyone would do. But there was no one. This longing to share her feelings had recently become as acute as her need to breathe.

Yes. There were her little friends who would talk for her. Her paper dolls. She kneeled on the rug and opened the bottom drawer of the desk. There were dozens of colorful figures lined up in neat rows like soldiers. One by one she took them out, handling each as lovingly as if they were made of Venetian glass. There was a king and a queen. Nobleman and ladies . . . all dressed in brilliant costumes she had made for them. There was one of her father that was larger than all the rest. Another of a man with strange spectacles, a few strands of straggly hair at the base of a bald head; he wore a simple black suit.

"Here, Benjamin Franklin. You must stand next to Director General Necker," she said with a giggle. She was in her element.

Germaine pushed her books and papers aside and set up a stage on top of the desk. Using the inkwells as thrones for the rulers, she arranged the other characters in a large semicircle in front of them. Playing truant was fun. Occasionally, she laughed aloud at her own cleverness as she spoke the lines she had written for her actors. It was as though she knew that this was a precursor of the life she would lead one day as a woman of influence.

She was so absorbed in her drama that she did not hear footsteps in the corridor. She did hear the door open behind her.

The color drained from Germaine's face. It must be her mother, arriving early. She would surely be punished, not just reprimanded. From the beginning she had been indoctrinated with the importance of her education. Her mother grew sharp over a misspelled word or a liberty taken with grammar. Germaine's mind went blank. She was as mute as the portraits on the wall. She could contrive no excuse for her play.

The door squeaked shut. She did not move.

"Minette! My little one!"

It was the deep voice of a man.

Germaine pivoted about, her dread evaporating as though a rainbow filled the room.

"Oh, Papa! I did not know you were at home."

Hugging her, Jacques kissed the soft curls on the top of her head.

Germaine was a Necker, her father's daughter. Features that were unattractive in the girl gave Jacques strength of character and virile dignity. To Germaine, of course, Necker was the handsomest of all men. Today, he wore a dark brown velvet jacket, tan knee pants and a soft, yellow, ruffled shirt. His white wig was held in place with a small ribbon tied at the base of his neck.

Standing back from her father, Germaine declared, "I must make a new ensemble just like this one for my paper doll of you."

Looking at the display of little figures, Necker said, "Have you finished your studies early today?"

"No," she shrugged. "Do help me, Papa—I must put these away before Mama gets here. She'll be cross with me if she finds I've been playing without her approval. She may not tell me about the special surprise she promised me today."

The Director General of France kneeled on the floor, his pants, unaccustomed to such activity hugged his buttocks tightly. As Germaine passed him her dolls, her father, handling them as carefully as precious gems, replaced them in the drawer.

When Madame Necker entered the library at noon, she found her husband and daughter, like political analysts, deep in discussion about France's financial aid to the new nation in America . . . the current controversial issue at the court of Versailles.

Germaine sat quietly, meek in a throne-like chair that encircled her with heavily carved protective arms.

Necker rose to greet his wife. They sat down side by side on a tapestry upholstered fauteuil across from their child. Necker leaned back comfortably, his wife held herself stiffly as though she were in pain.

"You have had a productive morning, Germaine, my dear." Madame Necker spoke crisply, assertively. She did not ask. She assumed. There was no question in her mind that Germaine had completed her lessons.

"Yes, Mama."

Madame Necker meticulously arranged the voluminous layers of skirts of her pale green silk gown, which was gathered into a band at her slender waist. She wore a broad white gauze fichu loosely looped between her breasts to form a deep V and accent her swanlike neck. Her heart shaped face was exquisite—her nose was slender, her mouth perfectly curved, her cheek bones well defined, her chin tapered. Her complexion was like fine porcelain, made even more transparent because of her delicate, declining health. Her long hair, sparkling with blonde highlights, was combed up from her wide forehead and drawn back to allow large soft curls to fall over her gently sloping shoulders. She was a distractingly beautiful woman.

Germaine felt vulnerable . . . intimidated not only by her mother's beauty but by her commanding presence as well.

"Your father and I agreed from the beginning to bring you up according to strict Calvinist ideals." Madame Necker spoke slowly and deliberately. She was also gentle. "I have done my best to train you within these guidelines. At the same time, we bring you into my salon to expose you to another world. Here we prepare you to understand and reject the frivolous, carefree ways of aristocratic society and to cope with intellectuals on their own ground." Madame Necker's tone grew kinder. She was breaking the rules of her own discipline.

"It is impossible," she went on, "to find families in Paris with the same Protestant background as our own. There have been no children that would be suitable companions for you. I have been searching for months and finally, I have found a girl who is a worthy of you, Minette."

Germaine's eyes widened in surprise and disbelief. "Would you like to have a young girl your own age to study and play with?" Madame Necker asked without changing her solemn expression.

Impulsively, Germaine shot out of her chair like an arrow and rushed to her mother. "Oh, Mama! This is a wonderful surprise!" Putting her arms around her mother's neck, she smothered her with kisses. Madame Necker, not responding to this show of affection, untwined her daughter's arms and held the girl's hands firmly in her lap. Germaine hung her head like a chastised puppy and tried to suppress her enthusiasm. She felt the physical rejection but was bursting with happiness.

"Having a friend of my own is an answer to my prayers, Mama! Who is she? What is her name? When can I meet her?"

Madame Necker put a forefinger to her lips to quiet her daughter.

"Her name is Catherine Huber," she answered. "She is the daughter of a woman who was my friend when I was a little girl. Her family has just moved here from Geneva. Catherine and her mother should be in the blue salon waiting for us now."

Madame Necker rang the bell cord. Three maids, a footman and her secretary filed into the room like a well-rehearsed chorus in a musical comedy. The rush of activity was palpable. Jacques Necker, who had decided to escape the domestic scene, walked out unnoticed in the flurry. While one of the maids brushed Germaine's hair and tucked it under a white lace cap leaving black ringlets to frame her face, Madame Necker gave detailed instructions to the rest of her servants.

"Minette. Here, my dear, is the friend I am giving you."

Catherine Huber was a quiet, pretty child who resembled her mother. Madame Huber was a proper Protestant but far less austere than her hostess.

Germaine watched her mother closely, fearing that if she spoke she would break the spell. Her face was animated as a mime's and her eyes were so filled with sparks they shouted her eagerness.

Poor Catherine was not prepared for this attention and Germaine's unspoken eloquence. She lowered her eyes and turned crimson.

Madame Necker approached the girl, brushed her lips against her forehead and gently placed her fingers beneath Catherine's chin.

"Go, my dear," she said to her. "Go into the garden and get to know my daughter."

Once they were out of earshot of their mothers, Germaine embraced her new friend as though she were her sister. "I've been hoping and waiting for someone like you for a long time," she said effusively.

Catherine drew back shyly as a wildflower in a spring breeze.

"I knew you would be kind and pretty," Germaine went on. She opened her heart to the other girl—that's what friends were for? "We shall be good friends and I shall love you all of my life till I die."

When the girls returned to the salon, the servants were hovering over the two mothers who were concluding arrangements. The secretary had taken pages of notes and gave them to Madame Necker to review.

"Before we begin the afternoon meetings next week," Madame Huber suggested, "perhaps the girls would like to get to know one another better. Germaine may come with us for a drive through the Bois de Boulogne and have lunch at our home. She will be back by the middle of the afternoon."

Madame Necker was appalled but her formal veneer showed no change. The servants' mouths dropped open in disbelief. Such audacity . . . . Germaine had never been out of the house without her mother!

Germaine, herself, was stunned but thrilled by the invitation. She quivered in suspense as Madame Necker stood silent. The few moments seemed an eternity before she replied.

"Thank you, Madame Huber," she said calmly. "Of course, Germaine may go. But . . . not till later this afternoon." Madame Necker would have the last word. "Would you come for Germaine later? Then, Catherine may come back and join *us* for dinner."

When the Huber carriage finally returned, Germaine shrieked joyfully and ran into the corridor, calling for her mother. Madame Necker admonished and calmed her. She took Germaine's hand and together they walked to the foyer. In the presence of the Huber coachman, Madame Necker talked to her daughter about the dangers of riding a carriage through the traffic of the city and along the busy roads of the Bois de Boulogne. She rambled on for so long, Germaine feared her mother would change her mind.

But at last the lecture was over and Germaine bounded down the stairs and into the waiting coach like a fleet-footed fawn.

Madame Necker stood in the portico waving as the driver urged the horses to start and the carriage pulled away. Germaine was in such rapture, she forgot to turn around and wave good-bye.

The child was so intense, so full of emotion, that she alternately kissed Madame Huber and hugged Catherine till they were well into the forest. Then, she grew calm and sat silently as a sleeping kitten. She was unaware of her new friends, the passing trees, the other carriages, the riders on horseback. She was in a world of her own, in a trance. She would permit nothing to mar this first taste of freedom. She treasured it like a jewel found by chance that would have to be returned . . . when she went home again.

Chapter 3
A Place in the Country

H er body felt as taut as the strings of an overtuned harpsichord. Twelve-year-old Germaine looked like a diminutive version of the fashionable women who frequented her mother's salon. She was not pretty, but she radiated the enviable freshness of a young girl. Sitting stiffly on a small stool near the chaise on which Madame Necker reclined, Germaine wondered if it was worth all the trouble it took to try to look like a grown up.

Germaine's chestnut hair was powdered, pulled back and piled up on her head five inches high in a cadogan. A bow of wide blue velvet ribbon, embroidered with pink and yellow flowers, was perched precariously at the very top. The style was becoming and softened her blunt features. She wore a matching blue dress with a white organdy collar that gave her complexion a sunny glow. It was the corset with whalebone stays pushing up the budding bosom beneath her ruffled bodice and squeezing in her waist, that made her stiffened body ache.

The guests showered her with compliments on how she looked. Germaine smiled shyly but was more interested in what they were discussing than in her appearance. She could do without all the primping but not the thrill of being treated as someone twice her age when the visitors included her in their conversations.

It was Friday evening. The capacious lower floor of the Controller General's residence was ablaze with light from hundreds of candles in giant crystal chandeliers like brilliant stars in a moonlit sky. There was a steady hum of subdued voices and quiet laughter. Intellectuals and aristocrats, bewigged and bejeweled, dressed in satins, silks, velvets and brocades in every hue, crowded elbow-to-elbow in the grand drawing room and overflowed into adjoining chambers. Footmen in elegant livery served vintage French wines in silver goblets and tempting delicacies from trays lined with Chantilly lace.

Germaine, in wide-eyed wonder, watched the admiring young men who encircled her mother. Listening, the girl anticipated what each would say. She was familiar with all the topics of salon conversation—politics, theatre, financial matters, love affairs and family scandals. But, dutiful as a lap dog, she remained silent.

Germaine marveled at the ease with which her mother changed from the rigid, demanding disciplinarian of the day to the genial, sophisticated hostess of the evening. Germaine often agonized over the love her mother extended to her friends but withheld from her own daughter. Madame Necker's charm and beauty attracted and aroused many of the young gallants who surrounded her. She indulged in innocent flirtations but never swayed from her Protestant morals. Germaine observed the interplay and, in wistful innocence, she approved. She was heartened to see that her mother was capable of warmth and gentleness.

One of the young men was the Abbé Raynal, a longtime friend of the Neckers.

"I would never miss a Friday evening at the Necker mansion," Raynal remarked with good-humored brashness, "unless I was so ill I could not move from my bed. Both our host and hostess are gracious, charming and lavish in their hospitality. I like men only for their money . . . and Monsieur Necker is very rich. I like women only for their beauty, and you, Madame, are ravishing."

Madame Necker smiled and countered with the charm the Abbé granted her. "You are a delightful monster, Abbé Raynal. You are almost as great a wit as Voltaire."

The aged philosopher was currently the most provocative topic of conversation in all Paris. The feisty iconoclast, who had just come back to France after years in exile because of his bitter attacks on the church, was being lionized by society. The great man's health was failing too rapidly to visit the salons, but he held private audiences in regal style perched high in his own voluminous bed. Madame Necker, who had maintained regular correspondence with him after the statue venture, was among the first to visit him. She took Germaine along.

"The grand philosopher plied Germaine with questions about the theatre," she said with pride. "She responded brilliantly. He told me she has had excellent training."

Abbé Raynal stepped aside from the circle around Suzanne to talk with Germaine.

"I've read your essay, *Reflections of the Edict of Nantes*," he said quietly. Madame Necker feigned interest in the ongoing discussion on Voltaire but tilted her head toward the Abbé. "I've told you I am writing a book on the philosophical history of the Two Indies," he went on.

"Yes," Germaine replied and said no more. She knew her mother would object if she engaged in a conversation. She had strict orders to answer only when asked a question and to reply as briefly as possible.

"You have handled the material brilliantly," Raynal told her, "I would like to include it in my history."

"Oh, Mama," Germaine exclaimed. "Did you hear?" Madame Necker glared at the Abbé whose back was turned toward her.

"Yes, my dear, you have written many essays. That is one of your best," she said charitably.

Other guests now moved toward Germaine. Their attention to his daughter flattered Monsieur Necker but irritated his wife. They made a game of asking her questions hoping to stump her. Her precocity always amused them. This evening they began with questions about Shakespeare's plays, turned to French history and then to the English system of government.

Germaine's dark eyes danced with delight as she responded simply, directly and correctly.

"Where in *De l'Esprit des Lois,*" the Abbé asked, "can Montesquieu's most noted doctrine be found?" He chuckled, certain she did not know.

"In Chapter 6 of Book XI," she replied, grinning with triumph.

The Abbé raised his hands stretching out his fingers in front of his face in praise.

Carried away by the spirit of the repartee, Germaine went on enthusiastically, "He declares that liberty is most effectively promoted by dividing political authority among three bodies—the legislature, judicial and executive. He cites England as the best example of his theory."

"Bravo!" The guests cheered her and commended her mother. Madame Necker smiled politely but regarded the praise as an affront. She considered the salon her stage and resented any attention paid her daughter. Germaine knew that by responding spontaneously she had gone too far. Feeling crushed, she began to cough.

"What's wrong, my dear?" her mother asked solicitously.

The child continued to cough, aware that her mother's show of concern was for the benefit of her friends.

Jacques Necker, in a nearby circle, rushed over to Germaine and calmed her, chucking her playfully under the chin and then holding her close for a few moments, the coughing stopped.

"Germaine is fine," he reassured the guests. "This happens from time to time. It passes quickly."

Germaine sat downcast, her chin in her hands. When the conversation turned to the current book by Edward Gibbon, her mother's former suitor, she straightened and her face brightened like a freshly sprinkled flower.

After Jacques and Suzanne had married, Gibbon became one of their most devoted friends and was a frequent visitor in their home until he returned to England and was elected to Parliament. Already plump when he courted Suzanne, he had grown corpulent and never married. Germaine shared her parents' affection for him.

"When do you expect Edward to return to Paris, Madame Necker?" one of her guests inquired.

"Not for sometime—Parliament is still in session. Edward is one of our favorite people . . . he is a gentle, sensitive, unassuming man. We miss his distilling English wit. I wish we could see more of him."

Germaine's confidence blossomed. Her fertile imagination conceived an idea that would win back her mother's good will. Edward Gibbon was a compassionate man. He liked Germaine and she enjoyed his company.

"Oh, Mama," she cried out. "I know how you and Papa can see Mr. Gibbon as often as you like—I'll marry him and he can come live with us!"

Despite her intellect that was far beyond her years, Germaine was still a child, given to childish but sincere notions.

"Magnificent!" the Abbé remarked, and the rest of the circle nodded in agreement. Madame Necker did not.

Germaine turned toward her mother. She was taken aback like a startled rabbit and was overwhelmed by the angry stare of disapproval. She began to cough again and shake uncontrollably.

Madame Necker took the distraught child by the hand and slowly led her from the room.

Alone with her mother in the corridor, Germaine tried to speak between frantic gasps for breath. "Oh, Mama. I do love you so much," she declared. "I try so hard to please you. I am jealous of every moment you turn away from me."

"You are very clever at twisting the truth," Madame Necker replied sharply. "I can see through your tricks as you try to attract attention. You will have to remember that these are my guests and they come here to see me, not to listen to you. I let you come to observe and learn. As for your love, if you want me to believe in your exaggerated expressions of affection, you'll have to use other ways and words to prove it to me."

Germaine lay very still, huddled under the covers of her bed. Just a few limp, tousled curls were visible against a lace-edged pillow. She snuggled deep, nursing her bruised and offended sensibilities with her own warmth. She had a fitful night of sleep. Her head still pounded and her entire body throbbed. Why had her mother pressed and encouraged her to concentrate on her studies . . . never to play? Why attend the opera and the theatre and listen to scholars . . . yet not respond to intellectual challenge? She burrowed deeper under the covers like a frightened mole.

"Minette! Minette! Are you all right?" Madame Necker spoke guardedly and with remorse. Germaine did not reply. "You coughed most of the night, Minette. We are worried about you."

The child would not answer, though the pleading in her mother's voice touched her heart.

"Minette! Please Minette!" It was Jacques Necker.

"Yes, Papa." But she would say no more.

"Dr. Tronchin is here with us. He wants to talk with you."

Germaine still refused to answer.

"You see, Dr. Tronchin," Madame Necker's voice was shrill. "She will not speak. She is stubborn and may stay this way for hours without saying a word. At other times she will chatter on and on without stopping. She will not listen to reason."

Dr. Tronchin was calm. He sat down on the edge of the bed.

"Germaine," he said softly. He placed his hand on her arm.

"Germaine, would you like to live in the country and stay at your home in St. Ouen? You would be away from everything you know here. There would be no lessons, no reading, no studying. You could play wherever and whenever you wished. Indoors or in the gardens . . . in the mornings, the afternoon, or the evenings. Your friend Catherine can stay with you for days at a time. You could wear loose comfortable clothes, never a bonnet or a corset. You could do exactly as you please. Your parents would visit you only once every week or two. Would you like that?"

Germaine pushed the covers from her head, turned and looked into Dr. Tronchin's kind face. Her huge eyes were sad and wet from crying but she managed a tentative smile. She glanced up at her mother who stood behind the doctor. Madame Necker's stunned expression extinguished the spark of hope that the doctor had fanned. Her mother would never permit it. She plunged back under the duvet and drew her body up into a tight ball.

Madame Necker was shocked at the doctor's prescription. She did not expect to hear that her daughter would have to be torn away from her.

Monsieur Necker worried in silence.

His wife protested loudly carrying on like a fishwife. "I will not allow it. I've sacrificed almost thirteen years of my life for this child. I have spent all my time with her . . . to educate her . . . to assure she is a credit to her Swiss heritage. She's ungrateful. She defies me. I've given her my love, my life, my breath. You want to take her from me. It cannot be!"

Dr. Tronchin stood firm as a family court judge. "The regimen Germaine has been subjected to is more than any adolescent can tolerate and is particularly damaging," he warned, "for a girl as intelligent and high strung as she is. Germaine is on the brink of a nervous breakdown. If her daily life is not altered she will sink into a complete emotional collapse."

Madame Necker knew her protests were futile. Despite her austere manner, Madame Necker loved her daughter deeply. She knew she had begun to alienate the child and, if she did not assent to the doctor's recommendation, she might destroy her relationship with her husband as well.

Grudgingly, she agreed.

Germaine, like Cinderella on her way to a ball, was driven off the next day in the family carriage to the freedom of the Necker's vast country estate in St. Ouen, a few kilometers east of the French capital. With her were her own maid, a housekeeper and a cook to supplement the regular staff of servants and gardeners who maintained the stately chateau, its lawns and parks . . . there was no tutor, no governess.

There was nothing to remind her of the disciplined life of Paris.

Monsieur Jacques Necker

Germaine Necker at age 13

Madame Suzanne Necker

Chateau de Coppet from the pond in the park

Chapter 4
A Daughter's Choice

Months later, when Germaine returned to her home in Paris, she was transformed . . . she had become a self-assured young woman of almost fifteen. She was exuberant, witty, good-natured, confident and, like her father, a little vain. Unlike ambition, a selfish drive, this vanity was a search for glory in service to others and Germaine, influenced by her father's example, was already contemplating a life dedicated to the people of France.

She had grown taller. Her figure, no longer that of a girl, had gentle womanly curves. The lines of her face were softer, her complexion had taken on a fresh glow in the country air but she still showed no signs of the Curchod loveliness. Her enormous dark eyes, with long, thick lashes, were her best feature . . . and disarmingly seductive.

Germaine's life at St. Ouen had been as carefree as the doctor had promised. The freedom did more than improve her health—it set free her spirit. Catherine Huber was her playmate. Together, they dressed in loose pastel shifts and ran through the gardens and among the trees at the edge of the forest like wood nymphs. They sprawled on the lawns with books of poetry and recited verses to each other. When a cloudburst drenched the countryside on a warm summer day, they reveled with joy as they pranced about in the rain, laughing as they got soaked and shivering with delight as they changed into dry clothes. They whispered about their developing bodies and speculated about love and virile young men. Their straight-laced Calvinist mothers never discussed sex with them so they were ignorant of the physical aspects of love. Their notions were sentimental and came from the popular romantic stories they read and from the gossip of trysts and clandestine love affairs they overheard in the salons.

Germaine had a vivid imagination, an innate grasp of words and an extraordinary talent for stringing them together. Besides her serious essays, she wrote her own love poems and stories. She also penned dramas which she and Catherine produced and performed (with servants in supporting roles) for her father and his friends. Though the doctor had forbidden her to work, Germaine could not and did not want to alter all the study habits Madame Necker had forced upon her from the time she began to speak. She had an avid curiosity and a compulsion to learn. She devoured the books in the chateau library and continued her education on her own.

Though Jacques Necker visited his daughter once or twice a week, his wife rarely accompanied him. Madame Necker's health was declining and she spent most of her time in bed. Whenever he could, Necker escaped like a schoolboy truant to the peace and quiet of St. Ouen, away from the pressures of court and his ailing wife. He and his daughter treasured the moments they were alone like a pair of illicit lovers. He listened in silence as Germaine discussed her lessons and read passages from her essays, marveling at her insight and intellect. Rather than praise or flatter her, he merely nodded his head like a sagacious Buddha. When she made a mistake, he chided her with the gentleness of a summer breeze.

Nothing escaped this phlegmatic man. Observing his daughter's enthusiasm, her intensity, her childlike frankness and her sincerity, he permitted her to speak her mind and to openly shower her affection on him. His joy was infinite as he watched her guileless nature assert itself.

Germaine understood and appreciated her father's passive encouragement and was sensitive to his problems and needs. As they walked hand-in-hand along well-tended garden paths or as they sat before the library fire on chilly days, she plied him with questions and coaxed him to talk. Then, she listened raptly to his analysis of the crises facing France and how he hoped to curb the extravagant spending of the nobility. She enjoyed most hearing about his early years, before he married, when he was a hardworking banker.

Germaine imagined her father as he was as a young man, handsome, lonely and loving. These daydreams were far too intimate to share with Catherine, though there was little they did not tell each other. If only she had been her father's contemporary, she fantasized, he would have selected her, not her mother, to be his wife. Germaine's love for Necker turned into passion, reverence and idolatry. He had released her from imprisonment like a crusading prince and she owed her life to him.

Madame Necker was still ill but no longer bedridden when Germaine returned home. She was well enough to observe that many of the qualities in herself that had attracted Necker were strikingly apparent in Germaine. She felt threatened, fearing that he might transfer all his affection to their child.

Feeling pressed to compete with her daughter for her husband's attention, Madame Necker grew bitter. Germaine had the advantage--her mind was quicker, her repartee brighter, she was more clever. But she used none of this against her mother for during the months of separation she had grown perceptive. Germaine understood and respected Madame Necker, loved her and appreciated the dedication she had given to training her when she was a child.

But the tension was palpable.

To the public and their friends, the Necker family was uniquely solid. On one occasion when the veneer wore thin, a guest was surprised to see Necker favoring his daughter and remarked to Germaine, "Your father appears to love you more than your mother does."

Germaine came to the defense of the family honor. "My father," she said with equanimity, "thinks more of my present happiness, my mother of my happiness in the future."

As Germaine exercised the restraint of a nun in her day-to-day relationship with her mother, the two women began to reverse roles. Germaine had recovered completely from her childhood breakdown and never slipped back into her early pattern of listless compliance. It was Madame Necker who now resorted to emotional outbursts that she had once condemned in Germaine. Convinced she had a terminal illness, her preoccupation with death became an obsession. Though he sympathized with her, his wife's complaining forced Necker to turn more and more to Germaine, treating her as a confidante rather than his daughter.

Germaine glided into her new life as easily as a breaking dawn. Her tutors for the sciences, math and languages were outstanding. Her coaches for singing, drama and elocution were without peer. At the Necker salon, she no longer sat next to her mother but mingled with the guests and like a queen bee led dazzling discussions in her own circle. Often, as they had done at St. Ouen, she and Catherine enchanted guests by performing in short dramas, Germaine taking the role of hero and Catherine acting as her leading lady.

In May, 1781, a crisis in Jacques Necker's career forced the family to reunite. Despite Necker's efforts to bolster the sagging French economy with loans rather than increasing taxes on the overburdened populous the nation continued on its road to financial disaster.

Necker felt responsible to his admiring public and believed he owed them an explanation. In an act of historic precedent, he published *Compte Rendu,* the first White Paper, an accounting of the faltering condition of the royal treasury caused by the misuse of funds by the nobility. The princely linens had never before been exposed to so much fresh air.

The public's acclaim for Necker was overwhelming and unanimous. Jacques attained glory and Germaine was overjoyed. The report was read by every French citizen who could get his hands on a copy. Printing presses worked overtime to meet the demand—more than 200,000 copies in less than a week. The illiterate gathered at street corners to listen as the paper was read aloud.

But Necker had aroused the wrath of the Council of Ministers and the hostile aristocrats. They opposed his liberal policies and envied his popularity. They pressured the King who was too weak to fight back and Necker was forced to resign.

It was a bitter blow to the Necker family pride. Suzanne and Germaine set aside their differences to rally behind Jacques. Necker left Paris quietly with his wife and daughter and went into self-imposed exile at his country estate, St. Ouen

But his popularity followed him—St. Ouen was invaded by well wishers and those who protested his dismissal. The roads from Paris were jammed with sympathizers come to pay homage. The outpouring of good will came from every level of society, from bishops, journalists, shopkeepers, peasants. The public adulation was gratifying but ineffective. The nobility still ruled France.

Popular support, however, did permit Necker to remain a power in France as leader of the opposition. He remained on good terms with the King and Queen and several members of the court.

Soon, the clamor evaporated and Necker was yesterday's news. The family left St. Ouen and toured the provinces for three years. Germaine's interest mounted and her education broadened as they learned first hand at meetings with provincial officials of the growing unrest among the people of France.

The Neckers traveled on to Switzerland, where Germaine was bored with her relatives and most of the Swiss whom she considered unsophisticated and dull. She was disillusioned further when her father bought a dilapidated chateau at Coppet, fourteen kilometers from Geneva on Lac Léman, and spent part of his fortune and endless hours in restoration. More disturbing for Germaine was her fear that they would never return to France. For Necker who had acquired a barony with the purchase was turning the property into the family estate.

But her parents were just as impatient as she to go back to Paris. Necker had been assured by aristocratic friends that the stigma of his dismissal had been forgotten and that he would again be welcome in the capital.

Early in 1785, when Germaine and her parents returned to Paris, she knew she had come home.

Madame Necker planned the evening with great care. She selected the intimate mauve drawing room for a quiet dinner and a critical private family council. The walls of the chamber were hung with damask panels in soft shades of violet in the mode of the era. Strong accents of gold leaf and deep purple tones were repeated in stripes and small patterns on the upholstered fauteuils and love seats. The fire in the white marble fireplace cast a vermillion glow like a late afternoon sunset throughout the room while its flickering flames were reflected like darting fireflies in the crystal goblets and candelabra on the dining table.

Madame Necker took painstaking precautions in arranging this meeting and in convincing her husband to keep its purpose a secret from Germaine. Such get-togethers were rare for the Neckers whose nights were usually filled with theatre, opera, receptions at the homes of friends and their own regular Friday salons. Germaine continually rebuffed any suggestion about a discussion of her future. "There is plenty of time," Germaine would reply and left her mother dangling and frustrated.

This time Jacques Necker submitted. He knew the resolution about his daughter's marriage was long overdue.

Germaine had matured far beyond her eighteen years. She had as casual an acceptance of her intellect and position as Mozart had of his musical genius. She was vivacious and gregarious and displayed an urbane arrogance that reflected her father's wealth, power and popularity. She had a mind of her own and easily deflected her mother's pressures with her gift of debate and persuasion.

As they dined, Madame Necker, secure in the presence and support of her husband, braced herself and broke into the lively conversation about the drama they attended the previous evening.

"It's time we made plans for your future, Germaine," she said. "You are a grown woman . . . we can no longer put off the question of your marriage. Your father and I are of one mind. You must marry, and soon. We have selected the Englishman, William Pitt, as the most promising candidate."

Germaine was stunned. She looked to Necker, who picked up his wine goblet to avert her glare. She felt she had been tricked and that her father was a party to it. She was cornered. Trapped.

She did not respond. She rested her fork on her plate, refused to eat and stared into space like a defiant, implacable child.

Ignoring her daughter's silence, Madame Necker went on to speak of the joys of sharing a husband's successes and the satisfaction of entertaining as a married woman.

As footmen cleared away the table, Madame Necker moved to a bergère near the fireplace. She began to pour coffee from a baroque silver service. Necker sat benignly on a sofa across from his wife.

Their daughter stood up, aloof, with her back to her mother. Selecting a green twig from a vase of flowers, Germaine fingered it petulantly. Once the servants left the room, she took a place beside her father. She held her shoulders back stiffly, her chin thrust forward with determination.

"I refuse to marry Mr. Pitt," she declared firmly.

The room fell silent as an empty church.

A log slipped from the andirons. The fire flared up.

Madame Necker gripped the arms of her chair, her face white, her eyes fastened on her husband.

Necker stared into the flames.

"Jacques!" she implored.

Necker would have preferred to face another dismissal from court than endure this painful scene. He knew his daughter had little interest in taking a husband. On the other hand, he was concerned for her welfare were she to remain single. As a woman alone, she would encounter insurmountable hurdles if she tried to exercise her intellectual interests and implement the political philosophies he passed on to her. The plight of women members of the royal family was no better unless married to princes or heads of state. Aristocrats arranged marriages for their daughters with officials in government or military men to maintain property and prestige. During their talks at St. Ouen, Necker had told Germaine that he, as a man, had to marry to find his way into politics.

Germaine decried society's limitations on women.

Though defiant, she was too perceptive to deny custom and tradition. She was aware of the advantages of having a man provide a base from which she could express her convictions. She also wanted children . . . she had to admit she had physical and emotional cravings which perhaps a husband might fulfill. But she continued to rebel against restrictions and conventions.

"Minette!" Monsieur Necker was firm but cautious.

"Yes Papa."

"You concede that you will marry?" he asked reading her mind.

"Yes," reluctantly. "But I will not have the Prime Minister of England as my husband. I know he has all the proper credentials," she went on well prepared for the inevitable. "He is not a Catholic. He is young, only twenty-five, and has an unprecedented series of achievements to his credit. He's a financial genius. He served as Chancellor of the Exchequer and has a predictable future of success ahead of him."

Madame Necker was encouraged. "Why do you reject him when you acknowledge he is a noble man, a man of character? Someone who appreciates your father and could carry on his legacy. There is no one else in Europe worthy of being Jacques Necker's son-in-law."

"He would be *my husband*!"

Madame Necker ignored her daughter's retort. "Your marriage to Mr. Pitt could strengthen relations between France and England."

"Papa!" Germaine did not want to turn the discussion into a disagreeable battle with her mother.

"Suzanne!" Necker tried to interrupt his wife. "We agreed the choice would be Germaine's."

Madame Necker refused to listen. "Two young people brilliant in international politics at so significant a time in history—it is prophetic—you will create a dynasty beyond your own lifetime and assure the peace and economic stability of Europe!"

"Papa!" Germaine pleaded.

"Suzanne!" Necker implored.

Madame Necker was adamant. "It must be Mr. Pitt!"

"Mama!" Germaine stood up, extending her hands toward her

mother pleading to be heard. "You must understand, Mama," Germaine's voice was commanding but gentle. "I refuse to marry Mr. Pitt. I do not wish to hurt you, but nothing you can say or do will change my mind."

Madame Necker leaned back in her chair, disbelieving. She had expected an argument, but not total rebellion and rejection. Germaine remained obdurate and her father was unwilling to attempt to persuade her. It suddenly struck Madame Necker that from the start she had never had her husband's complete support. Feeling outmaneuvered, she lashed out at Germaine.

"You are wretched and ungrateful! You will regret your decision." She said no more. She knew she had lost.

Jacques Necker felt that Germaine owed her mother at least an explanation of why she would not consider William Pitt.

"Why, Minette?" he asked.

"It is simple, Papa. I would have to make my home in England if I married him. I am French. I would be considered a foreigner in both countries. My visit to Switzerland convinced me that I can not live happily anywhere other than in Paris. I identify with the spirit of the French people . . . their intellect, their spontaneity, their sensibilities and their obsession with self-determination. I cannot leave France. Most of all, Papa, I cannot leave you." She saw her mother flinch. "Or Mama," she added quickly.

She and her father then went on to talk of other candidates for her hand. There were many men anxious to marry Germaine without ever having met the future bride, but few qualified. The first consideration was religion, which eliminated most Frenchmen since France was a Catholic nation and the Neckers were staunch Protestants. Then there were position, background, political sympathies and future career prospects to be weighed against the Necker fortune, which brought a substantial dowry.

The field of suitors narrowed to two: both were Swedish nobles and favorites of Queen Marie Antoinette. They were Count Axel Fersen and his good friend, Baron Eric Magnus de Staël who had sought Germaine's hand since she was a child.

Count Fersen had distinguished himself in the American Revolution and was honored by George Washington for service during the siege of Yorktown.

"He is a contradiction," Germaine said circumspectly. "I am sure he is a charming young man. Perhaps he has more charm than conviction. Though he fought beside the Americans he does not believe in their ideals of freedom and independence. I could not live with someone whose integrity I could not defend."

"That leaves the Baron de Staël," Madame Necker concluded dryly.

Since he first approached the Neckers about Germaine through his sponsor, Count de Creutz, de Staël had never relaxed his efforts to convince them of his eligibility. He was the most persistent of all Mademoiselle Necker's suitors.

"Well, Minette?" Necker asked.

"He is worth considering," Germaine replied. From the beginning, she had kept a record of everything she learned about Eric de Staël. She hid it among the pages of the journal in which she entered her activities, daydreams and random thoughts every day. Germaine knew the Baron had been born into a poor aristocratic family and used his beautiful face, trim figure and cunning to advance his station in the Swedish court. He began his career as a military officer and chamberlain to the Queen of Sweden. Believing his talents were wasted in this small court, he grew bored and sought to serve with his friend Fersen in the American army. He won the assignment but before embarking for America he made a detour to Versailles. At once, he recognized that he was destined for this most sophisticated, debauched court in the world. The women were charmed by this obliging young baron and he was flattered by their attention. He stayed, easily wangling a post in the Swedish embassy as Ambassador de Creutz' protégé, and was immediately accepted as a member of the court.

Germaine had never overcome her childish fascination with the handsome aristocrat who wanted to marry her. She combined a brilliant mind with the sensibilities of a supremely passionate and sensual woman. She was aroused by what she had learned of his physical charms, but her final decision was a product of her intellect. She was impressed with the Baron's liberal political leanings. While her father was in the service of the King, de Staël had used his influence with both monarchs to promote Necker's policies. He did not cease after Necker left office. Germaine was not so naive as to discount the rumors that his actions were deliberate—to pave the way to marriage and a share of the Necker millions. But would such a man make a devoted husband and a dedicated son-in-law?

"Your mind is made up, you will marry de Staël?" Necker asked, hoping the decision would be made this evening. He could not face another confrontation with the two strong-willed women in his life.

"Yes," Germaine said. "Under certain conditions. The contract must guarantee that he is Swedish Ambassador to France for life. De Staël himself must also promise that we shall always live in Paris and that I shall never go to Sweden against my will."

"You may marry the Baron de Staël," Madame Necker said with a heavy sigh of compliance. She would not deny herself the right to participate in her daughter's future. "I shall do everything in my power," she said, "to make sure that as the Ambassadress of Sweden in the French court you will have the most famous salon in all Europe."

"My dear Baron. Let me show you how to dance with the young woman you love."

Monsieur Necker whisked Germaine from de Staël's arms and whirled her around the Swedish Embassy ballroom. The new bridegroom melted away among the hundreds of wedding guests, watching his father-in-law and his bride glide as smoothly as ballet dancers across the polished floor.

Necker's eyes shone with pride and relief as he looked down at his daughter. The thickening waistline of his mature years had no effect on the lightness of his feet.

"How young you are, Papa! I will always love you best!"

The bridal bargain had almost failed when King Gustavus of Sweden demanded the island of Tobago from France in exchange for de Staël's ambassadorship. When he finally settled for a smaller island, Louis XVI and Marie Antoinette signed the marriage contract on January 14, 1786.

The shy child who once sat beside her mother at her glittering salon was now the Baroness Anne Louise Germaine Necker de Staël Holstein, Ambassadress to Sweden, assured residence in Paris for life . . . chatelaine of her own mansion. De Staël, after more than seven years of dogged determination, was married to the Necker fortune.

Chapter 5
Life at Court

Germaine stood motionless in a splendid bedchamber in her parents' mansion where she would spend her wedding night. She was neither the self-assured, efflorescent Germaine Necker she had become after St. Ouen nor the liberated Baroness de Staël she had expected to be as a married woman. The marriage ceremony conjured no magic. Instead, she shivered uncontrollably beneath her long white peignoir and negligée and felt as vulnerable as a lonely sunflower in a meadow during a windstorm. Her eyes, a deep fathomless violet, shimmered in innocent expectation. How would she endure the mysteries of marriage . . . with a man who was a paradigm of the dissolute society of Paris?

But was this not one of the reasons she married Eric de Staël? Or was her mother right after all . . . that she would regret the choice she made for a husband?

She hugged her body as if her arms would warm her and took a cursory look about the room which seemed foreign to her though she had helped her mother select its decor. The chamber had a quiet intimacy despite its spacious splendor. The flickering light of the candles on several small tables bounced off the crystal pendants of the chandelier above Germaine and dazzled like facets of diamonds on her black hair. The soft blue damask of the wall panels was repeated in the draperies, the upholstery and on the canopy and the spread of the bed. Gold leaf accents sparkled brilliantly on the ceiling and the doors like reminders of the Necker wealth.

It was an old French custom for a newly married couple to live their first days of marriage in the home of the bride's parents and the de Staël's would spend their nights in the most elegant guest room of the Necker's Paris manor house.

Germaine was startled as the door from her husband's dressing room swung open. A poised Eric Magnus entered and strode toward his bride as though this opulent chamber had always been his home.

De Staël exuded style and impeccable taste. His velvet lounging robe, emblazoned with his family's coat of arms, was royal blue, a tone he deliberately selected to complement the dominant color of the chamber. His thick, long blond hair cascaded in waves to the nape of his neck and was pulled back in a queue. His features were chiseled, his skin fair. His figure trim and erect. A golden sash with cerulean tassels was tied in a casual loop showing off his slim waist and slender hips. Though his azure, lackluster eyes evoked an aura of his jaded lifestyle, he appeared younger than his thirty-six years.

The new Baroness marveled at the beauty of this creature and understood why the ladies of the court fawned over him—what woman would not be eager to fall into his arms? She glanced uneasily at the marriage bed with its plump pillows, its blue satin sheets and blankets folded down in expectation.

Germaine felt a chill like spring water crawl up and down her spine. She closed her eyes and envisioned her father's face as he had looked earlier that evening. His eyes were full of love and omniscient, like that of a sage, aware of what lay ahead for his daughter. She felt his presence and the pressure of his arms around her. She loved her father, she wanted him—not this stranger.

But it was her husband who was standing beside her. Germaine opened her eyes and saw Eric Magnus hold out his hands to her. She trembled slightly, drew her peignoir close and turned her back to him.

Placing his hands lightly as a feather on his wife's shoulders, de Staël moved his fingers slowly along her neck. Never before had he been so moved by the emotion that overcame him now. This girl disarmed him. He felt a magnetic attraction, yet, at the same time he could not deny the powerful force that separated them.

"Germaine," he whispered with practiced gallantry trying to break the barrier that kept him from embracing her.

She drew away abruptly, then turned and faced the startled bridegroom who was unaccustomed to rejection.

"I am your wife," Germaine said, her eyes darkened to a brilliant midnight blue. She spoke coolly and without rancor: "I have every intention of fulfilling my marriage vows. I'm certain you will instruct me well. We are married in the eyes of the church and the law. I promise our marriage will be consummated." She hesitated.

"But not while we are in my father's house," she added with finality.

Eric was stunned, not by his new wife's ultimatum but by her directness and guileless honesty. He backed away, slipped into a bergère and stared up at her in amazement.

"I am tired," Germaine went on simply. "You must be too. We have many commitments and engagements during the next few days. We should rest."

Then she lay down in the bed, drew up the covers, turned on her side and pretended to sleep. Later, when her husband had quenched the candles and took his place beside her, she waited, afraid that he might defy her conditions. She fought to control her trembling.

At last, she heard Eric's regular breathing and knew that he slept. Near dawn, she dozed. He had not touched her.

The following night was no different from the first. Nor was the next. By the end of the week, Germaine's curiosity and sensuality were aroused. Had she spoken too brashly, too soon? How long would he lie there, night after night, in the darkness and ignore her? Was he less the gallant, less the lover of his reputation? Was there a weakness in his character that kept him from asserting himself, or even discussing what she denied him?

As the excitement of the post-nuptial activities filled the young bride's days there was little time for her to agonize over the tension of her nights. She entertained callers, supervised her move into the Swedish embassy and, with her husband, she attended dinners and receptions held in their honor. She was surprised and elated with the privileges society granted her as a young matron, the wife of an ambassador. She was extended special courtesies and was received with deference and respect. Slowly she was attaining the independence she cherished and hoped for. It wasn't by magic, it was by station.

Germaine's zest for life gained momentum with her new social commitments. Her periods of despair and depression were fewer but now they were more intense.

Her nights alone with Eric Magnus were both disturbing and tantalizing. Often she wanted to reach out and touch him in the dark, but she did not dare. She had made the rules and her pride was too great to break them.

The Baron de Staël was unaware of his wife's turmoil. He was as impassive as a sleepwalker. He had waited years for the Necker fortune--a few more days or weeks before he possessed his bride, who was barely beyond her girlhood, were of little consequence. In the short time since their marriage, he had grown to respect Germaine and was developing an unforeseen affection for her. He hoped to understand and please her.

That she had none of the beauty and sophistication of the ladies at court did not concern him. He found her manner refreshing. He observed that his friends and their guests were fascinated by her brilliance . . . she could keep an audience spellbound for as long as she chose. Her uneven features were immobile, but her amazing eyes, flashing suddenly, were a signal that her mind had been triggered with an idea. She would express herself precisely, entertainingly and without affectation.

The Baron de Staël was clever, manipulative and cunning. But his mind was slow. He admired Germaine's intelligence without comprehending her genius. The girl he married for her dowry (to pay his debts and permit him a life of extravagance) he concluded, was a complex and remarkable woman. Her rare intellectual charm transcended her appearance.

Eric de Staël was falling in love with his bride.

On a brisk afternoon late in January, the Baroness de Staël descended the stairway of the Necker residence on the arm of her husband.

She would no longer call this mansion home.

A sensation of déjà vu swept through her—the memory was of an early venture into freedom . . . leaving her mother behind for the trip to St. Ouen. Her emotion was also much the same as it had been when, as a child, she drove off with Catherine Huber and her mother. Now there was a finality to her departure. She was leaving to create a world of her own. In the future, when she returned to this mansion, it would be on her own terms, as her own mistress, no longer bound by the rigid routines her mother had inflicted upon her.

During the first ten days of her marriage, Germaine came to understand Eric Magnus. He would pose no barriers. He was dull and indifferent, but to his credit he had charm, superb manners and distractingly good looks. With such a man, Germaine knew she could do and live as she chose.

The couple stopped at the steps of the coach and turned to nod toward Suzanne and Jacques Necker, standing at a window. The expression on her father's face tore at Germaine's heart.

As she settled comfortably into the gold velvet seat in the carriage with Eric, Germaine felt a sense of loss, of doors closing behind her ending an irretrievable part of her life. She was saddened, but exhilarated. She shuddered slightly. Eric misunderstood her trembling. Thinking she was cold, he put an arm around her.

The carriage took them through the broad boulevards of Paris's fashionable districts and beneath the stark beauty of the bare plane trees along the Seine. Germaine was consoled by the warmth of Eric's body, so close to hers.

She did not speak. The sound of the horses' hooves and the rumble of the carriage wheels along the cobblestones seemed to be telling her of what lay ahead in her future.

Because he had become accustomed to his wife's eloquence, Eric Magnus was distressed by her silence. He tried to draw her out by talking of her father. He spoke of his efforts to keep Necker's name before the King and the possibility of her father's recall to the government.

But Germaine was putting her past behind her. As they drew nearer the Swedish Embassy, Germaine's feeling was one of elation.

Later, as she stood next to Eric in front of the marble fireplace in the master bedroom of their new home, her senses, already aroused quickened with the warmth of the fire. She looked up at her husband. Eric was stirred by the hypnotic depth in her eyes. He reached out to his wife, picked her up in his arms and lowered her slowly onto the bed. With joy and mounting ecstasy, Germaine de Staël fulfilled her promise.

Within a month of her wedding, the Baroness Anne Louise Germaine Necker de Staël Holstein was presented at court in Versailles.

Though she had practiced the ritual till her back ached, the Ambassadress curtsied awkwardly before the monarchs of France. On the third bow, Germaine tore the train from her gown.

She was horrified.

"You need not be concerned," Louis XVI remarked when he saw her flush in embarrassment. "We are your friends. If you cannot feel at ease here with us, you will never be comfortable anywhere."

Germaine smiled appreciatively. Leaving her throne, the Queen led the young woman to the royal apartments, where she put a chambermaid to work on the ripped seam and talked to Germaine about her parents and her husband.

The new Baroness was delighted with her introduction to the glittering life of the court. The nobles and diplomats, representing the great houses of France and Europe, were as kind and helpful to her as the King and Queen. They accepted her into their circles as a member of an extended family.

Germaine was in awe of the palaces in which she spent most of her days. The halls and corridors, with marble floors, walls and columns, were vast and filled with magnificent furnishings and spectacular works of art. Luxury and wealth were not new to the Baroness de Staël, but Versailles was grandeur.

Madame de Staël was swept up by a whirlwind of intriguing duties. The pace was an incredible merry-go-round of dinners, dances and entertainment that took her back and forth between Versailles and Fontainebleau. She felt like an actress on tour jostled about by wardrobe mistresses who adorned her in elegant gowns and then shoved her onto the stage to perform. She was carried along so swiftly from one affair to the next, she had no time to determine whether this was indeed the way she wished to spend her life. But she was grateful to Eric Magnus for his patience, affection and encouragement as he answered her questions about people and protocol. He was educating her to the subtleties of the French court.

Once her initial bewilderment passed, Germaine was quick to adapt to the gaiety and the pomp. Her inherent pride and self assurance surfaced. She rode the crest of the prestige which came with her role as Ambassadress of Sweden with confidence and aplomb.

Her husband was responsible directly to Gustavus, King of Sweden. When the Swedish monarch learned of Germaine's writing talent he asked her to report on the events of French government. She approached her assignment with the diligence of a dedicated journalist.

"The Queen of France," she wrote in one of her first dispatches, "received me with the same courtesy she shows all Swedish nobility. The dinner she held in my honor was far more elaborate than those she gives other ambassadresses.

"Unfortunately, the emphasis on life at Versailles is placed on entertainment and pleasure-seeking. Little business is conducted since the ministers and government officials avoid and refuse to make policy decisions. There is nothing important to report for nothing critical is discussed, no legislation is proposed or adopted and no appointments are made. The government appears to be floundering out of control.

"There is one major resolution that must be made each day which is the preoccupation of the nobles—where dinner will be held that evening. It is quite pointless since the schedule is repeated every week. We dine three nights with Madame de Polignac, three more at Madame de Lamballe's apartment and the last day, the evening meal is served in the royal suite with the King and Queen.

"Later in the evening, the noblemen gather round the gaming tables in several of the huge chambers of the palace. Their greatest pleasure, it seems to me, is gambling away their money. There is rarely an evening when, in the course of a few hours, one nobleman has not lost a complete fortune.

"Card playing and other games of chance are nightly pastimes. When the men tire of their surroundings or the game, the nobles leave and look for another in the apartments of the ministers, the captains of the guard or the officers of the crown. They do not stop at dawn but prowl the countryside for more amusement.

"You may have heard that the Queen is blamed for much of this frivolity and carousing. I do not believe she should shoulder all the responsibility for this wanton behavior, particularly since she does not approve of it. She has tried to restrict the gambling to a few hours a week and direct the nobles to the serious business of government. She has not succeeded for they refuse to listen to her."

The Baroness went on to describe Marie Antoinette's lavish affairs which contradicted her efforts to direct the court's attention to the nation's welfare. The Queen had a talent for setting the stage for the magnificent spectacles she contrived to amuse the court. She changed the backdrops for each event, with decorations she had workmen construct or with sets from the King's vast warehouse, the Hôtel des Menus-Plaisirs. For fancy dress balls, the interior of the palace could be transformed into a mystical fairyland, with thousands of yards of gossamer fabric, or made into a huge indoor garden, with fresh shrubs, flowers and trees. The parks surrounding Versailles became ballrooms for concerts, dances and fireworks displays.

The Queen wore elaborate costumes to match each of her themes.

Germaine hesitated to write about the amorous adventures commonplace among the courtiers and the ladies. What had been delicious fiction and rumor to the new Ambassadress before her marriage was now a reality as stark as a frigid day in winter.

Madame de Staël was not prepared to discard the Calvinist training and discipline of her early years and succumb to the profligacy that surrounded her now. She respected the sanctity of marriage and the example of devotion her parents had set. She was fond of the man she married and hoped to make her marriage a success. Though Eric Magnus was the darling of the court, he was a loving and attentive husband.

Germaine did not escape the attention of the courtiers. She was surprised, for she had no illusions about her appearance. The jaded aristocrats were attracted by her voluptuous femininity and her spirited repartee. Her attempts to discuss serious matters, which they ignored, were considered charming and precocious. They flattered her. She shrugged off whispered proposals of intimacy as gestures of friendliness. When they persisted boldly and proved their earnestness, she was embarrassed. At first. Then frightened. Then offended. Finally, resigned.

It took the Baroness two months to catch her breath in these palaces of wanton pleasure and look for a way to nourish her mind, now starved for stimulation. So she established a salon of her own, inviting a select group of friends to her home in Paris one night each week. Her guests found her wit, her sparkling conversation and her intellectual enthusiasm irresistible. Before long, her drawing rooms, as her mother's, were filled regularly with journalists, lawyers, philosophers, literary men and some of the nobility who also wanted a reprieve from the banality of the court.

The Baron de Staël was uncomfortable among his wife's erudite friends and avoided her salon. Germaine was unconcerned. She saw much of Eric at Versailles and spent her nights, happily, in his arms.

By the first anniversary of her wedding, the Baroness de Staël had grown disillusioned with court life and was disappointed in her husband. And she was pregnant.

Versailles no longer charmed or awed her. Nor did it pose a challenge. The artificiality bored her, and the obsession with self-adornment she found degrading.

Did it matter that the Queen could stagger under the weight of a two-foot tall headdress of fur, fabric and feathers—crowned by a miniature boat? Or that a duchess decorated *her* hair with the figurines of an infant, a Negro, a wet nurse and a parrot? It was all too absurd.

She lost patience with the women's petty prattle, their efforts to emulate the Queen's costumes and the coquetry to which they resorted to attract a partner for the evening or, perhaps, for a longer liaison. Most of the men were equally as shallow, pursuing their twin interests of gambling and seduction.

As for her husband, Germaine watched with chagrin as he slipped back into the patterns of a philandering courtier-bachelor. She had to admit (to herself but no one else) that he was as ineffectual and irresponsible as her mother had predicted. Germaine hadn't expected more, and considered herself fortunate. The early happiness in her marriage, she reflected, was a dividend, and, despite Eric's present behavior she preferred her new life to that of living with her parents.

The Baron de Staël's attitude toward Germaine had altered. He continued to love his wife but was listless and incommunicative, unable to express the depth of his affection. He felt inadequate, no match for Germaine's intellect and drive. He could not cope with her eloquence, aggression or passion. She frightened him with her fierce intensity, in conversation, in politics, in lovemaking. Intimidated, he withdrew from his wife and returned to the gaming tables and the ladies of the court. He ran up debts that were larger than those he had brought to his marriage and gave them to Germaine's father for payment. Necker paid.

To their friends and the court, the Baron and Baroness de Staël were of one mind. And they were. Germaine and Eric had a unifying and consuming interest—the political career of Jacques Necker.

Husband and wife conspired with hearty camaraderie—Eric Magnus to assure his source of income, Germaine for the love of her father and her own lust for glory. Working together on this shared goal, they blocked out their differences.

At all other times, there was tension in the marriage.

"There are rumors," Germaine said to Eric one day, "that you have a mistress. The hours you keep make me believe the talk is true. I warn you that I find this every bit as unprincipled and deceitful as if *I* were to take a lover."

Eric Magnus was unable to defend himself.

On July 22, 1787, after discomfort, but none of the agony her mother suffered during Germaine's birth, the Baroness de Staël delivered a daughter whom she named Gustavine, after the King of Sweden.

Watching his wife holding their child in a snow white blanket edged in Belgian lace, seeing the infant's tiny pink face, Eric Magnus felt a twinge of guilt about his philandering.

Germaine was stirred by other thoughts. She drifted back to the glorious moments of her own childhood which she shared with her father. Contemplating her daughter's future, she wondered if she would feel the same sense of love and attachment for Eric Magnus.

Germaine implored him to abandon court life and devote more time to his diplomatic work. "It's not for me," she insisted, "but for the sake of your daughter."

Eric Magnus again was defenseless. "If you can't understand me," he pleaded pitifully, "please be tolerant."

It wasn't long before Germaine had to admit that she would never be able to separate her husband from his profligate friends. She realized with horror that her marriage was beginning to disintegrate. She and her husband lived under the same roof on the rue du Bac but rarely spoke. When they did it was only to promote Necker's career. Germaine curtailed her visits to Versailles and Fontainebleau, attending only functions of state to maintain an appearance of family solidarity.

Madame de Staël succeeded in deceiving the court about her failing marriage, but she could not deceive herself.

Hers was a lonely struggle. She fought off depression, determined not to succumb to her frustrations as she had when she was a child. She was beyond turning back to her family. She deplored giving her mother the satisfaction of being proved right about Eric Magnus.

But the problem for Germaine was more than just a weak husband. Though she recognized the position of authority that society granted men, she refused to accept the subordinate role of women. What should a woman expect from a marriage or a liaison with a man—emotionally, physically, intellectually—within or without the context of the mores of the times? Germaine had to find an answer . . . to fulfill herself as a woman and a human being.

In earnest, she set about seeking the resolution: how should she plot the course of her life?

She turned first to books she treasured and then began to write herself. She found it therapeutic. Before long she had completed two plays, *Sophie* and *Jane Grey*, and moved on to *Zulma*, a romantic novel. As the character of her heroines developed, Germaine's own direction evolved. A woman, her protagonists demonstrated, deserved to have a lover. She was guaranteed spiritual growth and it was within her realm to pursue and dominate him for her own survival.

Though she wrote prolifically, Madame de Staël did not lead the solitary existence of a writer. She was determined to explore and act out her contention.

Expanding her salon, she scheduled receptions for two or three evenings each week, alternating the settings between the Swedish embassy and her own lavish town house on the rue Bergère.

Two of her earliest and most trusted servants were Olive and Eugene Uginet, who assumed responsibility for household affairs. Together they hired, fired and directed a staff of forty footmen, chambermaids, personal maids, dressmakers, carpenters, coachmen, cooks and kitchen hands.

Eugene planned all meals with Madame de Staël and then assigned their preparation to the chefs. He and Olive (who kept keys to the cabinets of all gold, silver, china, glassware and linens) together made table arrangements. For large receptions, tables twenty-five feet long and six feet wide were set on opposite sides of the ballroom. Each was covered with exquisite damask linens that draped gracefully to the floor.

Down the middle of each buffet table were magnificent centerpieces—baskets of fruits or flowers in cascading levels. Smaller tables, set in alcoves, held more exceptional centerpieces--a replica of garden statuary made of sugar, perhaps. Ornate porcelain or silver pieces held other dazzling arrangements. Food plates flanked the decorations. There were often as many as twenty entrées—roasted fowl, glazed hams, fillets of beef, loins of pork—and thirty entremets—cauliflower in volute sauce, asparagus in plain butter, orange jellies in mosaiques—along with side dishes of confections, fruits, cheeses, ices.

Though there were always enough liveried footmen to serve, salon guests often preferred to make their own selections of food from the buffet, choosing wines from goblets on trays passed among them.

The de Staël salon attracted the most influential and distinguished men of the times. The Marquis Paul Joseph de Lafayette, Charles Maurice de Talleyrand-Périgord, Viscount Mathieu de Montmorency-Laval, Count Louis de Narbonne and Hippolyte de Guibert were among Germaine's regular guests.

The appeal of an evening at Madame de Staël's went beyond that of food and drink and decoration. Her drawing rooms became the forum for ideas that could not be discussed with sincerity or abandon anywhere else—least of all Versailles.

While establishing her own domain within French society, Germaine never ceased working to enhance her father's reputation. She would wander from group to group among her guests and discreetly veer the conversation toward the talents and achievements of Jacques Necker.

"It is too late, now, Minette," Jacques Necker told his daughter.

"But Papa! How can you believe that? You are wrong. I have worked for months to achieve this for you."

Germaine was flush with triumph.

As she had campaigned among her powerful friends for her father's return to office, she had given Eric Magnus a directive to sway the court in his favor. In the seven years since Necker had left the government, Louis XVI had appointed three different Controller Generals and had dismissed them all. The last had persevered only fifteen months before failing as miserably as the others. In August of 1788, the King had no choice but to send for his old friend Jacques Necker and offer him the highest official post in France.

"Too much time has been lost," Necker said apocalyptically. "If I had been granted the last fifteen months I might be optimistic."

"But Papa! This is the chance you have wanted!"

"If it had come earlier, yes. The minister's daughter sees only the agreeable side of office. She lives in the reflected light of power," Jacques Necker chided his daughter affectionately. He knew he would accept the appointment. "But the power itself, especially now, is a fearful responsibility."

Jacques Necker was still the most important man in the Baroness de Staël's life.

Chapter 6
Liberated

"How alluring you are," Charles Talleyrand remarked dryly, "and how nonchalant you are about seduction! Were you really a virgin when you married your Swedish Ambassador?"

The recently appointed Bishop of Autun stood at the foot of the commodious *lit de repos* upon which Germaine de Staël reclined. Wearing only a gossamer-thin peignoir, she stretched luxuriously among a pile of damask cushions like an odalisque in a Turkish harem. Talleyrand leaned heavily on a cane that favored his crippled foot.

Charles-Maurice de Talleyrand-Périgord was the Baroness's first lover. But he was much more. Her confidant and mentor, he had introduced her to the delicate intrigues and dissolute ways of the French aristocracy. They had met in 1787, two years earlier, when she was twenty-one and he was thirty-three. A regular guest at her salon, he fueled Germaine's intellectual passion for politics. She was no longer an ingenue, she was master of her craft.

"Why is it," she had asked him one day, "that young girls are educated in convents and in ignorance? They are taught to suppress the freedom of their emotions. Then, once they are married, the atmosphere and attitudes change sharply. Marriage is no longer looked upon with reverence but is scoffed at and joked about. Women are encouraged to break their sacred vows."

To Talleyrand, this brilliant, guileless woman presented a challenge. Germaine could have fallen into worse hands than those of this profligate priest. He had a keen, incisive mind and was considered an authority and a sage on many subjects.

Unlike most of the debauched members of the court, Charles Talleyrand was no hypocrite. French noblemen of the eighteenth century conducted their love affairs with discretion, but Talleyrand lived quite openly with his young and beautiful mistress, the Countess Adélaïde de

Flauhaut. Because of a crippling childhood injury, he had been denied the military career due an eldest son. Neglected and ignored by his parents, he was forced to pursue a career in the church. He resented and hated his profession and developed a cynicism that would color the rest of his life. His intelligence and drive quickly took him to the top ranks of the church hierarchy and Paris society.

The Baroness de Staël looked up at her lover with amused defiance. "Did you envision me emerging full grown and worldly wise from the forehead of Jacques Necker as the goddess Athena did from Zeus's head? Sorry to disappoint you. I am the product of patient and dedicated tutors. And I learn quickly."

Talleyrand smiled wryly.

Germaine beckoned her hairdresser to comb and powder the long soft curls that fell loosely over her shoulders. She returned her hand to the young girl who had been manicuring her nails when Talleyrand interrupted her toilette. Another young maid was giving her a pedicure.

Though it was customary for noblewomen of wealth and rank to receive guests in their boudoirs, the Baroness de Staël often went beyond the accepted limits of propriety. She was far more casual than her friends about how little she was wearing.

"Come, Charles. Don't tire yourself by standing. Sit here beside me."

"Thank you for letting me enjoy the religiosity of a lady's toilette," he said.

Talleyrand stayed at a remove, resting his free hand on the elegant Gobelin tapestry-covered screen that separated the alcove from the rest of the enormous bed chamber.

Talleyrand was expressionless, not a muscle rippled in his rigid, ashen fact. Only his eyes moved—with appreciative familiarity. Starting at Germaine's perfectly manicured toes, he slowly toured her firm body, feature by feature, like a gourmet at a festive table, until he reached her compelling eyes.

He was not an attractive man. His face was masklike, his complexion chalky grey. Skillful at concealing all emotion, he somehow projected a mysterious charm and subtle masculine strength.

Raising herself into a sitting position, Germaine waved her servants away.

Charles Talleyrand moved slowly toward her. He was short of

stature but his carriage was compellingly imperious. He sat down near Germaine.

"Charles," she began earnestly. "I know now that I am in love. I am certain of it."

"Ah? You have told me many times of your passion for me."

"Of course, I love you. Devotedly. As my mentor . . . my confessor . . . my beloved antagonist. As I love my father."

"Fie!" His lips moved imperceptibly, his face was a sphinx.

"You know very well what I mean. Now, for the first time in my life I love a man who can be all things to me. He is someone you know well."

"I marvel at your extremes, dear Germaine. The brilliant, witty, sophisticated daughter of the financial wizard of Europe has the emotions of a lovesick school girl. Here you are, at twenty-three, married to one of the best looking men in court. You have already published learned treatises as well as romantic trifles. Yet, you are now carried away by a juvenile infatuation."

The Baroness smiled tolerantly.

Talleyrand slipped off his jacket, laid it carefully on a nearby chair, loosened his collar and unbuttoned his white ruffled shirt. "How can you, my dear, be so unkind to your husband? Eric Magnus may have married you for your fortune, but now he is genuinely in love with you."

"He's too late. You should know that. I can no longer tolerate Eric's intellectual vacuity."

"What compels you, Germaine, to want to surrender your soul to someone? It is *you* who does the possessing. It was inevitable. Shall I tell you who your man is?" Moving closer to her, he ran his fingers lightly through her soft curls.

"Don't be exasperating!" She touched his hand affectionately. "What was inevitable?"

"Your attachment for my good friend, Louis, Viscount de Narbonne-Lara. Well?"

"Charles!" For a moment, Germaine was deflated, but she was amused by Talleyrand's perception.

"I am happy I brought you together," he said. Narbonne and the new bishop had joined the inner circle of licentious French society together. He was a member of a close group of friends whom Talleyrand selected with great care. But the Bishop of Autun questioned Narbonne's sincerity. "You will not neglect me?" he asked Germaine offhandedly.

"You know better than to ask, Charles. I am much too attached to you."

The ambassadress and the bishop were of the same cloth. Talleyrand's will was as indomitable as hers, and they nourished one another's independence, intellect and ambition. He had objectives that did not include a binding relationship and she knew it.

"Louis Narbonne is sensitive, intelligent and attractive," Germaine went on excitedly. "I never hoped for such a man. He combines all the superb qualities of my father with the vigor of youth and a lover's tenderness. Most important, he is receptive to my suggestions. I will groom him and help him secure a government post."

"There is a shadow over his background."

"I know. He's Louis XV's illegitimate son."

"Some say, by his own daughter, Madame Adélaïde."

"Base rumors."

"Just so you know."

"He is a prince of the blood." Germaine looked up at Charles, her eyes kindling brightly. "He has been brought up with the royal fortune at his disposal. He is fluent in five languages. He knows intimately the laws and political systems of most European countries. He's an expert in the intricacies of diplomacy—the ideal partner for me! He has convinced me that he loves me deeply and can only be happy when I belong to him. He has broken all his other attachments and is dedicating himself to me. Without me, he cannot survive."

"Bravo." Cynically. Talleyrand's hand crept along her face and then down her neck.

Germaine was supremely happy, happier than she had ever been. "There's more . . . " she began.

"Of course." Talleyrand had the finesse to interrupt the workings of Germaine's mind by devoting attention to her body. Caressing her, he spoke hypnotically "Our friend Narbonne has infinite charm. His good looks are a match for Eric's and he is equally appealing to women. He has nobility and elegance . . . but take care, my love," Charles murmured, as Germaine drew him down beside her, "he is of royal blood, as you say. By heritage and instinct, he does not share our liberal ideals . . . "

Lulled by the sonorous tone of Charles' voice, the Baroness no longer heard what he was saying.

Chapter 7
The Year of Necker

It was early in 1789. The Baroness de Staël was delirious with optimism. The great Jacques Necker had performed miracles.

When her father was summoned to return to the government as Finance Minister, a year before, Germaine had written King Gustavus of Sweden:

> *If the circumstances were different, I would have taken pleasure in announcing my father's reinstatement to Your Majesty. But the nation has been placed under his command at so desperate a moment that all the admiration I have for him is barely enough to inspire me with confidence.*

At the time of Necker's appointment, a devastating crop failure threatened famine in most of France. This was followed by the coldest winter in more than eighty years. Yet Necker managed to stave off countrywide starvation and thwart—at least temporarily—the crisis in the state treasury.

Once again, Jacques Necker was the most popular and powerful man in France. He could do no wrong.

The Baroness's salon in the Swedish embassy was both the center of liberal political ideology and publicity headquarters for her father. Her receptions were the most sought after in Paris. She made certain that the writers and journalists among her guests learned first hand of Necker's good deeds: that he had arranged loans through his international contacts, that he declined his two-hundred-twenty thousand-franc annual salary, that he loaned the treasury two million francs of his own money, and that he alone was responsible for saving the nation.

Madame de Staël was emerging as a political force in her own right. She had learned how to fuse her awareness of intrigue, her intelligence, her wealth, her station as ambassadress with gentle . . . and not so gentle . . . coercion and persuasive charm in support of Necker's programs. Together, father and daughter manipulated the opinion makers to rally behind him. Their unity of strength was able, also, to fend off the angry factions both to the left and right that openly opposed him and had attempted to foment a revolution.

Germaine's energy was boundless. She worked with her lover, Louis de Narbonne, to prepare him for a post in her father's government. Success and supreme power, which Necker represented, were heady drugs. The Count bound his devotion to the daughter of the great man with his desire for personal glory.

Eric de Staël rode the same crest. Despite his philandering, his star rose with his father-in-law's fame. The Baron ignored his wife's political ambitions and was blind to her affairs of heart. Not until her relationship with Count de Narbonne became court gossip was Eric's pride punctured. He decided to act the wounded husband.

On one of their rare moments alone, the Swedish Ambassador confronted his wife with the rumors.

"Your indiscretions with the Count de Narbonne are the talk of Versailles," he told the Baroness. "Your actions are imprudent."

"Ridiculous!" Germaine was not surprised by her husband's awareness—she was piqued that he should dare approach her about it.

"I can no longer tolerate his presence in our home," de Staël declared.

"Do I object to *your* friends?"

"Friends!" de Staël fumed. "Your relationship with Narbonne goes beyond a simple friendship."

"Of course it does!" Germaine was indignant. "It is one of mutual understanding that grows each time we meet. Our political goals are identical . . . we seek to unify France and fortify her leadership of Europe. He supports my father's proposals and has influenced both the clergy and the nobility in his behalf."

"It is impossible to believe that you discuss only politics— yesterday you spent twelve hours together!"

"We were alone for only six hours," Germaine countered. "How can you know how I spend my time when you are at court twenty-four hours a day? The Count is a man of honor!" The Baroness lied with such conviction that she almost believed herself.

"Furthermore," she continued, "you committed the first transgression. Shall I tell you what I hear about you and your mistress?"

Eric Magnus winced. "She is a fine woman, a compassionate companion," he said timidly.

Germaine had no real desire to demean her husband. Three weeks before they had shared a personal sorrow when their eighteen-month old daughter died after a brief illness.

Madame de Staël was deeply grieved. She was stunned less by Gustavine's death than by the remorse she felt for the neglect of her daughter and the love she had not expressed while she lived. Germaine vowed that should she be blessed with another child she would not entrust her offspring completely to a nurse and would gratefully participate in its upbringing.

Eric Magnus' tenderness had been sincere, but brief. After the funeral, he vanished immediately, taking off for his usual haunts.

Now Madame de Staël was annoyed and felt justified in trying to humiliate him. Vulnerable, her husband turned away dejected and beaten.

Germaine, for the most part, had grown indifferent to Eric. She had infinite energy and more important demands on her time. Her priority was Jacques Necker who was seeking a broader political base—he hoped to convene the elected representatives of France, the lawmaking body that had not met in 175 years!

Louis XVI had resisted all attempts to summon the legislature because he feared interference and loss of power. Ultimately, he succumbed. He could not withstand Necker's urging nor the pressures from Germaine's powerful friends.

Elections were held in the provinces. During an oppressive heat wave in April, deputies poured into Versailles where they were greeted with pomp and pageantry. Banners hung from house tops, carpets lined the streets to the palace and the populace rallied by the thousands.

May 4, 1789 was Jacques Necker's day of triumph. His daughter exulted. For the first time since 1614, the Estates General was reconvened.

The people of France were jubilant. At last they were represented. Long-overdue reforms would be instituted. There were promises of lower taxes, an improved economy, the abolition of unfair feudal practices.

Jubilation turned to confusion after the first spectacular convocation as the assembly fell in disarray like a house of cards.

Madame de Staël despaired as she watched her father try to maintain the viability of the Estates General. It comprised three bodies: the clergy—the first estate, the nobles—the second estate, and the third estate whose membership Necker had successfully increased to represent fairly, the bulk of the populace.

As the Estates General went into session, the King refused to respond to its demands. All three bodies grew resentful and voiced their bitterness against Louis. The third estate protested loudly and vehemently for they were denied the one-for-one vote permitted the other two estates.

Large numbers of clergy and nobility, agreeing with middle-class objectives, defected and joined the third estate, swelling its membership. Fortified in quality and size, this body rebelled and withdrew from the Estates General.

Jacques Necker and his daughter supported the Abbé Emmanuel Siéyès, a close friend, who led the intransigents. Under the Abbé's guidance, they declared themselves the "National Assembly," the one body capable of representing and acting for the entire nation.

The next day Louis XVI refused to recognize the assembly as it tried to convene. He locked the doors to the meeting chamber and forced the members to stand outside in a cold, teeming rain. Angered and determined, they gathered in a nearby indoor tennis court. In a dramatic demonstration of unity and strength, the assembly vowed to enact drastic constitutional changes.

Their rage spread. The people of Paris, already desperate and hungry, were aroused and ready to riot.

Jacques Necker urged the King to recognize the National Assembly and to agree to meet its demands. Like a spoiled child, Louis refused and impetuously dismissed the body out of hand. Against further protests from Necker, the King called up seventeen regiments of mercenaries and stationed them strategically around Paris and Versailles.

Later that evening, as Suzanne and Jacques Necker dined alone in their apartment, a courier delivered a secret dispatch. Without official or public announcement, Louis asked Necker for his resignation and ordered him to leave France at once.

The Controller General was stunned, but then relieved. Quietly, he obliged the king and, with his wife, left the country taking no belongings.

When she received her father's message about the departure, Germaine made a quick, instinctive choice between lover and father. She summoned Eric and left Narbonne behind with a note that said she was leaving Paris. The de Staël's joined the Neckers in Basle, Switzerland. The family reunited, retrenched and made plans to return to Coppet.

In Paris, news of Necker's dismissal and flight enraged the populace. The milling mobs, already angered by Louis' earlier actions, exploded.

On July 14, 1789, they broke into army barracks and storehouses, stole guns and ammunition, mounted busts of Necker and the Duke of Orleans (Louis' brother was sympathetic to their cause) on pikes and stormed the Bastille. They butchered the timid governor of the prison, chopped off his head and carried it on a pitchfork through Paris.

The King was terrified. The Assembly shaken. They dispatched the swiftest courier available to Necker and asked him to resume his post.

Reluctantly, Jacques returned with his wife and daughter beside him in their coach.

As the Neckers approached Paris, joyous Frenchmen unharnessed the horses from their carriage and with brute strength pulled it to the Hôtel de Ville. The citizens of the capital jammed the streets, leaned out of their windows and hung over rooftops shouting out: "Vive Monsieur Necker, Savior of France! Vive Madame Necker! Vive Madame de Staël!"

Germaine mounted the steps of the city hall with her parents as hundreds of thousands cheered her father. Her mother stood at his side and shared the glory. The Baroness was so exultant and excited she almost fainted.

"My father could be king if he chose," Germaine said to herself. She warmed to the thought of her lover. One day, with her help, he would receive the same ovation, she would be at *his* side. The Count de Narbonne could *be* king since he was of royal blood.

Jacques Necker's popularity was infinite, but the barriers to the Bastille had been the floodgates to the Revolution.

Necker tried to reconcile the extremes of political ideology and was caught in a three-way vise—the apathy of the King, attacks from the Assembly and the unrelenting pressures of the larger, stronger mobs, who had no loyalties.

Madame de Staël's friends in the legislature tried to quell the unrest by abolishing the ancient privileges of the nobility and replacing them with the Declaration of the Rights of Man, which was based on the American Bill of Rights. Louis XVI, forced to share his power, no longer served as sole ruler of France. But the mobs continued to simmer.

On the morning of October 5, Paris erupted.

Germaine received an urgent letter from her friend, the Marquis de Lafayette, saying that hundreds of wild Parisian women had ransacked shops and government buildings for food and arms and had begun to march the twenty-three kilometers to Versailles. The Marquis warned Germaine of the imminent violence since he knew that her parents lived in the palace with the King. As Commandant of the General Guard, Lafayette had to make a decision worthy of King Solomon. He had to defend the King but he had no wish to attack a band of women.

Germaine, knowing the route of the marchers, traveled in her berline by a different, little-used road to Versailles. She found her mother among a crowd of nobles trembling with angst. Their customary arrogance had evaporated. They huddled like sheep within the palace surrounded by magnificent marble columns and walls hung with giant tapestries which, ironically, depicted the victories of Louis XIV. They had waited all day while the King conferred with Necker. Louis XVI could not decide whether to flee or wait for the mob. After hours of painful suspense, he decided courageously to stay and face his people.

The nobility's anxiety now changed to dread.

Shortly after Germaine's arrival, there was a report that the mob's numbers had increased to thousands as it passed through villages en route. Women and children carried pikes, scythes and guns. The men were brandishing axes and swords and dragging cannons. Like raving maniacs they screamed vengeance on Marie Antoinette, the foreigner they blamed for their poverty. Crying out their hatred, they promised bloodcurdling tortures for the Queen.

The irate marchers finally arrived at Versailles during a drenching downpour. They were filthy, soaked and bedraggled. The Marquis de Lafayette tried to head their columns with his national guard, but he could not stop them from forcing their way into the public galleries of the palace. They shouted abuse and obscenities and hung their sodden garments to dry on banisters, furniture and chandeliers. They were prevented, however, from penetrating the King's security.

Lafayette entered the upper level of the palace, where the terrorized aristocrats waited. Composed and at ease, he assured them the mob was under control and too weary from the long march to do violence. Relieved that the crisis seemed to have passed, the nobles dispersed to their apartments for the night.

Jacques Necker led his wife and daughter to the chambers of the Controller General which were connected to the palace by long, meandering passageways.

As dawn began to break, Germaine was startled in her bed by a small, fretting, aged noblewoman in nightgown and cap who was tapping her shoulder.

"The murderers have broken in and reached the Queen's suite!" she screamed in fright. "The Queen escaped but they massacred the guards and slashed her bed, thinking she was still there. I'm frightened—I cannot return to those horrors!"

"We are safe," Germaine said trying to comfort the woman. "You may stay here. The mob won't find its way to these rooms through the morass of buildings. They want the King and Queen, not us."

Jacques Necker had already left the King's chambers. Germaine roused her mother and guided her hurriedly through the endless corridors. They heard gunshots, saw splashes of bright red blood on the marble floors and encountered the King's bodyguards embracing Lafayette's men, who had saved them. As they walked past the soldiers, Germaine recoiled, quickly shielding her mother from the gory sight of two decapitated bodies.

Madame de Staël and her mother were drawn on by shouts and cries till they reached the huge chamber in which the nobles had gathered the night before and were reassembled now with their terrified families.

The Marquis de Lafayette walked among them with the supreme composure of a ministering priest, trying to bolster their spirits. An uproar rose from the monolithic Marble Court below, where the mob had broken in after crashing down the doors. Guards barred them from reaching the upper level. "The King and Queen—back to Paris!" they shouted.

Suddenly a hush fell over the chamber, while the roar still rose from below. The royal family had arrived to join the nobles. Marie Antoinette walked slowly, with regal dignity, her daughter and son at her sides. Her face, deathly pale, was serene.

Lafayette approached the Queen and suggested that she stand on the balcony in view of the mob. Unflinching, she did as he asked, and looked down on the crowd with her children, expecting at any moment to be attacked by flying rocks. Instead, the men and women who had tried to kill her a few minutes earlier, now cheered her wildly. Their fury subsided, but only for a few moments.

The Queen left the balcony and approached Germaine and her mother. Holding her children close and choking back sobs, Marie Antoinette whispered, "They will force the King and me to travel to Paris with the heads of our bodyguards impaled on pikes before us!"

Later that afternoon, the royal family was herded into its carriage, which inched its way to Paris among the filthy, foul-mouthed marchers flaunting the hideous symbols of their bestiality on long poles against the blue autumn sky.

The Neckers drove back to the capital along a quiet route through the Bois de Boulogne. The Baroness de Staël was moved by the serenity and splendor of the day which seemed to mock their distress and the horrors they witnessed. The sun shone with startling radiance and the air was still as a grave, not a leaf on the trees was stirring.

The seat of the government and the Assembly was officially moved from Versailles to Paris. The royal family was installed in the abandoned, dilapidated rooms of the Tuileries.

What Jacques Necker had feared when he resumed office was now a reality. The authority of the nation had left the hands of the King and the legislators and was passing to revolutionary factions that were cropping up all over Paris.

In the next months, a fresh group of leaders emerged. They were young, energetic, ambitious, vocal, unrestrained and able to ride with the restless populous. Their liberal philosophies coincided with Necker's. They wanted the same constitutional monarchy he hoped for. But they demanded quick change and drastic reforms. They disagreed with Necker's methods and began to challenge him openly. Many were Germaine's friends, regular guests at her salon.

The Marquis de Lafayette's display of courage during the October march on Versailles made the young general the nation's new idol. The dynamic, leonine Honoré Riqueti de Mirabeau, who envied Necker and fought zealously to replace him, roused the people with fiery oratory. Germaine's lover and mentor, Charles Talleyrand, to aid the state treasury that had been Necker's bailiwick, introduced a bill before the Assembly to confiscate the lands of the clergy. Germaine's influence with the deputies and Mirabeau's dramatic leadership of the legislature forced the bill into law.

Necker's glory was struck another blow. During the spectacular Fête de la Fédération on July 14, 1790, he watched as Lafayette and Talleyrand were given rousing ovations by thousands of Frenchmen who had come from all the provinces of the country to celebrate the anniversary of the start of the revolution. They had forgotten Jacques Necker, the man for whom they had once stormed the Bastille.

On July 21, the press and the Assembly harshly attacked Necker's report on France's financial condition. Thwarted in his attempts to raise money, under fire and shunted aside, Jacques submitted his resignation. No one objected. On September 4, he and his wife left for Switzerland.

Germaine de Staël was unable to leave with them. On August 31, she had given birth to Narbonne's son, whom she named Auguste. Eric Magnus proudly acknowledged the child as his own offspring and heir. Germaine did not dispute his claim.

In October, the Baroness, taking her son with her, reluctantly followed her parents to the family chateau at Coppet overlooking Lac Léman. Germaine deplored her father's decision to resign for she was convinced the country still needed a man of his vision and integrity. But she was not as devastated by his latest fall from power as she had been by his first. Germaine was only twenty-four, one of the new generation of liberal activists. Her father was nearing sixty, a member of the old guard. She had a vigorous young lover, the Count de Narbonne, who was eager for a place in France's destiny. As she traveled the countryside to Switzerland she lamented her lot preferring to have remained at Narbonne's side in Paris.

Chapter 8
The Year of Germaine

W ithin three months the Baroness de Staël was back in Paris. She revitalized her salon, set to work on a constitution with her friends the Marquis de Lafayette and Abbé Siéyès, and plotted the steps to launch her lover's career.

The capital of France was Germaine's city, the center of her life, her world. Its pulse was her pulse, its vitality, its excitement, its changing moods—all were hers. Here, her heart beat faster, her mind was clearer, her conversation more brilliant.

Madame de Staël had quickly become bored with the provincial Swiss and tired of her ailing, waspish mother. Madame Necker's health had declined further and she had resorted to taking opium, the drug widely prescribed by doctors for a broad range of illnesses. When not under sedation, Madame Necker argued with her daughter. She objected to Germaine's way of life and her indiscretions with Talleyrand and Narbonne. She tried in vain to persuade her daughter to stay at Coppet.

Even the joy of her father's company could not hold Germaine. They had spent hours walking along the winding paths under the great trees on the grounds of the chateau, discussing his years of government service and her ideas of what was best for the future of France. When the days grew cold, they continued their conversations in the seclusion of their spacious, book-lined library, with its spectacular view of Lake Geneva.

But for Madame de Staël, the magnetic magic of Paris was powerful. Entrusting her son to her parents' care, she left Switzerland.

"I find it all crass, unfair and in vulgar taste," the Duke Mathieu de Montmorency-Laval protested. The dashing nobleman was one of a small group of close friends who met two or three mornings each week in Germaine de Staël's private suite.

"I cannot disagree with you, dear Mathieu," the Baroness said to the tall, blond young man who leaned his slender frame against a silk-covered wall. Germaine stood up from the couch where she had been sitting with Louis de Narbonne and walked over to the somber Duke.

"In the beginning," she went on, placing her hand lightly on his arm, "I, too, was hurt and offended by the attacks the press made against me. Now, I accept them. They are the penalty I must pay for trying to serve the people. I still shudder at what I read."

The group had been discussing the recently published book that referred to Germaine as the "Bacchante of the Revolution," the votary of its orgies and the only person in Europe capable of deceiving the public about her sex. The same author wrote a comedy, *The Intrigues of Madame de Staël,* in which Germaine was a nymphomaniac who created dissension among her lovers in order to hold them.

The Baroness de Staël had become a controversial celebrity. The press delighted in printing racy, provocative stories about both her private and public life. But with a keen instinct for personal publicity, Germaine chose to be maligned rather than ignored. Her causes and campaigns were enhanced by oblique tributes like one paid her by Antoine de Rivarol in his *A Little Dictionary of the Great Men of the Revolution.* In the dedication of his book he wrote:

> *I take liberty to place your name in the front of my collection, for to publish a dictionary of the great men of today is merely to submit to you the list of your admirers.*

Mathieu's indignation about the invasion of her privacy moved the Baroness. The Duke's love for her was pure, slavish and platonic. Blind to her faults, he resented any slur cast against her character.

He was a member of Germaine's intimate circle, a paradoxical quintet that included Charles Talleyrand, Narbonne and Mathieu's youthful mother, the Viscountess Elizabeth Montmorency Laval, who had been Narbonne's mistress before Germaine. Together, they mingled pleasure with intrigue and influenced the unstable political scene of France.

Mathieu de Montmorency, a year younger than Germaine, was a sensitive creature with delicate sensibilities. He had fought with George

Washington and the Marquis de Lafayette in America and was now an elected member of the Assembly. His penchant for liberal causes endeared him to Germaine.

Some months earlier, Mathieu had been devastated by the death of his paramour, his wife's cousin. When Germaine responded to his grief with compassion and understanding, he fell in love with her. His devotion kindled in her the same ardor for him that she had for Talleyrand and Narbonne. She added him to her coterie as a queen bee admits her drones.

There was an enigmatic purity in Madame de Staël's passion for the three men. She craved perfection in love. What one man lacked she looked for in another—but did not forsake the first for the last. Sexual fidelity was not the key to her relationships. Loyalty was. But then, only if she were assured of ideological and intellectual compatibility.

The Baroness de Staël was a product of an era when morals were lax but immorality was rarely flaunted. Men were attracted to her for her femininity, her brilliance, her drive and her wealth, and shared her *largesse de bonne grâce*. Her zest for life was more dazzling than the beauty she did not have. Talleyrand and Narbonne had tutored her in the art of gracious and sensual living, had broken the bonds of her rigid upbringing and freed her to develop into an exuberant literary and political figure. They were closer than lovers, friends or family . . . they were inexorably bound by ardent and intellectual pursuits.

Charles Talleyrand listened to the conversation, his face immobile as a marble bust. He sat stiffly on a gold-encrusted armchair, his distorted foot moved slowly back and forth across the pattern of the exquisite carpet. His shoe heedlessly caressed the inscription "deS" woven into the delicate design of flowers and vines.

Charles smiled bemused as Narbonne sympathized with Mathieu.

"You take offense too readily," Talleyrand said derisively.

"The press goes beyond the bounds of decency," Mathieu insisted.

"Poor Mathieu. You are such a dupe," the Viscountess Laval said to her son. The burning idealism and self-sacrifice that endeared him to Germaine irked his mother.

"Would you suppress the voice of editors, Mathieu?" Charles pressed like an interrogating trial attorney. "You declare you serve the cause of justice and equality, and that all men should have freedom of expression."

Talleyrand was in tune with the times, for as the government floundered, censorship relaxed and more than one hundred and fifty newspapers had cropped up in Paris. They joined a rash of political clubs in attacking the government, the King and the nobility.

Louis de Narbonne defended Mathieu's position. "The Revolution has brought substantial changes. Well deserved and overdue. But there comes a time when they must be reigned in . . . now, these liberal policies have gone far enough. The freedom of action is beyond control . . . the King's authority has eroded."

The direction of the discussion was shifting.

"The reforms have been necessary," Germaine said. "The need now is for France to be unified. The émigrés should be permitted to return, rather than flee to other countries. I'm sure that even the King and Queen would do the same if they could find a way."

"Your blood is as blue as the royal family's," Charles taunted his friend Narbonne. "You are free to leave now, Louis. What makes you stay in France when you are in as much potential danger as the monarchs?"

"While they remain here, I must do so as well. Even if they abandon the throne, I will stay. The Bourbons must always be represented in France."

"You demonstrate remarkable visceral fortitude," Talleyrand said wryly. Louis deflected the jibe with a shrug as he would brush off a fly. The others savored the spice of Talleyrand's caustic wit. "Or do you have illusions of mounting that throne yourself?"

It was Germaine who had the illusions of making Louis de Narbonne ruler of France, and her circle supported her. Mathieu out of guileless devotion to Germaine, the Viscountess because she was still very much in love with Narbonne and would do all she could to win him back, and Talleyrand, himself, for selfish reasons.

The Baroness de Staël assessed the political climate and was ready to make her first move . . . manipulating a seat for Narbonne as a Minister on the King's Council. She always attempted to act with restraint but failed for her performances were inevitably uninhibited and flamboyant.

Germaine, with typical abandon, plunged headlong into the confusion and violence of the revolutionary fervor which gripped every Frenchman from the meanest peasant and the lowliest ragpicker. Every shade of political leaning surfaced, the extreme terrorist leftist to the reactionary monarchists and the counterrevolutionaries. Few agreed.

Opinions were debated in dozens of political clubs, among hundreds of splinter groups and by the rioting masses in the streets.

Madame de Staël knew that the leadership of the nation did not come from the working class deputies in the Assembly nor the brash leaders of the mobs. The political policy of France was constructed in the salons of the liberal aristocrats of Paris, and the Baroness de Staël's was far and away the most popular. Despite the country's cry for equality, the wealthy bankers and influential merchants at her salons felt privileged to rub elbows with the nobility. Germaine, simultaneously a dreamer and an activist, hoped to reconcile the extremes and rally sweeping support for Narbonne.

The press reported her efforts saying she wanted "to unite all parties by receiving Royalists at breakfast, Girondists at dinner, Jacobins for supper and everybody in her boudoir at night."

Late in the spring of 1791, Madame de Staël completed her groundwork for Narbonne's career. The Assembly was in sympathetic hands, no longer under the thumb of the fiery Mirabeau, who had died of overwork, overindulgence and over zealotry. It was controlled by a triumvirate that included Antoine Barnave, a close friend of Germaine's.

The Baroness was certain that she and her supporters were well entrenched. She felt secure enough to succumb to her father's pleas and return to the family estate in Switzerland.

Germaine de Staël had misjudged.

During the summer, the most significant incident of the Revolution took place and turned the confusion in France to frenzy and turmoil. To Germaine's chagrin, the event took place while she languished at Coppet.

It began when the King and his family, disguised as commoners, slipped out of Paris unnoticed in an attempt to flee France. The climax was played out in a small village near the Belgian border. The royal family had spent a long, arduous day traveling at high speed away from Paris. They stopped briefly at Varennes to rest and change horses that had been pressed to exhaustion. The King was immediately recognized, apprehended and forced with the Queen and their children to take the road back to the capital under heavy guard. The return journey, which stretched out to four days, was unbearable. The family suffered from the intense heat and the dust from the dry roads which billowed into the open coach. To add to the indignity, the family was taunted by jeering crowds who blocked their way.

Back in Paris, the King, as a virtual prisoner of the Assembly, created a situation that confounded the legislators. Louis was still head of the nation and promptly vetoed each measure the deputies tried to pass. All government business crashed to a stagnant standstill.

The populous grew irate and protested the deadlock. Demonstrations got out of hand. The national guard fired into a crowd and killed and wounded several rioters.

In her golden carriage, Germaine de Staël dashed back to Paris like a comet streaking across the midnight sky.

She found France a divided nation. Gentle, phlegmatic Louis XVI had been distressed by the escalating opposition to his lack of leadership. Under pressure and a sincere concern for his people he relented and had signed a new constitution that stripped him of most of his powers. A troubled calm followed.

The country's problems were aggravated by foreign unrest. The counterrevolutionary movement was gaining momentum. Aristocrats who had escaped the nation's violence were plotting against France with rulers of other countries who conceded that monarchist rule throughout Europe was threatened by the decline of Louis' reign.

Leopold II of Austria, Marie Antoinette's brother, who was now Emperor, joined with Prussia to mount an aristocratic mobilization against France. He aimed to restore Louis securely to the throne and wipe out the reforms that benefitted the largest segment of France's population.

The Baroness de Staël savored the threat of foreign invasion like a hawk soaring over its prey in the Bois de Bologne. War was a unifying issue, she deduced, with all domestic factions uniting to defend the nation. The raging strife at home would be thwarted.

Germaine's attitude was not completely selfless. A nation under fire would need a hawkish Minister of War. For the Baroness, Louis de Narbonne was the only man qualified to fill the post. She aligned herself and Narbonne with the Girondists who clamored for battle.

The Baroness agitated for armament to launch a ground swell of backing for Narbonne. She left no stone unturned. She met privately with men of influence and filled her salon with members of the Assembly. She made overtures to the King and Queen though she knew they opposed her lover's appointment since he had attacked Marie Antoinette for her spending and her Austrian sympathies. As she expected, she was rebuffed. Finally, Germaine got what she wanted by working through Antoine Barnave who had befriended the royal family during their ride from Varennes when he served as their sympathetic bodyguard.

On November 7, 1791, Marie Antoinette, Queen of France, wrote a friend: Madame de Staël is working night and day for Monsieur Narbonne. I never saw a stronger, more involved intrigue.

On December 7, 1791, the Queen wrote: Count Louis de Narbonne-Lara is at last, since yesterday, Minister of War. What glory for Madame de Staël and what a pleasure for her to have the whole army at her command.

The Queen did not jest. Madame de Staël took charge of the army like a seasoned commander-in-chief. She immediately assigned Narbonne to review the military installations and troops at the front. She sent Mathieu de Montmorency along as liaison officer to report back to her.

"Do you plan to cast about and find another lover to fill the void you have created in your life?" Charles Talleyrand asked Germaine as she conducted the affairs of the ministry from her library. He chided her with capricious affection as he bade her good-bye. He, too, was leaving Paris. Madame de Staël had maneuvered a diplomatic mission to England for the renegade bishop through the King with Narbonne's help.

"If it pleases you, my lord," she replied with equal cynicism. She did not look up from the desk and continued to write. "Our tight circle is being disbursed in the interest of France, precisely as we planned."

Talleyrand sat across from the Baroness, peering over stacks of papers and letters. He rested his chin on the back of his hands as he held his cane upright in front of him. He reflected on the past year, and its rapid turn of events that had won Germaine the prize she sought—Narbonne's appointment.

Charles viewed her with amusement, tinged with respect.

"Or will you concentrate on the momentum you have incurred to plot the next step on Narbonne's rise to the top?"

Germaine stopped writing. She put down her pen, selected a sprig from the vase on her desk and caressed it slowly. She glared at Talleyrand.

"France could fare worse, as it does now under a weak, vacillating king. Narbonne has already captured the imagination of the people and the Assembly. He has been voted, as you are aware, a twenty million franc allotment for his army . . . far more than we anticipated."

"He is straddling a popular issue—war on Austria and Prussia," Talleyrand pointed out. "How can he be faulted?"

"The strategy is sound. We must appeal to the rabble with issues they can understand . . . just as my father did."

"But Jacques Necker lost in the end."

Germaine's eyes narrowed. "He had his moments of glory and may yet return. Narbonne has an even greater advantage. He may be illegitimate, but he is a prince of the blood. He could be king."

Charles nodded in agreement. "You may be right, my dear. The people revolt against oppression. They fight for liberty and equality. Yet they are hidebound by centuries of traditions. Breaking with the monarchy could be more traumatic than they can tolerate."

"The masses want to improve their lot without complete rupture," Germaine observed. "They cling to the mystique of the monarchy . . . they could not let Louis leave. Yet, they would accept a *new* king. Narbonne's spectacular acceptance and his royal blood, could put us . . . *him*, on the throne."

Charles stood up and leaned over the Baroness, kissing her gently on the forehead. "I leave to convince our island neighbors to remain neutral when Austria attacks. I'm doing my share to help Louis Narbonne's cause—and mine."

Germaine's dark eyes radiated confident joy. "I will see him acclaimed, as was my father."

"Your dedication is admirable," Charles said. Reaching inside the pocket of his jacket, he drew out a flat narrow case and handed it to the Baroness.

"Here," he said with roguish good humor, "is a gift to remind you that with intelligence and finesse a woman can wield unlimited power."

Surprised and curious, she lifted the cover. A gold letter opener rested on a bed of dark blue velvet. The handle was carved ivory in the head of a regal Egyptian woman.

"It is Queen Hatshepsut!" Germaine exclaimed. "She ruled Egypt for more than twenty years during the eighteenth dynasty."

"She was as brilliant as you. Voluptuously feminine, if not beautiful," Talleyrand added. "Like you! Hatshepsut was the most powerful woman in history . . . until you!"

"Thank you, Charles. You exaggerate my influence," said Germaine, smiling benignly at her mentor.

"Your confidence betrays you, my dear," he replied.

She marveled at how her former lover flattered and patronized with such exquisite discretion. She could never deny him. The next day he left for England.

Baron Eric Magnus de Staël

Count Louis de Narbonne-Lara

John Rocca and his horse Sultan

Benjamin Constant

Chapter 9
The Reign of Terror

France was moving rapidly toward the war Germaine de Staël and her confederates had charted.

"Bravo! Bravo!"

Count Louis de Narbonne-Lara, Minister of War, acknowledged the applause with a smile of assumed humility and contained confidence. He stood before the Assembly, which cheered him without restraint on his return after spending two noteworthy months bolstering the troops at the French borders. He glanced toward Germaine, who sat in the diplomatic gallery. How handsome he is in his brilliant military finery, she reflected. His face has the distinctive features of the Bourbon kings!

The Count raised his hand and with a lambent gesture quieted the acclaim. He concluded his report with the same flamboyance that had won him the confidence of soldiers and their officers.

"Our defenses at the front are complete. The discipline of the troops is above reproach. The morale of the officers is magnificent. All lines of supply are open and shipments are on their way. France is ready for war!"

The members of the Assembly rose in a body with thunderous applause.

Germaine was exhilarated. This time it was *her* man who was being hailed. She was radiant. She was also pregnant again, by Narbonne.

With the sounds of the cheering Assembly ringing in her ears, Germaine plunged ahead with the next phase of her grand design for her lover. Skirting a reluctant and jealous Cabinet, she sought out the King and Queen directly and petitioned them to appoint Narbonne Minister of Foreign Affairs or, more appropriately, Prime Minister.

The Baroness de Staël had been heavy handed and over zealous.

The Cabinet turned antagonistic. Its members stood firm and fought back. Frustrating her attempts to obtain the post for Narbonne, the ministers went a step further. They forced the indecisive Louis to their will. Soon thereafter, Narbonne received a terse message from the King:

> *This is to inform you, sir, that I have just named Monsieur de Grâve to head the Department of War. You will hand him your portfolio.*

Germaine was stunned. She experienced another disappointment on the heels of the first. She hoped that the populace would protest Narbonne's dismissal as they had Necker's when they stormed the Bastille. The Count's downfall, alas for Germaine, occasioned no notice.

The Baroness was still powerful in her own right. She called a council of war with the leaders of the Assembly. That same afternoon, these men maneuvered the expulsion of the entire cabinet that opposed Narbonne. Within a month, the deputies in the Assembly rallied to Germaine's cause and voted a formal declaration of war.

All France was on fire! Frenchmen throughout the nation mobilized to the unifying war which Germaine supported.

Without Narbonne in command, the triumph was an empty victory for the Baroness.

And the victory over the domestic crisis was brief as the temper of the populace remained volatile. The mobs of the streets sought vengeance from the royal family, from Narbonne and all liberal aristocrats. They blamed Marie Antoinette for the threats of invasion and were convinced that she conspired with her brother, the Emperor of Austria, to attack France and restore total power to her and the King.

The control of the country was out of the hands of the government and was usurped by the rebellious rabble. The Assembly was unable to cope with the surging masses nor could its members comprehend or accept the evolution from royal power to popular rule.

France exploded!

On the night of August 9, 1792, the insurrection gained momentum. The wild mob, seething with rage against all its enemies—the King, the Assembly and the foreign powers—stampeded through Paris with unbridled fury.

On August 10, the hordes attacked the Tuileries Palace, where the royal family was living. Narbonne, Mathieu de Montmorency and other loyal aristocrats rushed to its defense. The frenzied rioting and shooting escalated rapidly and roared out of control. It was bloody and terrifying—most of the Tuileries guards were slaughtered where they stood!

At the Swedish Embassy, across the Seine, the Baroness de Staël could hear the horrifying sounds of the melée. For hours she waited for news. There was none. She grew frantic with anxiety.

In desperation, Germaine ordered her carriage to drive in the direction of the Tuileries. At the bridge over the Seine, she was halted by impenetrable crowds. One of her servants bulled his way through the human barrier to report that Narbonne and her closest friends had escaped unharmed. But where were they? Unable to move forward, she returned home, disheartened.

At midnight, when the rabble wearied and disbursed, Madame de Staël, undaunted and determined, donned an oversized dark cape, pulled the monklike hood over her head and set out on foot into the perilous streets. Stepping past wine-sotted men and women asleep in doorways and filthy gutters, still clutching the knives and axes they used in the assault, Germaine searched houses in wretched streets and alleys she never believed existed but had learned about from her servants. By dawn, she had located most of her quarry and offered them the sanctuary of the Swedish Embassy, in which she had immunity. Most accepted. Mathieu and Narbonne declined, refusing to jeopardize her safety. They stayed on the run moving from hovel to hovel in the decaying sections of the city.

As a month passed, Germaine had no time to regret her loss of power. She was consumed with efforts to rescue other friends from the powerful arm of the people's Commune, which had imprisoned the King, subjugated the Assembly and gained control of the populace.

France was under siege. The Prussian and Austrian troops had crossed into French territory on August 19 and were marching on Paris. The Commune, under the leadership of the Jacobins and a mole-like country lawyer, Maximilien Robespierre, arrested anyone who indicated a remote sympathy for the enemy. Hundreds were apprehended, given mock trials and sent to the Abbayé Prison, where most were either hacked apart by a waiting mob or sent to speedy execution under the swift blade of the guillotine.

The Swedish Ambassadress worked alone. Eric Magnus had been recalled to Sweden for interfering in France's domestic crisis. Talleyrand, to avoid the physical violence he detested, had maneuvered another mission to England.

Harboring as many refugees as her home on the rue due Bac would hold, Madame de Staël helped smuggle others to the provinces or out of the country. She was in constant dread of search parties, who conducted raids at will throughout the city. Narbonne and Mathieu managed to keep a few paces ahead of the searchers but in the end, both men had to turn to Germaine for refuge.

She hid them in a small room under the Embassy's altar where she had taken her wedding vows six years earlier. The day after they arrived, her factotum, Eugene, reported seeing Narbonne's name on a poster as a fugitive who would be put to death on apprehension. That same afternoon, two searchers, looking like hired assassins, appeared at the Embassy door. They confronted the Ambassadress insisting that Narbonne was on the premises.

She scrutinized the two callow, scrubby men of the Paris gutters who were enforcing the Commune's terrorist directives and decided to try to bluff her way out of a search. She knew her two lovers would be discovered if the building were ransacked.

"You are committing an outrage against the household of an Ambassador," she asserted as they forced their way into the vestibule.

"Sweden," she said with fire in her eyes, knowing they had no knowledge of geography or political protocol, "is a border nation and will retaliate with an attack on France—using the most destructive forces you have ever seen," she went on imperiously. "Don't you dare defy the international law of diplomacy! Sweden will strike in an instant!"

Startled and confused, the searchers stumbled back like a pair of cowardly dogs convinced they had overstepped their bounds. Germaine held tight her momentary success and relaxed her attack.

"Now," she chided, "you don't want to be unfair . . . you don't really suspect me of hiding something from you? Here, let my servants get you some wine before you go on your way!" She treated them with such kindness and put them so at ease, that the men felt chastised and chagrined. They appeared to enjoy the chaffing at the hands of this noble ambassadress.

Keeping up the light banter, she hustled them out the door, still holding their wine glasses.

"Adieu," she cried cheerfully.

They held up their glasses, drank a toast to her and left. They had penetrated no farther than the foyer.

But Mathieu and Narbonne were still in jeopardy since Germaine knew she could not again rely on such flimsy triumphs. She called on her contacts with underground connections to whom she referred as traffickers in human flesh. For an exorbitant price she obtained two forged passports. Within four days her lovers were on their way to England, Mathieu as a Swede, Narbonne as a Spaniard.

"She's stolen the gold of France! She's taking it to the enemy! Arrest her! Arrest her!"

A band of women flung themselves against Germaine's elegant berline drawn by six burly horses.

In the distance, she could hear the alarm bells that tolled the fall of two more French cities to the Prussian and Austrian invaders.

The Baroness de Staël was trapped. With her friends safe, she had decided it was time she take charge of her own welfare. Seven months pregnant and exhausted from her rescue efforts, she wanted to leave the oppressive tensions and violence of Paris and return to the haven of her parents' chateau in Switzerland.

The mob of women stopped her in front of the Embassy as her carriage tried to pull away. The horses bolted, their front legs held high, their hooves clawing the air. The Baroness's ploy to overwhelm the crowd with diplomatic authority, as she had the house searchers, failed.

The clamor attracted a swarm of wild-eyed, grubby men, who took the reins from the coachman and drove the carriage full tilt to the local precinct headquarters. From there, the Baroness de Staël was dispatched with her entourage to the Hôtel de Ville, where hundreds had been slaughtered the day before. She was horrified.

Germaine was given a police guard, but even he could not help the carriage through the raving, armed throng. After a three-hour trip—which should have taken thirty minutes—they reached the Place de Grève. Throughout the nightmarish ride, the Ambassadress had been mocked for her pregnancy, screamed at, spat upon and terrorized.

At the headquarters, Germaine was taken from the carriage and forced by the mob to pass under an arch of pikes. Her sympathetic police guard guided her. As she started to climb the stairs, Germaine slipped and one of the lancers thrust his pike at her heart! Instantly, and just in time, the guard diverted the pike with his sabre. Her eyes flashed her gratitude.

Germaine and her maid were led past bedraggled men, women and children who shouted "Long live the nation!" and were escorted into the Chamber where Robespierre, the member of the Commune largely responsible for France's bloodbath, stood in judgment.

"I am the Swedish Ambassadress," Germaine tried to explain over the shrieking around her. "My position gives me diplomatic immunity, I have passports here to prove it."

Robespierre was unimpressed. He was cocky, dressed as a dandy and presided with hygienic, self-righteous superiority.

She pleaded her case. He remained unmoved.

A door opened behind the judge's bench and another official entered the room. He was Pierre-Louis Manuel, another powerful member of the Commune, who was sympathetic toward Germaine and recently had helped free two of her friends from prison. He was astonished to see her and hear Robespierre haughtily pronounce a verdict of guilty.

Manuel cautiously intervened. "May I take Madame de Staël into custody while her sentence is being decided?"

Robespierre hesitated. Could he afford to deny the request . . . without reprisal? He replied coldly, "You have my approval."

Manuel quickly guided Germaine and her maid down the hall to his office and secured the door.

Germaine was grateful for Manuel's interference, but she was terrified. The hours passed. Hungry, thirsty and heavy with child, she suffered agonizing discomfort.

Through the solitary window overlooking the Place de Grève, she watched the bloody mobs as they bullied and attacked prisoners. Then she saw the familiar figure of a young woman being led down the steps of the building, forced between the pikes as Germaine had been. Germaine recognized her as the beautiful Princess de Lambelle, the Queen's closest friend. The mob let out a bloodcurdling cry, relishing their captive when they realized who she was.

Germaine saw the Princess hesitate and recoil as she approached the heaps of bodies that had been piled up in the square during the day. A guard pressed the woman to move on. Another struck her across the forehead with his sword. Blood burst from the wound and streamed down over her face and her long blond hair, which fell loosely over her shoulders. She stumbled forward. A raging ragpicker struck her from behind with a club. Knocked senseless, she was thrown on the growing pile of dead.

The mob fell on the body of the Princess like a pack of vultures.

They cut off her head and dismembered her body. They took one of her legs and shot it out of a cannon. They cut out her heart, placing it on a sabre, and speared her head on a long pike. Then the macabre spectacle was paraded in the square and off into the streets of Paris.

Germaine wept.

After six more hours of agony, Pierre-Louis Manuel returned. Darkness had fallen and the mobs disbursed. With Manuel was a wealthy brewer by the name of Santerre.

"Madame la Baronne," Santerre intoned to Germaine, "three years ago, in Faubourg Saint Antoine, I helped distribute grain that your father provided for the starving Parisians. I am honored to give aid to the daughter of so famous and generous a public servant. Together, we fight for the same cause—for the renewed glory of France."

Firm in his resolve Manuel took command. "I apologize for the delay. You know I could not expose you or myself to the mobs during daylight." He had taken advantage of weary authorities and wangled passports for Germaine and her maid. Before dawn the next day, Santerre smuggled them out of City Hall and assured them safe passage by driving the carriage through the south gates of Paris. The Baroness felt like a vagabond deserting her beloved city not knowing if she would ever return.

Chapter 10
Juniper Hall

Madame de Staël set down her cup and saucer and raised herself slowly from her chair. With a hand on her swollen belly, she walked across the informal family dining salon where she and her mother had been having breakfast. She drew back the crimson damask drapery and looked through the expansive window beyond Lake Geneva to Mont Blanc, its snow-covered peak glistening in the morning sunlight.

Germaine tried to absorb its tranquil magnificence. For a moment, she closed her eyes. No, there was no way to rid her mind of what she had just heard. Turning to face her mother, she said, "How could you believe I would ever welcome Eric here at Coppet?" Her voice was strident. ". . . now that I am about to deliver Louis' child?"

"You should be overjoyed," Madame Necker replied, glancing down at the letter she held and then looking up at her daughter. "Your husband is anxious to see you again. He has been reestablished as Ambassador and he has an income of 80,000 francs a year—enough to support you and the children."

"Bravo! Finally, after seven years of marriage he offers to share the responsibility of his family," Germaine said bitterly. "I have no intention again of sharing the same roof with Eric Magnus. When my child is born I plan to divorce him and leave for England to marry Louis Narbonne."

Madame Necker was mortified. Divorce in a Calvinist family was unthinkable and scandalous. "How could you say such a thing?" she cried, and left the room in childish tears.

Germaine found Switzerland stultifying. She did, of course, enjoy counselling her father on the document he was preparing for the defense of Louis XVI, now on trial in Paris. And she doted on two-year-old Auguste, who was developing into a bright, alert child.

She herself was at work on her treatise, *The Influence of Passions on the Happiness of Men and Nations.*

Madame de Staël was tormented by Narbonne's absence. It was weeks before she had word from him. She knew he was safe only through correspondence with other émigrés in England. When he did write, he said he wanted to return to France to testify for the King. Germaine flew into a rage. If he were apprehended en route he would be executed without trial. She sent off a tirade condemning him for his selfishness. He would risk his life and abandon her, his son and his unborn child. Typically, in contradiction, she filled pages of the same letter with expressions of her passion and devotion for the Bourbon aristocrat.

Jacques Necker walked briskly into the breakfast salon, kissed his daughter on the cheek and went to the serving cabinet. "Good morning, Minette, my dear," he said as he selected a croissant and poured himself a large cup of café au lait.

Necker had aged more gracefully than his frail wife. He had developed jowls but he stood erect and moved about like a young athlete.

"Your mother tells me you are not feeling well," Necker observed.

I am in perfect health!" Germaine snapped. "It is Mama who is ill and interfering in my life again."

"She worries about you."

Germaine did not reply.

"We would like you to stay here with us, but your place is with your husband in Paris. You can return to your passions . . . politics and intrigue."

"Without my friends, Paris is an empty shell." Germaine's eyes blazed with anger. "I will not be treated as a child! In spite of the hazards of a journey, I will go to London. I will not have the Swedish Ambassador calling *my* son Auguste, *his* son."

Shortly thereafter, in late November, the Baroness de Staël gave birth to another boy, whom she named Albert.

There was relative calm at Coppet. Jacques had forestalled Eric Magnus's visit and both parents strived to avoid aggravating their daughter.

In the bitter cold of Christmas Day, Madame de Staël left her parents' chateau on the pretext of visiting friends in Geneva. She had no intention of returning to Coppet. She rented a coach in the city and left for Paris, where she met her devoted friend, Mathieu de Montmorency.

Together, they planned a journey to London.

On the deck of the ferry, Germaine gripped Mathieu's arm tightly. She felt his warmth through their heavy garments. The wet salt air was delicious on her face. The cool breeze tossed her dark ringlets back against her bonnet.

Across the English channel toward Dover, dazzling white cliffs rose sharply from the shoreline—their brilliance in the sunlight, the Baroness discerned, was as startling as that of majestic Mont Blanc.

For the first time in months, Germaine permitted herself the precious emotions of anticipation and excitement. She radiated an inner glow in anticipation of seeing Narbonne. At last, the provincial Swiss, her hovering, solicitous parents and the perils of travel through France were behind her.

In January, Germaine and Mathieu drew up at the entrance of the mansion Germaine had rented for her friends at Mickleham in Surrey, twenty-five kilometers south of London.

The splendor of Juniper Hall, nestling at the foot of a gentle slope abutting a low hillside called Box Hill, was surpassed only by the vista of lovely formal gardens, lofty protecting oaks and fields that stretched far into the horizon. The Baroness was enchanted. "Yes," she mused. "I can be happy here in this serene setting. I'll make it my new home."

Entering the oak-panelled baronial reception hall, Mathieu and Germaine were met by more than twenty rejoicing friends, all of them émigrés from France . . . her guests.

Charles Talleyrand was the first to greet her.

"Germaine, my dear. Welcome to Juniper Hall!" He held her close.

Tears of joy streamed down her face as she embraced them all, looking among them for the man she loved. Slowly, almost reluctantly, a downcast Louis de Narbonne entered from a corridor and pressed through the others toward her.

Germaine was crushed by the sadness in his eyes. He was barely forty and still handsome, but he had aged markedly since she had helped him escape from Paris. Louis's embrace was warm but lacked the passion of a lover.

Others in the group were edged with similar sadness but none was as despondent as Louis. These displaced aristocrats were living in exile and poverty for the first time in their lives. For most it was a cruel blow to their pride. Some accepted their fate with grace, shared their resources and sought dignified employment to help pay their way.

Louis de Narbonne was a man apart. As a Bourbon, he keenly accepted a large share of the blame for conditions in France. Further, he felt deep remorse for leaving the royal family to face persecution alone in Paris.

The Baroness immediately took command of Juniper Hall, paying the bills and organizing its first salon. Soon the vaulted halls of the manor house echoed with laughter and gaiety as the émigrés made the most of their exile. Louis de Narbonne remained cheerless and reluctant to participate.

The straightlaced English on nearby estates were initially shocked by the communal living of the colony. Eventually, they were curious and could not resist the style and elegance of their *beau monde* new neighbors and eagerly accepted Germaine's invitations to Juniper Hall.

Not long after Madame de Staël assumed her role as chatelaine, two messages arrived that temporarily transformed the gaiety to gloom.

The first was a long letter from Monsieur Necker expressing his disapproval of Germaine's furtive departure from Coppet. He closed by saying:

> *Your behavior is unforgivable and reprehensible. I am enclosing a draft which is much less than you request. Under the circumstances this is all your mother and I will allow. Future sums will be equally meager . . . if we send any at all.*

The amount was substantial but not enough to continue to support the colony in the manner that Germaine had planned. She quickly sent off a request to her father for additional funds.

The second dispatch stunned and devastated everyone in Juniper Hall: Louis XVI had been guillotined. Narbonne was desolate.

The French exiles accepted the blow and bore their grief with courage when they learned of friends and relatives who met the same fate. They responded to Madame de Staël's constant efforts to lift their spirits and Charles Talleyrand's sharp wit and good humor. In the evenings they would gather in the grand hall, with its heavy oak furniture and huge upholstered chairs, talking of France and then taking turns reading aloud before the crackling fire on the great stone hearth.

When not with her guests, the Baroness buried herself in writing her next book, *The Passions*. One of her favorite diversion was riding in an old cabriolet she borrowed from her landlord. It was the émigrés' only means of getting about. On bright, warm days, Germaine dressed in a flowing, pastel decolleté gown and a matching bonnet that kept her dark curls from blowing in the wind. She mounted one of the open-air seats with Charles, Mathieu or Louis. The men alternated sitting beside her while the other two rode together in the groom's seat to the rear. They raced the horse along the roads, into the fields and over the moors of the countryside.

These were glorious days for the Baroness. She was with her dearest friends and close to the man who was her world—no one had ever stirred her more than Louis de Narbonne. She protected, comforted and made love to him with passion. But his ardor had cooled. She blamed his indifference on his sorrow over the death of his cousin. His melancholy only endeared him to her all the more, intensifying her attachment.

As their stay in England continued, Germaine's friendship and affection for Charles Talleyrand and Mathieu de Montmorency also strengthened. She leaned on Mathieu as a personal advisor and counsellor, and Talleyrand was her intellectual counterpart. They spent hours dissecting the news from France and making plans for the future. Louis de Narbonne took no interest in any of their discussions.

On a brilliant, sunny day late in May, the ancient cabriolet careened recklessly into the courtyard of Juniper Hall. Happy chatter and laughter bounced off the stone walls of the manor house. Germaine held a wide-brimmed straw hat with one hand and braced herself with the other as Mathieu pulled in the reins and the horse came to a sudden stop behind an unfamiliar coach-and-four. Who could be here? The carriage belonged to none of their English friends.

Mathieu helped Germaine dismount and together they climbed the steps into the mansion.

The visitors turned out to be Madame de Staël's cousins Louis and Albertine Necker de Saussure. They had arrived, unannounced, from Switzerland. Germaine stiffened with anxiety, her first concerns were of her parents and children.

"Your family is well," Albertine reassured her. "Your mother is failing but continues to persevere. Your sons are healthy and growing. Dear little Albert, he is still only a baby but already he shows remarkable spirit."

Madame de Staël was certain her cousins must have been dispatched to England by her father. Her money was almost exhausted and she hoped the purpose of the trip was to bring her additional funds. Since they did not raise the issue, Germaine got up the courage, while she and Albertine toured the gardens, to ask if the Saussures brought a message from her father.

"Your father wants you to return to Switzerland," Albertine said.

"I'm delighted you're here," Germaine said, "but that message could have been sent by courier."

Madame de Saussure was apologetic. "You are dear to me," she said, "which is why Monsieur Necker selected me to make this journey—he knew you would hear me out. Neither of your parents approves the life you lead here in England. They insist you come home."

"And if I refuse?" Germaine sensed an ultimatum. Her cousins had not come this far to make a social call.

"You will receive no further funds. In fact, your father has provided just enough to take us all back to Coppet."

Germaine de Staël had no choice. The next morning her friends assembled for a tearful departure of their benefactress. Even the stoic Talleyrand was disheartened. Only Narbonne was dry-eyed.

Chapter 11
Benjamin Constant

The Baroness de Staël's gleaming golden carriage swayed with easy rhythm on the Geneva-Lausanne highway as it wove its way through the glorious Swiss countryside. On the perches, Eugene Uginet, her factotum, and four footmen in green and gold livery sat tall and erect. The six sleek black horses, reined firmly in the strong hands of the skilled driver, galloped sure-footed along the smooth dirt road.

Inside the luxuriously appointed coach, the Baroness was absorbed in a book, ignoring the spectacular scenery. To the right, broad meadows sloped down to the tree-lined shores of Lac Léman. Rich green foliage was interspersed with the brilliant browns, oranges, russets and yellows of autumn. The fathomless blue waters of the lake stretched broadly southward, glistening in the afternoon sun. In the distance the French Alps rose to merge with the infinity of an azure sky.

It had been sixteen months since Germaine had taken leave of her lover and friends in England. France had been ravaged by internal atrocities and foreign invasion. The entire nation seethed under mass suspicion as the fanatic, waspish Maximilien Robespierre presided over the Reign of Terror. Speedy trials, execution by guillotine, deliberate drownings and murder were routine.

No one was immune from prosecution . . . the clergy, aristocrats, ordinary citizens and laborers . . . anyone who opposed the Paris Commune as well as those who were merely suspect.

Trying to forestall Marie Antoinette's execution, Madame de Staël published an anonymous paper in her defense, but her efforts failed. Ten months after King Louis's death Marie Antoinette followed her husband to the guillotine.

The long arm of the witch hunt reached across borders into Switzerland, forcing the Neckers to move from Coppet. Germaine set up her own household in a rented chateau at Mézery, outside Lausanne, where she resumed her rescue work. She harbored refugees, defended their residence to Swiss authorities and arranged forged papers to help those who were permitted to leave.

Only Louis de Narbonne and Charles Talleyrand declined her protective cloak. Talleyrand had decided to try to rebuild his fortune in America. Boarding the ship to take him there, he wrote Germaine: "Adieu, my dear friend. I love you with all my soul."

Narbonne remained in England, avoiding contact with his mistress. For months, Germaine wrote him daily, expressing undying devotion and her wish that he join her. After a year, her letters stopped.

The ploy had its intended effect. Narbonne promptly hastened to Mézery, where Germaine welcomed him with affection. He was annoyed and bewildered to find that her smothering passion had abated and that he had been replaced by a handsome young Swede, Count Adolf Ludvig Ribbing. Smitten by the blond nobleman, Germaine lured him to live with her at Mézery.

By December of 1793, the Reign of Terror had begun to subside. The port of Toulon, which the British held, was recaptured by a young adjutant general named Napoleon Bonaparte. Robespierre rewarded the Corsican by appointing him commandant of the artillery of the army in Italy. The invaders of France were gradually repulsed on all fronts. The perpetrators of the Terror, including Robespierre, whose vile acts had run their course, met the same fate as their victims, and the final bloody reign came to an end in July 1794. Calm settled over France. A new group of tyrants, many of them Germaine's friends now led the nation. She waited for signs that would clear the way so she could return to Paris with impunity.

It was a day in September, 1794, that found the Baroness de Staël reading in her carriage on the Geneva-Lausanne highway. She had just spent two days with her father at Coppet. Together they had completed the entombment of her mother's body. To Jacques Necker's despair, his wife had died five months before. The poor woman had been a necromantic with a dread of being buried alive. Necker willingly carried out her last wishes and preserved her body in a large open stone coffin filled with brandy. Unfortunately, the family mausoleum in the wooded park on the grounds of the chateau was still under construction. Necker sat vigil daily beside the sarcophagus which he kept in the library until the tomb was finished. Germaine and her father held a service for the pickled corpse and walked away with a sense of both guilt and loss.

Madame de Staël's musings were jarred.

The carriage slowed and then came to a complete stop. She was far from Nyon, where she planned to spend the night with a friend before proceeding to her chateau at Mézery.

Outside her coach, a horse whinnied.

"Madame la Baronne," Eugene Uginet called down to her, "a young horseman wishes to speak with you. He says that he stopped at Coppet and was told he would find you on your way back to Mézery. Will you talk with him or shall I drive on?"

Germaine's curiosity was aroused. Drawing the curtain aside, she saw a thin, awkward young man slouched astride an ungainly horse. She told Eugene to move on.

The horseman came closer to the window. His animal's neck oozed foam and sweat from its long, hard dash in pursuit of the Baroness.

"Madame la Baronne de Staël!" The voice was commanding but courteous.

"Yes," she replied. She opened the window to scrutinize the rider more closely. He was dismally unattractive. His face was pale, freckled. His red hair, braided and tied at the nape of his neck, accented a long but rather distinguished nose. His eyes squinted behind spectacles, his lips narrow and his mouth taut. His long legs hung limply from a tall, thin trunk. Yet, there was something noble and fleetingly familiar about him.

The Baroness withdrew her directive to Uginet.

"I have been trying to overtake your carriage," the horseman said. "I started out early this morning from Geneva. I stopped at Coppet but you had already left."

Germaine was both amused and curious because she now recognized the features and mannerisms of a long-established Swiss family named Constant. The red hair was unmistakable.

"Why have you been pursuing me?" she asked. Her eyes, bright with interest, took in the full measure of this man.

"I'm Benjamin Constant."

Of course, she recalled. He was the precocious one of the family, a child prodigy who lost himself somewhere.

"We have never met," he said, "but you know my family and friends. I have been eager to meet you—for years! This morning I determined that this would be the day!"

This young man is so unattractive, almost ugly, Germaine reflected, that he has a contagious appeal. His brash, imperial manner was refreshing. She was not accustomed to such directness on a first encounter.

"Now, that we have met, where do you plan to go?"

"Wherever you do. If you will permit me."

Germaine could not refuse. "Will you join me?"

"Most certainly. Thank you."

As one of Germaine's grooms secured the bridle of Constant's horse to the rear of the carriage, the young man climbed into the coach and settled his lanky body onto the seat beside Madame de Staël.

The coach-and-six resumed its journey eastward.

The Baroness wondered why she was drawn to this untidy, impetuous presumer. His long black riding coat and knee pants were wrinkled and ill-fitting. His boots were scuffed and covered with dust.

But when he spoke, Germaine was roused.

"I am fascinated with your involvement in the cause of liberty," he said. His eyes came to life behind the pale green lenses of his spectacles. His voice was sonorous and convincing. "It is my fondest dream to help eliminate the gross injustices, autocratic rule and tyranny that is rampant in Europe." As he expanded his ideas, it was obvious that his mind was indeed quick and keen.

"There is much to be done," the Baroness responded. "The principles of the Revolution are being grossly, blatantly, violated. The new leaders of France are as insidious as those they have replaced. They have come as close as Geneva, they have even penetrated Lausanne. They continue to imprison the innocent. This morning's paper, *La Quinzaine*, attacks my father and accuses me of harboring 'constitutional mongrels.' They have no basis for such statements."

"Ah! If you are a true liberal, you will not question the freedom of the press. You must be prepared to defend yourself against such calumny."

"Every individual has the right to express his opinion, I agree. But attack without proof is irresponsible."

Germaine went on. She drew Benjamin out, encouraging and manipulating him. Their conversation continued heatedly until they reached Nyon and the home of her friend de Vincy.

When the three sat down to dinner, Madame de Staël reopened her discussion with Benjamin. They exchanged political theories, discussing the war, the leaders of the Terror and their demise, the current regime and

Germaine's personal allies—Abbé Imannuel Siéyès, Count Paul de Barras, Jean Tallien and others. Their host was astonished by the interchange. They went on to literature and books she had written. She smiled broadly when Benjamin confessed that he had just read her most recent book, *Zulma*. Germaine wondered if the story had prompted him to find her . . . the novel was based on her relationship with Narbonne. She had poured out her soul in this fictional treatise.

The tapers in the candelabra on the dining table flickered and burned down to their holders. Monsieur de Vincy suggested they adjourn to the drawing room. Shortly thereafter, the weary host retired and left Benjamin and Germaine to continue alone.

The Baroness eased herself into a small velvet marquise and relaxed for the rest of the evening. Toying with a green twig she had plucked from a vase in the hallway, Germaine scrutinized Benjamin closely as he reclined loosely on a pillowed bergère. How could this brilliant, eloquent young man, with so penetrating and incisive a mind, have avoided an ennobling profession? The Constants traced their family to the fourteenth century, They had titles, wealth, intellect, moral fiber, stamina . . . and eccentricity. Why was Benjamin so uncommitted?

Constant took off his glasses, rubbed the bridge of his nose and blinked. Dangling his spectacles loosely from his fingers, he seemed to sense Germaine's thoughts.

"I'm almost twenty-seven," he said simply. "I've lead a desultory life. It is time I had a firm direction. For years I have followed your politics and your writings and found little with which I disagree. Our conversations have confirmed my convictions. I hope we may work toward the same goals."

The Baroness de Staël was captivated by this stranger, only a year younger than she, who was artfully spinning a web to entrap her. She had more than enough commitments and his personal appearance offended her. She should probably turn him away. But his mind—his determination! Not since her exhilarating confrontations with Charles Talleyrand had she been so stimulated.

Early the next day, Madame de Staël departed Nyon with Benjamin. When they reached Lausanne, she left him at his lodgings with an invitation to visit her at Mézery sometime in the future. But not soon.

Before dawn the following morning, Benjamin Constant was on Germaine's doorstep. He was unimpressed by her wealth, the luxury of the chateau and the panache of her French guests. Nor was he put off when they treated him with disdain and patronizing civility.

Benjamin knew what he wanted. He was determined to stay.

Chapter 12
Chateau de Mézery

T he day was serene. The air was clear and unusually warm for an October morning in Switzerland. From the low-pitched gable of the Chateau de Mézery, the round tone of the tower clock chimed ten times.

In the sunlit drawing room of the chateau, the Baroness de Staël glanced away from the Viscountess Elizabeth de Montmorency-Laval with whom she was sipping café au lait. She looked through the French doors, beyond the broad terrace to the shaded garden where several of her guests were enjoying the balmy weather.

"Are you concerned about Adolph, Louis and Benjamin?" the Viscountess asked. The men were not among Germaine's friends in the garden.

"No," the Baroness replied unconvincingly, "not at all!"

At breakfast, Germaine had learned from Eugene Uginet that the trio had gone out together before dawn. They left no word, and now, seven hours later, their whereabouts remained a mystery. Germaine was anxious. A smoldering antagonism had developed among the three men over her attention. Louis de Narbonne, though reluctant, was still her lover. Count Ribbing alternated with him in that role. Benjamin Constant's intellectual attachment for the chatelaine of Mézery rankled both her ardent swains since he took up so much of her time. The Baroness feared their animosities would erupt and destroy the tranquility of her extended family.

Elizabeth smiled complacently.

"Do you think Louis has challenged Ribbing to a duel over you?" she asked. "And that Benjamin has gone along as a second?"

Germaine ignored the remark. Across the room, her sons Auguste, now four, and Albert, almost two, played under the watchful eye of their governess. "Please take the boys for their walk," Germaine said to the servant with unusual curtness.

The Baroness returned her attention to the Viscountess.

"Louis has such dark, intense moods. He broods," Germaine said. "He objects to Adolph and Benjamin more strongly than a husband would."

"Don't condemn him," Elizabeth replied with sincere concern. "Louis has been through difficult times. They have made him wary and sensitive to your attachments . . . even jealous. He still despairs over the death of the King and Queen. He cannot shake the burden of guilt that weighs upon him. He feels he should have been in France to defend and save them."

"And endanger his own life!" Germaine refused to be sympathetic. "Two years have passed. He should be planning his future. Every noble has lost at least one friend or relative. You, dear Elizabeth, have suffered as much as anyone and you have handled your grief with courage and dignity." The Viscountess had lost a son, Mathieu's brother, during the Terror. She and Mathieu owed their lives to Germaine for helping them escape from the holocaust of Paris.

"Louis's anxiety over Benjamin's interest in me," she said with annoyance, "is baseless."

"I'm not so sure. Benjamin is entranced with you. He's hopelessly in love with you."

"That's ridiculous!" Germaine took a sip of coffee and set the cup down with a nervous clatter in the saucer. "Our political objectives are similar, but he has no personal appeal whatever," she protested. I could never take him as a lover . . . that shaggy red hair! Those beady eyes behind the green spectacles . . . "

"But the two of you talk incessantly."

"The way he looks and dresses has nothing to do with what he thinks. He has much to offer intellectually." Germaine was preparing a pamphlet with Constant's help that she hoped would pave the way for her return to Paris. "He has one of the best minds in all Europe." Her voice softened. "Ribbing is quite another matter. He is tantalizingly seductive."

"But he's a regicide!"

Count Ribbing's role in the assassination of the Swedish King Gustav III made him an undesirable foreigner. The Swiss government was attempting to deport him, ending his stay in Switzerland and forcing him to conclude his affair with Germaine. Since the Viscountess was still in love with Narbonne and hoped to win him back, she wanted to divert Germaine to a new liaison. Constant struck her as an excellent candidate.

"Adolph was doing his duty," Germaine replied in the Count's defense. "It fell to him by lot to go with John Anckarstroem when John shot Gustav."

"But it was his *king!*"

"Gustav's rule was absolute and unfair. Adolph's act was one of valor and conscience. He had no choice. He's all the more heroic because of it. Just as Napoleon Bonaparte, that brilliant military officer who was assigned to Toulon . . . "

"That was a different matter!"

"Not to me," Germaine insisted. "He had his orders. He attacked the fort and slaughtered soldiers defending it. I have been following the career of this young Corsican. He started corresponding with my father when Papa was Controller General. He is a man to watch."

"And so is Benjamin Constant," said the Viscountess, "turn around and see for yourself."

And indeed, Benjamin, looking like a bedraggled peasant, entered the room. Behind him, in meticulous morning attire, were Ribbing and Narbonne. All three walked up to Germaine and without a word, kneeled in front of her and each, like a noble knight presenting an offering to his lady, deposited a freshly caught fish at her feet.

The Baroness de Staël was both amused and relieved.

The trio stood. Then, shoulder to shoulder, they linked arms and wandered off.

A wild and terrifying scream suddenly sounded in the darkened Chateau de Mézery slicing through the bitter cold of a January night.

Startled, the Baroness sat up in bed and shuddered. The agonizing cries were repeated again and again. She could not shut out the sounds.

After lighting the candle on her bedside table, she quickly threw on a robe. Just as she was about to leave her room, the Vicountess de Montmorency opened the door.

"Germaine it's Benjamin . . . he has taken poison and asks to see you before he dies!"

The two women dashed through the passageway to Benjamin's room. Everyone in the household was roused. Dressed in their nightclothes, they clamored into the corridors and headed in the direction of the screams.

Crowding around Constant's bed, they watched as he tossed in agony. Germaine was overcome with dread and concern. "Benjamin!" she said, leaning over him, "what have you done?" She broke into sobs. "Quickly! Someone call a doctor!"

"Ah," Constant whispered. "Is it you, dear Madame de Staël? You have called me back for another moment of life!"

Convinced that he would die at any moment, Germaine whispered back to him, "Yes! Live, dear Benjamin!"

Clutching her fingers Constant drew her to him with unexpected strength. "Since you command it, I shall try to live." He then covered her hand and arm with passionate kisses of an adoring lover.

Suddenly, the Baroness realized this incident was a sham, and that Benjamin would recover . . . what they all had just witnessed was an inspired charade. When the doctor arrived, sometime later, he confirmed her suspicions.

As the guests disbursed, the Viscountess accompanied Germaine back to her room and watched as she filled a porcelain wash basin with water. After adding the contents of a large bottle of scent, she plunged her hands and arms deep into the bowl of the refreshing solution. She breathed more freely as if she had escaped suffocation.

"That is the first time Benjamin ever touched me," Germaine told Elizabeth, "I find him repulsive!"

"There has been a dramatic change in Benjamin since his midnight histrionics," the Viscountess de Montmorency commented to Germaine a few weeks later.

"I have not been aware of any difference," the chatelaine of Mézery replied, arranging the sheets of her manuscript for the *Passions* on a small bureau plat. She left her work to bid Elizabeth good night at the door of her bedroom.

"His hair is neatly trimmed. He brushes it now, so it falls softly down to his shoulders."

"His mind is as keen as it ever was," Germaine said flatly.

"He has acquired a number of white ruffled shirts and a well-fitting pair of yellow trousers," Elizabeth persisted. "Even his eyes seem clearer behind those dreadful spectacles."

Madame de Staël would not admit that Benjamin's campaign of pursuit had reached her. The suicide incident had appealed to her penchant for the bizarre. To keep him from repeating his act, or acting out something equally outrageous, she now allocated an hour or two before midnight for conversation alone with him in her bedchamber. They discussed politics and reviewed the progress on a tract she was writing called *Reflections on Peace*. Germaine imposed a rigid restriction . . . he was required to leave when the clock struck twelve.

As the Viscountess and Germaine reached the door, there was a gentle knock from the other side. Benjamin entered the room as Elizabeth departed.

Even without Madame de Montmorency's prompting, Germaine could not ignore Benjamin's appearance. He was taking particular care with his dress. Tonight, he also wore a light fragrance. For the first time, she was made pleasurably aware of his lean, sensual figure that had been concealed behind his usual, loose-fitting attire.

The evening passed more quickly than usual for Germaine. Shortly before midnight, Benjamin stood up and leaned against the fireplace. Germaine was reclining on the soft satin pillows of her chaise. The mantle clock chimed the hour and the Baroness reminded her guest that it was time for him to leave.

"That was only eleven," Benjamin asserted.

Germaine scowled. "Look at your watch!" she commanded.

He pulled the timepiece from his pocket. His squinting eyes opened wide behind his green spectacles. "It appears you are right," he replied.

Constant tore his watch from its chain and smashed it against the marble mantle. As it scattered into a thousand pieces on the floor Benjamin ground the twisted remnants onto the tile with his shoe.

He moved slowly toward the chaise and embraced Germaine. Finding his ardor as irresistible as his mind, she responded with fervent passion.

The next morning, a radiant Germaine entered the breakfast room and found Benjamin sharing coffee and croissants with Narbonne, Ribbing and Mathieu. As she joined the group, Benjamin announced, "I shall never again need a watch."

That evening the two new lovers set politics aside and Benjamin prepared a solemn contract:

> *We promise to consecrate our lives to each other; we declare that we regard ourselves as indissolubly bound to each other, that we will share forever and in every respect a common destiny, that we will never enter into any other bond, and that we shall strengthen the bonds now uniting us as soon as it lies within our power.*
>
> *I declare I am entering into this engagement with a sincere heart, that I know nothing on earth as worthy of love as Madame de Staël, that I have been the happiest of men during the four months I have spent with her, and that I regard it as the greatest happiness in my life to be able to make her happy in her youth, to grow old peacefully by her side, and to reach my term together with the soul that understands me and without whose presence life on this earth would hold no more interest for me.*

Chapter 13
A Stormy Liaison Begins

Madame de Staël tried to recall why she had given in to her mother's pleading that she adjust her son Albert's birthdate so Baron Eric Magnus de Staël would acknowledge the boy as his heir. At the time, the possibility of reconciling with her husband was as remote as having an Austrian prince on the French throne. She had resisted, finally complied and forgotten the incident . . . until now. Was family pride and the need to prevent a scandal her reason for acquiescing or was it merely to appease her parents? She could not remember, nor did it matter.

How fortunate that I agreed, Germaine reflected as she read a letter from Eric Magnus:

> *My dear Germaine:*
> *It is my sincerest wish that you join me once again and serve beside me as Ambassadress. I am certain we can live together happily as a family.*
> *There are other considerations you must weigh as you make your decision. Jean Lambert Tallien and Count Paul de Barras talked with me in confidence about their hope to establish a constitutional monarchy in France which you have long advocated. They are certain you will be invaluable in influencing men of disparate views to help unify the nation.*
> *I look forward to your favorable reply.*

Germaine was alone in her boudoir. Her eyes flashed brilliant embers at the stirring visions racing through her mind. The request from her husband had reached Mézery at precisely the right time.

The Baroness de Staël was ready to conquer Paris—with Benjamin at her side. The invitation from Eric gave her the excuse for her return. More importantly, the letter revealed that the leaders of the current government were eager to have her reestablish herself in Paris.

Germaine, herself, could not have devised a better scheme.

When Benjamin Constant had finally seduced her five months earlier, she found that he was a match for her sensual appetites. From the beginning she had been dazzled by his mind, and now she had a willing partner who was both a passionate lover and a dedicated political collaborator.

The Baroness did not abandon her former lover, the reluctant, despairing Narbonne, who now found solace in sharing the bed of the Viscountess de Montmorency. She continued to house, feed and entertain her full coterie of acolytes. She merely realigned her priorities. Ribbing soon had to leave by order of the Swiss government. Mathieu remained devoted, adoring and supportive.

Benjamin, who was twenty-seven to Germaine's almost twenty-nine wanted to make his mark in French society and politics. Madame de Staël obligingly offered to serve as his mentor and share his destiny.

Young Constant had an extensive education but had led a lonely, pointless life. His mother had died at his birth and he rarely saw his father, a career officer in the Swiss army. Colonel Arnold-Juste Constant de Rebecque recognized his son's potential early and enlisted tutors to guide and develop his precocity.

By the time he was ten, Benjamin had written a novel. When he was thirteen his father put an end to a long string of freakish private tutors. One was a homosexual, another an atheist, another a rapist and the last, a defrocked monk who shot himself.

The next phase of Benjamin's education took him to France, Belgium and Switzerland where he traveled extensively and learned to speak and think in three different languages. This was followed by formal training at Oxford, the University of Erlangen and Edinburgh.

At fifteen, Benjamin Constant had acquired a mistress and launched a career of love-making with married women, chambermaids and harlots. At twenty, he entered into a liaison with a woman twenty-seven years his senior who had a steadying influence on the rootless young man and helped develop his bent for literature and philosophy. The relationship survived an ill-fated five-year marriage to a shrew and continued until he moved in with Germaine.

Shortly after they signed their binding contract, everything began to fall into place for Benjamin and the Baroness as smoothly as the glistening waters of Lac Léman. Mézery became their private haven when the Swiss government served notice on Germaine that her friends were no longer welcome in the canton of Vaud. Unwilling to abandon the émigrés, she set them up in another refuge. This left the tempestuous pair alone to make love and to concentrate on their mutual passion . . . serious work on the regeneration of France.

Already a staunch liberal, Benjamin had soon developed an insoluble identity with Germaine's political theories and philosophy.

He conferred with her as she completed a paper, *Reflections on Peace*, in which she set forth her premise that the moderates of the right and the left should unite behind the republic and effect a peace between revolutionary France and the European Coalition.

Within days after the final draft of the tract was sent to Paris for publication, Germaine received de Staël's letter. The timing was serendipitous.

Eric Magnus's earlier sympathies for republicanism had put him in good stead with the people of France. He was the only diplomat of a monarchist state accredited by the French government. Installed again in the Swedish Embassy in Paris, the Baron had even more prestige.

On May 22, 1795, Benjamin Constant and Germaine de Staël set out for the French capital.

The Ambassadress was warmly welcomed by her husband. Her lover discreetly sought and found separate lodgings nearby.

Paris was not the same city Madame de Staël had left two-and-a-half years earlier. The French capital had always had its poor, but now, a large segment of its population was destitute, people were starving. Their faces were haggard, their souls tormented.

No one wandered the streets. Only an occasional carriage rattled along the filthy gutters. The sidewalks of the once fashionable boulevards were a continuous flea market lined with exquisite furniture, fine china, delicate porcelains and invaluable works of art scavenged from deserted homes of the aristocrats and wealthy émigrés. The elegant manor houses and chateaux, left bare and in disrepair, had been confiscated by the government. Their facades were plastered with signs reading: For Sale—National Property.

The Baroness was disheartened by the desolation.

The Paris Commune had lost its grip on the populace and control returned to the National Convention, but the fortunes of the people had not improved. Slaughter continued in the provinces, even without the suspects' list and the guillotine. The *jeunesse doré*, the gilded youth, who were responsible were no less bloodthirsty under the white terror than their red-terror predecessors.

Though the change of leadership permitted her to return to Paris, Germaine had no illusions about the men in power, many of whom were her friends. They took advantage of the mood of the nation and practiced flagrant abuses that nutured the deplorable living conditions, famine and runaway inflation.

The new leaders included Jean Tallien, with his seductive wife Thérèse, and Paul Barras with his lustful, greedy mistress, Josephine de Beauharnais. They ruled France by openly peddling patronage to the highest bidder and flaunting their lubricity like music hall performers.

The men in power dressed as dandies. Their women, led by Thérèse, who often appeared half nude in public and was called the Queen of Debauchery, exposed themselves in short, diaphanous gowns. Every degree of lasciviousness was rampant . . . dancing, gambling, drinking, free love. Nightly, Parisians indulged in the frenzy of dance . . . those who did not fill the more than six hundred dance halls that had sprung up in the city staged dancing orgies in churches and graveyards.

As Tallien and Barras had hoped, Germaine again threw open the doors of her salon to publicists, diplomats, literary men and the most powerful politicians of every persuasion in the capital.

Her receptions were soon as glittering and provocative as before.

There was gaiety and entertainment. The damask-draped tables of the Embassy were laden with tempting displays of food and fine wines flowed as freely as the Tuileries' fountains.

Benjamin Constant was seen at the de Staël gatherings every evening. Involved and ambitious, he became a man-about-town. Together, he and Germaine caused a prodigious stir on all levels of society and became the preoccupation of journalists.

Benjamin was learning to be charming and delightful; his eyes twinkled behind fashionable new spectacles and he developed a distracting, mischievous smile. Many of the Baroness's friends considered him handsome and regaling. His political career as a vocal advocate of liberal ideas was launched with brilliance.

Madame de Staël spent her days in the diplomatic gallery of the Convention where she kept the legislative pages busy running back and forth with messages for the deputies. Her nights were devoted to entertaining. She dedicated the rest of her time, what little there was, to uncover ways for her exiled friends to find their way back to Paris from all over Europe.

❖

In the distant United States, Charles Talleyrand suffered from boredom and a life empty of the amenities he craved.

"If I must spend another year in this country," he wrote in desperation to Germaine, "I shall die."

The consummate aristocrat was wretched in the thriving young country where a pioneering spirit was essential for survival and success. Talleyrand's elegant manners and polished diplomacy were not requisites for building a fortune in the wilds of America. He required the trappings of luxury and social intercourse much as an aging beauty needs cosmetics and flattery.

Charles asked Madame de Staël for a loan that would secure his return to the most civilized nation in the world.

Without slighting her other interests, Germaine made Charles' request her *cause célèbre*. It was a monumental order. His name would have to be struck from the list of undesirable émigrés by decree of the National Convention.

Germaine knew that most of the deputies thought of Talleyrand as an untrustworthy, degenerate defrocked priest. Over a period of weeks, she paid personal calls on as many deputies who would open their doors to her. She persevered until she felt confident enough members were swayed in his favor.

Madame de Staël convinced the legislators that Talleyrand was not the typical émigré but a fugitive who had been misunderstood and unfairly treated by the Convention. He had worked for the Republic, she maintained, in both England and America and his loyalty deserved reward.

She sought a deputy of prestige and honor to address the Convention on Talleyrand's behalf and called on Marie-Joseph Chénier, the most eloquent of the legislators. Goading him without success, Germaine then enlisted the help of his mistress, a good friend of hers. Chénier was finally seduced into believing that Talleyrand was a worthy Frenchman.

After days of discussion and a powerful plea by Chénier, the deputies assembled for the vote. Ambassador de Staël and his wife attended the session and sat in the diplomatic gallery.

The presiding officer responded to a final request from Louis Legendre, a deputy and an ex-butcher who wished to speak to the issue.

He moved that the petition be referred to the Legislative Committee for further investigation. Germaine was prepared. Earlier, she had briefed three deputies with arguments to oppose the move. They spoke against the motion and defeated it.

But the Baroness was not prepared for what was to come.

"Madame de Staël has requested that Bishop Talleyrand be permitted to return to France," Legendre continued speaking with great hostility. "But she is an enemy of France. The Directors charge she's leading a conspiracy against republicanism by financing and abetting nobles to come back from exile."

Following an extensive tirade against her political machinations, the ex-butcher went on to assault her personal life. "She has the audacity to sit in the gallery beside her husband, the fine Swedish Ambassador, whom she has cuckolded with Charles Talleyrand, the very man she champions, Count Louis de Narbonne, and now, Benjamin Constant."

He went on to describe the affairs with amazing accuracy.

Germaine was stunned. The Baron de Staël was mortified. The Baroness could not believe that her efforts to help her friends and further the cause of France had made such violent enemies.

The audience, enjoying every humiliating revelation of this very public woman's private life, clucked and tittered.

Eric Magnus and Germaine sat motionless and stoic, staying through the session to learn the results of the vote. The bitter barrage had not diluted the case that had been presented for the former statesman. The legislators cheered Talleyrand, removed his name from the list of émigrés and reinstated him with full French citizenship.

Madame de Staël was not so fortunate.

Legendre's denunciation fanned resentment and envy against this indefatigable defender of aristocrats. The tension between the royalists and the republicans increased to explosive proportions, and pressure from the press forced the deputies to debate the loyalty of Madame de Staël. Their vision was too narrow to allow them to see that she was trying to strengthen and unify the nation by consolidating the best minds among the liberals and the moderate monarchists.

The Convention precipitously voted to expel her from France and issued a decree that would haunt her for the rest of her life.

Germaine's exile was delayed for weeks when the royalists staged an insurrection and distracted the deputies. Her friend Paul Barras, the strongest member of the five-man executive team of the new Directory government, took bold steps to suppress the uprising. He called young General Napoleon Bonaparte to confront the rioters and shoot blanks into their ranks where they were holding up on the steps of the Church of St. Roch. Instead, Bonaparte discharged live ammunition—"a whiff of grapeshot," the General declared—into the crowd and blew the dissenters to pieces.

In the eyes of the Directory, the populace and Germaine, with his "courageous" act, he saved the nation and was called the Man of the Hour.

In late December, 1795, the decree for Madame de Staël's exile was instated and Germaine was forced to leave Paris. Six months had passed since her triumphal re-entry.

Harboring no bitterness, the Baroness accepted the resolution as a thoughtless act passed in haste and without sufficient grounds. Fortunately, Benjamin, whose republican loyalties had become impeccable, would remain in Paris. She counted on him to continue their work till she returned.

Chapter 14
Albertine

Madame de Staël held her father's arm as they walked slowly along the tree-lined path bordering the gardens that spread north from the Chateau de Coppet.

It was a glorious autumn day. The heady scent of venerable evergreens wafted through the air. And a soft breeze sent bright colored leaves from the tall oaks and maples swirling around their feet and onto the rich green lawns.

Father and daughter were deep in conversation.

Ahead of them, Benjamin Constant strolled with six-year-old Auguste beside him. Albert, almost four, trotted along behind them, wandering from one side of the pebbled path to the other chasing the brilliant errant leaves.

"Eric Magnus is trying only to please you," Jacques Necker said to Germaine.

"He fails. He has no concept of what is important to me," she replied, annoyed.

"You expect too much of him," Necker said. "You should consider his limitations."

"I accept them. But I don't have to tolerate and cater to them. His vacuity never ceases to amaze me. During his brief visit, he spent his time trying to convince me that it was *he* who had swayed Paul Barras to favor rescinding the order for my exile. Barras is a friend and has always been ready to help me. If he had convinced one of the other four Directors, I might have been sympathetic."

"Come along Albert," Constant called to the boy who had plopped down on the path to gather a pile of leaves. "Stay out of your mother's way—she and your grandfather wish to be alone to talk."

The child raced back to his brother's side, gripping Auguste's hand

and swinging it to and fro as high as he could reach.

Benjamin was visiting Coppet for several days. Traveling back and forth between Switzerland and Paris, he kept Germaine informed on the volatile political situation in France.

"I'm optimistic," Germaine told her father. "The climate will change and Barras will prevail, he'll convince his colleagues. I can count on Benjamin for what I must know. There was no need, at all, for Eric to have come."

"He wanted to see you, Minette," Necker said. "You are his wife and he is still fond of you . . . and the boys."

"He came to see *you*. For funds to repay his debts. You should have given him nothing."

Just before Benjamin's arrival, the Baron de Staël had left Coppet for the baths at Aix. He had again been relieved of his duties as Ambassador. This time, young King Gustavus IV, having changed his policy toward France, no longer required the services of a full diplomat, and appointed a low-level chargé d'affaires to replace Eric. Without an income, the profligate Baron was again deeply in debt.

"I was not generous," Necker replied. "He went off with far less money than he asked for."

"It was blackmail!" Germaine said sharply, remembering the parting. Eric had threatened to take Auguste and Albert away with him if Necker refused to pay. "I could not believe he would resort to such irresponsible tactics."

"You must remember, Minette, that Eric Magnus is no longer the dashing young courtier you married. His years with you have only delayed the full toll his dissipation will ultimately take on his health," Necker said with compassion, "but I am glad he has gone."

Germaine and Necker approached Benjamin and the two boys who stood at the edge of a large, clear, round pond. Auguste and Albert, throwing small stones into the water, watched ripples spread across the mirror-like reflection of the chateau with its towers and tall iron fence and gate. The image looked like a gigantic painting within a frame of brilliant saffrons, russets and reds of the foliage.

Near the shadow of a tall pedestal graced by a marble statue of a bare bosomed Greek goddess, Olive Uginet had arranged a table with tea, coffee and a platter piled high with pastries which held the boys spellbound. Well-mannered, they waited till they were served and munched little cakes with princely decorum.

"Neither the press nor the people can get enough of Bonaparte," Germaine said, accepting a small tray from Olive as she sat on a cushioned ladder-back chair between the two men. "He's dazzling all Europe with his campaigns as commander of the French army in Italy. My father and I follow his achievements closely and appreciate the insightful reports you send us about him," she told Benjamin.

After Napoleon Bonaparte suppressed the royalists he was named Commander of the Army of the Interior with headquarters in Paris. Now, for the first time, he was in a position to penetrate the fringes of politics. He was readily accepted into the tawdry society of the Directory. Paul Barras's mistress, Josephine de Beauharnais, who was casting about for a new liaison since Barras had lost interest in her, arranged to meet the celebrated Commander. Though years older than he, Josephine was still a ravishing beauty despite the decaying teeth she displayed when she smiled. Bonaparte was easy prey. Within weeks, the couple married. After a two-day honeymoon, the General left his bride to assume his new duties as Commander-in-Chief of the forces in Italy.

Josephine, hardly pining for her new husband, continued to share the bed of her most recent lover, Captain Hippolyte Charles.

Learning of this infidelity, the Commander turned violently jealous and dispatched angry letters of protest. He went further. He had the offender jailed for embezzlement, of which he was guilty, with a sentence of death by firing squad. Josephine screamed and fainted. The bewitched Bonaparte reversed the charges. Charles went free and Josephine continued her dalliance with the captain. This domestic upheaval had no impact on Napoleon's military strategy. He went on to win a series of spectacular victories: Millesimo on April 13, Dego which led to an armistice with Sardinia on April 28, Lodi on May 10, the occupation of Milan on May 15, all of Lombardy at Verona on June 3, central Italy in two weeks on June 30, Castiglione on August 5, and Mantua on September 15. His successes had no end.

"Bonaparte has demonstrated an instinct for political affairs which he combines effectively with his skill for the military," Germaine remarked to her father. "No one . . . no one since the Revolution began has so captured the imagination of the masses."

"His genius cannot be denied," Necker said, "but his brashness could be dangerous. His signing the treaty with the Piedmontese was not authorized by the Directory. If government directives do not suit him, he disregards them. His acts do not ingratiate him with the Directors."

Germaine chuckled. "He knows how to appease them by feeding their greed. He blackmails them with works of art that he has confiscated from local museums."

"He's also a talented writer. His rousing proclamations give hope to the people of France," Benjamin interjected. "But are these words a means rather than an end? Some say he wants to make himself King of Lombardy."

"If he is looking for greater rewards and more power, he deceives us all, even those close to him," Necker told Benjamin. "General Augereau, who has just come from Italy, told us that Napoleon is a zealous Republican. He is too noble a young man, he said, to want to be king."

"I've written Bonaparte, expressing our admiration and offering assistance," Germaine added. "I was also frank about his hasty marriage to Josephine. I suggested that he might have been wiser to select someone more worthy of his genius who could act as a political partner."

"What was his reply?" Benjamin asked.

"I have not yet heard from him."

"Perhaps he resented your criticism about his personal life."

"A man of such stature must be open to suggestion and impervious to attack."

Auguste and Albert had grown tired of their games and vied with each other for Necker's attention by climbing up on his lap.

"Grandpapa," Auguste implored him, "let us all go to the library. It is time for you to read to us."

Jacques Necker complied. The boys kissed their mother, gave Benjamin affectionate hugs and headed back toward the chateau racing ahead of their grandfather.

"The joy of watching my sons grow relieves the solitude I feel here at Coppet. I'm fortunate that my father is such an fine tutor."

"Auguste has a excellent mind," Benjamin offered.

"He is eager to learn. Albert is too young for regular studies. I will not rush him as I was forced to study. I was younger than he when I had to start formal lessons."

"I would be proud to have such sons," Benjamin said as they watched the shadows lengthen across the park while the sun set over Lac Léman.

Madame de Staël gripped his arm, held it fast and smiled. "By next fall, you will have a son or a daughter who will be your own."

Surprised and elated, he drew her close and kissed her passionately.

Several days later, Benjamin Constant left for Paris in high spirits. With him, he carried a carton of copies of Germaine's book *The Passions*, which she had just completed and published. He also had a generous loan from Necker for the purchase of property in France.

Within two months, Madame Germaine Necker de Staël Holstein was acclaimed by literary critics throughout Europe who were lavish with praise of her treatise, calling it "the finest work published in the century."

Benjamin had diligently placed the book in the hands of scholars, writers and journalists. His efforts had been rewarded.

Among the letters of commendation Germaine received was one she prized above the others—it was from Wolfgang Goethe in Weimar, Germany.

The acceptance and renown of Madame de Staël's book impressed and influenced the Directors of France. One by one they capitulated, and announced she could return to "any location forty kilometers outside the capital."

Germaine would have preferred Paris, but the relaxing of the decree was timely and suited her plans.

Madame de Staël was discreet in conducting her extramarital affairs. She wanted to preserve the dignity and the solidarity of her family so she readily accepted Benjamin's offer of a hideaway where she could complete her pregnancy.

To establish his political base and residence, Benjamin, with funds provided by Necker, had purchased, reconstructed and sumptuously refurbished the sturdy ruins of an ancient convent in Hérivaux, a small hamlet north of Paris.

It was here, on this quiet, secluded estate, that Benjamin and Germaine settled in January, 1797.

"Such audacity!" Germaine declared. "He dares to challenge me with divorce proceedings!"

"What did you expect him to do?" Benjamin asked peevishly. "You cut off the poor man's allowance without warning. He's in debt over his head with loans he'll never be able to repay. There are no carefree, philandering comrades he can turn to—the royal courtiers have scattered all over the continent."

"I don't understand why both you and my father defend Eric and fail to accept *my* suffering. It is I who have been talking of divorce for years," Germaine protested. "It is not my intention to free *him* but to free *myself!*"

An undercurrent of tension had been developing between Benjamin and Germaine for months without either choosing to acknowledge the rift. At times their arguments became so unbearable for Benjamin that he escaped to his study and worked on research for a book he was writing comparing religions of the world. Bound to each other by intense intellectual and emotional passions, the lovers' high-strung psyches, as taut as violin strings, clashed in the close confinement of their hideaway. They missed the stage of social intercourse and political intrigue on which they performed and thrived.

Word from Eric Magnus had increased the friction.

Both their families objected to the unconventional, solitary way of life they were leading. Jacques Necker had refused to send Germaine's son, Auguste, to Hérviaux to stay with his daughter as she petitioned. Benjamin's relatives were shocked to learn that they might marry.

Madame de Staël fretted more about her political ostracism than the judgement of her personal life. That Benjamin had been defeated in an election in his district discouraged her. She was being condemned for her liberal leanings by the royalists who had gained seats in the legislature. "The republicans," she wrote her friends, "exile me and the counter revolutionaries will hang me."

Germaine's pregnancy made her irritable and thwarted her. It was a hindrance, keeping her from openly declaring her position. She could not defend herself from the gossip mongers and against the press who were responsible for alerting Eric Magnus to her whereabouts. The journalists looked on Benjamin and Germaine as public property, personalities in the public domain and easy prey to attack. They delighted in bandying about their indiscretions.

The lovers permitted no visitors at Hérivaux but when their loyal friend, Mathieu de Montmorency, called on them, they welcomed the distraction and invited him to stay. Mathieu, still devoted to Germaine, was her self-appointed personal advisor and was prompted again to protect her from the newspaper attacks.

"The rumors in Paris are unsettling to me," he warned Germaine. "They can harm your future and destroy your reputation if you persist in having your child here. You will convince everyone that Benjamin is the father. The reports so far are still unsubstantiated rumors. You can avoid open scandal by asking Eric Magnus to take you back."

"Impossible! I don't want him back! I won't dignify his threats by begging a favor of him."

Mathieu, like a ministering priest, tried calmly to reason with Germaine. "I'm concerned for you, dear Germaine, and for the future of your children . . . not for your husband."

Madame de Staël stood up slowly. It was clear that she would soon deliver her child. Picking a pen from her bureau plat, she rolled it between her palms as she began to pace up and down.

"Eric Magnus will not be able to dispute the paternity of this child. The baby will be born nine months after he visited me at Coppet—he and Benjamin were both there within days of one another," Germaine said smugly.

"Will the journalists believe that if you stay here for your confinement?"

Mathieu had always been a steadying influence on Germaine. She stopped pacing. Her eyes glowed deep violet as she looked at him.

"Dearest Mathieu," she said softly. "As always, you are right."

"I understand how you feel," he said, "but first you must make peace with Eric Magnus. He has been deeply hurt by the attacks against you . . . they reflect on him. You must remember he has been revealed as a cuckold. He prevailed over Legendre's outbursts in the Convention, but his pride continues to take a battering."

Germaine was silent. She had already begun to plot her political strategy for Paris.

"Your best move is to reinstate his allowance," Mathieu offered. "Assure him the rumors are false and he will be happy to have you back. Though his status as a diplomat is still in question he lives at the Embassy."

"But my exile . . . what of the forty kilometer limit from Paris?"

Mathieu was relieved. Madame de Staël, once again, was yielding to his suggestions.

"You are in luck," he said enthusiastically. "The surging success of your book has brought you celebrity status. While the gossip columnists dwell on your personal life, the critics are hailing you as the 'Woman of the Age.' I'm certain the Directors will not enforce the decree against you when they learn that you have returned to the city."

The Baroness de Staël moved back into the Swedish Embassy just in time. Within a week of her arrival, on June 8, 1797, to the delight of the Ambassador (and Benjamin Constant) she gave birth to a girl whom she named Albertine.

Close by, in his Paris apartment, Benjamin waited his turn to call on Germaine. He was eager to see his daughter and resume his political collaboration with the Baroness.

He did not have to wait long. Within three days, the Swedish Ambassadress was again conducting her affairs from her boudoir. By the next week, she had opened her salon and was entertaining "republicans in the morning, émigrés in the evening and everybody at dinner."

Chapter 15
Talleyrand's Return

"I have never witnessed so stunning a scene of domesticity," Charles Talleyrand remarked unctuously, sniffing the smell of a newborn as he entered the boudoir of the Baroness de Staël. He was among the first of her friends to call on Germaine after the birth of her daughter.

The Baroness had been reading to her sons who sat next to her on a chaise. A nurse attended Albertine, now a week old, in her cradle.

"Charles!" Germaine exclaimed. "Charles! It has been too long," she said, greeting her old lover with a warm embrace. Turning to her sons, she took each by the hand. "Auguste! Albert! Bishop Charles Maurice de Talleyrand-Perigord, one of the most brilliant men of France—of the world. You have heard me speak of him often."

The Baroness glowed with the freshness of recent motherhood. At thirty-one she was at the height of her sensuality. When she had time to be a mother she concentrated on that role. Talleyrand observed that she loved her sons and that they adored her.

Talleyrand, who was now forty-three, looked grotesque. His limp was more pronounced, his complexion ashen, his face distorted and puffy. His grooming, however, was meticulous. His gaze had not changed—it was as steady and overpowering as it had been when she had last seen him in England four years earlier.

Charles leaned heavily on his cane with one hand and extended the other, first to the older boy, then to the younger. He spoke to them with indulgence and charm about their studies and listened attentively to their replies.

"Here, Charles, is my daughter," the Baroness said, nestling the baby against her breast.

Talleyrand, like a doting uncle, touched the little strands of red hair on the infant's forehead. "Beautiful child," he said wryly. "An unusual shade of auburn." He had read between the lines of Germaine's letters . . . Benjamin was no stranger to him.

The nurse left the room with Albertine and the boys followed.

"I made a vow," Charles said, settling into a comfortable bergère, "that I shall never stay away from you for so long again. I shall spend the rest of my life near you, wherever you are."

Germaine leaned back on the cushions of her chaise and eyed Talleyrand with skeptical amusement.

"I shall hold you to your promise."

The Baroness had missed the sparkle and sting of Charles' wit and the challenge of his rhetoric. She was delighted that he was still attached to her but was not beguiled by his gallantry. The sizeable loan she gave him had brought him back from America and reestablished him in Paris. Now, he was seeking more than money—support, no doubt, to regain political influence.

The Baroness de Staël and Charles Talleyrand both craved power, the power to bring world leadership to France and peace to Europe . . . and personal satisfaction.

After that their motives diverged.

For Talleyrand, power was a means to achieve the property and stature of a nobleman lost to him when he was deprived of his birthright. A true aristocrat, he was a Sybarite with a love for elegant clothes, opulent furnishings, lavish entertaining and works of art. He disdained violence and confrontation. His rigid, masklike exterior was a sheath that concealed a sharp, stiletto talent for manipulation. He wielded a diplomatic genius for power that could afford him the lifestyle he coveted.

Power to Madame de Staël was an end in itself, with glory and adulation its rewards. Her wealth, a weapon for her intellect and boundless energies, was directed to challenge and achieve power. She accepted the rules of society that placed men in positions of authority. She was eager to assist them and was fearless as she used them. Talleyrand was a tantalizing prospect to be helped and manipulated to gain her ends.

The tergiversatory Bishop would not jeopardize his position by being hasty.

He began by enchanting his former mistress with tales of his adventures in America. He knew Germaine planned a visit to the new nation to invest in property for her father.

Talleyrand had traveled from Virginia to Maine, stopping in rapidly growing cities that impressed him and riding through vast wildernesses that overwhelmed him.

He found the people industrious. He was surprised that the men of influence he visited . . . Aaron Burr, Robert Morris, General Philip Schuyler and Alexander Hamilton, among them . . . were cordial and gracious, "so much like Frenchmen" he declared.

"I deplore, however, the American preoccupation with wealth," he told Germaine. "There is something unbecoming in the luxury they exhibit. We French indulge in opulence and demonstrate extravagance and frivolity. But there, luxury serves to emphasize their defects and only proves that refinement does not exist in America.

"There is a bewildering, enigmatic facet in American politics," he said. "Hamilton, once Secretary of the Treasury, had to resign his post since he could not afford to serve. He went into law practice to support his family. It is mystifying. Everyone in government has the same attitude, unlike France, where those in office become rich or richer. Money is venerated in the United States but the officials do not use their offices to line their own pockets. They are either naive or stupid, or perhaps both."

Germaine did not remind her canny friend that her father had never profited from his position. He served without pay and went further by granting France a huge loan.

Charles talked more of his personal experiences than of his failed business ventures and had Germaine in tears of laughter when he related an incident he'd had with his servant, Courtiade, when they were lost in a dense forest in the middle of the night.

"'Are you there, Courtiade?' I called out, "for it was so dark I could not see him and was afraid we had been separated. My trusted servant replied sadly, 'Unfortunately, I am, my lord.' There we were, miles from civilization, bedraggled, our clothes torn, our beards heavy and we carried on with court formality. Our plight and our attempts at propriety were so absurd that we reached out to each other, grasped hands and sat down on the ground together bursting with laughter."

Charles Talleyrand recounted the way they safely reached a small village the next morning. Then he abruptly turned serious.

"I am ready to return to public service," he informed Germaine.

"Even though there is growing unrest with the current regime?"

"The time is right," Charles said. "I am not identified with the Directory since I have deliberately avoided all contact with politics during the months I have been back in France."

"Your absence in the government has not escaped me."

"Any affiliation with this incompetent administration, up to now, would have been dangerous for me."

"The masses are beginning to demonstrate against the corruption."

"That is why the time is right. The country is heading for another crisis. With a plan . . . "

" . . . another *coup d'etat*?" Germaine asked.

"Of course!"

"You will need military support . . . a sword."

Talleyrand could read Germaine's mind, but asked, "Whom would you suggest?"

"There is only one man who can help France. He has heroic qualities, he is the best republican of them all. There is no one else . . . it must be Napoleon Bonaparte!"

"Again, my dear, we agree."

"Can you convince him? I have tried to correspond with him without success."

"He would respond to me if I were in a post of authority. I must have a seat on the Council of Ministers."

Germaine laughed heartily. "Impossible."

Charles' expression did not change. "Not with your influence."

"Mine?"

The Baroness left her chaise and walked across the room to a small marquetry table. Picking up the Egyptian letter opener Charles had given her years before, she stood facing him.

"There are legislators who delight in demeaning me," Germaine declared. "That they listened to my arguments and voted for your return was short of a miracle. Now, with the clergy and the aristocracy both in disrepute, and you represent both, I question your chances. There is little I can do."

"You are a powerful woman, my dear," Charles replied with characteristic, seductive guile. "There are many women like Thérèse Tallien and Josephine Bonaparte who envy you. Men in power respect and fear you. Why else would they exile you?"

Undeceived, Madame de Staël basked in Talleyrand's flattery. She was eager to work for her one-time mentor but decided to play his game. She toyed with him making him believe she had to be convinced.

"I have avoided the Directory but I have not been idle. I delivered a paper before the Institute of Sciences and Art . . . " Talleyrand said.

"On the commercial relations between England and the United States," Madame de Staël finished for him.

"Ah! So you know. Yes. It was received with great enthusiasm and applause," he said handing her a copy of the address. "The audience filled the chamber . . . there were members of the society and of the diplomatic corps."

Together, they reviewed the contents of the paper in which the major issue focused on the fact that the English language, used by both nations, was a unifying influence.

"The Institute has invited me to deliver another paper," Talleyrand went on with brash confidence. "There are those who remember my past record favorably."

"Very well, Charles," Germaine said smiling benevolently. "How should we proceed?"

The former Bishop of Autun outlined his strategy. Madame de Staël's enthusiasm intensified for Talleyrand's agenda matched her own and would bring her close to Bonaparte.

"First," the Baroness offered, "I will introduce you to the Club de Salm." This organization was the political base through which she, Benjamin Constant and her longtime associate, Abbé Siéyès, wielded influence. Within a week, Talleyrand maneuvered himself into a position of leadership in the prestigious society.

Germaine then approached Count Paul Barras who was still one of the most powerful men in France.

"I have not changed my opinion of your friend," the Count told her. "He is a man of great intellect and talent. But my associates consider him a vile and licentious unfrocked priest. I can do nothing for you."

Madame de Staël refused to accept the rebuff. She persisted, pleaded and cajoled like a spoiled child. She harassed the reluctant Director until he politely asked her to leave.

Germaine retrenched.

Two days later, refreshed and fortified, she returned to ask for one more hearing and secured it. She staged a *tour de force* in Barras's apartment, working herself up into such a frenzy that tears welled up in her eyes.

"Bishop Talleyrand has suffered deeply throughout his life," she declared. "He was neglected by his parents and forced to take up a vocation he despises. He has been accused of vices he never committed and has endured exile."

Her voice reaching a piercing crescendo, she proclaimed, "If you deny him the post of Minister of Foreign Affairs, he threatens to throw himself into the Seine!"

Astonishingly, Germaine then calmly enumerated Talleyrand's contributions to France with cool eloquence. "Above all," she concluded, "he has an uncommon ability to survive, a quality our nation needs."

Count Barras was amused.

"We can't have France deprived of this man's genius," he told Germaine. "Go tell him to stay clear of the river."

Within days, in mid-July, Talleyrand was appointed Foreign Minister. His first move was to initiate a restrained correspondence with Bonaparte.

The General replied immediately. Accepting Talleyrand as a reliable, trustworthy channel to the Directory, he wrote:

> I *will be flattered to exchange letters*
> *with you often, so as to keep you fully*
> *informed and also to persuade you of*
> *my esteem and respect for you.*

Six weeks later, the new Foreign Minister was ready to test the relationship that evolved from the exchange of letters.

Paul Barras wanted to concentrate his power and needed military assistance. When he turned to Talleyrand for advice, the Foreign Minister directed a hasty dispatch to Bonaparte. The General responded by sending one of his top commanders to Paris.

On September 4, 1797, the coup d'etat of Eighteen Fructidor made Barras master of France and solidified Talleyrand's position both in the government and with the military. He was a step closer to his ultimate goal: toppling the man he helped elevate to the highest post in the government and removing the entire corrupt Directory.

Madame de Staël's status was secure. She had hoped for Benjamin's appointment as Secretary General in the foreign office as tangible evidence of appreciation. Instead, she settled for a ceremonial post for him. Constant was named President of the Canton of Luzaraches, in which Hérviaux was located.

Chapter 16
"Genius Has No Sex"

The Baroness de Staël looked calm. She was not.

Her excitement was evident in the slight trembling of the hand with which she held a note she received the night before from Charles Talleyrand. Her eyes darted from word to word like glowing embers as she read the message again:

> *The Office of the*
> *Foreign Minister of France*
> *5 December 1797*
> *My Dearest Germaine:*
> *I have just been delivered a letter from General Bonaparte who arrived in Paris this evening. He requests an audience with me tomorrow morning at eleven. If you would like, you may meet him in the anteroom of my offices before our conference.*
>
> > *Devotedly,*
> > *Charles*

It was nine o'clock in the morning. Germaine had risen at dawn to allow more than enough time to dress for her first face-to-face encounter with the man all France was acclaiming.

She was wearing a flimsy yellow Directoire gown, the most becoming she had selected from more than a dozen that were strewn about her boudoir on chairs, the floor and her chaise.

The Baroness smiled approvingly at her reflection in the full-length mirror. The current styles were well suited to her Rubensesque figure. The low décolleté revealed the round fullness of her breasts. A matching turban, trimmed in orange, held her curls close to her face, accenting her dark eyes. Taking one final glance at her image, she requested her maids to place a long, deep green velvet cloak over her shoulders. The Baroness was ready. She rushed from the room like a nubile young woman on her way to her wedding.

Germaine's two-wheel calèche delivered her to the government offices before ten. She was dismayed to find the reception room at the Foreign Minister's suite crowded with visitors. Talleyrand had not yet arrived.

Disconcerted, she sat down to wait.

Germaine was uncharacteristically nervous. Her palms grew clammy, perspiration formed between her breasts.

Just before eleven o'clock, Talleyrand emerged from his office. At the same moment, there was a clamor on the cobblestones in the courtyard. Rapid footsteps resounded in the hallway. The door flew open. General Bonaparte in full military regalia burst into the room like an opera tenor making a stage entrance!

Germaine panicked. Instead of removing her cloak to create the stunning effect she had planned with her low-cut gown, she bolted up from her chair and hurried to the center of the room where all three stopped short of collision.

Talleyrand handled the near-calamity with dignity, introducing the breathless Baroness to the imperious General.

Germaine found herself looking directly into Bonaparte's eyes—he was no taller than she. He was not handsome, though he had the swarthy good looks of a Corsican. His face was thin, pale and drawn from the fatigue of his long journey. His stark white uniform, with blue and scarlet braid, fitted his sturdy figure tightly. She felt strength and virility radiate from this arrogant genius.

"It is my pleasure to meet you, Madame Baronne de Staël," Napoleon said. He hesitated, waiting for a reply.

For the first time in her life, Germaine could not utter a word. Her mind was as empty as a clean slate.

"When my caravan left Austria," the General went on, "we traveled by way of Switzerland. I was near your home at Coppet and stopped to visit. I was disappointed that your father was away for the day."

At last Germaine was able to reply. "I also am sorry. My father holds you in high esteem." She could say no more.

"I have admired Monsieur Necker since my early days at the Academy," Bonaparte continued. "I am impressed with the heritage of public service he began and you continue."

Charles Talleyrand observed the brief exchange with amusement—he had never known Germaine to be speechless. As the crush of visitors began to irritate Bonaparte, Talleyrand led the General away and left the Baroness standing alone among them, bewildered.

On her way home in her calèche, Germaine was distraught. She could not understand why she had been unable to speak. True, she had felt overwhelmed by this man of obvious genius, but there was something else, something disturbing. When she stood next to Napoleon, she remembered, she had difficulty breathing.

She was chagrined, but thrilled. My God, she mused, could she fall in love with this man?

The encounter had been too brief. The pressure of the crowd, the suddenness of the meeting, her loss of words! How could she, the brilliant, powerful Baroness de Staël have performed as a naive maiden. She braced herself. What a fool I was? This will never happen again. I'll be prepared the next time, she vowed. I'll arrange a private meeting and set the stage. I'll be alone with this great man who would save France. I'll declare my admiration and exult in his achievements.

She paused to reflect on what she observed in those fleeting moments. Though Napoleon showed great strength of character, she had to admit he lacked nobility.

Nonetheless, here, at last, was a man worthy of her intellect and dedication—worthy of the daughter of Jacques Necker!

The next week, the Baroness de Staël was thrilled to see her hero again . . . but from a distance and along with tens of thousands of other French men, women and children. Together, they shared the excitement of an awe inspiring event held on the expansive grounds of the Luxembourg Palace to honor Bonaparte's battlefield victories. Germaine sat among the fashionable elite on a cordoned-off estrade. Far across the courtyard and over the heads of the shabby throng, she had a clear view of Napoleon and other dignitaries on the speakers' platform. A uniformed band of hundreds accompanied the choir dressed in red, white and blue robes. The music was deafening.

The choirs sang hymns. The speeches were lengthy. Paul Barras paid tribute to the Corsican's past successes. Talleyrand predicted a brilliant future for the warrior in glowing terms.

"One day soon," Germaine's former lover proclaimed, "we will tear Bonaparte away from his military pursuits and direct his genius toward building greater glories for France!"

The assemblage was aroused like Roman hordes welcoming the victorious Caesar. Their wild cheers reverberated off the walls of the lofty marble structures.

Napoleon was the Man of the Hour.

"Bonaparte is maintaining a low profile," Talleyrand told Germaine a few days later. "He's clever. He has keen instincts. He's responding readily to my suggestions."

"True. I saw him at the opera," the Baroness interrupted. "When the audience started to applaud him he slipped out of view to the rear of his box. He appears modest and unassuming. Even the journalists laud his quiet life. You are to be commended for the counsel you give him. But then, my dear, you have no peer."

"Bonaparte takes on the semblance of an experienced performer. He is superb. But we cannot wait for him. We have to move quickly and he is due to return to his troops. We must select an alternate military commander. The incompetence and corruption of the Directors is creating bitterness and discontent. We lack a viable organization to take command when they are overthrown. We cannot delay any longer. We must build a base and commit our leadership."

Talleyrand paused. Then with typical capriciousness, he went on. "Ah . . . I meant to tell you sooner. I plan a magnificent affair at my mansion to honor Napoleon and build support for him. Will you come?"

"Charles! How ridiculous! Of course I'll be there." Germaine's eyes flashed like sparks from a blacksmith's anvil. "We've worked together for just such a coup. I wouldn't miss it!"

"You will have to fend for yourself."

"Fend? What on earth do you mean?"

"I have learned that Bonaparte does not treat intelligent women kindly. His attitude toward all women is condescending and that of a peasant. As for those who are brilliant, like you . . . ."

"He was gracious when we met in your offices," she replied, stroking the Egyptian letter opener Talleyrand had given her.

"I cannot promise a similar performance—he envisions himself invincible . . . a superior human being. You'll see."

The gala took place shortly after the New Year in 1798. It was the most lavish reception held in Paris since the reign of Louis XVI, and startled even the jaded bon vivants of the Directory.

Germaine wandered around the massive fresh floral decorations that transformed the drawing rooms in the Hôtel Galliffet, the mansion of the Foreign Minister, into summer gardens. Fawning guests, three and four deep, encircled Bonaparte and his Josephine. She caught occasional glimpses of the General's face. Except for a frozen smile, it was a marble mask.

The Baroness de Staël would not stand on the fringes of lionizers. She took the arm of Vincent Arnault, a mutual friend of hers and Napoleon's, pushed her way through the cordon and maneuvered herself and Arnault next to the honored guest.

After a brief exchange of greetings, Germaine set aside the amenities and confronted him.

"General Bonaparte," she said, "I've heard you have a somewhat arbitrary attitude toward members of the opposite sex. Do you like women?"

"I love my wife," he replied, his face still granite.

Josephine nodded, approving.

"Ah. Whom do you most admire?" Germaine persisted.

"The woman who takes best care of her house."

"Of course. But, whom do you consider the *first* woman in the world, the woman who has made the greatest contribution? Who is your ideal woman?"

"The woman who produces the most children."

To her consternation, Germaine, again, was speechless. Napoleon bowed, took her hand in his, kissed it, turned to Josephine and guided her to another circle of adoring acolytes.

Disconcerted but quick to rebound, she walked to the opposite side of the ballroom with Arnault asking herself . . . Why can't I talk with that man? Why couldn't I elevate the banal conversation? I should have said that the great Thebian military strategist, Epaminondas, might have given the same answer?

The Baroness de Staël had encountered no insurmountable problems in captivating such erudite politicians as Talleyrand, Narbonne, Constant and the entire staff of government officials. Napoleon's military instincts and basic Latin passions needed more exposure and training in a society in which women influenced their men in the subtle arts of diplomacy, amorous adventures and intrigue. Undaunted, Germaine was ready to take him on and teach him.

Determined to see Napoleon alone, the Baroness ordered her calèche and instructed her driver to take her to his headquarters on the rue de la Victoire later that first week of January.

She intimidated the sentries and forced her way into the vestibule. A startled valet told Germaine his master was in the bath.

The Baroness was unruffled. "I can wait."

The flustered servant returned to Napoleon's chamber. Germaine heard the General's angry tones through the walls but she could not hear what was said. After a muffled discussion, she heard Bonaparte bellow so loudly that the rafters shook, "Tell that woman that I am naked!"

His words were clear, distinct and unmistakable. He wanted her to leave.

Madame de Staël walked up to the door and tried the knob. The latch was locked. Persevering, she knocked and called out with force equal to his, "What does it matter, General Bonaparte? Genius has no sex!"

The valet emerged, subdued and shaken. "Please, madame," he implored, "the General will dispatch a message to you in a few days to arrange a private interview."

While waiting to hear from Bonaparte, the Baroness de Staël received alarming news.

The French Army of the East had been ordered by the government to invade Switzerland, acquiring territories along the way. Its ultimate mission was to seize the abundant treasury at Berne.

Germaine was horrified—the family estate at Coppet lay in the army's path. The fees from the holdings comprised a large part of the

Necker income. She summoned Benjamin, whose family had similar properties, and together they called on Director Barras.

The powerful official apologized profusely. "The matter is out of my hands," he told them. "The Directors and Council voted approval of Bonaparte's venture. Since there are no funds available, they sanctioned the sacking of the Berne treasury. I can do nothing to help you."

Germaine was devastated.

Returning to her town house, the Baroness found a message from Bonaparte waiting for her. He had set up an appointment—for the next morning. The interview had lost its appeal. She was distracted from her interest in the well-being of France. When it came to her family's personal welfare and a threat to her life-style, Germaine was less a patriot and more a concerned member of the aristocracy. She did not intend to sacrifice the Necker fortune to her ideals. She would ignore the invitation.

On the other hand, she reflected, perhaps a meeting with Bonaparte would be opportune. Though he lacked political authority, he was in a position to exploit his popularity and prestige. She would keep the appointment and ask him to coerce the Directors to finance his campaign by other means.

The meeting began auspiciously. Napoleon greeted the Baroness cordially and dismissed his aide. They were alone. He led her to a comfortable armchair and sat down behind his massive desk. Seated, the General appeared more prepossessing, more commanding, taller.

The stage was set.

He listened attentively as Germaine began to plead her cause. "I am disturbed that the French Army will soon march into Switzerland. The Swiss are a peace-loving people," she contended. "We should not encroach on their liberty and freedom.

Madame de Staël's plea struck Bonaparte like a spate of cold water. His mood changed completely. She had not come to pay a social call and glorify his past accomplishments as she had seemed to promise. No! She was there to seek intervention in a military action!

His eyes chilled, his face turned to stone. He stood and looked down on his visitor. His voice was deep, deliberate and authoritative.

"The Directors," he said, "are sending troops into Switzerland in the name of the principles of the Revolution which you yourself advocate. The Swiss are under the heels of the aristocrats of Berne. No man should live without political rights."

"But the Vaudois are perfectly free," Madame de Staël countered. "When liberty exists in fact, it is unnecessary to obtain it by law and expose it to the great tragedy of all—an invasion by foreigners!"

Ignoring this, Bonaparte went on. "Men must participate in the government of their country. It stimulates their imagination and builds self-respect."

"Switzerland has maintained its contentment and beauty for centuries," Germaine insisted. "Its tranquility should not be violated."

"Men's rights must be preserved," Bonaparte ended, cutting her off with an imperious wave of his hand. "This discussion is academic, my authority is military, not political. It is not my duty . . . nor do I choose to influence the policy-making of France."

The Baroness was reduced to silence . . . not by his argument but by his overwhelming presence. She was angered with herself. It was happening again. It was she who was accustomed to dominating conversations. She marveled at Bonaparte's ability to take command. He appeared to build an impenetrable barrier around himself and block out all sensitivity to any other human being.

Napoleon considered the matter closed and went on to another. Strangely, he seemed drawn to the Baroness, impressed, perhaps, by her, her social position, her prestige, her literary fame. Dropping his guard mercurially, Bonaparte began to talk of art.

"My armies have confiscated the greatest masterpieces of the Italian museums," he boasted, "and are bringing them here to become part of the French collections."

She let him pontificate, in awe of this coarse Corsican's cunning and instinct to sense the cultural value and worth of great works of art. Mon Dieu, why, he's a scavenger, striving to be a patron of the arts by pilferage and force!

Bonaparte went on to speak of his love of country life, his disappointment that he had no time for such luxury.

It occurred to Madame de Staël that this military genius was a man without refinement, a peasant. He was terrifying, yet he had brusque charm. Germaine was fascinated . . . and challenged.

The next day, disheartened and despondent that she had failed to dissuade the General from sending the army into Switzerland, Madame de Staël packed her bags, gathered her children together and departed for Coppet to face the inevitable invasion at her father's side.

Chapter 17
Coppet Under Siege

The twenty-eighth of January, 1798, dawned magnificently on the tranquil hamlet of Coppet. Like a vulnerable fortress, the Necker chateau, glistening in the sunlight, grew precariously out of the hillside above the village.

Within the luxurious chambers and marble corridors, the family gathered somberly with a few trusted servants in the spacious library that faced south overlooking Lake Geneva. The room bristled with tension and anxiety.

A maid helped the Baroness de Staël slip on her cloak. Germaine tied on her bonnet and drew on a pair of woolen gloves.

Jacques Necker, in a long, heavy riding-coat and hat, stood between his grandsons, holding them protectively about their shoulders. They leaned against him to draw comfort from his closeness. Olive Uginet held six-month-old Albertine, wrapped snugly in blankets. Eugene stood attentively with two footmen beside him.

"We must wait," Madame de Staël said. Her voice was firm but gentle. "The troops are expected some time this morning. They have orders to take the lands. We may be permitted to remain in the chateau. I am not certain."

Eugene cleared his throat. "Everything is ready, Madame la Baronne." He was solemn. "The chambermaids are closing the trunks . . . the stablehands are ready to lift them onto the carriages. The horses need only be harnessed. I will wait for your orders."

"Thank you Eugene, Olive. We appreciate your loyalty and devotion. You know how much we rely on you."

Germaine turned to her sons. "Albert. Auguste. Have your coats close by. We may have to leave our home quickly."

The boys did not understand but they sensed the urgency in their mother's voice. Even Albert who balked at discipline was calm and held his grandfather's hand tightly for reassurance.

"Papa and I will go outside for a short time," the Baroness told them. "Monsieur Eugene will stay here with you."

Auguste and Albert reluctantly let their grandfather go.

Madame de Staël and Jacques Necker walked out onto the terrace balcony. The sun was bright, the sky cloudless, the smell of winter cold and dry. The brisk breeze forced them to draw their warm garments close. They had a clear view of the sparkling waters of Lac Léman, the distant summit of Mont Blanc and the road from Geneva that stretched out below.

Father and daughter looked to the southwest. They did not speak. Germaine took Necker's arm as they paced the terrace waiting for a sign of what might lie ahead. The minutes passed. An hour went by. Then another.

Still nothing.

At mid-morning, without warning, the initial suspense was broken. Rolling drums from the direction of Geneva shattered the stillness. Moments later, the French Army came into view. At first the procession, a long red, white and blue snake, was winding its way along the highway in the distance. As the marchers drew closer they became more distinct. It was a glorious sight. A glimmer of hope flashed through Germaine's mind as she remembered the respect the Directors and Bonaparte had expressed for her father. Momentarily, she was mesmerized by the rhythm and the military splendor.

Two spirited drummers led the way, followed by officers in full regalia on white chargers. The foot soldiers, in blue jackets, white pants, red plumes in their headdresses, marched forward in perfect precision, their swords glistening like gems in the sunlight.

Germaine grew tense as the army approached the foot of the hill below the chateau. Jacques Necker was unflinching.

The long column halted. An officer dismounted from his horse, left the foot soldiers and with an escort began to climb the path to the gate of the chateau's courtyard.

Madame de Staël and her father went to meet the spokesman of the invading troops. The handsome young soldiers were shown into the spacious marble foyer by a green-liveried footman.

"Monsieur Necker?" the Unit Commander inquired.

"Yes. Welcome to the Chateau de Coppet."

"Thank you, Monsieur." The officer hesitated.

"Would you join us in the library?" the Baroness de Staël asked. Eugene, standing behind his mistress, opened the large double doors to the bright chamber. "We will be more comfortable here," she went on, removing her gloves and bonnet.

They walked across the highly polished parquet floors and sat in a small group near the windows.

"I am honored," the commander continued, "to be assigned to call on you. We have been ordered by the Government of France and the Commander General of the Armies to express concern for your safety."

Germaine, who sat close to her father on a sofa, felt him sigh imperceptibly. Neither spoke.

"General Bonaparte wishes to stress that no form of harassment or discomfort will be caused you or your family by the presence of the French forces in Switzerland."

"We appreciate the consideration," Jacques Necker replied.

"Further, the Directors want to assure you that your lands will not be confiscated."

Germaine and Necker were astounded. Both concealed their shock and relief.

Standing, the Baroness then held out her hands in a gesture of welcome.

"You must be tired from your long march. Would you and your staff stay for luncheon?"

The repast was a joyous celebration. Toasts were drunk to each of the Directors of France and to Bonaparte. Jacques Necker gave a short speech in which he enumerated the battles Napoleon had fought and won, praising his accomplishments and predicted a great future for him.

After the soldiers had departed, Germaine discussed their good fortune with her father.

"Bonaparte must have interceded on our behalf," she said, feeling secure for the first time since she had left Paris. "The General has begun to influence the policies of France."

Later, Germaine tried to reconstruct the conversation she had with Bonaparte. What had she missed? Had he held her in greater regard than she believed? Had he deliberately misled her? She was confused, but her dreams of playing a role in France's destiny, at his side, were restored.

Chapter 18
Juliette Récamier

"We must move quickly or lose our advantage," Germaine confided anxiously to Juliette Récamier. "Charles is pressing hard to set the coup in motion."

Madame Récamier was a young woman of ethereal beauty and beguiling innocence. In the past year, she and Germaine had become intimate friends, sharing private hopes and passions. Outside of her own family, there was no one dearer to the Baroness.

"Abbé Siéyès has completed the constitution," Germaine told Juliette, "and we are ready to oust the Directory. If we delay much longer the people themselves will revolt against the inefficiency and corruption and install their own leaders. Fortunately, we convinced the Abbé to accept Napoleon Bonaparte's military support. Now, we are waiting for word from the General."

"The great man reciprocates your admiration," Juliette teased, hoping to calm and distract Germaine. "Bonaparte, they say, is reading your book, *The Passions,* on the battlefields of Egypt."

When the contingent of the French army had returned from Switzerland eighteen months before with the spoils destined to finance his expedition, Bonaparte set out for Africa hoping to cut off British routes to India. His strategy was grand, his victories meager. Admiral Nelson won the Battle of the Nile and sank the French fleet at Aboukir Bay. News of the definitive defeat had not yet reached Paris.

Napoleon made the most of the exotic aura of the locale to enhance his image. Frenchmen avidly awaited his glowing dispatches. When they learned that just before the Battle of the Pyramids he had pointed to those architectural wonders and cried out "Soldiers, forty centuries look down upon you!" they cheered him in the streets of Paris.

Madame de Staël sat beside her friend Juliette, who was dressed in a long Grecian gown of white chiffon and reclined on a resplendent Directoire chaise. Madame Récamier was only twenty-two, eleven years younger than Germaine, but was already one of the leading hostesses of Paris. Considered the most beautiful woman in France, she was beginning successfully to challenge the leadership for the "scepter of beauty" held by Thérèse Tallien and Josephine de Beauharnais Bonaparte. In her drawing rooms, which were tastefully lavish, she presided over receptions with simplicity, reserve and a gentle personal charm.

"That news has also reached my father in Coppet," Germaine replied, drawing a letter from her handbag. "'So your glory has spread to the banks of the Nile,'" she read. "'Alexander of Macedon called on philosophers and wise men from the four corners of the world to dispute with him. The Corsican Alexander, to save time, enters only into communication with the mind of Madame de Staël. He knows how to get things done.'"

"Yes. The General is as focused as his sharpshooters and he knows how to do things. But he does them all so dispassionately." Juliette remarked.

"Those traits which make him a man to be feared are those that will make him succeed," Germaine replied.

"I was once the object of one of his cold, silent attacks."

"You?" Germaine said in surprise, leaning over Juliette to touch her face gently. "My sweet, innocent Juliette! How? When?"

"It took place at the celebration held for Bonaparte at the Luxembourg Palace on the tenth of December in 1797 before you and I met."

"I was there!" Germaine exclaimed. "And so was all Paris!"

"It is still vivid in my mind," Juliette began. "The colorful procession, the soldiers marching into the courtyard to martial music. Captured foreign flags fluttered in the breeze . . . such a magnificent scene!"

"I remember it clearly."

"I was in the stands with a direct view of the dais. I was overwhelmed by the spectacle and watched as Barras paid tribute to General Bonaparte. I wanted to see the hero clearly. Without thinking, I stood up abruptly above the crowd. Everyone turned and looked at me. They whispered and pointed. I felt as if those many thousands of eyes were all on me!"

"Oh!" Germaine cried out. "Of course! It was *you*! I was too far away to see you clearly, but I heard the murmurs of the admiring spectators who were dazzled by your beauty and your costume."

"I was horrified," Juliette recalled. "I sat down quickly when I realized what I had done. I was confused and blushed bright red. I had not meant to cause a stir."

Germaine's dark eyes flashed with approval. "But you did!"

"I tried to bury myself among the others. But I could not stop watching Bonaparte. I was fascinated. He had turned in my direction when he heard the commotion. He looked directly into my eyes. The piercing shot of his sharp glance went through me. I felt disintegrated. He wanted to destroy me for distracting the attention from himself."

"He acted in character," Germaine said. "He dominates with his presence and projects power with a gesture. He is a man of genius . . . ambitious and fearless. We need him as the military arm of the new government. But he is a being without human compassion . . . we cannot permit him to govern alone."

"He is so different from any of his brothers." Madame Récamier was often a guest at Germaine's receptions, which regularly attracted the most influential literary and political figures, including Napoleon's siblings. The most dashing and impetuous of the Bonapartes, the younger Lucien, was smitten with Juliette. Though she did not want to encourage his advances, she enjoyed flirting with him.

The Baroness de Staël and Madame Récamier had met in the summer of 1798, when Germaine returned to Paris to manage the family investments in France. She first called on the Directory for the return of the two-million livre loan her father had made to the government in 1789. Then she turned to Juliette's husband, Jacques-Rose Récamier, for help in disposing of her father's real estate holdings in the city.

She fared better with Jacques-Rose than she did with the Directors who acknowledged the debt and Necker's generosity but made no promises. Récamier wanted to purchase two of the town houses for his own use and introduced the two women during the negotiations.

A wiry, energetic Frenchman in his late forties, the successful banker had married Juliette Bernard when she was only fifteen. It was rumored that she was his illegitimate daughter and he wanted to make sure she would inherit his fortune.

The women knew each other by reputation. When they came together for the first time in the drawing room of the banker's sumptuously furnished chateau in the suburbs of Paris, there was an instant spark of mutual attraction.

Germaine was enchanted with the young Juliette, who glided across the floor as though on a cloud. Her skin was pale, almost transparent, and she had a delicate porcelain beauty. Her rich black hair was held by a bow on the top of her head and ringlets framed her lovely heart-shaped face. Her white gown was tied beneath her firm, small bosom with a narrow black ribbon. Juliette always wore white.

When Récamier left the two women alone, Juliette smiled and beckoned to Germaine with a graceful movement of her hand, suggesting that they sit together on a silk cushioned canapé.

"I've heard so much about your beauty," Germaine remarked, "but compliments do not do you justice." When Juliette remained silent, Germaine continued. "I have wanted to know you for some time. Your salons are the talk of Paris. It's no wonder. You give them a refinement the others lack . . . they reflect the freshness of your loveliness."

Juliette blushed, and seemed nourished by the sincerity of Germaine's effusive compliments.

Then Madame Récamier spoke softly, "I am reading your *Lettres sur Rousseau.* I am moved by their brilliance."

"Your beauty is as much envied by women as they envy my intellect!"

Germaine replied with typical self-assurance.

For the first time, Juliette dropped her reserve and they both burst into laughter. They knew, somehow, that Juliette's vanity was equal to Germaine's. Madame de Staël embraced the shy young woman.

During the next months, they developed a spiritual and intellectual relationship as well as one of the senses. The retiring Juliette took delight in the new world of ideas introduced by the erudite Baroness. Juliette lost her temerity, but not her freshness. She quickly grasped the art of conversation from Germaine and together, they became the focal point of all the Paris salons with their clever, contagious repartee.

Germaine learned from Juliette as well—the value of tenderness, dignity of control, the eloquence of a smile, of modesty and most surprising to her, of silence.

The friendship deepened, surviving frequent distractions and separations while Germaine helped Benjamin Constant in two unsuccessful attempts to win office. She also worked to exonerate Talleyrand from charges that as Foreign Minister he tried to extract cash gifts from American envoys (which he had). Constant, although he lost, broadened his political base, and Talleyrand, with typical deviousness, managed to extricate himself.

Juliette's sensitivity to her friend's drives and ambitions were heightened by their intimacy. "Proceed with caution, my dearest Germaine," she warned as the Baroness intensified her efforts toward the overthrow of the government with Talleyrand and Siéyès, the prime movers of the intrigue.

Germaine failed to take the sound advice and, in her eagerness, proceeded too boldly. Her clandestine activities soon were reported to the authorities.

Juliette and their entire circle were shocked and dismayed when the Directors invoked the long-standing order of exile of October, 1795 against Madame de Staël. It had never officially been removed from the records. Despite secret attempts on the part of influential politicians, who could not openly seek her reprieve, Germaine was forced to exit Paris in July, 1799, leaving Juliette and her own spirited salon behind.

At Coppet, Germaine followed the progress of the coup's strategy in dispatches that Talleyrand funneled regularly to her. Charles had resigned from the Ministry to concentrate on the conspiracy and to disassociate himself from the floundering Directory.

In Egypt, Napoleon was losing ground and was hard-pressed to withstand assaults by the Turks. Even though the absent Bonaparte had been his first choice, Siéyès began to consider other generals for his military support.

Germaine rushed to Bonaparte's defense with a pamphlet that advocated a government administered by philosophers under the protection of a great soldier, whose qualifications were, not surprisingly, identical to Napoleon's.

Madame de Staël need not have worried. While Siéyès ruminated in Paris about "another sword," Napoleon surreptitiously slipped away from Egypt, leaving his struggling armies in the custody of his field marshals. In early October, 1799, he landed at Fréjus, near Marseilles, traveling north to cheering crowds and passing through the western tip of Switzerland on his way to Paris.

It was then, as Bonaparte rode through Geneva, that the Baroness de Staël, fourteen kilometers away at Coppet, heard the cannons salute him.

Germaine confirmed the political climate of Paris by courier with Benjamin and arranged a rendezvous with him at Charenton, near the gates to the capital.

Ignoring the restrictions of her exile, a jubilant Madame de Staël set out for Paris in the luxury of her yellow berline.

Chapter 19
Bonaparte Falters

The overburdened de Staël carriages followed the same route Bonaparte had taken. As she sped through the villages, Germaine exulted in the intoxicating spell he had left in his wake. The people had mobbed the Commander's coach trying to get a glimpse of their hero and celebrated by dancing in the streets. Often, when his entourage was brought to a standstill, his fear of crowds angered and overwhelmed him. Incensed, by the delays as he neared the city, he detoured along back roads, where he was not recognized, to hasten the last leg of his journey.

The Baroness learned that the conspirators were to strike on November 7. By mid-afternoon of that day, she was still thirty kilometers south of Paris. "Press the horses harder," she called up to Eugene through the talk box. Eager to reach Charenton before dark and meet Benjamin Constant according to plan, Madame de Staël had suffered six days and nights of riding on rough country highways. The comfort of her luxurious carriage only increased her impatience and restlessness.

The vehicle careened precipitously along the dirt roads, stirring up a choking dust storm that followed along like a phantom cavalry. To maintain the pace and hold the ground, the driver forced approaching vehicles into ditches and fields.

The Baroness's servants were terrified. The maids blanched at each turn. The grooms and the footmen gripped the perch railings so tightly their knuckles turned white.

Suddenly, Germaine's boredom evaporated.

An agitated Eugene knocked on the front window of the coach to point out the blur of another dust cloud visible on the crest in the road ahead. A huge carriage with a convoy of mounted grenadiers was rolling down toward them from the north.

Her eyes widening with curiosity, Germaine pulled the blind aside to see who was riding in the coach as it passed.

Whish! She saw only the flash of grenadiers' uniforms—a blaze of red and gold—and their magnificent stallions. No more! Clouds of dust encircled both entourages as they converged. The sun disappeared. It was black as midnight.

There were stampeding hoofs, muffled cries, harsh commands and the piercing shrill of braking wheels.

The carriage with the army escort emerged from the dust storm triumphantly and fled southward.

The de Staël berline plunged into a ditch at the side of the road. For an isolated moment, grim silence gripped the countryside.

Germaine was stunned. She could not move, yet she felt no pain. The dust was settling and sparkled in the sunlight that slowly reentered the interior of the coach. Madame de Staël lay in a heap on the floor--her servants, like a pile of neglected laundry, surrounded her.

"Olive! Julie!" the Baroness cried out, trying to stand. "Mimi! Marie! Answer me!"

The women stirred and started to untangle their limbs. The carriage wobbled unsteadily as they moved. "Hold still," Madame de Staël warned. "We may topple over. If the grooms were thrown and injured we may have to make our own way. Let us wait and see."

They did not have to wait long.

"Madame la Baronne! Are you all right?" It was Eugene.

"As far as we can tell," Germaine called out. "We were thrown to the floor. We are shaken but not hurt. How are you and the others?"

"Don't concern yourself about us," Germaine's factotum encouraged her. "Just stay where you are. Don't move! We must keep the wheels from burrowing deeper into the ditch and the coach from toppling. We'll get back on the road as quickly as we can."

Germaine comforted her female servants and convinced herself to wait patiently. Could they free the coach in time for her to keep her rendezvous with Benjamin?

The fleeing carriage that forced hers off the road might be an indication that the coup had begun. The passengers must have been military or government officials—Grenadiers were not commonplace escorts.

Her lackeys put their shoulders to the coach. It would not budge. Any hope of getting to Charenton before dark began to dim.

"Take heart, Madame la Baronne," Eugene called. She heard a commotion outside. "A farmer and his field hands are here to help us."

As the berline began to rock, Germaine felt the strength of these men . . . their powerful backs . . . their muscled arms . . . developed by heavy labor. The coach jockeyed once. Twice. On the third heave, the wheels made a full turn. Then another. The carriage was back on the road.

The doors opened and the women struggled from the floor, easing themselves to the ground with the footmen's assistance. Madame de Staël was relieved to be free but wanted to be on her way.

Straightening her bonnet and adjusting her clothes, she reviewed the damage and discussed the welfare of her servants with Eugene. Satisfied that no one was seriously injured, she turned to the farmer as her factotum took charge of reloading the baggage that lay strewn about.

"We could not have managed without you," she told the ruddy fellow as he refused the purse she offered him.

"My men and I are happy to be of help," he replied with awkward grace. "We wish we could go on to Paris with you and see Bonaparte's triumph."

"Do you know what's happening?" Germaine de Staël grasped at this improbable source of information like a drowning sailor reaching for a floating plank.

"Bonaparte has been named Commander-in-Chief of the military forces in Paris. The deputies expect rioting in the streets. He is assigned to defend the government officials."

"The Directory is still in power?"

"I don't know. The carriage that forced you off the road . . . one of the directors was the passenger. He was going to Grois Bois, a few kilometers south."

"To Gros Bois?" Germaine exulted. "It was Paul Barras, that is his country estate!" Charles Talleyrand had written Germaine that Barras's removal as the most powerful Director was essential to the coup's success. Had that, in fact, been accomplished? What of the other four Directors? They had to be ousted along with the entire legislature! Only a clean sweep and a new start would open the way to give France the constitutional government it needed to survive.

"Is he out of office?" she asked hopefully.

"Yes. He has resigned and was escaping from the capital."

"What of the others? Did they resign as well?"

"I don't know. Paris is in turmoil. We heard only about Bonaparte and Barras."

Madame de Staël had learned more than she expected. It was good news. Her appetite was whetted. She paced impatiently as Eugene checked the horses and the carriage and inspected the last piece of luggage being tied back into place.

After a two-hour delay, the de Staël entourage was rolling again. Germaine trembled with anticipation. The coup *was* underway . . . it might be over. Despite Barras's ouster, however, her colleagues could still fail. Bonaparte could be forced out of his command. Barras could be replaced with another equally corrupt member of the Jacobin Club. It was possible that the Directory survived and Germaine might have to remain in exile.

But first things first.

It was now beyond the appointed hour of her meeting with Benjamin Constant. Would he have given up waiting and returned to Paris without her?

With the Capital in foment, there was no one else to turn to. Her friends, involved in the coup, would be scattered all over the city. Eric Magnus, who was in failing health, had again been dismissed from his post. He had moved from the Embassy, but she did not know where.

Dusk began to close in. Finally, flickering lights and large dark shapes loomed in the distance. The relay post of Charenton lay directly ahead.

Charenton was a smattering of sand-colored stucco buildings loosely thrown together. It was set back from the road by a courtyard, surrounded by a high stone wall.

The de Staël equipage drove into the enclosure and was forced to a full stop in the midst of milling carriages, horses and humanity. The courtyard reeked of sweat and dung and reverberated to a deafening din.

Germaine opened the blind and looked down into the seething crowd below her.

Over the clamor a man's rich, deep voice called out, "Germaine! Germaine! Over here! Minette!"

She reeled in relief. To her left, on horseback above the jostling mob, was a figure with a familiar slouch and wavy red hair falling loosely on slender shoulders. The man maneuvered his mount to the carriage and leaned toward Germaine. She put her hand out the window to grasp his.

"You're late. I was concerned," Benjamin said.

"I was afraid I would miss you!"

Constant rode alongside the carriage as it inched its way to the front of the inn.

Eugene hopped off his perch with the spring of a fencer and helped his mistress from the coach. One of the grooms took Benjamin's horse as he dismounted.

Madame de Staël fell into her lover's arms.

They were an incongruous pair. Benjamin, tall and imperially thin, his face gaunt and haggard . . . his high cheek bones beneath wire-framed tinted spectacles. Beside him, Germaine, short and plump, black ringlets edging her bonnet, framing her round face . . . her eyes, dark, clear and beautiful.

"Tell me, Benjamin, quickly! What is the situation in Paris? Where do we stand?" She was urgent, demanding.

"The plan . . . " he began, but got no further. They were scuffled by agitated strangers. Eugene Uginet, like their royal guard, pushed his way forward and guided them into the inn. They filed through the packed public room to a private area in the rear.

Uginet bargained with the innkeeper and secured a small alcove furnished with a few pieces of well-worn furniture. Eugene saw them served, then drew the shabby curtain over the opening and left.

Constant drew Madame de Staël down to the threadbare sofa, took the cloak from her shoulders, touched her lips, her chin. His hands slipped down over her neck to her bosom. He put his arms around her, drew her close. His lips met hers. She raised her arms and pressed her fingers against the back of his neck. She drained his emotion.

Abruptly, Germaine broke the embrace, loosening Benjamin's arms and drawing away without a word. Her dark eyes turned a fathomless purple.

After five years, Constant had never grown accustomed to her candor. She resumed her inquiry as though there had been no interlude. She would not be content till she heard a recounting of the events in explicit detail. She had to know.

Pouring wine from the carafe on the table, the Baroness handed one glass to Benjamin and took the other.

Benjamin did not speak. The spell of the initial thrill of their meeting had been shattered.

Germaine broke the tension.

"Your daughter is a joy," she told him. "She is the most beautiful child. She's two, now, you know. And her head is covered with a mass of auburn curls."

Benjamin smiled in spite of himself. "And your father?" he asked. Of all the men in Germaine's life, Constant was Jacques Necker's favorite. They shared a deep affection for each other as father and son.

"Papa is well. He loves and cares for the children more as a father than a grandfather," Germaine replied. Having relieved the strain she returned cautiously to what concerned her most. "He tried desperately to keep me from leaving Coppet."

"He should have succeeded. You may have to go back tomorrow."

"Why? The people are celebrating. The coup must be going well." The Baroness had to raise her voice to be heard over the noise from the public room. "Barras has been eliminated. Bonaparte . . . "

"There is no doubt that the General has a position of power. But he has bungled his part in the plot."

"Bonaparte? Bungled?" Germaine was incredulous.

"Yes. The man of our hopes. He was given the ideal opportunity to take over the government. He entered the chamber of the Ancients with a cordial reception. Abbé Siéyès, who presided, called on him to speak. The legislators were eager to accept him. In return, Bonaparte was petrified. He mumbled a few words and left. There was a disconcerting void. He could have completed the conquest with a dynamic speech. No one heard him. If his supporters in the gallery had not cheered, Bonaparte would have been thrown out!"

"He is not an orator," Germaine said defensively remembering her own muteness in Bonaparte's presence "but a military man. Can we recover our loss?"

"If we are lucky. As president of the Ancients, Siéyès, and Lucien Bonaparte, who presides over the Council of the Five Hundred, manipulated the legislators. They have moved the debate outside the city to St. Cloud. The final effort of the coup is set there, for tomorrow."

"What of the Directors?"

"Fortunately, all five have resigned. Talleyrand was magnificent—it was he who convinced Barras to leave the government and the city. I am certain he offered him a huge bribe . . . and Barras accepted it."

"And Bonaparte?"

"The General did redeem himself. Later, he substituted action for words. In the courtyard, he intimidated the Council of Five Hundred with a show of strength—by parading ten thousand troops in full battle dress and with rifles."

Germaine breathed more freely. "Then we may still succeed."

"Absolutely!" Benjamin replied. "But we cannot count on it. The legislature—both bodies—are still intact and must be dissolved. The delay until tomorrow is a mistake. The coup should have erupted in one dramatic, bloodless convulsion. The Jacobins and the deputies have been alerted. They sense they have been tricked and have time to retrench and counterattack. Another blunder could be a disaster. But we have no choice."

Visions of the horrors of the Terror, the flight from France by her friends, the execution of others and her own brushes with death flashed vividly through Madame de Staël's mind.

"Is it wise to drive to Paris tonight?" she asked.

Benjamin hesitated. "Perhaps. But only because the action will take place out of the city. You must stay at your house on the rue de Grenelle until the final outcome. I will go to St. Cloud and keep you informed. If we lose, you must be prepared to flee."

Germaine could not suppress her optimism. "Despite your criticism, I have confidence in Bonaparte. He has captured the imagination of the people of France. He has been victorious on the battlefield. He has negotiated difficult treaties with amazing success. He's young. He's entitled to a few mistakes."

"Today's was a near catastrophe."

"You agree that we still have the impetus?"

"Yes."

"Bonaparte's military tactics can work to our advantage in this new crisis. Later, when he moves up to posts of broader responsibilities his dictatorial attitudes can be curbed . . . because of his youth. An older man could not adjust."

"What of his vulgarity and lack of finesse?" Benjamin asked. "They could harm him as a political leader."

"I do not deny he is uncouth and without judgment in his personal life—he married beneath his potential. Though Josephine is my friend, she is not the one who can help him. She is empty-headed, unworthy and debauched. He needs a partner equal to his genius, someone with a strong hand to guide him."

"You?" Benjamin suppressed a twinge of jealousy.

"Of course."

Together, they left the inn. Eugene had arranged for another carriage for the servants. Benjamin joined Germaine in her coach and they set out for Paris.

The Baroness was exhilarated. Her passion churned. Deep in the cushions of the wide seat, she succumbed to the intimacy Benjamin continued to seek with gentle persuasion. As he took her, she fantasized the future . . . she saw Napoleon in the luxury of her manor house where the gala celebration would take place to honor him and the successful conspirators.

PART II

THE CHALLENGE

Chapter 1
18 Brumaire

There was a chill in the air of the expansive marble foyer of Madame de Staël's town house on the rue de Grenelle. The Baroness shivered, but not from the cold. Dressed warmly in a plum colored traveling cloak and a matching velvet turban, she sat on one of the trunks piled in the middle of the floor. She had pointedly instructed Eugene to light none of the fireplaces or porcelain stoves, except for those in the servants quarters, until she knew whether she would stay or leave.

Insensitive to the weather, Madame de Staël felt confined, thwarted. She had come a long distance to be involved in the coup, yet she was far from the proceedings that would take place at Saint Cloud. She might as well be back at Coppet!

Her decision to remain within the city limits of Paris contradicted Germaine's impetuous nature. She knew she was taking the wise course by staying behind. For the sake of her children, she had to consider her personal safety. Her children were dear to her, but why must it be she who was always bound to them? Why could she not be free as a man who was permitted to pursue challenges? Permitted? It was expected of them! Why not of a woman—an intelligent, worthy, ambitious woman?

It was often difficult for the Baroness to reconcile her drives with her obligations. She had allowed Benjamin to sway her, thus denying herself the excitement of the culmination of the coup. She had created her own constraints, but she would rather she were with him!

Constant had left on horseback before daybreak that morning, November 8, the 18 Brumaire. The gray shades of dawn had faded, and now shafts of sunlight penetrated the panes of the tall windows. A good omen? Germaine was not cheered.

Thousands of Frenchmen and women were drawn out by the good weather and the promise of an inciting confrontation at Saint Cloud.

Benjamin had to make his way slowly through the snail-paced procession of carriages, carts, horsemen and pedestrians jamming the roads. Unlike the mobs that marched on Versailles ten years earlier, the people were dressed in their finest and were in a festive mood, eager to be on hand as the fate of their country was decided.

Germaine was braced to leave immediately, if the news from Benjamin indicated the conspirators had failed . . . or to reestablish her residence if the coup was successful.

Waiting was painful, boredom was torture. Not knowing terrified her.

Reaching for her portable desk, Madame de Staël propped it on her lap and impatiently fingered the feather of her quill before writing a letter to her father.

At mid-morning she was interrupted by a messenger from Benjamin. The lawmakers at Saint Cloud would be unable to convene for hours. The halls of the chateau were bare and were being set up with benches and tables that had to be carried in from nearby storehouses. The work was slow and tedious. The legislators and the assembled crowds, growing impatient, milled about in nervous groups on the cobblestone paths of the enormous courtyard.

Messages reached the rue de Grenelle hourly. The news did not change.

At noon, Olive Uginet brought in a tray and set it down on a trunk beside Madame de Staël. The Baroness left the food untouched.

Early in the afternoon, a dispatch revealed that both legislative bodies had been called to order. The Elders and the Council of the Five Hundred were, at last, in session.

Germaine exulted. Her waiting would soon come to an end.

But she was wrong. The afternoon began to drag. She finished her letter and put her desk aside. Could the conspirators have lost their nerve, she pondered, and decided to forego their chance to strike? What was taking so long?

Daylight dimmed.

"Shall I light some candles?" Eugene asked his mistress.

"No, not yet," Madame de Staël replied savoring the aroma of the hot cup of herb tea Olive brought her.

"Would you like some dinner, Madame?"

At that moment, Germaine and Olive were startled by rapid banging on the door. Thrusting the cup and saucer into her servant's hands, the Baroness dashed across the foyer.

A shaken courier burst in as she released the latch.

Olive, Eugene and the courier hovered close to Madame de Staël as she broke the seal of the parchment. The note was short, written in haste.

> *Germaine:*
> *Napoleon Bonaparte committed another blunder—even more detrimental than yesterday. The situation is hopeless. Flee!*
> *Constant*

There was no time to weigh the words or dispute the command. Madame de Staël accepted Benjamin's judgment.

"We must leave!" she told Eugene. "Prepare to return to Coppet at once!"

Eugene called out instructions to the servants. "Bring round the carriages! Load the trunks! Bridle the horses!"

The air bristled with alarm.

The Baroness deplored leaving Paris, but she was relieved that her waiting had come to an end. Better a bad outcome than further frustration of indecision. Deeply concerned about Benjamin, she turned to the distraught messenger and asked, "Monsieur Constant? Is he all right?"

"Yes, Madame la Baronne. He was anxious that you know."

"Tell me quickly, what took place at Saint Cloud?" Germaine gathered together her writing materials.

"It was all that delay, Madame. Bonaparte stood by all day with his troops. He finally showed his irritation and entered the chamber where the Ancients were deliberating. He was not invited. Even so, they were willing to listen to him. He stood up before the deputies and scolded them for taking so much time. He was so arrogant that the Ancients became irate and screamed back and shook their fists at him. He ignored their protests and continued to criticize them. It was embarrassing for our Commandant."

"Was that the end?" the Baroness asked in disbelief.

"Oh, no!" the young man exclaimed "That was just the beginning. Bonaparte went to the Orangerie where the Council of Five Hundred were assembled. They were in a vicious mood, and complained about being deceived. As soon as Bonaparte came in, a deputy seized his arm and shouted, 'Get out! You don't belong here! You are a member of the military.

How dare you violate the sanctity of the legislature!'

"Other deputies climbed over the benches and rushed at him. I could see the General from where I stood. He was terrified! His face turned white. The legislators began to strike him and tear at his uniform. 'Down with the tyrant!' they called out. 'Hors la loi! Outlaw him!'"

"My God!" Germaine was alarmed. "At the end of the Terror Robespierre was attacked with the same cries. It signalled his end! No wonder Monsieur Constant admonished us to leave."

The courier rushed on to relate that Bonaparte's brother, Lucien, who was presiding, rapped the gavel, but the deputies paid no heed. Bonaparte tried to escape through an overwhelming human wall. His way was blocked. Then out of nowhere, five powerful Grenadier guards appeared in their red uniforms and towering black fur headgear. They bulled their way through and came to his rescue. They seized Napoleon by his shoulders, almost carrying him as he stumbled from the chamber, blood running down his face.

There was terror in the young courier's eyes.

"At that moment, Monsieur Constant dashed off this note," he said breathlessly. "He watched to make sure I got on my horse and started to ride toward Paris. He stayed behind to see what would happen next."

The Baroness suppressed her own fears and tried to calm the courier. "Go inside and rest. The cook will prepare some food for you."

"Oh, no!" he protested. "I must report to Monsieur Constant that you have left safely."

Madame de Staël's courtyard bustled with activity. The luggage was being tied into place, only one more trunk had still to be loaded. The servants were starting to take their places on the perches. The driver restrained the six-horse team that pawed the ground restlessly.

Then suddenly, the urgent clatter of galloping hoofs penetrated the wall from down the road. The sound soon engulfed the courtyard. Germaine was gripped with dread. Was this worse news?

The entire party froze like a bronze sculpture in the Tuileries garden . . . the driver, holding the reins outstretched over the horses, the footmen, halfway up the sides of the carriage, a maid lifting a box to another servant who leaned down from the perch.

All eyes focused on the gate.

The horseback rider loomed into view, another courier. He wheeled up to the Baroness and reined in his horse to an abrupt halt.

"Madame la Baronne!" he exclaimed, bounding out of his saddle to land at Germaine's feet. "I prayed I would arrive before you fled!"

Had harm come to Benjamin?

Anxiously Madame de Staël ripped open the dispatch and took in the contents in one quick glance. Slipping down onto a trunk, she wept . . . for joy.

Again, the message was brief.

> *Minette, ma chérie,*
> *The day is saved. We've won! Stay in Paris! I*
> *will be with you as soon as possible.*
> > *Fondly, Benjamin*

What could have brought about so complete a reversal, Germaine wondered. And so quickly?

"It all took place in a matter of minutes," Benjamin explained later. Wearing a mauve dressing gown, he reclined among blue satin pillows on a broad *lit de repos*. Exhausted, he indulged in the comfort and the warmth from the blazing fire. Germaine poured hot brandy into the cup he held toward her, then replaced the fragile porcelain pot on a trivet within the gallery of a small polished wood table.

The Baroness walked to the hearth, turned her back on the fire and faced Benjamin. A long, turquoise silk peignoir fell loosely from her shoulders.

"I have had only small bits of information about Saint Cloud." Germaine's voice was husky and urgent. She had not pressed Benjamin for details when he had arrived an hour before in the darkness of early morning.

"We have triumphed," Benjamin replied wearily. "That is what matters."

"Of course," she said, trying to control her impatience. "But I must know how . . . I must, in order to plan my next moves."

Germaine's agile mind took her far beyond the events of the day. She must now prepare for her role in the new government. Two or three hours of sleep was all she needed and then she'd begin at dawn. First she had to learn every detail on how the success was achieved. She could not proceed until she knew.

Constant had dozed. Germaine sat down close to him on the edge of the sofa.

"I must know precisely what happened," she said gently. Benjamin opened his eyes sleepily.

"Sometimes I wonder why I yield to your dominance!" he said.

"You have no choice. Nowhere else would such luxury and attention be lavished on you. Nor your intellect and ambition be so stimulated and encouraged."

The cutting remarks, stirred him. He could never deny Germaine when he was with her. When he was alone, he dreaded their next meeting and fought desperately to summon the courage for the next encounter. He was a man bewitched. Life was intolerable with or without her.

"Forgive me."

"Forgiven!" she said, climbing under the quilt beside him on the *lit de repos*. "Now!" she insisted.

"When I sent off the message that you should flee Paris," Constant began, "we were convinced all *was* lost. We were devastated. The truth was, no one had counted on Lucien Bonaparte. He had tears in his eyes as he sat in the President's chair, presiding at the session, listening to the Deputies condemn his brother. Suddenly he stood up and ripped off his toque and red toga. 'I hereby remove myself as first officer of this Council,' he announced. His voice was edged with an effective, poignant tremor."

"He should not have done that!" Germaine was horrified.

Benjamin laughed. "That is exactly how the Deputies reacted and what Lucien had counted on. They howled their objections—they admire and respect this Bonaparte."

"Ah!" Germaine understood. "A ploy! Lucien is impetuous, but clever. He knows how to manipulate a mob."

"I learned later," Benjamin continued, "that during the commotion, Lucien sent a message to Napoleon which said, 'You have ten minutes to act!' Napoleon did. He sent a contingent of soldiers into the chamber. They carried Lucien, bodily, out to the courtyard.

"The brothers were of one mind. They did not have to confer. Each mounted a huge white charger. Napoleon addressed the troops while the Deputies stood at the windows of the Orangerie shouting, 'Outlaw! Outlaw!' The soldiers were confused, baffled. Napoleon . . . shockingly . . . lost his grip for military rhetoric . . . he could not convince them to action. But Lucien did. He rose to the provocation. He displayed a perfect sense of timing and drama. Whipping out his sword, he rode up to Napoleon and thrust it at his brother's breast. 'I swear,' he bellowed, 'I will run my brother through his heart if he ever interferes with the freedom of Frenchmen!'"

"My God!" Germaine cried out.

"Yes! A cry of awe came up from the crowd. The blade of the sword sparkled brilliantly in the sun. The troops were mesmerized. Taking the initiative, Bonaparte ordered two generals to lead the men forward. 'Clear the Deputies from the Orangerie,' he commanded. The soldiers were inspired. They plunged forward on their horses yelling, 'Let us die for freedom.'"

Caught up in the anxious expectation of danger and confrontation, Germaine could hear Bonaparte spit out his orders. The cries of the men rang in her ears. She could see them following their leaders on horseback through the vast doorways of the chateau. She pressed hard against Benjamin.

"The rout was terrifying," he went on, "but the scene was dramatically comic. The horsemen were not out to kill but to evict."

Bonaparte had won!

"Napoleon has redeemed himself," Germaine said, glorying in his success. His triumph was hers. She would have the thrill of working with this genius who would help to restore order and bring liberty and justice to the people of France.

"It was Lucien who made it possible," Benjamin remarked.

"No. Napoleon." Germaine said almost inaudibly.

Benjamin's full, rich voice was gentle as he came to the end of his narrative. Soothing. "Later," he said, "when it had turned dark, some eighty of the Deputies sheepishly slipped back into the chamber. They accepted their defeat but did not shirk their responsibility. They declared the Directory at an end and voted a provisional government with three consuls equal in authority to rule France. Roger Ducos, the former director, Abbé Siéyès, your dear friend, and Napoleon Bonaparte."

Flames in the fireplace had given way to glowing embers. Candles flickered. The room dimmed.

Germaine's body fell limp. Her happiness was complete, her ardor was stirred. She would share ultimate power with Bonaparte. She dug her fingers into Benjamin's shoulders. He responded to her passion.

Chapter 2
The First Consul

Germaine de Staël wanted all Paris to know that she had returned and would reestablish her position of authority in French society and politics. She would be the first to celebrate the success of the coup with a gala resumption of her salon.

There was no time to repair and refurbish her neglected mansion, but it did not really matter. Her furnishings, though bruised, were opulent. Carrying on in the tradition of her mother, she felt supremely secure in her flair for entertaining.

The Baroness toured the chambers with Eugene as servants stripped protective muslin coverings from the furniture. She gave instructions to wipe down the walls and the ceilings, oil the panelling and polish the floors.

With Olive and several maids, she checked linens, china, crystal and silverware. There were dates to schedule, invitations to send, menus to review, wine lists to approve.

By the end of the day, Germaine was still brimming with energy.

Continuing to work after the rest of her household retired for the night, Madame de Staël sat at her desk in her boudoir and wrote by the light of the tapers in a bronze candelabra. She penned intimate notes to her dearest friends . . . engaging messages to men who were regaining power . . . another long letter to her father.

She smiled contentedly as she sealed the envelope to Jacques Necker. She knew he would rejoice at her news and approve her strategy.

Five days later, Germaine de Staël threw open the doors of her home. Her guests crowded the drawing rooms and the hallways which sparkled brightly from the lights of hundreds of candles through the lower level of her residence. They were enchanted and dazzled, oblivious to the worn upholstery, faded draperies and the tarnished gilt woodwork.

Bewigged footmen in trim green livery kept goblets filled with champagne. A steady flow of tempting, aromatic dishes came from the busy kitchen . . . hors d'oeuvres artistically arranged on large trays, poached fish, crisply browned fowl, succulent roasts. Desserts of delicate pastries, tiny cakes, mousses, cheeses from nearby provinces.

Glowing with confidence the Baroness de Staël had never been so charming, so gracious. She moved among her guests, speaking warmly of Napoleon Bonaparte and praising him without restraint. His wisdom, his glory, his virtue, his clemency, his tolerance . . . all were infinite. She was creating a temple for the man of the hour.

Night after night, Germaine's salon was filled with people of influence. Men and women of elegance dressed in the latest Directoire fashions, drove up in splendid carriages to the portico of the town house of the rich and famous Baroness de Staël. There were generals, Murat, Junot, Bernadotte . . . members of the cabinet, Joseph Fouché, minister of the police, Talleyrand, reappointed foreign minister . . . publicists, Suard, Fontanes, Roederer, Fauriel . . . the Bonapartes, Lucien, Joseph, Pauline, Eliza. Benjamin Constant, of course.

Everyone came. Those who were not invited called on those who were, scrambling about for extra places on the guest list.

Everyone came . . . everyone but Napoleon Bonaparte.

His co-consuls, Abbé Siéyès and Roger Ducos, were regular guests. The Baroness reasoned that as a military officer, a man of rigid discipline, he would take time to adjust to his civilian post. One day, once he had a strong hold on his duties, he would come to her salon . . . or send for her. She made sure his subordinates and his brothers and sisters were in her circle when she talked of him, they would carry back favorable reports about her.

A week went by, then another. The popularity of her salon did not wane, but Napoleon had not ventured beyond his home where he confined himself like a monk.

During the third week, Germaine felt that the least she deserved was the courtesy of a reply to her invitations. Even a note expressing regret and explaining his delay.

At the end of the fourth week she approached Lucien and Joseph.

"Your brother would do well to mingle with his supporters . . . those responsible for putting him in a position of power," she suggested. "Tell him he's welcome here any evening."

"I agree that he should make himself more available," Lucien replied. "He won't break away from his study. It would do him good to get out."

"I've advised him to visit you," Joseph intoned. "He insists that the precarious conditions of France prevent him from coming. He cannot tear himself away."

"Of course," Germaine agreed. "He's dedicated. But do try again."

Before dawn on a day during the fifth week, the diminutive Abbé Siéyès arrived at the home of Madame de Staël and banged on the massive entrance door.

"I have urgent news for the Baroness," he said to Eugene Uginet who let him in to the foyer and accompanied him down the marble corridor to Germaine's boudoir.

Uginet, announced the Abbé to his mistress who was already at work at her writing desk. She looked up to greet him and observed that his gentle eyes were saddened. His wrinkled brow dramatized his hooked nose and bald, domed head.

The Abbé embraced Germaine, then walked to a small white porcelain stove in the corner of the room. He warmed his hands, his back to the Baroness who sat down on a sofa upholstered in gold velvet.

She poured him a cup of coffee from the pot on the tray which Uginet had brought and waited for him to explain his early morning visit. His silence distressed her.

"Emmanuel?" she asked intently. "Coffee, my friend?"

Siéyès turned slowly and faced the Baroness. Together, these two intensely political human beings had lived through difficult times, but Germaine had never seen his face so grey, so somber.

"Napoleon Bonaparte is *First* Consul of France," he announced grimly, accepting the steaming cup.

"*First* Consul?"

"Yes." Without emotion.

"How can he be *first* consul. The constitution calls for three consuls to share equal authority . . . you, Ducos and Napoleon!"

"France has a *new* constitution."

"Of course. The one you drafted."

"No. There is another, more recent one . . . written by Bonaparte."

"Just yesterday the government was operating under your document!"

"That was yesterday."

"When . . . how did this happen? Amendments must be approved by the legislative committee." Germaine was adamant.

"It took place early this morning. I could not prevent it. During the first Council meeting following the coup, Bonaparte took charge of the proceedings. As the weeks went by, I, of course, objected to the changes he proposed in my constitution. I did not let you know, for I hoped in the end to succeed. But my efforts were useless."

Emmanuel Siéyès slipped down to the sofa beside Madame de Staël, like a disheartened, defeated gladiator.

"You fought him?"

"Vehemently."

"And Talleyrand? He protested of course."

"No, I'm sorry. He stood with Napoleon."

"Just like a windmill that alters its course with every wanton breeze!" Germain declared, stunned then angered. "Did anyone else stand by you?"

"No! I was alone. No one else dared disagree. His energy and endurance are debilitating. We worked late every night without a break. Last night, he pressed us. I was near exhaustion but I strongly opposed these latest revisions. I was not prepared for his next move. I did not know that he had summoned the legislative commission to stand by in the chamber down the hall.

"Your Bonaparte is keen, clever, crafty. Just before midnight, he called in the commissioners, feigning weary patience. He read the changes to them, holding his draft in one hand. With the other he passed out quills for their signatures. They submitted without a murmur. All my years of hard work! This constitution is an abortion. All is over!"

"It cannot be! Though he may be First Consul, you and Ducos still serve with him," she said pacing back and forth across the room.

"We will continue as consuls, of course. But in name only. We have *no* authority. The ultimate power rests with the First Consul. He will direct foreign policy and continue as commander of the military. He rules through a Council of State and appoints all its members. This handpicked Council nominates members of the two chamber legislature, the Tribunate and the Senate, which can debate legislation but propose none."

"Incredible!" Germaine gasped.

"There's more. This monster appoints all ministers, envoys, prefects, officers and judges."

"He has walked off with France!"

Madame de Staël had wanted Bonaparte in a position of power. But he was wresting away complete authority. Unchecked, Bonaparte's thrust could lead to tyranny . . . an autocratic leadership like the one-man rule of Louis XVI. A strong-willed despot could destroy France. What possessed the men who surrounded the consuls to permit Bonaparte to usurp control of the government? Had the corruption of the Directory dimmed their memories to the horrors of the bloody decline and the aftermath of the Bourbons?

Germaine understood now why Bonaparte had avoided the ritual of the salons. He could not tolerate an open forum where ideas were discussed and policies determined by mutual understanding and agreement. He refused to acknowledge consensus. Bonaparte approached the council table as he did the battlefield. He was the commandant. He readily shifted his autocratic military tactics to civil affairs. There was no denying his wilfullness . . . he was a man to be feared.

Madame de Staël tensed as she recalled the general's overwhelming will when, in his presence, her chest and throat had grown tight and she could not speak. She had been hypnotized by his glory and his charm. It was no wonder the Commissioners submitted . . . they were also repressed by his menacing manner. Only Siéyès had not been taken in, but he could not battle Bonaparte alone.

"Mon Dieu, Emmanuel! Absolute power is returning again to one man!"

The Abbé was bitter. "Bonaparte is a tyrant. There is no hope of liberty for France now."

"But the people must approve the new constitution. The final draft must be sanctioned by popular vote."

Siéyès grimaced. "My dear friend. Do you truly believe the citizenry . . . the volatile mobs of France who finally believe they have a leader who has their best interests at heart . . . would deny their hero what he asks?"

Germaine could not refute his words. Nor could she accept his conclusion. She had waited too long and worked too hard. Though she felt her hold on France's destiny slipping from her hands like sand through a sieve, she would fight to retrieve every grain.

"Bonaparte has unvarnished instincts for propaganda . . . they are uncanny," Siéyès said with grudging admiration. "Make no mistake, he is afraid of mobs and knows he cannot control them by personal appeal alone. Yet, he can manipulate his officers with absolute authority behind the scenes. When his troops floundered in Egypt, he left them when they needed him most. He assumed the image of a triumphant, valiant general and returned to Paris at the most auspicious moment. He is a megalomaniac . . . he will not be distracted from his objective. He is efficient down to the smallest detail. Did you see the posters that were plastered all over the city after the coup . . . those which credited Bonaparte for the victory?"

"You and Ducos arranged that with him."

"That is what he would have the public believe. Bonaparte did it himself, using his military subordinates to get the broadsides printed and posted. There is much more I could reveal that would astound you. He conceals his acts by appearing benevolent and humble to the masses."

Madame de Staël felt betrayed. Her eyes blazed in anger and determination.

"The men who have supported him, and there are hundreds of them, will not tolerate his autonomy," she said. "Once they learn what he is doing they will oust him."

"The situation is beyond recovery," Siéyès replied with resignation.

Chapter 3
Decision

Germaine de Staël stepped down from her calèche and looked up at the imposing facade of the splendid residence at 7 rue de Mont Blanc. The December sun cast gentle grey shadows over the familiar building, mellowing its austere carved-stone facing. A sense of warmth and belonging surged through Germaine as she approached the wide stairway that led to the entrance.

This mansion had once been her home, owned then by the man she loved beyond all others, her father. Now, by coincidence, it was the home of the woman who was dearest to her. How undeniably fulfilling, she reflected, to have so deep a passion for another woman. The closeness she felt for Juliette Récamier was what she had hoped to find with a man and was still seeking. Instead, she had come upon everything she desired in this haunting young woman whose beauty was blissfully spiritual. They shared a deep understanding, honesty, sincerity and sympathy. Juliette's compassion was strongest when Germaine was troubled, as she was today.

The Baroness climbed the marble stairs, feeling the worn, smooth surfaces she knew well through the soft leather soles of her shoes.

The heavy, intricately carved wood door opened expectantly as she reached the upper landing. A liveried footman greeted her and ushered her into the vestibule. The perfumed fragrance of fresh flowers filled the air. Green shrubs and clusters of small potted plants were arranged in planned symmetry around the room, creating a magical garden.

The Baroness accompanied the servant down corridors lined with paintings and statuary and passed exquisitely furnished drawing rooms whose floors were covered with rich Oriental carpets. The banker Récamier and his wife had transformed the beautiful townhouse, already opulent, into the most luxurious in Paris. They had engaged the famous architect Berthaut and the best menuisiers, drapers and upholsterers in France.

The footman left Germaine in the foyer of Madame Récamier's apartments. The white and gold panelled door, slightly ajar, moved open slowly. Juliette emerged, flawlessly lovely, a vision in white. Germaine took her hands and kissed her gently on the cheek.

Madame de Staël followed her friend into her bedchamber that echoed shades of violet, gold and ivory. The mistress of the mansion stepped onto a low dais and lay down on a bed that was partially enclosed with a billowy cloud of white muslin descending from a gold damask canopy.

Shining bronze swans perched majestically on the mahogany bed-posts high above Juliette, defended their fragile charge as she sank into a lavender coverlet.

Violet gryphons mounted close to the ceiling cast fluttering shadows as the candles flickered. Molded gold-leaf garlands circling high along the walls appeared to sway.

Germaine paced the room, stroking a sprig she had plucked from a vase on a tall, slender stand. For a moment, she stopped in front of the nude marble statue of a beautiful woman, *Le Silence*, by Chinard, which graced the sanctuary as the goddess of rest. She gazed thoughtfully at the sculpture, her mind elsewhere.

"Germaine?" Juliette said softly. "Is it Bonaparte? You are distressed."

Madame de Staël moved toward the raised platform. She hesitated beside one of the candelabra that stood on either side of the bed and looked down on the child-woman.

She began to speak, slowly, deliberately. "The people of Paris have overwhelmingly approved the First Consul's mandate for one-man rule with only a handful of opposing votes. He plans to act immediately under the provisions of this new constitution without waiting for the results from the rest of France."

"He moves quickly," Juliette said, "but is it fair to condemn him? You are not certain. You are torn . . . "

It was a week since Germaine had met with Emmanuel Siéyès, and she had grown more discouraged as each day passed. She could no longer shrug off the gnawing apprehension she had about the autocratic behavior of the man she once believed could, with her guidance, return France to glory. The truth was too real. She had to admit that Bonaparte's posture was destructive to the principles of the revolution. It had taken Siéyès, who had never been blind to Bonaparte's obsession for power, to make her see her hero for the tyrant he was.

The Baroness de Staël agonized, struggling with her conscience as her disillusionment with this Corsican upstart grew. But she did not openly alter her attitude toward the First Consul. To her friends and guests she was still his most enthusiastic advocate. She continued to entertain lavishly and to praise Bonaparte with verve. Criticism of him by the guests at her salons was scattered, restrained and cautious.

The First Consul, Germaine learned, was championing equality while he denounced liberty. "Both the savage and the civilized man need a lord and master," he was saying. "They seek a magician who will hold their imaginations in check, impose strict discipline, and, when necessary, bind man in chains, so that he may not bite out of season. Obedience is man's destiny; he deserves nothing better."

Bonaparte would deny liberty to man!

Should Germaine continue to wait for Bonaparte to summon her? Though he scrupulously guarded his autonomy as First Consul, he was an administrative master and a consummate politician. He selected ministers and heads of departments with no regard for family background, social position or political leaning. He chose men of stature and ability. Jacobins and aristocrats shared equal responsibility and sat side by side in his Council of State. He demanded energy, diligence, loyalty and dedication . . . all the traits he acknowledged in Jacques Necker. Surely, the Baroness rationalized, he would recognize them in the former finance minister's daughter. Bonaparte could not be so much a peasant as to permit his weakness for insipid, beautiful libertines to stand in his way of calling on an intelligent woman who could strengthen his position without resorting to tyranny. Or could he?

Or should she respond to her conscience and challenge Bonaparte's right to autonomous rule? She could gather together the men who had opposed him from the beginning with those who were now starting to question and fear him. They could confront this dictator and unseat him, or at least curb him. A dangerous but tantalizing course.

"Lovely Juliette," Germaine said at last, smiling through her gravity. "What should I do, my heart?" She slipped down to the bed and gently caressed Juliette's graceful, slender fingers.

Together, they sat without speaking. An hour passed. The serenity in Juliette's presence cleared her confusion. There was only one course for Madame de Staël.

And Madame Récamier sensed it. She had observed her friend's increasing anxiety and frustration. First, it was Bonaparte's neglect. A rebuff. Then, his bold actions. An affront. Juliette feared Germaine's decision would be harmful to herself and her children.

When they had first met, Madame de Staël was inclined to act impetuously, agitating the voracious journalists and government officials who responded by maligning and condemning her. Soon, she learned to respect Juliette's entreaties and held herself in check.

This time, however, Juliette wondered if she would succeed in calming Germaine. Even if she could deter her friend, was it in Juliette's domain to try? They had a binding relationship built on sensitivity and trust. Attempting to warn her, to restrain her from the course she was convinced she should take would be false and self-serving.

"Bonaparte has performed miracles in the domestic affairs of France," Germaine admitted. "He comfortably straddles the worlds of politics and the military. He's the darling of the populace. He has brought order to the economy. He has stabilized the tax system by establishing a collection office in every department . . . sorely neglected and ignored till now. He has granted religious freedom to Jews, Protestants and those of all faiths. He saw the need for a unified legal code . . . on the day after the coup, he assigned a committee to prepare a set of laws and regulations."

Madame de Staël felt compelled to go on as though she were introducing a head of state. "He has ended profiteering in the military, reduced the national debt, and is organizing a national bank. Manufacturing has rejuvenated, productivity has increased. The chambers of commerce have reactivated. Our First Consul *has* breathed new vitality into our nation."

Juliette knew from first hand that Bonaparte was performing miracles . . . her husband was reaping huge profits as optimism swept through the financial community. But Germaine spoke reluctantly . . . unconvinced that the spectacular success was in the best interest of Frenchmen or that this run of good fortune would continue.

"Bonaparte has made swift, dramatic changes," Juliette said, "he shocks the senses. He wins the blind devotion of the compliant masses. His appointed officials are cowed into submission by this clamor of approval and support."

"Using the tactics of a dictator," Madame de Staël added with rancor as tears filled her eyes. "He runs the country on his terms, not as a republic."

"You speak these truths," Juliette said gently, placing her arm around her friend to comfort her. "But you will not believe them. You envision Bonaparte's destiny. The glory. The adulation. They are inevitable. You want to share them with him."

"I cannot deny what you say," Germaine replied.

"Nor can I fault you. You are attracted to him. Drawn intellectually and ideologically. And, as a woman to a man . . . ?" Juliette posed cautiously and waited for a reply.

At last, Germaine looked into her eyes and smiled. She leaned toward Juliette and kissed her on the lips. "Oh, my dear," Germaine said enigmatically, trying to hide the truth which was written clearly on her face. "I've always been stimulated and aroused by the most brilliant minds . . . worthy of Necker's daughter. My passionate dream was to guide Bonaparte through the awesome politics of Paris . . . nothing more."

Sensing she had gone too far, Juliette took Germaine's hand and said, "My darling, don't blame yourself. We've all been taken in by him."

"Blame?" Germaine went on, standing as she spoke. "Mon Dieu, he has proven his superiority . . . he manipulated the coup and created conflict among all who supported him."

Juliette feared that any action her friend might take against the government, no matter how surreptitious, was dangerous.

"So . . . ma chérie, what shall we do?" she asked.

Germaine paced back and forth, still reacting to Juliette's intimations of her feelings for Bonaparte. "I can separate my passions," she said coldly. "I will not be misled by a personal rebuff." Then taking up Juliette's concerns, "I would relish the satisfaction of retaliation, of course. But have no fear Juliette, my angel, I shall not act out of wounded pride and lead a crusade to eliminate Bonaparte. I would defeat my own purposes. The way would be open for the corrupt Jacobins to return. Back in power, they would destroy France. I would be exiled. At least, Bonaparte's immediate goals coincide with ours. We must settle for him . . . now. I do not agree with Emmanuel Siéyès that the situation is hopeless. Bonaparte is vulnerable, he has enemies. He has slaughtered royalists . . . and the Jacobins hold him responsible for the coup and their loss of control."

"But how will you work against him?" Juliette asked discreetly.

"Oh, I'll not be alone," Madame de Staël assured her. "There will be others. I will act guardedly. Rejection and scorn will not get in my way. But Bonaparte cannot go unchallenged."

Juliette, trembling slightly, drew Germaine close and embraced her. She knew it would take more than her arms or counsel to protect the Baroness from herself. Madame de Staël was as single-minded in her mission as Bonaparte. They were worthy adversaries.

Chapter 4
Action

Madame de Staël reclined alone on a *lit de repos* before a fire in her boudoir, comfortable under an azure blue satin duvet. Stroking a quill, she contemplated her conversation with Juliette.

Germaine's indecision and despair had vanished. No longer held back by false expectations of being called to action by Bonaparte, she felt unencumbered, free to act on her own. She performed best when she responded to her instincts. Personal rebuff was a convenient catalyst. Jacques Necker's daughter would not tolerate the actions of a despot who threatened the integrity and survival of the country she loved. She would mobilize her forces against the First Consul. With restraint, in the manner of Juliette.

The Baroness's mind raced rapidly as she set about devising her plan which she separated into two distinct assaults.

Germaine propped herself up, placed her portable writing desk that lay beside her on her lap and set out on the first . . . a private gathering of men and women who doubted and distrusted the First Consul as much and more than she. Her pen could not keep pace with her mind as she compiled her list, weighing each name with care. If she had any doubt about the loyalty of a candidate she scratched it out with a firm, deliberate stroke.

Her first choice was General Jean-Baptiste Bernadotte, a distinguished general who had narrowly missed playing Napoleon's role in the coup and might now have been Consul instead. Bernadotte was convinced he could serve France better than the Corsican intruder and resented the lost opportunity. He would be eager to join any action against Bonaparte.

Then, there was Honoré Duverrier, an outspoken member of the new legislature who was already causing a stir by expressing opposition to the new regime. He would be a reliable ally.

Madame de Staël drafted invitations to Mathieu de Montmorency, her devoted confidante, and to his liberal cousin Adrian. There were Siéyès, Benjamin Constant and Juliette, of course, and about a dozen others whom Germaine knew she could rely on.

Charles Talleyrand? Why did she hesitate? She had written his name and then quickly drew a bold line through it. Reviewing the list, she added his name again. Again, she crossed it out. For the first time in their long relationship, Germaine questioned the constancy of her former lover and mentor. She sensed a coolness in his manner toward her that had never surfaced before. For years, she observed the duplicity he practiced against others. She pitied those who suffered it. He had never before turned on her. Had he forgotten her efforts to support him? How could he? She had risked censure to defend him and secure appointments for him. She had dipped into her father's accounts to finance his endeavors. Were his detractors more accurate in their assessment of him than she? She relied on her instincts, she could not invite him.

Despite its solemn mission the affair was lively and held in the privacy of Madame de Staël's boudoir.

Germaine wavered between distress and excitement. Her guests were at ease, they trusted one another and knew why they had been brought together. They were lighthearted, creating epigrams of ridicule about Napoleon and his family, and about Josephine's blatant affair with Hippolyte Charles, turning Bonaparte into a cuckolded fool.

"Our plebeian leader is so short and small," intoned Mathieu, "he harbors impossible dreams of growing tall."

Even Juliette was drawn into the fray. "Mama Letizia meddles in important government affairs," she offered. "While the graceless Bonaparte sisters put on parvenu airs."

Germaine opened the sober business of the meeting by calling on the Abbé Siéyès with an issue more titillating than serious. "There is a rumor, Emmanuel, that the Consuls are involving themselves in the moral behavior of Frenchmen."

"You refer, no doubt, to the prostitutes in the Palais Royal? It is Bonaparte . . . he has ordered Fouché to turn them out and clean up all of Paris."

"Is it a question of morality?" Juliette asked. "Is there a dual standard when it comes to the military? On one hand the poor women are forced off the streets of Paris and then others are being shipped off to entertain, as it is called, the troops in Egypt."

"That order has been rescinded," Siéyès cited. "At least in part. The Council pressured Bonaparte. The women cannot solicit in public places but they can still practice their trade. He explains away the Egyptian edict as a complete misunderstanding."

"That's reassuring," the decorous Mathieu de Montmorency remarked with bitter sarcasm. "So, the great Bonaparte is capable of reversing himself."

"Perhaps, on a minor issue," Siéyès noted. "But not on vital matters that affect us all and deny us due representation."

The Abbé went on to explain how Bonaparte had manipulated the constitution to his own ends. "He voided the participation of the electorate and has arrogated leadership of France for the next ten years."

Germaine's guests were not surprised.

"Bonaparte has directed Joseph Fouché, the Minister of Police," said Honoré Duverrier, "to establish an espionage network to monitor movements of all citizens and societies. We may be under surveillance here, this afternoon."

"Despicable!" Germaine said. "He's turning France into a police state. We must find ways to suppress Bonaparte's greed for glory and power."

"We should throw in our lot with the Royalists," Adrian de Montmorency declared, advocating a return to the monarchy. "A Bourbon must be placed back on the throne. It is our only hope."

"I oppose such a reversion," Duverrier interjected. "We must preserve the consular system and assault Napoleon's methods in an open forum."

"I object to both those alternatives," Bernadotte bellowed angrily standing and raising his fist. "We must show power. I advocate another coup."

Benjamin Constant was cautious. "Bonaparte's position," he reminded the dissenters, "is tenuous and defensive. He knows his government is far from secure. The Jacobins blame their defeat on him. They are prepared to attack and displace him as soon as he flounders. We know that Bonaparte is not stupid. He can learn of the plots against his life just as we do."

"We must prevent a confrontation that would force the hand of the Jacobins," Germaine warned. "Bonaparte's objectives are closer to ours than theirs. We should support his programs but restrict his authority." She was treading warily, guided by Juliette's influence of restraint, as she attempted to incite her friends without pushing them too far.

Duverrier agreed. "We must work within the perimeters of the new Constitution. It has shortcomings, of course. In time, we will amend it, eliminate the post of First Consul and elect just leadership that permits freedom of action. We cannot risk more corruption or more bloodshed."

Bernadotte disagreed again, his long, dark Gascon countenance clouding as he spoke of his former comrade-in-arms. "Bonaparte must be overthrown! I know him. He has gone too far and will not stop!"

"The lawmakers are restless," Duverrier cautioned the General. "They resent being rendered ineffective. I can rouse them to support a drive to strengthen their influence within the framework of the Consulate but not to form a new government. They would be out of office and forced to start again."

The heat of the discussion escalated. Both Bernadotte and Adrian de Montmorency refused to back down, insisting that Bonaparte should be removed from office.

How sweet vengeance can be, Germaine said to herself. But she knew that any attempt to use force would be fatal. Further, the First Consul who deserved credit for his achievements would be inclined to retaliate. He could summon up the military.

"We are enjoying peace and stability for the first time in years," she said. "We can thank Bonaparte in large part for bringing order to France." She spoke persuasively and with conviction, not by rote, as she had when she enumerated the First Consul's accomplishments for Juliette out of pique and disappointment. Her eyes were alive, sincere, mesmerizing. "The economy has firmed, the stock market rebounded. There is religious freedom for all sects. The dim-witted citizenry look to Bonaparte as their savior. His popularity with almost every segment of the population cannot be discounted. The people would rise up as a revolutionary mass to destroy us if they are provoked by any attempt to oust him."

Madame de Staël was convincing, using the green stem she fingered like a baton to orchestrate her message.

"We can act neither boldly nor openly," she affirmed. "We must support the government. We should form a loyal opposition and pose our objections as constructive criticism," she concluded giving a steel spine to her argument.

Constant and Duverrier supported Germaine's recommendations. They suggested that the groups' membership be increased to include others who were also disillusioned with the First Consul. Opposition would be subtle and meetings would be held regularly and continue in private to plan strategy. Overt action would center in the legislature under Duverrier's leadership.

Bernadotte continued to resist.

"Please, my good friend," Germaine implored. "The day will come when we may have to use force."

The General looked about the room and realized he stood alone.

"I'll support your proposal, for now," he said reluctantly. "I hope I shall not regret it."

Madame de Staël was gratified. Her first move to establish a power base from which she could operate against Napoleon was accomplished. Now, to the second step, securing a direct voice within the government.

Germaine composed a letter to her friend Chabour-Latour, a member of Bonaparte's nominating committee. She sought him out and requested he consider Benjamin Constant for a seat in the Tribunate.

The next day, Madame de Staël received a letter from Joseph Bonaparte, Napoleon's eldest brother, asking for a private audience in her home the following morning. Germaine was elated!

The oldest Bonaparte was an intelligent, gentle, engaging man with a taste for fine wines and beautiful women. He was more Italian than French and, clutching securely the traditions of his heritage, was resentful that his rank as the first son now counted for so little. Nonetheless, he was Napoleon's favorite sibling with whom the First Consul shared his private hopes and initiatives.

Germaine knew all this and knew, too, now that Joseph's message arrived, that news of the clandestine meeting must have reached the First

Consul.

The Baroness was fond of Joseph, and he in turn, appreciated her position of influence and her brilliance. He was a frequent visitor at her salon where they talked long about his family and his interest in literature.

"Napoleon suggested I call on you," Joseph said when he arrived. He displayed none of his customary geniality. "He knows of the deep regard I have for you."

"You are always welcome, Joseph," Germaine said gently, attempting to put him at ease. "You don't have to have a reason to call."

It was obvious that his mission weighed heavily on Napoleon's sibling.

They walked the marble corridor to the small drawing room in the rear of the mansion.

"Of course, of course," Joseph said, rattled. "I must repeat that this visit, however, is at Napoleon's request. He has no time to meet with you himself. Affairs of state put him under great pressure."

"I'm sure they do. His position is a heavy burden," Germaine said impatiently since she would have preferred to address Bonaparte himself rather than his conciliatory brother.

"There are the wars with England and Austria he must chart . . . the treasury is bankrupt . . . domestic affairs are ripping the country apart."

Joseph's words came in a rush as he tried to defend Bonaparte's position, hoping to gain Germaine's sympathy. He was not succeeding.

"Yes," Germaine said, picking up Talleyrand's Egyptian talisman from the bureau plat next to her chair. She caressed the handle.

"The solution to these problems falls to my brother."

"He would have a great deal of assistance, if only he would avail himself of it. But, he refuses to share authority with others."

"He needs support for his policies."

Now, Germaine wondered, will he question me about the meeting? "The people support him," she said. "The vote for his constitution was all but unanimous."

"There is something he considers more valuable than the approval of the populous . . . "

Germaine waited.

"He wants the unqualified respect and support of the intellectual and political circles," Joseph explained. "These are your circles, your friends. They are among my brother's closest advisors."

"Why must he ask me to gain their favor for him if they are so close to him?"

Joseph's preoccupation with his assignment prevented him from hearing what she said. He went on. "My brother says your attitude harms his position. Just yesterday, he asked me why you do not support his government."

"*My* attitude?" Germaine said indignantly. Joseph was startled by his hostess' tone. "It is *his* attitude that harms France," she went on. "The people are vulnerable to his demagoguery. He hides behind eloquent promises of liberty, simultaneously performing acts of tyranny. Support? I've offered my help many times . . . he ignores me!"

Joseph had heard this before, but not with the wrath the Baroness exhibited this morning. He had asked Napoleon on several occasions to see her, but the First Consul flatly refused.

"He's preoccupied . . . involved . . . busy."

"Busy? So am I, on his behalf! You yourself have witnessed the receptions I hold where my guests and I praise the progress he's made. Bonaparte is welcome . . . as you are. But he never attends."

Joseph stopped pacing across the opulent rug and sat down in a large, carved wood chair across from Germaine. His failure to reach her showed in the deep furrows between his brows. He could not return to his brother without firm assurance that the Baroness would no longer encourage her friends to work against him. The rumors of her closed meeting were having an insidious effect on Napoleon's temper. He vented his rage on Joseph and other members of his family.

"I am here to apologize for Napoleon," his brother went on. "He has no time. And if he did, he would not know how to appreciate an intelligent woman. Women to him are wife . . . mother . . . sister . . . mistress . . . nothing more.

"Yet, he is sincere in his appeal to you. He seeks your understanding. He asked me, 'What does Madame de Staël want? The return of the two million livres her father loaned the government? To live in Paris without harassment?' He will order anything done you wish. I implore you, Madame, what shall I tell him?"

Germaine was moved by Joseph's plea, if not by Napoleon's request. She had the advantage, so she did not reply.

"When I left Napoleon less than an hour ago," Joseph went on desperately, "he was deeply agitated, asking the same question again and again. 'What on earth does she *want* from me? Go find out!'"

"That's absurd!" the Baroness declared. "Tell the First Consul that it is not a question of what I *want*, but of what I *think*."

Joseph was at a loss. Feeling that he could not go on, he stood up and started to leave. Madame de Staël, knowing that a sudden departure without satisfaction could mean a break in her line of communication to the center of power, hastened to repair the rift, quickly.

"Come now, Joseph," Germaine cajoled, gesturing with the hand that held her talisman and changed the subject to distract him.

"How is your lovely wife Julie?" she asked knowing Napoleon envied his brother's happy marriage. "Please give her my warmest regards."

Joseph beamed with pride. "She's planning a reception next week," he said and talked animatedly about the preparations.

Then, returning to what concerned them most, the Baroness said, "An interview with Napoleon would set matters straight between us. But he refuses. I do not want his obstinacy to harm my friendship with you." Germaine hesitated. "I may have a solution."

"You are kind and most understanding," Joseph replied with hope and relief.

"Your brother has control of appointments to all offices and government posts . . . "

Joseph nodded.

"Ask him," Germaine said, "to have Benjamin Constant appointed to the Tribunate."

Joseph Bonaparte's face lit up. "Of course, of course," he agreed.

"You are the most admirable woman in France," he said convinced that she was. He had accomplished his brother's directive and he had performed as expected of the first born of the family of Bonaparte.

He left the de Staël residence bolstered with a sense of self-importance. It did not occur to him that the Baroness de Staël had made no commitments to him.

Benjamin Constant's myopic eyes gleamed cannily. His lips were narrowed in a sardonic grin. He had just returned from the interview with Napoleon Bonaparte that Germaine's friend, Chabourd-Latour, had arranged for him.

"The First Consul was most cordial," he told Germaine, who reclined snugly among the cushions of her chaise. She was amused. Bonaparte had taken the bait. Everything was proceeding according to plan.

"He told me," Benjamin went on eagerly, "that he has read many of the papers I have written and was fascinated. I countered by saying 'Your treaties and your constitution are brilliant.'"

Germaine sat up, startled. Her dark eyes flashed disbelief. "You said what?"

"Yes. I said they are brilliant. Two can play at this game. There is too much at stake. It was hardly the time to be candid. If I had not returned the compliment I might have shown my hand. It was a golden opportunity I did not want to lose. After all, I *am* seeking Bonaparte's confirmation to the Tribunate."

"Of course," Germaine now reasoned, "you made the right move."

"Bonaparte talked on and on. I was beginning to wonder if he would ever get to the purpose of our meeting. Finally, I found an opening. I came directly to the point and asked him if he would submit my name as candidate for a seat in the legislature. His reply was equally forthright. 'And why not?' he said. 'It can be arranged.'"

"As simple as that!" Germaine's eyes sparkled triumphantly.

By week's end, the nomination was made and Bonaparte gave his approval. On December 24, 1799, Benjamin Constant was sworn in as a Tribune in the Consular legislature.

Benjamin and Germaine celebrated that night by developing a strategy that would curb Bonaparte's lust for power.

Chapter 5
Convictions

The Baroness de Staël radiated confidence and satisfaction. Her guests were arriving in droves. After she greeted them in the grand foyer under a glittering crystal chandelier they strolled into the splendid drawing rooms.

"Pierre!" Germaine exclaimed. "I'm so pleased you could come." Pierre Roederer, the famed publicist, now a member of Bonaparte's Council of State, often sent notes of apology since he was on twenty-four hour call by the First Consul.

"I decided to stop briefly," he said, embracing his hostess affectionately. "I must leave early, not by choice."

"You will come tomorrow night?" she asked. "I'm planning a celebration for Benjamin. He makes his maiden speech in the Tribunate in the morning. Everyone will be here."

"My dear Baroness, the First Consul *himself* could not keep me away." The party was the talk of French society.

"I'm delighted, Pierre."

"Here is your man of the hour, our freshman legislator," Roederer said as Constant approached them.

After a brief exchange, Constant took Germaine by her elbow and gently guided her away, up the circular staircase. Near the upper landing, they stopped and stood observing her guests below.

"You are truly a remarkable woman, Minette," Benjamin told her. "People throng to be near you. When they leave they take part of you with them. You give them courage and inspiration."

Germaine turned and looked at her lover. "You did not take me from my guests to flatter me, Benjamin. What is it you want to tell me?"

"Have you heard what happened after Duverrier attacked Bonaparte in the Tribunate today?" he whispered solemnly.

"I know Honoré was eloquent in his pronouncements, but I have been too busy this evening to hear the latest gossip."

"Bonaparte is irate. He dictated a crushing rebuttal to Roederer, who has spent the day preparing drafts and delivering them to the papers. The First Consul's statement will appear early tomorrow. I was surprised to see Pierre here."

"Ah! We are making inroads," the Baroness said with a throaty laugh.

Benjamin was somber. "Look . . . there," he said, indicating the shimmering sea of people below.

"You savor each guest like your favorite paté. You relish the excitement of this insane pace you keep."

"Of course. It is my life . . . any other would be unbearable."

"Tonight," Benjamin said, his voice barely audible, "your drawing rooms are filled with the most fascinating and influential people in the world. Tomorrow, after my speech in the Tribunate, your house may be deserted. Have you considered that possibility?"

Madame de Staël eyed Benjamin coldly. She knew his address attacked the First Consul's proposal which gave Bonaparte the authority to set the date and limit the time on debate of all bills placed before the legislature. Germaine had helped prepare the final draft of Benjamin's speech and approved it enthusiastically. Was he intimidated by the rebuke given Duverrier? Does he fear reprisal?

"One must have the courage of one's convictions," the Baroness said sharply, and left Benjamin to stand alone on the staircase as she walked back down to rejoin her guests.

The next day, January 5, 1800, was clear and crisp.

The Baroness de Staël left her home before sunup in her calèche and was one of the first to reach the chamber of the Tribunate, a stately half-rotunda in classic design. She took a front row seat in the visitors' gallery from which she had a clear view of the long, narrow podium below. It was flanked by two huge marble statues of Roman senators presiding in solemn dignity over the empty hall. Behind them, heavy red velvet draperies, with gold braid and fringe, hung between tall, white ionic columns lining the curved wall.

There was a sense of expectation among the spectators as they began to fill the gallery.

Germaine watched the Tribunes, eighty men in dark brown or black frock coats and knee pants, Benjamin Constant among them, as they took their places. She was struck by the drabness of their dress compared with the flamboyant costumes the Directory Deputies had worn only a few weeks earlier.

The presiding officer rapped the gavel with such force the sound echoed through the chamber. The session was open. The preliminary formalities proceeded smoothly and quickly.

Bonaparte's legislation to restrict debate was introduced.

The members were called upon to speak to the issue. One by one, the first four delivered uninspired messages of support for the measure like parishioners reciting the rosary.

Benjamin Constant was the fifth to be called. As he strode to the podium, Germaine wondered if he would keep to his script or submit to the pressure of conformity and consent.

Despite the natural droop of his shoulders, Constant was prepossessing. The assembly knew him by reputation but not by performance. They knew him as a writer, a brilliant man of spirit and wit, as a republican, as the lover of the Baroness de Staël, and as a cosmopolite . . . but not as a Frenchman.

The Tribunate's newest member mounted the speaker's platform, set down his papers and glasses on the narrow lectern and slowly surveyed his audience. He stood tall, straightened his shoulders and assumed the stance of a military commander. Germaine squinted, apprehensively.

He raised his arms and thrust them forward.

"Fellow Tribunes!" Constant's voice thundered, reverberating against the walls as loudly as the gavel sounded earlier.

The audience was startled. Even Germaine was taken aback by the power in his voice.

"It would have been most advantageous," Benjamin went on forcefully, "to have the first law being discussed here adopted unanimously and without protest!"

He stopped abruptly. After a long silence, he resumed.

"However, I must challenge that law! I do so within the limits of the Constitution and my rights as a Tribune!"

Germaine was thrilled. This was the speech he had written. She felt an urge to applaud but sat motionless. Not since the people of Paris hailed her father at the Hôtel de Ville in 1789 had she felt such overwhelming pride.

Constant paused while his colleagues and the members of the gallery absorbed the impact of his statement. Then he went on, and for twenty minutes, held his audience spellbound.

He clarified the bill, challenging Bonaparte and explaining that the First Consul had proposed it with exaggerated urgency.

"We are being hustled along as if we were an enemy army or a squadron of Cossacks," Benjamin declared, clenching his fist and pounding the lectern. "If the supreme authorities in our republic are in complete agreement we demonstrate a weakness in our system and signal a contradiction of our principles."

Some Tribunes stood up in protest, others in approval. Constant waited patiently till the chamber calmed.

"It is my hope," he said, "that we serve as a sustaining body in the government, as its conscience and its 'loyal opposition,' to debate *all* proposals . . . good or bad.

"Nothing is more harmful to the liberty of the people than an act that deprives the Tribunate of its rightful influence. Unless we invoke the right to resist such laws that limit our duty, we will be looked upon with indifference and disdain."

Constant concluded by proposing a compromise with a series of amendments. "Without these modifications," he said, "our liberty is in jeopardy. Without the independence of the legislature there can be no harmony . . . there can be no constitution. There will only be servitude and silence . . . a silence that will be heard throughout Europe. And France will be judged accordingly."

The legislators, jarred by Constant's logic and eloquence, were dumbfounded . . . and fell silent.

The vote must be taken now, quickly, Madame de Staël muttered beneath her breath . . . we will win by an overwhelming response.

Suddenly, the silence was broken. A rigid Bonapartist Tribune named Riouffe demanded the floor. With fist held high pounding the air he launched a vicious diatribe against the bold, new legislator. He ignored the bill under discussion. He shouted down appeals for order from the podium and the other Tribunes. For two long, tedious hours, he alternately showered Bonaparte with praise and bombasted Constant with a steady stream of invectives.

Finally, he concluded his tirade by shouting, "Who are we to question the wisdom of the First Consul?" A shudder of doubt and fear rippled through the assembly.

Germaine clenched her hands anxiously. Would Riouffe's irrelevant remarks and assault against Constant intimidate the Tribunes?

The bill was rushed to a vote.

The Baroness was stunned by the results.

Though Constant had managed to capture twenty-six Tribunes, the other fifty-four supported the bill. Later that day, in the Senate which voted without benefit of debate, the Deputies passed the resolution as Bonaparte had proposed it . . . 231–200!

Germaine and Benjamin were crushed, defeated.

PART III

THE SKIRMISH

Chapter 1
Fouché, Minister of Police

The Baroness de Staël stood riveted in the middle of her grandest drawing room. She was numb, unnerved.

Servants bustled about, completing arrangements for the party in celebration of Benjamin Constant's maiden speech in the Tribunate. It was only five o'clock in the afternoon, hours before the elaborate affair would begin. Already, ten of her guests had cancelled their earlier acceptances.

Ever since her return to Paris in November, Madame de Staël had worked intently on refurbishing her home. Craftsmen had painted, hung wallpaper, plastered, gilded woodwork, panelled, redraped windows, refinished and reupholstered furniture. Everything, was now ready for the one, most fitting occasion, a significant event to celebrate.

Germaine had accepted the loss of Bonaparte as a partner with bitter but good grace. Now, even Benjamin Constant, her alternate prince, was threatened. Could she endure it?

Madame de Staël surveyed the fresh opulence of the large chamber. No! She would not permit the rejections to mar the evening she planned for Benjamin . . . and herself. Over a hundred others would attend.

Spinning around to reach a bell pull, she almost collided with Olive Uginet, who approached her from behind.

"Pardon, Madame la Baronne. Here is another message for you."

Germaine tensed. Another regret?

She walked to the corner of the room, leaned against the wall as if to brace herself for the contents of the letter. The crest of the Foreign Minister was emblazoned on the back of the dispatch. She ripped through the seal swiftly with Talleyrand's Queen Hatshepsut letter opener.

> *My dear Baroness de Staël:*
> *Germaine . . . I regret that an unexpected*

*emergency prevents me from attending your
dinner party this evening. Please accept my
deepest apologies.*
                                    Charles T.

That made eleven regrets so far: Joseph Bonaparte, Lucien, Pierre Roederer. She could bear them, but this last, from Talleyrand, was a severe blow.

She folded the note slowly, impaled it with a thrust on the tip of the letter opener and placed it with the other messages on the narrow table.

Later, at ten o'clock that evening, a somber hush hung over the handful of guests in the drawing room. The magic and sparkle of elegant men and women who usually filled the de Staël mansion were missing. So was the din of provocative, erudite conversations and lighthearted banter.

Juliette, Mathieu, Adrian and Benjamin were there, of course, as were a few others not intimidated by possible threats from the First Consul. But they had not touched the food nor drunk the wines. Their voices were subdued.

The Baroness had received several more messages of regret. But most of the guests had not extended the courtesy of writing to decline. Was Madame de Staël becoming a pariah?

By midnight, the de Staël town house was empty. Footmen in green livery walked the floors, extinguishing the flames of the tapers in candelabra and chandeliers with brass candle snuffers. An eerie silence echoed from chamber to chamber.

Early the next morning the Baroness de Staël was delivered another message, flaunting the seal of a different member of Bonaparte's Council. It came from Joseph Fouché, Director of the Ministry of the Police, summoning her to his offices.

Fouché and the Baroness were friends of long standing. He had been a regular guest at her home, where they talked long, often and intimately about France and his political aspirations. He had been one of the first to turn down her invitation to dinner after Benjamin's proposal was defeated in the Tribunate.

Madame de Staël was outraged by the summons. She responded immediately, arriving early in the afternoon at the plush ministry headquarters at the Hôtel de Juigné.

The lean, pale Minister greeted her with urbane courtesy. Madame de Staël knew Fouché was ruthless and ambitious, one of the two most powerful men in the Council of State—the other was Talleyrand. She also considered him a toady.

Joseph Fouché had served Robespierre in the same capacity during the Terror as he now served Bonaparte. An intrepid organizer, he was establishing a police state, as Germaine had feared, that was more controlling than any in European history. He took joy in probing into private affairs of citizens for the thrill of discovery rather than for the need to conduct an investigation or to prosecute.

"It was not my decision to call you here today, Madame la Baronne," he said, caressing the carved arms of his chair with long, thin fingers.

"You submitted to Bonaparte's orders."

"The First Consul does not approve of the opposition you are arousing against him," he said, ignoring Germaine's remark.

"I? Opposition? I defy you to name anyone who is more enthusiastic about Bonaparte!" she declared indignantly. "You know very well how hard I pressed Talleyrand and Siéyès to select him, above all the other competent generals, to serve as military leader in the coup! Since then, my salons have celebrated his successes and glorified him!"

"Perhaps, Madame, the First Consul has been misinformed." The Minister of Police was amiable. His wan skin, stretched too tightly over his sharp features, looked as if it would crack if he smiled. "The speech Monsieur Constant delivered . . . " His voice trailed off.

"What about it?" Germaine asked sharply.

"Bonaparte believes that it was you who wrote it and influenced Constant to deliver it."

"That is absurd!" Germaine insisted haughtily. "Monsieur Constant is his own man. He has too creative a mind and is too dedicated to his own principles to blindly accept the views of another human being . . . man *or* woman!

"The First Consul . . . "

Germaine would not listen. "Why should Bonaparte object to constructive criticism?" she railed. "He is a man of strength, brilliance and foresight. He holds the most powerful position in France. No greater genius could make our nation the foremost in the world."

Fouché listened with forbearance.

Madame de Staël went on. "He should welcome suggestions from a *loyal* opposition. We can enhance his role and move France to a quick recovery."

"My dear Baroness," Fouché interrupted, lowering his voice and maintaining aloof control. "You must realize that Bonaparte does not have the hold on the government with which you credit him."

"I will not accept that. He inspires everyone . . . from the poorest street hawker to the craftiest politician. You, yourself, my dear Joseph, were swayed from attending from my reception."

"It was an expedient gesture."

"And effective with Bonaparte," Germaine replied with disdain.

"As you wish," Fouché said. "The First Consul demands open support and will resort to any method to assure it. He has already confiscated Siéyès' paper, the *Moniteur*, to use as the voice of the government and will soon cut the seventy papers of Paris to thirteen."

Earlier that day, Madame de Staël had been the object of attack in several of the censored publications. One reported, "It isn't your fault that you are ugly, but it is your fault that you are an intriguer. Mend your ways. You know the road to Switzerland. Take it and Benjamin with you. Let him try his hand in the Swiss Senate."

Germaine wondered if Fouché was responsible for the tasteless news item. He had been.

"Perhaps, Madame," he said, bowing low as he led her to the door, "you might spend a few weeks at your chateau in the suburbs at St. Ouen. I'm certain when you return the furor will have subsided. By then, other issues will preoccupy Bonaparte."

The Baroness de Staël obliged the Minister of Police by leaving Paris for her country estate. Benjamin stayed behind to attend the sessions of the Tribunate.

Germaine made most of the solitude of St. Ouen concentrating on her writing. She sent a letter to her father, asking him to tell her more in his letters about the children. They also corresponded at length about the settlement they wanted to make on Eric Magnus de Staël.

Madame de Staël had learned that her husband was ill and that his aging mistress, the actress la Clairon, had taken his furniture in lieu of payments he promised her. Eric Magnus never stopped making demands for money. Father and daughter, working through a lawyer in Paris, were trying to prevent the constant drain on the Necker fortune with a definitive separation, if not a divorce.

The Baroness's greatest pleasure during her enforced holiday was finalizing a manuscript she had been writing for more than a year. The book, *De la Litérature,* expanded her premise that all events in history lead to the "perfectibility" or "the civilization" of the human race and that literature is the most significant manifestation of this evolution.

By mid-February, Germaine's outlook brightened. Her book was ready for publication and an agreement had been worked out for payment to Eric Magnus. The Baroness, ignoring Bonaparte's directive, was ready to return to Paris.

Chapter 2
Joy and Despair

"Go by way of the Champs-Eluseés and the Rue Saint Honoré," the Baroness de Staël instructed her driver.

As the horses drew her coach along the Champs-Eluseés, Madame de Staël opened the windows to breathe in the cool brisk air of the Paris afternoon.

The people of the city were in a lyrical mood.

It was unusually warm for February and Parisians were basking in the hint of spring. The boulevard was lively with horse-drawn carriages, many of which turned off to drive through the Bois de Boulogne. People sauntered in twos and threes along the walkways laughing and chattering. Some gathered in clusters under the leafless giant plane trees that lined the avenue.

Madame de Staël thrilled to the strains of music. First from a harpist through the door of a café, then further along, from a violinist, next a guitarist. On a corner was a quartet, and then, from the Tulieries Gardens, the sounds of a concert.

Paris was glorious!

Germaine's carriage left the wide boulevards for the narrow, shop-lined streets. Swarms of pedestrians pursuing their business of buying and selling forced the moving vehicles to a crawl.

Germaine leaned out her window to share the delicious bustle and clamor. Women in beautiful gowns made the rounds of the shops, mingling with little dressmakers and merchants. Carts and wagons drawn by horses, donkeys and human power. The perambulating dealers, with their goods spread out on huge flat trays suspended by straps from their shoulders, others with capacious boxes or wicker baskets harnessed to their backs. Their costumes, drab or colorful, typical of their trades. There were men in tricorner hats, loose fitting coats and knee breeches, women wearing huge aprons over layer on layer of skirt sweeping to the ground, their heads draped in matching caps.

The discordant cries and singsong of the vendors, the clinking of their wares, the smells of the produce and cooked foods, the pungent aroma of spices and the fragrance of flowers were tantalizing to Germaine's starved country senses. The streets of the city had not changed.

Nor, unfortunately for Madame de Staël, had the political climate. When she reached her residence, she was greeted with rumors that the First Consul would exercise the decree of exile against her.

Early on the day after her return to Paris, Germaine called on her friend Juliette Récamier.

"Bonaparte persecutes *me*," she told Juliette, "when it is *Benjamin* who openly challenges him."

"You have a friend in the First Consul's wife," Juliette said.

"Josephine?"

"Yes. She is sympathetic to you as a woman and she has an understanding of what you are trying to say in your writing. Life with Bonaparte can be agonizing. She has offered to help you."

"Help me? How?"

"Would you like to take your case directly to Napoleon and discuss it with him in person?" Juliette asked.

"Of course. But will he see me?"

"Your friend Charles Talleyrand is planning a ball for Josephine and the First Consul on February twenty-fifth. She will arrange that you talk alone with him that night."

Madame de Staël was encouraged. She accepted the offer and waited expectantly for an invitation from Talleyrand. Two days before the event she still had no word from the Foreign Minister.

Germaine sent him a note. "In the name of our old friendship," she wrote her former mentor, "Would you kindly invite me to your ball."

By the hand of the same messenger, Charles Talleyrand sent back a brutal reply: "In the name of our old friendship, would you kindly stay away."

Germaine was shocked, unbelieving.

For most of the ten years of their intimate friendship, Talleyrand had flourished in the luxury of her home and her boudoir. She had willingly jeopardized her family's reputation and her own political position by helping him return to France and regain power. She had scores of letters in which he swore he owed his life to her.

She did not expect gratitude . . . only a small favor that he could easily grant and would mean little to him. Instead, he chose to be obsequious to Bonaparte. Was he a coward or an opportunist? Or both?

Germaine knew Talleyrand too well to ask again. But Talleyrand's affront was only a taste of what followed.

Madame de Staël was learning that Paris could be a lonely city. No one responded to her invitations. Nor was she welcome at the social functions held by the hostesses for the luminaries of the Consular government.

The few friends who called on Germaine were cautious enough to arrive at her home after dark. Benjamin stopped by every day but she sensed that it was with grudging compliance. She became impatient and irritable and began to test his loyalty.

"You have asked your relatives to help you find a wife," she said reproachfully.

"That's nonsense," he lied, for Benjamin had indeed decided to marry. Germaine's ostracism was not responsible for his attitude toward her, it underscored what he had been feeling for months. He had achieved a level of political sophistication and acceptance and felt that her dominance in his life would now be a liability to his career.

At the end of each of his visits, Germaine threw a tantrum and resorted to tears in the desperation of her loneliness.

"How dare you leave me," she screamed. "Have you forgotten that I am the mother of your daughter?"

"You must try to understand," Benjamin implored. "It is time I held the tiller of my own life."

Germaine recalled bitterly how, early in their friendship, Benjamin had improvised a humiliating campaign and seduced her intellectually, physically and emotionally.

Though Benjamin fought to resist her goading, he never failed to return on the following day. He could not stay away from her. He was a magnet to her iron will.

The First Consul was drawn to Madame de Staël, similarly, but with unfathomable resentment. He was obsessed with her and contributed to her despair. Since she avoided political intrigue, he harassed her personally by criticizing her management of her family's finances. He sent his brother Joseph, again, as emissary to censure her. The eldest Bonaparte called on

Germaine with this letter from his brother Napoleon:

> *Monsieur de Staël is destitute while his wife lives and entertains in luxury. When you see her, advise her to grant her husband an allowance of 2,000 francs a month. Madame de Staël's conduct must be judged as a man's. Would a man in the same position—heir to the fortune of Monsieur Necker and having enjoyed the privilege of using the distinguished name of de Staël—leave his wife in penury while he lived in abundance and expect to be received in decent society?*

Germaine was offended and deeply wounded. What would the First Consul know of the inadequacies and philandering of her husband and the grief he had caused her? Even if he knew, what right did he have to interfere in her personal affairs?

In April, Madame de Staël's emotions plunged. She nursed her injured sensibilities by completing her book, *De la littérature,* and followed it through to publication.

Soon thereafter and suddenly, her luck changed. Simultaneously, Bonaparte's leadership was being challenged.

Once again, her writing received public acclaim and was commended by the critics. *De la littérature* was a success.

Madame de Staël's spirits lifted and she regained popularity on the social circuit. The influentials returned in droves to her soirées.

"My brother tried to read your book," Lucien Bonaparte told her one evening at a dinner party at her home.

"I'm flattered," she laughed, reassured. "I did not think the First Consul would bother." Germaine sensed that despite his dismissal of her advances, Bonaparte was unable to control a subliminal attraction to her.

"He had difficulty understanding it," Lucien said with amusement. "He told me, 'I was hoping to make something of this work but I was unable to make sense of even one of the ideas . . . which are proclaimed to be so deep.'"

"If he had more time," Germaine replied charitably, "I am certain he would have no trouble with what I try to say. The Austrians are monopolizing his time now."

For the first time since he usurped the reins of government, Bonaparte's authority was being put to a definitive test. He knew his position had never been completely secure. Now, he was forced to subordinate his duties as head of state, call on his military genius and proceed to Northern Italy where the Austrians were besieging France, to advise his beleaguered commanders.

If he won the battle his power would be supreme. If he lost, his regime could topple.

With the French armies engaged in war against most of the countries of Europe, France could not afford the threat to its Italian front. The Austrians had taken Genoa with the help of the British fleet and were moving north. The loss of the Alps was imminent.

After a short period of false security Paris was plunged into grim sobriety. In the streets, drums rolled relentlessly, encouraging men to enlist. Unhappy women watched grimly as husbands and sweethearts trudged on their way to battle with children clinging desperately to their marching fathers.

Madame de Staël deplored another war that took Frenchmen beyond the borders of their beloved France. But she exulted in a confrontation that would decide Bonaparte's fate. As Bonaparte's influence wavered, Madame de Staël's strengthened.

The Baroness, usually reluctant to leave the city, was eager to begin the journey to Coppet for her annual summer sojourn. She looked forward with joy to seeing her growing children. Here, reports from the field of battle would reach her sooner than they would in Paris.

Germaine left the solemn city the day after Bonaparte's departure, taking the same route south, by way of Dijon, that he had followed. At relay posts where she stopped along the way, innkeepers and travelers talked animatedly about Bonaparte, hoping for his victory against the Austrians. The Baroness de Staël remained silent, praying for his defeat.

Chapter 3
Interlude at Coppet

The weight of his heavy body was a burden for Jacques Necker's swollen legs. He leaned against a column on the portico of his baronial chateau to relieve the pressure as he watched his grandsons race to greet their mother descending from her coach. He was worried about how his daughter would react to the news of his meeting with Bonaparte.

The Baroness de Staël embraced her sons warmly. She held them at arms' length, one at a time, and admired each of them proudly. Then with Albert on one side and Auguste on the other, her arms around their shoulders, she walked toward her father.

Necker reached over the boys to kiss his daughter. "Albertine is taking her nap," he said. "The dear little girl was eager to see you and tried to wait but she could not stay awake."

It was a happy reunion for Germaine.

Later in the evening, father and daughter stood on the south parapet facing Lac Léman and looked down on the dark blue water, sparkling like a sea of diamonds in the brilliance of the setting sun.

"Bonaparte spoke well of you," the retired statesman told Germaine. "He sees no reason why you should feel you cannot reside in Paris whenever you choose."

Madame de Staël was unimpressed and skeptical. The two men had met in Geneva for more than two hours when the First Consul stopped in the city on his way through Switzerland.

"He'll promise anything," the Baroness said caustically. "I don't trust him. He knows he is facing a bitter contest that is crucial to his career. If he loses to the Austrians he has a formidable struggle ahead of him, and he will need all the support he can rally. I am not deceived by his pretense at generosity."

Germaine had been hopeful when she reached Coppet, but a few days later she grew wary. Excitement was spreading through the country to the news that the French army was crossing the hazardous St. Bernard pass. When the troops reached the far side of the mountain the feat was compared to Hannibal's conquest of the Alps.

Madame de Staël was relieved when she learned that, in Paris, opposition was mounting against the First Consul. Preparations were underway for a government takeover if he lost, even his brother Lucien, who had been muttering disapproval of many of Napoleon's actions, was ready to defect.

By early June, Bonaparte had led his troops into Milan and labored long, arduous hours planning his strategy for the Battle of Marengo.

Fighting started before dawn on June 14, mounted viciously and was over by noon. Germaine learned this early on the day of the battle from the prefect of Léman, an old friend and former deputy in the Constituent Assembly who arranged for couriers to deliver hourly messages far ahead of regular, sluggish news channels. The Baroness concealed her jubilation from the prefect, who would not understand why a defeat for the French was in the best interest of France.

But Germaine's joy was premature.

Later that afternoon, the courier reported that Bonaparte had pulled back and retrenched. Then, with the fury of an angry Greek God of War, he hurled the full force of his artillery against the unsuspecting Austrians, routing them.

The day that had begun with defeat for Bonaparte ended in glorious victory. Unfortunately, the constitutional republicans and royalists in Paris had learned only of the report of the Austrian success but not the devastating reversal that followed. They put their plans against the Consular government into motion without waiting for a confirmation. When Bonaparte returned to the capital, only Lucien escaped punishment and the First Consul's wrath.

In the tranquility of the Chateau of Coppet, Madame de Staël marvelled at Bonaparte's success. Her admiration for him, which she had suppressed, flared again like dying embers bursting into flame. She was elated and felt justified in her early judgment of his talent, genius and resourcefulness. The Marengo triumph reaffirmed his mastery. He would now be secure, entrenched, indestructible. Nothing could capsize him. She lamented that she could not share his fame. Nor could she dare oppose him again. It was hopeless to try.

The Corsican had won. The Parisian had lost.

Madame de Staël admired Bonaparte's ambition and envied his achievements. But she despised the man.

Bonaparte always rose to the occasion but was still the tyrant she feared.

Madame de Staël's dream for a free France and for her own personal glory fell like limp shafts of wheat in autumn. Barely thirty-four, she saw her life in shambles. Everything she had worked for with such intense passion, was gone.

She had failed in politics and in love. For Germaine, one had no meaning without the other. Bonaparte had escaped her. Benjamin was slipping away.

Madame de Staël anguished over the grief that filled her life. She lived with heartache as others lived with physical pain. Her heart was never free of the sorrows that hounded her. She thought of the men she had loved best . . . Narbonne, Talleyrand and Mathieu were no longer close to support and comfort her. Narbonne, still graceful and attractive, had returned to his earlier mistress, the Viscountess de Montmorency. Talleyrand, the grotesque charmer, had chosen allegiance to Bonaparte. Elegant Mathieu, still a devoted friend, had turned to religion. And, her father was too old to share a meaningful part of her life.

Why could she not hold a man's interest as other women did? Did her intellect and her genius place a burden on her that ordinary women did not have to face? Madame de Staël brooded and turned to her writing and her family. She titled her new book *Delphine,* a novel in which her heroine champions liberty and the rights of women.

To the surprise of her friends she undertook the training and education of her children, applying herself to them with the single-mindedness she had devoted to politics.

Auguste, who was plodding but eager to learn and please, she realized was already a handsome gentleman at ten. Albert, now eight, was lovable, precocious and impatient. She gave them lessons and drills in languages and the classics. For science and mathematics, which held little interest for her but fascinated the boys, she hired a tutor, a German named Gerlach.

Three-year-old Albertine who inherited her grandmother's delicate beauty was alert and responsive. Germaine introduced her daughter to literature and enchanted her with stories of Rousseau and Voltaire from her own childhood. She played with her, read to her and to the child's delight, plucked simple tunes on the harp so she might learn the nuances of music.

Gradually, as the summer waned, Madame de Staël's spirits lifted. Once again, she was vivacious, enthusiastic. Her children responded to the attention she lavished on them. Though their lessons were constantly interrupted by visitors and the demands of managing the household, Germaine felt a sense of family and closeness she had not experienced before.

Toward the end of August, Benjamin Constant came to Coppet. He acted remote and detached. He evaded discussion with Germaine by spending most of his time with the children. When she questioned him, he withdrew. Then, abruptly cutting his stay short, he said he had to visit relatives in Lausanne before returning to France.

Madame de Staël worried that their relationship was floundering beyond recovery and was distressed for she counted on him. She was ready to return to Paris, but she could not do so without a man to serve as her escort and host at her receptions. She was reluctant to call on Benjamin.

Without an alternative, Germaine turned to her father asking him to move to France and offer his services to the French government. He could serve as her host and be a buffer against the First Consul.

Jacques refused to accept the role of elder statesman.

Germaine begged, pleaded, cajoled. In vain.

"I'm too old," Necker said. "I'm nearing seventy. Bonaparte would not want a doddering royalist peering over his shoulder."

Germaine watched the green mountains and the foliage in the parks surrounding Coppet turn to bright yellows, oranges, reds and browns. The air was brisk and filled with the scent of autumn. Servants lighted fires in large porcelain stoves and fireplaces to heat the sprawling chateau.

Madame de Staël could tolerate the wondrous summers in Switzerland but the cold, dreary winters lent Coppet the aura of a luxurious army barracks.

Desperate to repair her relationship with Benjamin and starved for intellectual and social stimulation, she decided to take on Paris alone. She had no intention of relinquishing her hold over Benjamin without a resolute effort to keep him. She sent Eugene Uginet ahead to make inquiries into his activities and to prepare her mansion on the rue de Grenelle.

In December, Germaine found a gentle governess for her children and entrusted their instruction to Gerlach, their tutor. To reassure her father, she listened patiently like a subdued, dutiful child, as Necker warned her to stay out of politics and avoid Bonaparte's wrath.

Then, under grey skies that threatened a heavy snow fall, Madame de Staël set off for Geneva and Paris in her carriage burdened with sturdy trunks and bulging boxes.

Chapter 4
The First Consul and Juliette

Paris, during the winter of 1800 and 1801, had recovered from its wartime grimness. Signs of prosperity and peace were uplifting for the people of France. All the nations of Europe, and even England, wanted to sign treaties with the conquering Bonaparte.

Madame de Staël was encouraged to find the streets, by day, bustling with buyers and sellers. At night the clatter of horses's hooves and carriage wheels on the cobblestoned boulevards echoed the gaiety of French men and women of every class as they made their way to the theatre, opera, concerts, restaurants and private parties.

The Baroness's first visit was to the Récamier mansion where she and Juliette gossiped about their mutual friends.

"I expect to hear from Benjamin soon," Germaine told Juliette. She had recovered from her angst about her lover knowing he was obsessively bound to her. "I wrote him that I would be back this week."

"If I do not tell you," Juliette offered cautiously, "you will hear about him less kindly from someone else."

"About his infatuation with Anna Lindsay?"

"You know?"

"Yes," Germaine replied without emotion. "It is a ridiculous attachment for him to make. He has no idea of what a shabby situation he is getting into. She is a harlot with two bastard children."

Juliette had feared Germaine would fly into a rage. Instead, her friend was accepting Benjamin's dalliance with the calm of a disinterested observer. Eugene had given the Baroness a detailed report on Constant's activities as soon as she reached Paris. He had learned that Mrs. Lindsay was the cause of Constant's distant behavior at Coppet and had given her a dossier on the woman. Madame de Staël was convinced that the Englishwoman was hardly a formidable rival.

"Is their affair common knowledge among our friends?" Germaine asked.

"They have been discreet," Juliette told her. "But the loud whispers can't be ignored."

Though Madame de Staël was harsh on Benjamin's paramour, Anna Lindsay was an elegant, intelligent woman of classic beauty. She had led a difficult life and it was true that for a short period in her youth she was forced to sell her charms to the highest bidder. She was thirty-seven, lonely and despondent, when she accepted Benjamin's blind passion. She had just been discarded by a French aristocrat when they returned to France after living together in London for eight years. Germaine was certain that Mrs. Lindsay was a fatuous conversationalist and that Benjamin would become bored and disillusioned, particularly when he learned that she had no money and he would have to support two small children.

"Benjamin will be back," Germaine said. "I have little to fear about his attachment to me. My concern is the First Consul. I want to enjoy the season by entertaining my cousin, Albertine Necker de Saussure, who is here from Switzerland on a holiday. I have vowed to avoid Bonaparte, Charles Talleyrand and all French officials and keep them from interfering with my affairs."

Juliette's porcelain skin turned grey.

"What have I said to upset you, my dear?" Germaine asked.

Juliette hesitated, her delicate features flinched. "Nothing. Directly. You have reminded me of something I wish to forget. I have met your nemesis."

"Bonaparte?" Germaine exclaimed.

"You met him? Face to face?"

"Yes. It was disturbing. I did not expect to see him."

Germaine took Juliette's hands in hers. "How did it happen?"

"Lucien Bonaparte invited me to dinner at his new residence on the Rue Verte," Madame Récamier began. "I was seated in the corner near the fireplace and was aware that someone was standing in the shadows of a large leafy plant. I turned and thought it was Joseph Bonaparte whom I've met so many times at your home. I nodded and greeted him eagerly. Then, to my chagrin, I recognized him to be the First Consul. I blushed and bowed my head.

"I saw that he was talking with Joseph Fouché. A few minutes later, the Minister of Police came up to me and whispered. 'The First Consul finds you exceedingly charming.' I was relieved that Lucien came by at that moment to escort me to dinner.

"We walked past Elisa Bonaparte, who served as her brother's hostess. She mumbled something to me which I could not hear. I looked for an empty place at the table as far from Napoleon as I could find and sat down. The new Second Consul, Cambacérès, took a seat beside me. When everyone was seated, Napoleon called out so everyone could hear, 'Ah ha! Citizen Consul, next to the most beautiful of them all!'"

"How pompous and vulgar!" Germaine interjected. She had listened intently but could stay silent no longer.

"Later, after dinner, when we left the table," Juliette went on, "Napoleon strode boldly up to me. 'Why did you not sit beside me?' he asked.

"'I would not have dared,' I demurred.

"'It was your place,' he said.

"'That is what I told you before dinner,' Elisa added as she walked by.

"We went into the music room to listen to Garat sing a scene from *Orpheus*. Napoleon's gaze was fixed on me with such persistence that I began to feel quite ill. At the end of the concert, he tried to engage me in conversation. For the first time, I was grateful for Lucien's open jealousy. He took my arm and walked me away."

"Now, you, too, have defied the First Consul," Germaine observed.

"Bonaparte repels me. I'm concerned that he will not let the matter rest there."

Germaine selected a green sprig from a vase and fingered it delicately.

"That man," she declared, "is an insensitive despot who will never return the government to the people. He is as boorish in social situations as he is dictatorial in matters of state. Now, he forces his attention on *you.*"

Germaine snapped the twig in two. She felt a sense of shame and shock at the fleeting moment of envy that rushed through her. Did she still have a lingering attraction for Bonaparte? For a brief instant, she craved the attention that he wished to lavish on Juliette. She shuddered at the notion and quickly vanquished this very private sentiment.

"Bonaparte is an unbearable hypocrite. He exerts his authority as it pleases him," Germaine said. "He curbs the morals of the public to a point of prudery yet he indulges his own sexual fantasies with anyone he chooses."

"Yes," Juliette answered with loathing. "He has his servants bring the actresses from the *Théâtre Français* to his apartment at all hours."

"And the gossip is that they comply. They are eager to go to bed with him," Germaine replied with equal disgust. "And his sister Pauline. He has even slept with her! He contradicts himself," Germaine went on. "He will not permit Josephine's dearest friend, Thérèse Tallien, in his home because he objects to her revealing garments and her immoral behavior."

"Even more sanctimonious is his current decree," Juliette said scornfully, "that requires all government officials to break with or marry their mistresses."

Germaine's eyes sparkled capriciously. "Ha! Charles! My dear Charles Talleyrand! It will be amusing to learn how Charles will respond to the order. Will he marry his beautiful but stupid Catharine la Grande?"

The idea of the licentious, self-indulgent Talleyrand bending to the will of Bonaparte and restricting himself to one woman relieved the tension the two women were enduring. Juliette and Germaine fell into each others arms in laughter.

Months later, the former bishop married his paramour.

Chapter 5
Benjamin Returns

I have had no time," Benjamin said penitently.

"Your duties in the legislature have never kept you away before," Germaine scolded.

As Madame de Staël had expected, a subdued Benjamin had returned to her. She looked at him curiously. His hair was no longer red and long but blond and cropped short.

"What have you done with your hair?" she asked, amused.

"It is a wig," he replied sheepishly. "Red hair is for passionate heroes."

Madame de Staël remembered Benjamin's sensitivity to the color of his hair. He was wearing a natural hairpiece that looked like his own, not the powdered peruke that was going out of fashion. He appeared more sedate, less flamboyant.

"You are no longer a hero?" she queried callously.

"I plan to give up the wig," he replied.

"You may wear any color hair you choose," she said imperiously. "But I expect you here every evening while I'm in Paris."

Benjamin obediently returned to the fold.

He and Germaine resumed their private life and happily revived their amicable debates. Occasionally he escaped to make love to Anna Lindsay or to a prostitute in a Paris brothel. He did discard his wig.

But publicly they went their separate ways.

Madame de Staël entertained the diplomatic, literary and arts communities, and attended public and private receptions that steered clear of Bonaparte and his staff. One day she received an invitation to dine at the home of General Berthier where the First Consul was to be a guest. She knew she could not refuse. With the odious memories of their earlier encounters, which left her breathless and mute, Germaine prepared herself with several dignified but biting answers to the insulting questions he might pose. She recalled only one woman who could rebuff Bonaparte's insults. Her friend Madame de Condorcet was approached at a ball by Bonaparte. "Madame," he addressed her, "I do not like women to meddle in politics." "General," the glib Countess replied, "you are right. But in a country where their heads are cut off, it is natural for them to want to know why."

Germaine hoped to equal one of her own successes when Napoleon had told her, "Madame, I do not like women to write." He had no reply when she said, "General, if I had the honor of calling myself Madame Bonaparte, I would not seek personal glory."

Madame de Staël attended the Berthier affair with confidence.

When the guests proceeded to the dining room, Bonaparte with his brother Lucien at his side, stopped in front of Germaine. He avoided her eyes and peered at the décolletage of her stunning dress.

"Doubtless," he said with pointed crudeness, "you nursed your children yourself?"

Madame de Staël was struck dumb. As he strutted off with Lucien she heard him say, "You see, she does not even want to say yes or no!"

Bonaparte's attitude toward Germaine did not affect his brothers' respect for her. Their friendships, in fact, grew more intimate. While Josephine and the First Consul held dull formal affairs at Malmaison, Germaine was often a guest at the carefree weekend parties at Joseph's splendid estate at Mortfontaine.

With Madame de Staël back in Paris, Benjamin was emboldened to make daring moves in his role as Tribune. Rumors of conspiracies against Bonaparte also bolstered his courage. He ventured to speak out once more against the First Consul in the chambers of the legislature.

Madame de Staël tried to dissuade him.

"The Tribunate is falling into degradation as Parliament did under Cromwell," he exhorted. "I must defend my principles."

"To my detriment," Germaine protested. "Bonaparte is certain to blame me."

Constant was not deterred. He continued his attacks against the Consular government.

On Christmas eve, while entertaining friends in her drawing room, the Baroness's house was jarred by a loud explosion as though an earthquake had undermined all of Paris. The conversations stopped abruptly, then continued as before when the the shaking ceased. Everyone believed a cannon had been fired in a military exercise. A few hours later Germaine learned that a group of dissidents had made an attempt on the First Consul's life. A bomb, hidden in a water cart and placed on the rue Nicaise, along the route Bonaparte was taking in his carriage to the opera, exploded as he drove by. Several people were killed but Bonaparte and his party miraculously escaped injury.

Unshaken but irate, he continued on to the opera. Later he demanded the death penalty, without trial, for the two hundred suspects in the case. Benjamin challenged this arbitrary stand on the floor of the Tribunate.

It was Germaine who was reprimanded. "It is to your benefit, Madame," Bonaparte wrote her, "that you cease inciting Benjamin Constant against my policies. I warn you to stay out of matters of government."

As it developed, one hundred and thirty men, made up from a random list of Jacobins were deported as hardened criminals to Madagascar and never heard from again. The true culprits were known to be Royalist.

In the spring, dreading further harassment from Bonaparte, Madame de Staël journeyed to Coppet for the summer earlier than usual.

Benjamin Constant followed her a few days later and found her despondent. She tried to overcome her despair by devoting herself to work and her family. She helped tutor her children, took lessons in German (which she found tedious and constraining) from Gerlach, worked on her novel *Delphine* and convinced her father to begin a political thesis that she hoped would influence Bonaparte to recall him to service.

She was tired, overwrought and deeply depressed. She dwelled on the First Consul's unwarranted persecution of her and feared he would exile her permanently from France.

Benjamin agonized with her. He no longer loved Germaine, but was addicted and could not tear himself away from her. When she suffered, he felt responsible in some way for her torment and tried to console her.

As a last resort, Constant persuaded her to take opium. For the first time in months, Madame de Staël slept peacefully through the night and most of the next morning. When she awakened she was in a state of calm contentment which lasted through the day. For weeks thereafter, she relied on the drug to sustain the improbable (for her) quiescent mood.

Benjamin was delighted. When he returned to Paris, he told their friends that Germaine was once again the gracious, affectionate, intelligent woman she had been when they first met. He convinced himself that he had never stopped loving her.

Months later, in the fall of 1801, Germaine wrote to Joseph Bonaparte to ask how Napoleon would react if she set up residence in the city. Joseph approached his brother and praised his friend. The First Consul surprised the eldest Bonaparte by remarking offhandedly, "I suppose you are right. There has been no talk of her lately."

The Baroness acted cautiously when she returned to Paris, keeping her opinions to herself and advising Benjamin to do the same.

Unfortunately, as before, he did not heed her but joined other members of the Tribunate in an attack on Bonaparte. This time there was no appeasing the First Consul. "I shall shake them from my clothes like vermin," he declared.

He silenced his opponents by withdrawing their forum. Bonaparte, using the authority of his office, dismissed Constant and nineteen other recalcitrants from the legislature.

Madame de Staël ingested another dose of opium.

Chapter 6
The Baroness Withdraws

A few days after the mass dismissal, Joseph Fouché paid an unannounced visit to Madame de Staël at her home on the rue de Grenelle.

"The First Consul plans to spend more time on domestic problems," the Minister of Police informed her.

"I would expect him to redirect the emphasis of his duties," Germaine replied. "The English are about to sign a peace treaty and he will be free of pressing foreign affairs."

"Bonaparte plans to devote at least one or two hours a day with me on police matters. He wants to be informed of everything in the greatest detail."

"Are you trying to alert me to a directive from the First Consul that will affect my welfare?" the Baroness asked with a touch of irony.

"We have been friends for many years," Fouché flushed evading her question.

"Exceptionally good friends," Germaine replied.

"You know how dedicated I am to my . . . duties."

"Of course."

"Bonaparte has reports that you discuss neither him nor politics," Fouché informed Germaine. "He's exasperated. 'Just by being in her company,' he says, 'is enough to disturb people's minds.' It infuriates him. He feels that after your guests leave your home, they somehow always think less of him. He calls you a bird of ill-omen that signals trouble."

"What do you suggest I do?"

"Nothing that will add to his fury. You will be watched closely. All you do and say will reach the First Consul."

During her soirées the Baroness continued to act with discretion guiding conversations away from politics to theatre, literature and opera.

The next week, it was Joseph Bonaparte who called on Germaine.

"Napoleon insists you are calling him an ideophobe," he told her.

"He has called the friends in my circle ideologues," she laughed good naturedly.

"I denied you called him anything," Joseph assured her.

"Lucien was also there with me at the time and defended you as well."

"You are both kind and loyal friends," the Baroness said warmly.

"Napoleon called us in while he was taking a bath and berated us for your behavior. He screamed at the top of his lungs. 'I can smell Madame de Staël from a distance of three kilometers! Ideophobe, eh!' He railed on and on, his voice grew louder, his anger hotter. When I thought he would explode, he brought his fist down into the tub with such power that a sheet of water splashed high and wet me from head to toe."

The Baroness suppressed her amusement.

Joseph shook his head sadly, "I hesitate to tell you what he said then."

"But you must," Germaine said smiling with catlike curiosity. "That is why you are here."

"Yes. He has ordered me to do so. Napoleon said, 'Forcibly remind this woman, Her Illustriousness, that I am neither Louis XVI nor Paul Barras. If she stands in the way I wish to go, I'll crush and break her. The best course for her is to be mute. I won't hurt her if I don't have to.'"

"Yet, it seems my silence is more irritating to *His* Illustriousness than my candor," Germaine replied.

Both Fouché and Joseph Bonaparte admired Madame de Staël's fortitude. Neither guessed she was alarmed by the warnings. If Bonaparte wanted her silence, she would continue to maintain it. She had not opposed him nor did she plan to. The atmosphere in France was too favorable to the Consular government.

Acting with calculated prudence, Germaine attended her social engagements in the elite arrondisements of Paris and conducted her own salons with equal low key. Her guests packed her manor house several evenings each week. Her circle of close friends, Juliette Récamier, Benjamin Constant and Mathieu de Montmorency now included the writer-poet François René de Chateaubriand, the country vicar, the Chevalier de Boufflers, the regal Roman beauty, Madame Visconti and scores of other notables.

The Baroness de Staël guided her guests away from the usual intimate groups which encouraged talk of politics. Instead she provided entertainment to distract them. There were musical ensembles, authors read from their works, Germaine herself enchanted visitors by playing a harp . . . she had become a talented musician.

Madame de Staël's actions concealed the depth of her anger and resentment.

Germaine despised the arbitrary manner in which the First Consul treated her and, in private, strongly objected to his tactics. The royalists and republicans who gathered at her home respected her silence, shared the opinions she did not express and felt betrayed, too, by the Corsican demagogue.

She grew even more incensed when Bonaparte attempted to heal the ten-year-long breach between France and the Catholic Church in Rome. Madame de Staël abhorred his hypocrisy. He was not motivated by religious conviction but by a lust for even greater power.

"When I was among the Turks," a friend told Germaine he had said, "I was a Mohammedan. Now I shall become a Catholic. The church has kept the Pope from supporting me. With my unchallenged grip on Italy, I shall bend him to my will."

One evening in the middle of April, Madame de Staël attended a reception at the Récamier mansion. It was a quiet, sedate affair that reflected the dignity of its hostess.

Germaine circulated among the guests searching for Juliette. When she failed to find her, she wandered into a corridor that led from the foyer.

She saw Juliette, alone, pale and shaking. As she approached, her friend, Germaine heard angry, muffled voices from behind the closed door Juliette was leaning against.

"You are trembling, my dear," Germaine said taking her friend in her arms. "What is going on in there?"

"I cannot tell you," Juliette whispered.

"It sounds like Jean Baptiste . . . General Bernadotte," Madame de

Staël exclaimed with surprise.

"Yes," Juliette conceded. "It is he and General Moreau."

Germaine walked her down the hall to a small chamber, where, inside, Germaine closed the door behind them.

"I've done my best to keep this from you," Juliette said. "I have not wanted to implicate you You are already condemned for so much in which you are not involved."

"Implicate?" Germaine asked. "In what?"

"They, the entire group, have been meeting here regularly for weeks."

Germaine was horrified. She had heard of a plot involving twelve of Bonaparte's comrades-in-arms in a conspiracy against the First Consul. She had stayed clear of the intrigue that was whispered about as the Generals' Plot.

"They put *you*, my dear Juliette, in jeopardy!" Germaine cried.

"They have never talked violence before. I came in to warn them to keep their voices down—they were disagreeing on how to assassinate Bonaparte."

"They have gone that far?" Germaine was stunned.

"I know nothing of the details. I allow them to meet here. It was by chance that I heard."

"This will reach the First Consul, I'm sure."

"We have been cautious."

"We must return to your guests before they begin to miss you as I did."

As they walked down the corridor, Juliette and Germaine came upon the handsome Bernadotte, pacing agitatedly.

"Madame de Staël," he said, "I would like to talk with you."

"I would be delighted," she replied, "but only in the company of my friends. I wish to know nothing of your scheme."

"You disapprove?"

"You do not understand," she replied. "You must be guided by your instincts and your sense of duty. I cannot, however, be a part of any plot. I encourage you to proceed as quickly as possible, for soon our evil genius will have forty thousand priests at his command. Au revoir, my friend."

Madame de Staël tenderly embraced Juliette.

"Good night, ma chérie," she said, and left.

Chapter 7
"*Delphine*"

I t was a clear afternoon on the first of May. The sun was high.
Madame de Staël rode south toward Switzerland, her golden carriage
swaying along the rugged rural highways of France. She looked out the
window to observe the splendors of the changing countryside. No other part
of Europe, she mused, can boast this dramatic panorama of beauty . . . miles
of undulating landscape, vast fields of newly planted wheat, screens of tall,
slender poplars, time-honored vineyards. Clusters of unpretentious
farmhouses were surrounded by groves of trees in full leaf, striking
silhouettes against magnificent skies, unique to France. Giant cloud
formations, serene, limpid, soft and pure in their whiteness like mountains
of fresh cotton, traveled languorously across an azure sky.

Germaine de Staël felt the carriage slow as the horses hesitated.
Down the road, she saw a round tower signalling a hamlet lay ahead. The
horses slipped into an easy canter, passing stucco houses that forced the road
to a one-lane thoroughfare. The berline quickly reached the village square—
with its fountain, its trough to water the animals, its monument to honor an
illustrious citizen . . . like scores of others she breezed through on her
journeys.

Germaine turned from these familiar, picturesque sights to the man
who sat slumped in the opposite corner of the coach. She shook her head in
disbelief. Was this the stunning diplomat she had married, the darling of the
court, with gracious manners and an engaging smile women could not
resist? Eric Magnus was a shadow, a wasted man, the product of his own
debauchery.

A few days earlier, Madame de Staël had received a plea from her
estranged husband begging for help. She responded immediately, calling at
his meager quarters the following day. She had not heard from de Staël
since she had made the settlement on him and believed he was managing on

the allotment.

She was aghast at what she saw. His rooms were bare except for a few sticks of furniture and the bed where he rested. He was ill, penniless, destitute. Though he recognized her, he was incoherent. Eric Magnus de Staël was senile. He was barely past fifty but appeared many years older than her father.

Without rancor Germaine accepted him as her responsibility. Only at Coppet could he recover, or, if his health could not be restored, he could live out the few years he had left in comfort. She flew into action. Within hours she had made the necessary arrangements . . . paid his debts, wrote her best friends that she was leaving, asked Benjamin to follow as soon as possible and left Paris with her charge.

As Madame de Staël boarded her carriage, she was delivered a reply to one of her notes.

> *Germaine, my dear:*
> *You and I leave Paris separately, taking opposite directions without the joy and the sorrow of a farewell. Yet, I doubt I could bear a parting. As you leave for Coppet I go to London. A rumor has just reached me that Bonaparte has learned of the plot. It is best that I leave the city . . . I do not know how long I will have to stay.*
> *I am saddened and dread the separation from you.*
> *Your dearest friend, Juliette*

The Baroness took out the letter and read it again, wistfully.

When she looked up, the berline was again in open country, speeding along a sun-washed landscape that seemed to mock her loneliness.

On the sixth of May, the de Staël carriage drew up to a small inn in Poligny, a village several kilometers north of Switzerland.

Eric Magnus, weary from the strenuous journey, complained of dizziness and pain. As they prepared to leave the next morning, he was delirious. Then silent. He had suffered a stroke. While Germaine nursed him, waiting for him to regain strength, Benjamin Constant arrived. Together they watched over the Baron who was sinking rapidly. He never recovered. Slipping into unconsciousness, he died three days later.

Benjamin accompanied Germaine as she took the body in a separate coach over the Alps to Coppet. Before he was buried in the parish cemetery, Germaine removed from his finger the ring made of her hair, intertwined with fine strands of gold, which Eric Magnus had worn since their marriage.

"No, I have no feelings of guilt or remorse about Eric Magnus," Germaine told her father solemnly. "I did all I could for him. Often, more than he deserved. He squandered his life."

"Do you have any regrets about your own life, Minette?" the aging Necker asked his daughter.

"None. I have expressed what I feel within the rigorous code society has placed on me and on other women like me." Germaine hesitated. "None except perhaps that I was not born a man. If only both sexes could be judged by the same set of rules. I don't seek equal political or legal rights . . . just that women be entitled to express themselves beyond their expected roles of mother, wife or mistress."

"Now, the man on whom we once placed our hopes for the freedoms of which you speak is imposing an even more stringent morality on people," Jacques said with a wry smile.

"Bonaparte!" Germaine shot back. "Ask of my chagrin for permitting him to intimidate me! If I continue to suppress my opposition to his tyranny, I shall suffer tremendous guilt."

Four months earlier, on the same day that the Baron de Staël had died, Bonaparte's term of office had been extended ten years. Shortly thereafter, the people elected him Consul for life with the right to choose his own successor.

While he was being honored and glorified, Bonaparte was attempting to deal with the officers who took part in the Generals' Plot. Juliette's suspicions were justified. He had learned of the cabal. Since he feared the public would lose confidence in his leadership if they learned of the dissension among the military and high level officials, the First Consul punished the plotters leniently. He dismissed one general from his post, sent Bernadotte for a vacation to Plombières and chastised the rest with a warning to stay away from the influence of Madame de Staël on whom he placed full blame for the conspiracy.

Germaine was rankled by Bonaparte's presumption, his arrogance and, even more, by his success. She encouraged her father to complete a paper, *Last Views on Politics and Finance,* in which Necker analyzed the Consular government. It was a dull, learned treatise portraying Bonaparte as a necessary man who should relinquish leadership of France to others and serve in a guardian role. When the First Consul read the report he went into another diatribe, condemning Germaine for inciting and misinforming her father. She denied the accusation, telling her friends, "It is impossible for anyone to guide the pen of a man who thinks so nobly."

Bonaparte's reaction prompted Germaine to alter her plans of spending a leisurely summer getting to know her children better before taking full charge of their development. They had matured enough to be able to leave the insulated confinement of the family estate and travel with her. Her sons, twelve and ten, had progressed far beyond Necker's tutelage. Albertine, now five, was ready for her mother's coaching, molding and fashioning.

Madame de Staël felt compelled, instead, to work on the manuscript of her novel *Delphine,* denying herself the full pleasure of her children's company till she finished her book.

"My novel shall speak for me," Germaine told Necker. "It will not be political, nor will I accuse Bonaparte. I hold society responsible for what we endure . . . I shall condemn our social institutions for subjecting men to harsh, inhuman treatment, for imposing limiting, puritanical codes on women and for permitting despots to rule."

"Is fiction the best vehicle for so powerful a message?"

"It will reach those who understand . . . the silent but enlightened people of France," Germaine replied confidently.

Her novel was published in December and had a readership that extended beyond the borders of France to all of Europe.

Delphine was a sensation. Readers clamored for copies.

Madame de Staël knew what her public wanted. The book was a roman à clef about international celebrities with Germaine herself, subdued and sympathetic, the model for the heroine. Her friends and lovers, loosely disguised, played other leading roles.

Delphine was destined to be a best seller.

One of the most thoroughly defined characters was Madame de Vernon, a feminine Machiavelli, ruthless, indolently egotistical and passionlessly dissipated. She was patterned after Charles Talleyrand. Germaine gained satisfaction and reprisal with the revealing portrayal of her former mentor.

When he read the book, the Foreign Minister remarked with sarcasm, "The Baroness de Staël has disguised us both, herself and me, as women."

Germaine's book carried her thinly veiled vendetta further. *Delphine* was filled with attacks against the principles of Bonaparte, but skirted any reference to the First Consul. Her characters spoke out against the consular government and favored the English parliamentary system. In contrast to the prudish morality that Bonaparte inflicted on France, her players upheld divorce and equality for women, opposed loveless marriages and ridiculed the bigotry of Catholicism.

On the day after Christmas, as she sat in the library at Coppet reading stacks of glowing reviews of her book and reports of its widespread acceptance, Madame de Staël found a letter from Joseph Fouché in her mail. "When I responded to a summons from the First Consul," he wrote, "I found him in his office standing with his feet spread wide apart, his back rigid, his jaw grim, holding a copy of your novel. He screamed out in anger, 'Madame de Staël attacks my policies and has instigated my comrades-in-arms against me. I hope this woman's friends have advised her not to come to Paris. I will be obliged to have her driven back to the frontier by the gendarmarie. Never again will the ink-stained daughter of Monsieur Necker be permitted to enter this city,' Then he hurled your book across the room like a shot from a musket."

Napoleon Bonaparte exiled Germaine de Staël not only from Paris but from all of her beloved France.

Chapter 8
The Dichotomy of Benjamin

"If you won't marry me, why won't you let me go?" Benjamin lamented. He was haggard and distraught. His hands clasped behind his back, he stood facing Germaine, who reclined comfortably on a cushioned chaise under a down quilt.

"What would I gain by marrying you?" she asked disparagingly.

"You might put an end to Bonaparte's attacks on your morality . . . or immorality," he replied, piercing Germaine's sensibilities.

The Baroness's eyes flared defiantly. In the months since her exile, she had grown despondent. She had tried repeatedly to reach Bonaparte through his brothers hoping to obtain permission to return to Paris. They had tried, again and again, to present her case, but had failed to sway the First Consul. Rejected and isolated, Germaine vented her frustrations on Benjamin. And he responded in kind.

"I will not yield to a tyrant who has two moral codes . . . one for himself and the other for the rest of the world," she snapped back.

"Then do it for your own sense of decency and for my well being. I'm thirty-five. It is time I found peace and solitude. I want to devote myself to study and writing. I can no longer have a political career, for which I have you to thank." It was the sharp thrust of an épée.

"I did not expect to hear that from you!" Germaine was infuriated. Leaping up from the chaise, she took hold of Benjamin's arms.

"When a man no longer wants to give happiness to a woman," she raged, "he must have the courage to break with her!"

"Do you not see that I lack the fortitude for it?" he challenged. "It is up to you, since you do not love me, to find the strength to release me! I beg you!"

"Oh, Benjamin! Benjamin, my dearest!" Germaine was pleading now. During their eight-year-long relationship she knew how to appeal to his sympathy and his sense of duty. She summoned a flood of tears. "Sometimes I feel like a bird buffeted about by a violent storm."

She slipped to the floor onto the soft quilt that had fallen at her feet. She pulled Benjamin down beside her. He responded by kissing her as fiercely as he had condemned her, and the heat of their passions was once more transposed into an act of love, as it was each time they quarreled.

Later, as they lay quietly together, Germaine placed her hand on his bare chest. "Why is it, Benjamin," she whispered, "you no longer speak tenderly to me of love?"

"I ask you to marry me. What more do you want?"

"That was not my question. Why?" she repeated softly.

"Your love continues to be demanding, oppressive. That kind of love is for the very young."

"A woman must be loved all her life."

"Not with such fury. You live everyday in a whirlwind . . . if the day is calm, you stir, you *stampede* everyone around you until it becomes a tempest."

"Then why don't you leave?"

"Because you will not let me go. The power of your intellect dominates me."

"You are free! Go!" she commanded

"I will! I'll marry Anna Lindsay."

"You wouldn't dare. That Irish whore could never give you the home and the luxury you have with me," she said reopening the argument. "She would suppress your talents and restrict your creativity. Your friends would forsake you. And what of the money you owe me?"

"Then marry me so I may have peace of mind."

"And lose my title? Threaten my children's inheritance and my sons' careers!"

The Baroness knew perfectly well that Benjamin's ardor for her had cooled. Did she really love him any longer? Perhaps he was right. Perhaps *she* should marry. Someone else, not Benjamin. It must be a man who could give her the kind of happiness she had dreamed of but had yet to experience. But could she let Benjamin go? His keen mind continued to rouse and inspire her. Only he could challenge her intellectually and spark the eloquence and depth of passion that she never could reveal except with him.

Benjamin, at the same time, never realized the full potential of his brilliance with anyone else, and this frightened him.

"I cannot go on living as I have been with you," Benjamin said. "I feel like a vagabond without a place to call home. Since you refuse to be my wife, I'll marry the young heiress, Amélie Fabri, whom my family has selected for me."

"And forsake your daughter?"

Benjamin winced. He loved Albertine to distraction. He worshiped her, and dreaded ever being separated from her without the privilege of visiting her when he wished.

"Why do you torture me so with your threats," Germaine said accusingly. "You push me to the point of suicide. You know my despair is deeper than any *you* have ever suffered."

Benjamin closed his eyes, trying to shut out the scene. Living with Germaine was unbearable, but the guilt he felt each time he left her was harrowing. Why had he allowed himself to slip under the yoke of her dominance? Was this what Bonaparte had instinctively sensed about Germaine . . . an overwhelming power of intellect which he rejected and suppressed with continuing acts of oppression against her? Could this be the root cause of the First Consul's antagonism? Was he both drawn to and repelled by her?

"Benjamin! Don't dare turn from me!"

The diatribes and recriminations went on until four o'clock in the morning, at which point they were interrupted by another unrestrained bout of love.

Exhausted, Benjamin dropped off to sleep.

Madame de Staël awake and overwrought, paced the floor like a lioness searching for a lost cub. Momentarily she hesitated, then walked to a commode and reached into a drawer to find what she wanted. Unaware that she was becoming addicted, she took a dose of opium.

That afternoon, Benjamin regretted his truculence when Germaine greeted him with gracious calm in the sun-filled library.

"I submit," he told her. "What do you wish me to do?"

"I cannot return to France, of course, but you have Bonaparte's permission to do so."

"But I cannot live in Paris," Benjamin replied. "There are restrictions on where I can travel."

"I know," Germaine spoke with such understanding that all the bitterness of the night was erased. "But you will be close enough to communicate with Joseph Fouché. Perhaps you will be able to convince him to persuade Bonaparte to end my exile."

Benjamin agreed to try. He would stay in a small house he had recently purchased, Les Herbages, only a few kilometers from the capital.

Several days later, when he parted with Germaine, the thought of his freedom softened the harshness of his enslavement to her. He repented their disagreements and knew he would miss their stimulating repartee. He was saddened by his sensation of elation that he would see her no more. Knowing he would no longer be subject to her will, Benjamin was genuinely tender and solemn at their parting.

Germaine was convinced that he still loved her.

Chapter 9
A Definitive Directive

"Bonaparte has lost interest in harassing me," the Baroness de Staël told a group of her friends who had gathered in the shade of a huge elm tree on the parklike grounds at Coppet. "He is concentrating on his expedition to invade England."

During the summer of 1803, following Benjamin Constant's departure, a steady stream of visitors found their way to the Necker chateau and made life bearable for Germaine. But her longing for Paris, deeper than the yearning for a lover, did not diminish.

"While he is boarding his ship to cross the channel," Madame de Staël remarked, "I will return to France." Germaine had persuaded herself that the First Consul no longer kept track of her movements. "If he learns I am back, he'll hesitate to take action against me. My writing, my reputation and my banishment are too widely known for him to chance criticism."

Coppet had become a center for the gathering of scholars from all of Europe. Amicable debates and provocative discussions in the bucolic setting of Switzerland had given Germaine a false sense of security.

Most of her guests were people she had known and loved for years.

She spent the mornings tutoring her children and having quiet, unhurried conversations with her cousin, Albertine Necker de Saussure, and her childhood playmate, Catherine Huber Rillet. Both had become prominent in literary and social circles in Geneva. The three women shared hopes and plans for their families. "Auguste is destined for the diplomatic service," the Baroness informed her friends. "Albert, for the military. As for Albertine, I'm determined she shall not suffer a marriage like mine. I shall see that she marries for love."

Mathieu de Montmorency, devoted, supportive and now deeply religious, often joined this causerie in Madame de Staël's boudoir. She was delighted to have him back.

Afternoons were spent in the company of her guests, strolling in the lovely gardens or languishing on the parapet overlooking the lake. There was always talk of literature, of politics, of philosophy. Evenings were dedicated to dinner parties, receptions and more conversation within the walls of the chateau.

Though she was denied the excitement of Paris, the Baroness de Staël could exult in the company of her friends.

Charles-Victor de Bonstetten, an eternally youthful Swiss Voltaire who had frequented her mother's salon and had become attached to Germaine over the years, told her, "I feel electrified when I see and hear you. More intellect is displayed here in one day than in many countries in a whole year."

Other brilliant minds inspired Madame de Staël. There was Candolle, who was making great strides in botany. De Chateauvieux, who wrote perceptively on Italian society. Pictet, the professor who adopted a new approach to physics. Prevost, who wrote on philosophy in a popular vein. The writer Camille Jordan, the philosopher de Gérando, and Madame Julie de Krudener, who introduced Germaine to mysticism.

Jean-Charles-Léonard Simonde de Sismondi was another regular at Coppet. Two years earlier he had intrigued Germaine with a problem of the heart. He asked her if he should defy his mother's objections and marry Lucille, a penniless consumptive far below his social station The girl had since died and solved his dilemma, but he fell in love with Germaine and brought on another. Madame de Staël held him at arm's length because Jean-Charles lacked the aristocratic panache she demanded in a lover.

Yet, she admired his remarkable mind.

One day as Germaine was writing on her lap desk and having tea with her father in Coppet's library, Sismondi appeared at the doorway.

"There are many who are willing to openly oppose Bonaparte's tyranny," she was telling her father.

"I, for one, will stand and fight at your side, my dearest Germaine," Sismondi declared.

"Oh!" Germaine intoned unaware of the presence of the smitten young man, "Jean-Charles, I knew I could count on you. Do join us."

"We need not worry," Sismondi went on, taking a chair beside Germaine, "a man who does not understand political freedom in his soul will ultimately destroy himself. Don't you agree, Monsieur Necker?"

"I'm no longer a soothsayer for France, Monsieur Sismondi. Your book, *On Commercial Wealth,* is fascinating. You forsee a new mercantilism?"

"Yes, the bourgeoisie will grow. There will be . . . " Sismondi groped for a word, " . . . an industrial revolution that will demand an enormous work force."

"As a result, " Necker said, "the owners and workers will be in conflict."

"It is inevitable. Human nature," Sismondi replied.

"Bonaparte is so busy spending the little money France has on military exploits," Germaine interjected, "he has no time to construct a unified economic plan based on principles of freedom."

"Germaine is right," Necker added. "Perhaps you should send the General a copy of your book."

"I doubt he's ready for my ideas," laughed Sismondi.

Though she rejected this brilliant scholar as a lover, the Baroness de Stael, as usual, did not want for admirers.

She found the travelers who were coming in droves, from the British Isles to Switzerland most appealing. Even before Benjamin departed, a young Irishman, Sean O'Brien, attached himself to her and never seemed to leave. In late spring, she switched her affection to two gallant Scotsmen, Lord John Campbell, the Duke of Argyll, and his physician, Dr. Bruce Robertson. They became an intimate trio and then a quintet when another Scotsman, William MacCulloch and a Swiss diplomat, Ferdinand Christain joined them. All professed their love for Germaine, who displayed a marked partiality for the handsome young doctor. The five traveled the country side from Geneva to Montreux, with Germaine acting as tour guide, more perhaps as a queen bee, with her carriage the hive for her buzzing drones.

The excitement of this rondelay and the demands of her erudite visitors diverted Germaine from the reality of what was in store for her as, once more, she made plans to take up residence in France.

Jacques Necker tried to dissuade her even as she mounted her golden berline to leave Coppet.

"What a miserable gypsy life you live," he declared.

"*Paris* is my life."

"Why must you be so obstinate?" Necker asked. Germaine glared at the man who meant more to her than any other, turned her back on him and settled in the coach with her children. Necker, deeply concerned for his daughter, returned to the chateau without watching the carriage pull away.

The only house that the Baroness de Staël-Holstein could find was small, damp and dismal, but cramped quarters did not disturb her. She was in France. Her current residence was in the village of Maffliers, only twenty-five kilometers northwest of Paris. She was close to her friends who had country houses in the same district. Juliette Récamier lived at Saint-Brice. Benjamin Constant at Les Herbages. Mathieu at his family estates on the edge of the Forest of Montmorency.

"During the month I have been here," she told Régnault de Saint-Jean d'Angély, a friend in a high government post who came to call, "I have spent all my time trying to untangle the maze of my husband's unpaid bills and arrange to register my sons in French academies."

When Germaine had left Switzerland early in September, she had enrolled Albert in a boarding school in Geneva in an attempt to curb his high spirits and prepare him for the disciplines of formal training.

D'Angély fidgeted uncomfortably. "I understand your concern with your sons' education," he interrupted. "But there is an urgent matter that I must reveal to you." D'Angély was cautious, hoping he would not alarm his hostess.

Madame de Staël showed no surprise. She knew her friend had not come from the capital without good reason.

"We can avoid an incident if we take proper precautions," he said preparing her. "But your move back to France has attracted the attention of the First Consul."

Germaine braced herself. "I thought he was too busy to bother with the whereabouts of a defenseless widow and her children."

"He has reports that you entertain widely, mostly dissidents who oppose him. And that you have made clandestine trips to Paris."

"That is preposterous!" Germaine replied on the verge of hysteria. "I have confined myself to this miserable house and have gone no farther than a few kilometers to visit friends."

"I believe you. I do not doubt that you have acted with discretion, my dear Madame de Staël. However, there are those who stoop to curry the favor of the First Consul by denouncing those he despises with false information. I must warn you that if you are not out of the country by October 7, he will send the police to remove you."

Madame de Staël was severely shaken. "*Who* could have told lies about me?" she demanded.

"There is one," Régnault replied, "whose letters have had great impact on Bonaparte . . . they come from an authoress."

"Stephanie de Genlis!" Germaine cried out. "Of course! That witch! She has always envied my popularity and the fame *Delphine* has brought me!"

"You must leave at once. I have arranged for you to stay with a friend whom I trust implicitly . . . Madame de La Tour, who lives in the vicinity. You can decide there on more permanent plans.

Madame de Staël calmed herself. She knew the urgency of her plight.

"Thank you, Régnault, for warning me."

Germaine spent the next days with her children and a maid hiding at the home of Madame de La Tour. Unable to tolerate the confinement, she wrote to Joseph Bonaparte, asking him to intervene for her with his brother.

Then, she sent a letter directly to Napoleon. "If you want me to leave France," she wrote, "let me have a passport to go to Germany and grant me eight days in Paris to obtain necessary funds I will need for my journey. I must also take my daughter to a doctor. She is only six years old and the voyage has made her ill.

"There is no country in the world where such a request would be refused. I beseech you once more, give me the benefit of your leniency and allow me to live in my father's house at Saint Ouen. I shall leave in the spring, when the season will allow my children to travel safely."

It was Joseph who replied by the same courier saying his brother had denied the request. Without official word from the First Consul himself, however, Madame de Staël ignored Joseph's report and boldly returned to Maffliers.

Though she refused to be intimidated, the Baroness was terrified, seeming neither to sleep nor work.

On the third day, when no gendarme had appeared, the Baroness put aside her fears by inviting women friends for dinner. She took a seat at the table where she had a clear view of the highway through the tall windows overlooking the garden.

Suddenly, in mid-sentence, Madame de Staël started from her chair as though propelled. There was a stranger dismounting from his horse in the road in front of the house. At the iron gate, he rang the bell. Though he wore no uniform, she knew from the horseman's stiff-backed posture that he was the gendarme she had expected.

The Baroness took leave of her guests and walked to the garden to meet the caller.

"Good afternoon, Madame de Staël. I am Lieutenant Gaudriot of the gendarmarie of Versailles. In deference to your station, I wear civilian clothes. I have an order signed by Consul Bonaparte to say you must leave France immediately."

Germaine nodded. Turning from the lieutenant, she stood silent, her senses recording her surroundings as if this were her last day on earth . . . a garden basking in the warmth of an October sun, the fragrance of autumn flowers and rich green grass, a scattering of white clouds drifting lazily across the clear blue sky.

Within moments, she faced the gendarme resolutely.

"You cannot order a woman and her children to leave her home at a moment's notice," she declared. "I need several days to make arrangements."

"Madame, you are a foreigner under police jurisdiction," he replied apologetically.

"You will return with me and my children to Paris," she commanded, "and try to secure a three-day extension so I can plan my journey."

He bowed graciously. "Very well, but you must leave immediately."

Within a half hour, Madame de Staël and her son and daughter crowded into the carriage with as much luggage as the coach could hold.

The accommodating lieutenant was impressed with his illustrious charge. "I have read all your books," he said to her as he closed the carriage door. "I have just finished *Delphine.*"

Madame de Staël had managed to conceal her true feelings and maintained her dignity. She felt that her heart would break . . . she could not leave France again for she feared she might never return.

"You see, Monsieur," she replied, "the consequences of being a woman of intellect. If there are any females in your family who aspire to self-expression, independence and fame you might best prepare them for what to expect for their pains."

Lieutenant Gaudriot consented to stop at the Récamier home in Saint-Brice where General Junot was waiting for his wife.

When Juliette met the carriage in the courtyard, she and Germaine fell into each other's arms in tears. Also there, as a guest of the Récamiers, was General Junot, who had been Bonaparte's aide-de-camp at the first Italian campaign. Touched by the pathos of this scene, he comforted Germaine as she was about to leave. "I will go to St. Cloud tomorrow to visit the First Consul. I'll speak to him on your behalf."

In Paris, Madame de Staël rented an elegant manor house at 540 rue de Lille. Lieutenant Guadriot arranged to extend her stay three days. After the extension passed, he dropped in every morning to remind her that she would have to leave the next day. Each time she swallowed her pride and asked for another day. With these entreaties, Germaine gained a week.

As he promised, General Junot reported on his interview with Bonaparte.

"I pleaded with him as I would for my sister," he said sadly. "The man stamped his foot like a frustrated child and demanded, 'What interest have you in this woman?'

"'The interest I always take in the oppressed and the brokenhearted. If you tried, General,' I told him, 'you could make this woman your devoted admirer.'

"'I *know*,' Bonaparte shouted. 'When the devil is sick, the devil a saint would be. When the devil is well, the devil a saint was he. No! No more truces with her. She asked for it. Let her suffer the consequences.'"

Germaine contemplated her exile as she would death.

It is easier to brave the prospect of the scaffold than loss of country, she mused. In all legal codes, perpetual banishment is considered the severest penalty. Yet, here in France, one man casually inflicts this sentence as a whim while honorable judges impose lesser punishments on ordinary criminals. No statesman, no writer will express his opinion freely if he might be banished for his honesty. No man will dare challenge the state if it cost him his family's happiness. I shall try to draw attention, in my exile, to show why no sovereign should ever be allowed to have the arbitrary power of banishment.

On her last day in Paris, Madame de Staël still had no plans for her future. Julie Bonaparte, Joseph's wife, called on her at the rue de Lille.

"Joseph is with Napoleon," she told Madame de Staël, "making a final appeal for you. Would you and your children wish to spend your days in France with us at Morfontaine?" Germaine could not refuse.

When Joseph returned to his country estate, he called his guest into his study.

"We have all tried . . . all of us . . . Junot, d'Angély, Fontanes, my brother Lucien, and many others . . . to help you. None of us has succeeded."

"It is a bizarre destiny," Germaine told her benefactor, "to be exiled by one brother while the other is a dear friend. I cannot understand Napoleon's dogged determination to be rid of me."

At that moment, Germaine suddenly experienced an exquisite thrill coursing through her veins. She had a sense of power she had never fully realized: Bonaparte feared her! "That man," she murmured to herself, "that intrepid soldier, is afraid of me!"

Joseph was unaware of Germaine's intense emotion. He grew thoughtful and then said, "My brother is convinced of the ascendancy of the salons over the minds of the people of Paris. He despises their hostesses for exercising manipulative power. He worked himself into a state of panic over being forced to accept the influence that drawing rooms had on the pens of philosophers, writers, politicians and journalists. He vowed to prevent the repetition of this concentration of authority. For him, you and your methods are formidable enemies to be eradicated."

Resigned to her exile and bouyed by her sense of power over Bonaparte, Madame de Staël expressed her gratitude to Julie and Joseph for their understanding and hospitality and undertook making arrangement to depart.

With passports Joseph obtained she decided to go to Germany where her books had been acclaimed and she was certain she would be welcome.

Benjamin Constant, hearing the news, rushed to Morfontaine to comfort her. He coveted his solitude but agonized over her suffering. When Germaine left with the two children, Benjamin went along, promising to travel with her till they were well within the borders of German territory.

En route, the evicted Baroness instructed her driver to go through Paris. She cherished every moment, savored each street, each building, each tree, each bridge across the Seine, the noisy hawkers, the bustling crowds. The rich, upholstered interior of her berline had become more her home than chateaux or town houses.

As the carriage passed through the last city gate, Madame de Staël contemplated her conversation with Joseph.

My pride and my ecstasy is that Bonaparte fears me, she reflected. This is also my terror. I sink at the prospect of my exile and am not prepared to endure its boredom. But I want no humiliating remedies. I have a woman's fears. But they cannot make a hypocrite or slave of me.

Chapter 10
Germany

The shadowy solemnity of the Cathedral of St. Etienne in Metz was suffocating for the Baroness de Staël.

"I'll wait here," she told Benjamin. "Go on ahead with the children and get a close view of the altar."

Germaine leaned against a marble column at the rear of the dimly lit nave and watched Albertine and Auguste, hand in hand with Benjamin, move slowly toward the apse. The trio was dwarfed by the stately Gothic splendor of the huge structure that had been completed after three hundred years of loving labor by generations of craftsmen who lived in the Moselle Valley surrounding the city.

A swift, cool draft brushed past Madame de Staël like the ghost of a deceased parishioner.

"Hurry," she called out in a hushed tone to Benjamin and her children. "Let us leave this dismal place. I have enough of sight-seeing."

Benjamin held Germaine's elbow as they followed the children down the steps of the cathedral.

"In the synagogue we visited," Madame de Staël lamented, "it was the piercing wails of those mourners. Here, the dark and gloomy tombs. They tear at my nerves. I feel that death is stalking my father, my children, my friends."

"Your anxiety is understandable," Benjamin said trying to calm Germaine as they walked back toward their hotel. "You are going to leave a country you love to travel among unfamiliar surroundings—another culture, a strange language. But your fears are baseless."

"No. The challenge of change excites me," Germaine replied. "It is what I sense that distresses me. I have a premonition that someone dear to me is threatened. I don't know whether to go on or stay here in Metz."

"You should be tempted to remain here indefinitely," Benjamin said, "and enjoy the overwhelming ovation you have had."

The Baroness's reputation as a celebrated woman of letters piqued the curiosity of the people in the department of Moselle. Her persecution at the hands of a tyrant aroused their sympathy. The district prefect, Count Colchen, had greeted Madame de Staël when she drove into Metz and arranged a round of gay parties, soirées and fêtes in her honor. She extended her stay from a week to twelve days to accommodate the literary elite of the city and to satisfy her own fascination with Charles de Villers, a young French writer who had become an authority on German philosophy and letters.

Madame de Staël had detoured from her original itinerary to rendezvous with him. Departing from Paris, she learned that Villers, with whom she had carried on an intensive correspondence for several years, was on his way from his home in Germany to visit her. They decided to meet halfway.

Villers reached Metz first. He took over the entire spacious first floor of the Hotel de Pont-à-Housson with his robust mistress, Frau Senator von Rodde, her husband and children. Arriving later, the Baroness had to settle for the second floor, where she and her entourage of several servants, were crammed into more modest quarters.

Germaine, who was now thirty-seven, was charmed by Villers' brilliance and youth. He was ten years younger than she. They met alone each morning in her small boudoir to discuss the philosophical movement that was emerging in Germany.

She presided over the tête-à-têtes with urbane majesty, dressed in striking ensembles which she crowned with colorful turbans, more fashionable headgear than bonnets.

Villers expounded on Immanuel Kant's work in metaphysics and epistemology. Germaine listened with rapt attention, eager to prepare herself for meetings with the German intellectuals.

"And Goethe? Schiller, Wieland and Klopstock? How do they project the theories of the romantic movement?" she asked.

"In drama," Villers replied, "they can expand their concepts with greater passion and grandeur and not be bound by pragmatic reality. The theatre is the center of culture around which the arts revolve."

During their second meeting, Germaine sensed that young Villers' interest in her went beyond the mind. By their third encounter, he pursued her as a lover. Benjamin and Frau von Rodde were chagrined by the sudden turn in Villers' attitude. Herr von Rodde, indifferent to his wife's paramour, whom she had entertained long before their marriage, was amused by the absurd ménage.

The daily talks between Germaine and Villers escalated into violent arguments when the young man, a confirmed Germanophile, attacked French politics and literature. "The Germans have far outstripped your intellectuals in France," he maintained.

Madame de Staël was intrigued. She vigorously defended her countrymen and skillfully deflected Villers' advances. The disagreements and the rejection intensified his passion and made Germaine more desirable.

The Baroness was tempted by Villers, but uncertain. To clear her mind she took a tour of the sights of Metz with Benjamin and her children.

By the time she returned to the hotel that evening she had made up her mind about the ardent Villers. Germaine's exile and her future were hardly secure. She needed someone more familiar, someone she could count on. This was not the time to launch a new relationship.

She decided to leave Metz.

"Oh, mama!" Albertine said plaintively. "I'm so cold and the snow is falling again."

Madame de Staël drew her daughter close beside her on the seat of the coach and tucked a lap robe around her. In the distance the horizon had been obliterated by the same white blanket that covered the earth. The snow was heavy enough to force the de Staël postillion to drive with extreme caution. When they reached the villages, their slow pace stirred the householders to come to their windows. Curious eyes in somber, vacant faces peered at the coach as it went by.

Albertine shrank back from the stares and snuggled between her mother and Benjamin.

After traveling almost two hundred kilometers in bleak, dismal weather, the entourage reached the murky waters of the Rhine. Crossing the river by barge, they were greeted by the first raging snow storm of their journey. As they grew closer to Frankfurt, hardly a day passed without a heavy snow fall. They stopped only at night, persisting through deep drifts that often slowed the horses to a halt.

"Shall I read you another story?" Benjamin asked Albertine, "or do you want to hear about the standing ovation I once received on stage when I was no older than you?"

The red-haired child brightened. "Tell us about *you*," she enthused, "when you were little."

"You have been an actor?" thirteen-year old Auguste asked.

"It was at the home of my aunt when I was visiting my cousin Charles in Lausanne," Benjamin began. "The family turned their main drawing room into a theatre and invited several distinguished citizens to see Voltaire's comedy *Nanine*. The great philosopher, himself, was in the audience. It was a formal affair with dinner to be held later in the evening after the performance. I was dismayed, for at that age I had a voracious appetite.

"Both my cousin and I were starved. I could not wait so I went into the kitchen and searched every cupboard till I found some bread. I was so excited with my discovery that I ran into the drawing room with the loaf under my arm, looking for my cousin. I sailed onto the stage from the wings into the scene of the play, which was already in progress. I was oblivious to what was going on. I saw the boy among the guests and called out, 'Charles! Look! I found something to eat!' I waved the bread at him. I have never heard such applause since."

Albertine and Auguste clapped their hands.

"Oh, Benjamin," Albertine exclaimed. "What would we do without you? I am so bored with Germany. Only *you* make us happy. I would rather go back to Switzerland, so we could be with dear Grandpapa."

As the carriage lumbered slowly along, Benjamin told of more boyhood experiences, embellishing them all with twists of humor. Running out of true stories he fabricated others. When Albertine grew tired and dozed, he entertained Auguste with word games. By the time they reached Frankfurt, Albertine had developed a fever.

Madame de Staël rushed her daughter to bed in their hotel. There was no question but that Albertine needed medical attention, and that neither she nor Benjamin knew anyone in the city to whom they could turn. They had to rely on the hotel to recommend a doctor.

The physician, a heavy-set, brooding man with a full beard and piercing grey eyes, examined the sick child as Germaine looked on anxiously.

He shook his head. "Scarlet fever," he announced without feeling.

"How serious is her illness?" Madame de Staël asked.

"It is too early to tell," the doctor replied. "There are several cases of the disease in the city. One little girl down the street from here died yesterday."

Germaine shuddered.

"What can you do for my daughter?"

"Very little. Keep her warm and comfortable. I'll come back."

For two days, the fever persisted. Madame de Staël did not move from her daughter's side. She sat motionless, haunted by the feeling of foreboding she had had at the Cathedral.

On the third day, the fever broke and Albertine showed signs of recovering.

"It is just a bad cold," the impassive physician remarked when he returned.

"There was reason for worry," Benjamin told Germaine. "I was deeply concerned. But you see now that your presentiment was imagined."

"Perhaps," she replied, but could not shake the gloom of her premonition. As she waited for Albertine's full recovery she wrote her father. "I don't know how I would have survived without Benjamin," she told him.

Madame de Staël made preparations to move on to Weimar.

"I'm returning to Paris," Benjamin informed her.

"You cannot leave us now!" Germaine was frantic. "You have come this far, why not continue all the way?"

"I promised to see you safely into Germany. I never planned to go farther than Frankfurt," Benjamin said adamantly. "You knew that. I have business to attend to."

Constant did not confess that his business was personal, and with another woman. She was Charlotte von Hardenberg, with whom he had fallen in love when they first met, eleven years earlier. Though they divorced their respective spouses, they were never able to consummate their affair and had lost track of each other except for an occasional letter or news they had through friends. Benjamin learned that Charlotte had remarried, divorced again and remarried for the third time. She knew of Constant's attachment to Germaine . . . the main reason she and Benjamin were apart. Away from Charlotte, Benjamin forgot her until one of her letters caught up with him and his old passion resurged. Charlotte was a pretty, gentle, undemanding woman with no disposition for the intellectual. She was interested only in devoting herself to a loving husband. After his erratic gypsy existence with Germaine, Constant yearned for a quiet domestic life with a submissive wife.

Just before Madame de Staël's last banishment, Benjamin had received a note from Charlotte asking him to visit her in Geneva. He had agreed, but then Germaine's predicament diverted him.

Now, in dreary surroundings of a small chamber in a Frankfurt hotel, Benjamin agonized. Yearning for Charlotte, he had to make his break from Germaine.

"You cannot leave us among strangers," Germaine said petulantly. "I cannot face the brutish, insensitivity of these people alone. You saw the callousness of the doctor."

"He is not typical. You should not judge the German people by one man and a handful of overworked hotel servants. You chose to come to Germany when you could have gone to Coppet."

Germaine refused to listen to reason and played on Benjamin's sense of duty as she would the strings of her harp.

Benjamin, bullied and beaten, caved in. "Very well," he promised, "I'll meet you in Weimar in January."

But, in truth, it was Albertine, with silence and wistful eyes, who had convinced him.

Chapter 11
"Delphine est Charmante"

I am received like a sister of the First Consul," Madame de Staël wrote her father from the palace of the ruling family of the Duchy of Weimar, "and I am treated like a royal princess."

The Baroness was exhilarated. She was at last encountering the attention in Germany that she had hoped for. The headlines of newspapers showered her with praise that would certainly reach Bonaparte. He could not deny her international acceptance. The smallest detail of the movements of this "famous French woman of letters" was reported by the journalists who trailed after her like lemmings.

Germaine was taking Weimar by storm.

The aristocracy of this remote duchy had awaited her arrival with apprehension, fearing the overwhelming presence of a worldly Parisian eager to flaunt her sophistication.

Instead, they were enchanted.

Madame de Staël immediately put the entire court at ease.

"There is a poetry of the soul that characterizes all Germans," she said graciously to the Duke and Duchess of Weimar.

She flattered them with comments about their daily life, children, music, literature and whatever was being discussed by the nobles as the Duchess introduced her.

Germaine had experienced a change of heart about the country after she left boorish, desolate Frankfurt and journeyed on to Weimar.

Her entourage had crossed snow-covered mountains under clear open skies, penetrated thick pine forests and found quaint, medieval villages nestled deep in protected valleys. The Christmas season had begun and the spirit was joyous.

At night the de Staël party stopped at rustic country inns or stayed with townsmen or farmers in homes darkened by tobacco smoke. Together, they joined in the gaiety as the master and mistress of the house improvised on the harpsichord and the children sang or played tunes on the mouth organ. Occasionally, Madame de Staël took Auguste and Albertine, bundled warmly against the cold, to walk the snowy streets to listen to carollers as they trudged along serenading the villagers. Families opened their doors to offer the singers spicy, steaming holiday punch.

Germaine was moved by the sentimental warmth within the families and their dedication to music. She extended her stay for two days in Gotha, less than fifty kilometers from her destination, to take lessons on the harmonica.

The usually staid and aloof Duchess of Weimar was as charmed as the lesser aristocracy by Madame de Staël's easy style and her unabashed enthusiasm for Germany.

As in Metz, Germaine was feted at dinner parties and soirées. Asked to lecture on her writings, she learned that everyone who could read had devoured *Delphine.* The book had been published in three different translations and was completely sold out. "La Delphine est charmante," her new friends told her in guttural French that jarred her sensibilities. She smiled warmly.

Madame de Staël also conquered the reluctant intellectuals of Weimar, though the conquest was neither instant nor complete.

"They create remarkably believable excuses to stay away from us," Duke Charles Augustus explained to Germaine. The scholars deliberately avoided aristocratic dilettantes by retreating to obscure havens in outlying villages of the duchy.

But eventually the Duke succeeded in summoning the best minds of his dukedom. One by one they arrived . . . Goethe, Schiller, Wieland, Böttiger, Fichte, Klopstock.

Madame de Staël was gracious and agreeable. She drew out the scholars by absorbing them in parallels between German individualism and French urbanity, then with the similarity in the social life of the two cultures. She waited patiently, pondering on the translations of their responses. Then, she pressed on to inquire about the romantic movement in the arts that was emerging among German philosophers.

The scholars were flattered. The talk bristled with ideas that were new to Germaine. As she listened she took pages of notes.

Turning to literature, Madame de Staël tried to persuade them of the superiority of French writers and poets. The Weimar intellectuals disagreed sharply. Several times Goethe drove her to despair with his obstinacy as they parried, neither able to claim a touché. The German genius finally had to admit that "Madame de Staël is amiable and displays her mental and vocal agility with brilliance." His colleagues grudgingly agreed.

Within days, the Baroness presided over the crusty sessions with the brainy flock encircling her in her own quarters. Dressed in heavy green, gray, or burgundy velvet robes, with her inevitable turban, she brandished her Queen Hatshepsut sceptre. Stimulated and aroused, she encouraged the discussion of theories on Romanticism knowing these concepts had not yet penetrated beyond the borders of the German states.

Germaine was no longer haunted by ominous premonitions. By the time Benjamin arrived in Weimar in January, back from his clandestine visit with Charlotte in Geneva, she had filled several notebooks with quotations and her own impressions and analyses.

"I'm planning a book which I shall title *De l'Allemagne*," she told Benjamin. "It will explain the revolutionary thinking that is evolving here in Germany. There is much I disagree with but the rest of Europe must be introduced to these exciting concepts."

Constant joined the intellectual circle and handled himself with greater restraint than Germaine. With his grasp of the language, he was able to translate quickly and clarify the nuances of the language that gave Germaine better insight into the theories. Now, interchanges with the Germans were smoother and carried off in an atmosphere of stronger mutual respect. Only on occasion, did the differences grow bitter as the Weimarians clashed with their visitors and among themselves.

The Duke continued as a gracious host, filling the social calendar with gala events, and included special theatre performances to demonstrate the innovations in German drama. He even catered to the youthful tastes of Auguste and Albertine by arranging comic-opera productions. The children were thrilled.

Madame de Staël's exile was no secret to the Germans, who feared the long arm of Bonaparte's police force but respected her efforts and Benjamin's to avoid discussing international affairs. Though both sides maintained a discreet silence about Bonaparte, they grew more and more anxious about the fate of Europe as his tyranny escalated. Napoleon was increasing the size of his armies, extending the borders of France, forcing the British to declare war again and aggravating more plots against his life.

Germaine felt secure in the vast distance she had put between herself and the First Consul and was counting on her foreign triumphs to agitate him.

They did.

He issued orders to the French Ambassador in the Duchy of Saxony to prohibit the display of Germaine's *Delphine* at the book market in Leipzig.

"Bonaparte will not accomplish what he hopes," she told Benjamin with complaisance. "Forbidding the sale of my books will only increase the interest in and demand for them."

Early in March of 1804, Madame de Staël knew her frenzied pace in Weimar had to come to an end. She had prolonged her stay to prevent breaking ties with Benjamin, and through him, her ties with France. But she was ready to depart for Berlin.

This time, reassured by the glory of her lionization, she was better prepared to respect and accept Constant's wish to leave for Switzerland and Paris.

"You have never been more kind, loving and devoted," Benjamin said sincerely, for her acclaim had mellowed Germaine. "I am profoundly sad that we are parting, but you have achieved what you were seeking among the Germans. They welcome you as the priestess of liberty, love and duty. You will not be lonely. Even Bonaparte cannot stem your influence."

"Lofty praise," Germaine shrugged. "It is you I want. But, since you are determined to leave, I must extract a promise from you for the sake of our daughter."

Free to go, Constant would agree to anything. "I promise whatever you ask."

"Then tell me you will never marry another woman."

Benjamin was shaken but showed no signs of his emotion.

"I promise," he replied.

The next day, on the morning of March 6, Madame de Staël left for Berlin with her children and servants.

That night, Benjamin found a brothel and dispelled his gloom.

Chapter 12
Berlin

The Baroness de Staël sleepily lifted her head from her pillow. There was a loud, rapid knocking at her door.

She opened her eyes. The knocking persisted.

Now, she was fully awake in the apartment of her hotel on the quay of the Sprée in Berlin. She was again the idol of a court, feted and favored as a distinguished visitor. Her deep sleep was brought on by exhaustion after that evening's social affair, which climaxed the gala festivities since her arrival in the city. The events of the ball tumbled into her consciousness. A lingering hint in her room of the perfumes of the ladies of the court was another reminder of the extravaganza. The Baroness had been celebrating the Queen's birthday. She had ordered an elaborate gown that was completed just in time for the occasion. She had entered the ballroom where two thousand men and women in the finest, most fashionable attire, glistening in gold braid and diamonds, had assembled to greet King Frederich Wilhelm and Queen Louisa of Prussia.

The monarchs arrived to the sound of clashing cymbals. The hushed excitement burst into gaiety and spread through the crowd.

The Baroness was presented to the royal couple who welcomed her kindly and without pretension.

The Queen was charming and distractingly beautiful. "What a stunning gown," she told Germaine. "The color is most becoming." She hesitated, then went on. "Madame de Staël, we are flattered that you have chosen to come to Berlin. You have been highly regarded here for a long time and you have no more sincere an admirer than myself."

The memory of this exalted encounter with the Queen flashed through Germaine's mind like accelerated scenes of a play, and now abruptly vanished with the banging on her door.

"Madame la Baronne," her maid called as she knocked, "there is someone outside, beneath your window. He's anxious to talk with you."

Germaine threw off the covers, pulled on a warm wool robe and hurried across the room to let her servant in.

"Who is out there?" she asked.

"It is Prince Louis Ferdinand."

"What time is it?" Germaine asked.

"It is morning, Madame. Eight o'clock," the young woman replied, lighting the candles on the walls and on the commode.

Germaine took off her lacy head covering and ran her fingers through her black curls. She tossed her head about, looked in the mirror and shrugged. The Prussian prince had seen her often enough at public affairs and in the privacy of her apartments where they dined alone. If he was eager to talk with her he would have to see her before she prepared her toilette.

Separating the heavy draperies, Madame de Staël opened the large glass doors and stepped onto the balcony.

Prince Louis was just below, astride a sleek black stallion. How stunningly sedate he is, she observed.

"What can be so urgent this early in the morning?" Germaine called down. "We left the ball just three hours ago."

"I have horrendous news," the Prince called up to her. "The French kidnapped the Duc Louis d'Enghien on Baden soil and transported him back to face a military commission. He was preemptively shot twenty-four hours after being taken to Paris."

"That's impossible," Germaine said in disbelief. "It can only be a rumor that the enemies of France are spreading to incite animosity against us." She was unable to believe that even Bonaparte would order or sanction such an atrocity.

"But it is *true!*" Louis cried. "I'll be back with proof," he said, urging his horse into a gallop. Germaine heard him shout, "Revenge or death!" as he rode off.

Madame de Staël was still dressing when Louis returned less than a half hour later. She invited him into her chamber while her maid hastily adjusted the closings on her gown.

"Here," the Prince said, jamming a copy of the *Moniteur* into her hands. "You can see the decree for yourself." He hovered over Germaine as she read about the heinous act that was carried out by General René Savary.

An article in the newspaper, the government-controlled publication, revealed that the Duc d'Enghien, a Bourbon aristocrat descended from the same line of royal blood as Prince Louis Ferdinand, had been executed by official decree two days earlier, on March 21.

Germaine was horrified. "The Duke has been linked to the Pichegru-Cadoudal conspiracy, but he was not at all involved."

In February, Georges Cadoudal, a commander in the Breton rebellion, had collaborated with General Pichegru to assassinate Bonaparte during a ceremonial parade. The two men and several others had been encouraged and financed by the British. The plot failed. Cadoudal was arrested and confessed, implicating a Bourbon prince. The nobleman he involved, the Count d'Artois, had managed to evade apprehension.

"Bonaparte needed a scapegoat—any available Bourbon would suit him," Louis told Germaine. "The Duc d'Enghien had no inclination for intrigue. He was in Baden visiting his mistress when he was snatched from his bed in the middle of the night. The First Consul violated Bavarian sovereignty by sending agents across the border to kidnap him. It was a plot coldly planned by Bonaparte and abetted by Charles Talleyrand."

"I should have expected it of Talleyrand."

"The gendarmes took d'Enghien to the fortress at Vincennes," Louis went on. "He was given a mock trial that lasted five minutes. Then, in the moat of the castle, by the light of a torch held close to his head, he was summarily shot by a firing squad. He was denied the last rites and buried immediately in the ditch next to the spot where he fell."

Every court in Europe was aghast at the horror of Bonaparte's act.

"This monster," Madame de Staël told the King and Queen, "has violated the international law of nations, the constitution of France and public decency and humanity everywhere. I was the first to defy this enemy of mankind," she declared.

The Baroness contemplated going back to Coppet. She believed that the execution was a sign of the return to revolutionary atrocities and that the guillotine would be resurrected. As days passed, she sensed that though Bonaparte would again resort to murder, he was more inclined to terrorize through suspense and fear rather than carnage. He was forcing the French to be grateful for the evil he did not commit and for his mercy when he allowed a man to live. What he might and could do was more terrifying than the deed itself. He had staged a drama to prove that he was capable of any infamy.

Madame de Staël missed the intellectual community she had enjoyed in Weimar. She weighed her options: Berlin, Weimar again or her father in Switzerland.

Remembering an introduction Goethe had given her to Augustus Wilhelm Schlegel, she called on the famed philosopher-writer.

There was an instant spark of affinity between two brilliant minds, two lucid conversationalists. For Germaine, it was exclusively an intellectual attraction. For Schlegel, it became a physical passion as well.

"I have met a man who is supremely well informed," Germaine wrote her cousin Albertine Necker de Saussure with whom she corresponded regularly to learn of her father's health. "He is the most profound, literate human being I have ever known."

To Jacques Necker, she wrote, "I have become increasingly captivated by Schlegel's genius and am trying to persuade him to come back with me to Coppet. He would be invaluable in providing background for my book on Germany, and he could perform minor tutoring duties for the children for which I would pay him well. But he hesitates to leave Berlin because he has a distinguished career here."

At thirty-six, he was the pedant of the romantic movement in Germany, a respected critic, an exacting scholar familiar with all the literature of modern Europe, an authority in every field of knowledge he pursued, a poet of merit, and a linguist. As fluent in French and English as he was in his own tongue, he had translated sixteen Shakespearean plays into German.

For Madame de Staël, Augustus Wilhelm did not qualify as a lover. He was small and unattractive, if not altogether ugly. He was also vain, self-important, quarrelsome and poor.

Less than a month after the execution of the Duc d'Enghien, Madame de Staël's indecisiveness about her next destination came to an abrupt halt.

She received a letter from her cousin Albertine, telling her that Jacques Necker was dangerously ill. "It is imperative that you return at once," her cousin urged.

"My father is dead!" Madame de Staël screamed in panic, and set about assembling her children, her servants and her belongings. She sent off a message to Schlegel, telling him to prepare to leave with her the next morning. She was so overwrought that it didn't occur to her that he would not be eager to console her or that he might refuse to accompany her to Switzerland.

At dawn, in a jam-packed berline, Madame de Staël reached

Schlegel's lodgings. He sat waiting for her with two small bags and a trunk of books. The coachmen succeeded in tying these extra pieces to the roof and Germaine made a place for Schlegel between herself and her son, keeping Albertine close at her other side.

Teetering precariously under its weight, the carriage finally adjusted and rolled steadily forward to the south.

Germaine was near hysteria with concern for her father.

"Here," Schlegel said, handing her a letter. "This will tell you what I feel for you, and that I am someone to count on in your despair."

Germaine was calmed as she read the document outlining the conditions Schlegel made for placing himself in her service.

> I *declare that you have every right over me and that I have none over you. Dispose of my person and of my life; command, forbid—I shall obey you in everything. I desire no other happiness than what you see fit to give me. I want to own nothing, I want to owe everything to your generosity. I am proud of being your property. I do not know whether it is right to surrender so completely to another human being. Do not abuse your power over me. You might easily make me miserable while I would be defenseless against you. Above all, I beseech you, do not ever banish me from your presence.*
>
> *Your slave,*
 A. W. Schlegel

"Benjamin! I did not expect to find you here at Weimar!" Madame de Staël exclaimed with surprise. She introduced Constant and Schlegel in the public room of the hotel where she and her entourage planned to spend the night. "I was sure you would have been in Switzerland long ago."

Constant flushed.

"I traveled slowly to enjoy my journey," he said evasively. "When I finally reached Lausanne, I learned your father was failing. I thought only of how distressed you would be and I returned immediately to wait for you here. I could not endure the thought that you would have to bear the strain alone."

"You are very kind, Benjamin, my dear," Germaine replied, grasping his hands. "I have not been alone. Herr Schlegel has been at my side since we left Berlin."

"Countess Elizabeth has offered to stay with you while you are here in Weimar," Benjamin told her. "She is waiting for you in your apartment."

Augustus Wilhelm and Madame de Staël went up to her suite. Germaine was unaware that Benjamin had detained the children and remained behind with them.

"Monsieur Constant has asked me to talk with you," the Countess said warmly. "He is too distressed to tell you the news himself."

"What news?" Germaine asked, the color draining from her face.

"Your cousin," the woman chose her words carefully, "was with your father night and day."

"*Was?*"

"Your father called for you again and again. It was on April 10, with your name on his lips," Countess Elizabeth faltered for a moment, "that he died."

"He *is* dead! I knew it all along!" Germaine cried in anguish. "I was not with him when he needed me most."

Madame de Staël crumpled and fell to the floor with piercing screams. Benjamin rushed in when he heard her cries and, with Schlegel, tried to restrain her as she flailed about like a woman possessed.

"I should never have gone to Germany," she called out in self-reproach, striking the floor with her open palms. "I should have acknowledged my presentiment and gone back to Coppet. Instead, I went off selfishly in search of inspiration and glory."

Benjamin fled the room in search of a doctor. When they returned, the physician tried to give Germaine a sedative but she pushed him away.

Finally, after four hours of exhausting self-condemnation, Germaine lapsed into silence. Schlegel helped her off the floor and onto a chaise. Dishevelled and pale, she looked at her friends.

"Today is April 22, my birthday. I am thirty-eight and my father is dead."

The Duke of Weimar and Goethe came the next day to pay their condolences.

"There was no one like him," she told them. "There never will be anyone like him. I have lost not only my father, but my friend, my brother. He was the best part of me, the only noble part of me."

The steady stream of visitors who came to her apartment served as a tonic to Germaine. She forced herself to be gracious and accepted their gestures of sympathy as a tribute. By the end of a week, she was able to control her grief. She also regained sufficient strength to resume her quarreling with Benjamin.

When her guests left late in the afternoon, she had dinner with her children, Benjamin and Augustus Wilhelm. Later, feigning weariness, she sent them all off to their rooms. Then, making certain that Benjamin had retired, she called Schlegel back and they talked long into the night.

But the walls of the rooms were thin, and the sounds of their voices reached Benjamin. He tossed about in bitterness.

"You betray me," he told her one morning. "It fell to me to break the sorrow of your father's death to you. I set aside my own plans for you . . . willingly. I have carried out my duty as a faithful, devoted member of your family. You treat me as you would a servant."

"You have no right to condemn me in my grief," Germaine protested. "Augustus Wilhelm has become a dear friend. He supplies me with impelling ideas for my manuscript and will tutor my children." She was offended by Benjamin's accusations. "He means nothing else to me."

They left Weimar after a nine-day stay. As they crossed the flat plains and low mountains of Saxon Germany, Benjamin repented, moved by Germaine's suffering and determined to be compassionate. With Schlegel, he tried to distract her from her sorrow. There were pleasant intervals when they discussed politics, literature and religion, often slipping into provocative, amiable arguments. Most of the two-and-a-half week journey was fraught with dissension. Benjamin avoided direct confrontation with Germaine by encouraging fourteen-year-old Auguste to join the conversation and by playing games with Albertine.

In the larger towns where they stopped to spend the night, Benjamin would disappear, not to return until the next morning as the party was ready to leave. Occasionally, he succeeded in finding what he looked for . . . a prostitute in a local brothel.

When the entourage crossed the borders into Switzerland and drove through familiar villages and hamlets, Madame de Staël began to envision with dread her arrival at the large empty family chateau. On the outskirts of Coppet, suddenly overwhelmed with what lay ahead of her, she panicked.

Disturbed by her uncontrollable shaking, Benjamin urged the driver to press the horses. With the whip cracking above them, the animals galloped swiftly along the main street, lined with villagers hoping to see their celebrated resident.

Inside the courtyard at Coppet, a cluster of servants gathered to meet their chatelaine. Madame de Staël started to descend the coach and then let out a heart-rending scream. "I cannot bear to be here without him!" She fell, crumpling limply to the cobblestones before anyone could reach her. The servants carried her, almost unconscious, into the building.

It was May 19, 1804, Germaine de Staël was home at last.

The day before, May 18, had been a momentous one for the man she despised. Napoleon Bonaparte had been declared Emperor of France "by the Grace of God and the Constitution of the Republic." The French, who had guillotined Louis XVI to rid themselves of royalty, had been subdued by the Corsican's terrorism. Unwittingly, they had permitted the birth of another dynasty.

Madame de Staël was too grieved to notice.

Chapter 13
The New Aristocracy

S
he screamed in anguish . . . the torture was beyond endurance. Thrashing and writhing like a madwoman, she stripped her bed of linens and blankets. Her eyes watered, her cheeks burned, her mouth was dry, her hands clammy and cold. Pain pressed against her temples like a vise and lay on her chest with the weight of a boulder.

Germaine had thought she was prepared to face her father's death. She was wrong. The torments of hell could be no worse than her sorrow.

Why could she not die and escape this agony? Was she being punished for selfishness, for fleeing to Germany instead of returning to Coppet? Was she being condemned for irresponsibility, for the willful way she had lived her life, relying on her father to reveal her shortcomings and forgive her her mistakes? No matter how far from him she had lived, she heard his voice, she felt the power of his influence, guiding her with his protecting genius.

While he lived, nothing was impossible.

But he was dead! She should have responded to her premonitions and rushed to his side.

Germaine howled like a wounded animal.

Her cousin Albertine Necker de Saussure hastened into the chamber with Constant and Schlegel. She waved them off. They replaced the bed-covers and left.

Germaine put her hands to her throbbing head. Her mind burst with memories of her father . . . of herself as a small child when he first loomed large in her life, the furtive plotting against her mother, the private times at St. Ouen when she fell in love with him, the wonder of freedom when he encouraged her to express her passions, his tutoring during their travels when he taught her to know and appreciate France and its people, his sympathy and understanding before and during her marriage, his nurturing her genius, sharing the moments of his apotheosis when Frenchmen fell to their knees cheering and glorifying him, his comforting advice during the bloody terrors of the revolution, guiding her efforts in politics, his joy and patience in acting as father to her children.

Again, the reality of Necker's death, his absence, penetrated her consciousness. This time she was silent in her despair deep under the blankets like a frightened fawn under a cover of leaves.

The tapers had burned down to their holders, the eerie light of dawn filled the room. Germaine slipped out of bed and glided over to a marquetry commode. She picked up a small bottle, emptied its contents in her palm and took the dose of opium. In the haze of the mirror in front of her, she saw an aging woman with shaking hands. With the death of her father, Madame de Staël had lost her youth.

Back within the temporary security of her canopied bed, Germaine slowly came to realize that although she would never be completely happy again, there was still much in life to live for. Her children. Their education. Preserving the substantial Necker fortune, acting as its guardian to pass it on to his grandchildren. The greatest challenge was the Necker political legacy . . . restoring the liberty of the French people, freeing them from the tyranny of Bonaparte.

The memory of Necker, in death as in life, had a quieting effect on his daughter. She lapsed into a deep, drugged sleep.

Madame de Staël awakened in mid-afternoon. Sun streamed into the room. A maid responded to her ring on the bell pull. She went through the ritual of her toilette, put on a blue velvet robe and a matching turban and sat down at a bureau plat.

"Have Eugene Uginet come in," she requested of her servant.

"I'm ready," she told her faithful factotum. "I have much to do. My first task is to prepare a collection of my father's works and publish them with a preface I must write about his character and private life. Bring in Monsieur Necker's papers. It is time to secure his proper place in history."

"It is barely two weeks since you returned to Coppet," Benjamin complained. "This is the first moment I have had alone with you. Your home swarms with people and is as spirited as a gypsy camp."

Germaine and Benjamin passed through an iron gateway and walked northwest of the chateau down a narrow path into a wooded glen.

"I need friends to share my grief," she replied firmly.

"Your father's passing deserves a period of quiet respect."

"My mourning is no less than that. But I cannot grieve in solitude."

Madame de Staël's visitors called to express their condolences. She asked them to stay on as guests. They did. Besides Constant and Schlegel there were her cousin Albertine, her childhood friend Catherine Huber de Rilliet, Benjamin's cousin Rosalie Constant, a tidy spinster, professors from the University in Geneva, several aristocrats and scholars she had befriended in Germany, along with other intellectuals she had known for years.

"You drive yourself so . . . you work on your father's papers, analyze his finances and investments, manage your household. Then you spend the night entertaining."

"If I did not I would die of despair. The reality of my father's death never leaves me."

They reached a clearing in the forest where the towering trees created a natural cathedral. Long slanted rays of the sun filtered through shimmering leaves down to a small stone structure, a sylvan chapel.

Benjamin held back. Germaine approached the barred door through a carpet of blue and yellow wildflowers.

"The silence of a tomb," she murmured, "always overwhelms me. The solemnity of this one, where my father and mother lie, is unbearable."

After a few moments, Germaine retraced her steps to Benjamin and walked back with him to the chateau.

Madame de Staël was inconsolable in her grief. She fought to hide her pain but as she talked about Necker, tears welled up in her eyes. The guilt she felt for ignoring the premonitions of tragedy drew her to the mystical and compelled her to respond to every sign of clairvoyance. With any favorable incident or good fortune, she would say, "My father has obtained this for me."

Benjamin, caught up in her frantic activity once again, could not leave her.

Germaine's intellect was unaffected by her sorrow. For the first time in her life she was the head of a family and responsible for its wealth. She handled financial matters with amazing skill, made decisions without hesitation and made them soundly. She had not changed, Benjamin observed, she had simply become more intense, more determined to achieve her objectives, as though Necker were at her side. She lost none of her volatility but she no longer acted capriciously, like an impulsive child. She was more the daughter of Suzanne and Jacques Necker than she had been when they were alive.

Her desire to return to France and her preoccupation with Bonaparte became more acute.

Madame de Staël closely followed the trials of the conspirators who had been involved in the plot against Napoleon for which the Duc d'Enghien had been murdered. She was appalled by their treatment. Several were tortured, at least one maimed, and another, on order of the Emperor, smothered in his jail cell. George Cadoudal, the leader of the group, was guillotined on June 24. Only her friend General Moreau was spared, his prison term was commuted to banishment.

"Bonaparte," the Baroness de Staël told Constant and Schlegel, "has a genius for timing. Another man would have waited till the storm had passed. Not the Corsican tyrant. Taking advantage of the upheaval, he proclaimed himself Emperor at the height of the tempest. He cleverly diverted attention and succeeded where he might have failed during a calmer period."

When the weather grew balmy, Germaine and her guests gathered to converse on the lawns of Coppet. News from Paris was of an elaborate coronation to be held at the cathedral of Notre Dame.

"Napoleon is creating his own nobility," Germaine's cousin Albertine remarked. "It's ridiculous. The new Emperor demands that his family, all novices at manners of the court, parade in gaudy costumes."

"Paris mocks the efforts of this freshly minted aristocracy," Rosalie Constant commented.

"The Emperor's minions search the archives for documents on etiquette. Artists are designing coats of arms for the new royal family," Augustus Wilhelm Schlegel said.

Germaine laughed. "It is all worthy of a Molière comedy," she said. "Yesterday they were citizen and citizeness. Today they are 'your lordship' and 'your highness.'"

"It takes substantially more than a proclamation to rise above humble beginnings," Benjamin noted. "Yet, Bonaparte has named his brothers and sisters princes and princesses."

"He has baptized them with the blood of the Duc d'Enghien," Germaine added solemnly.

Bonaparte went beyond giving birth to his own nobility. He

introduced members of the former aristocracy to mingle in his court. Most of Madame de Staël's friends refused allegiance to the new regime. Several, like Mathieu de Montmorency, obtained vows from members of their families to do the same. One who deserted Germaine's camp and deeply wounded her by agreeing to serve the Emperor was her former lover, Louis de Narbonne, the father of her sons.

The Baron Claude-Ignace de Barante was an intelligent, courteous man of great distinction, a dedicated public servant with a loyal but objective view of the Consulate. He was the French Prefect, stationed in Geneva, to handle administrative and police matters in Vaudois territory.

Since Germaine de Staël resided within his jurisdiction he was assigned to keep surveillance on her.

On his first call to Coppet, he was impressed with the Baroness's cordiality. He already knew of her fame.

"Won't you join me and my other guests?" she asked.

"Perhaps the next time I'm in the village," he replied warily.

"Tomorrow?"

"Well, thank you. I will." He found it impossible to refuse.

The next day he joined a circle of eight or ten others who listened to a discourse on politics, literature and philosophy. Fascinated, he soon became a regular visitor at the chateau.

"There is no one kinder than Madame de Staël," Barante told his twenty-one-year-old son, Prosper, later as they drove together in the Prefect's carriage along the Geneva road to visit her. The young Barante whose mind was as keen as his father's was on leave from his post as attaché in the Ministry of the Interior in Paris. He was a handsome, slender youth, but shy and retiring and his father had to coerce him to accompany him.

"You will be inspired by the conversations in the Baroness's home," Baron Barante said. "Madame de Staël speaks brilliantly. Her criticisms of the Emperor prevent her from returning to Paris. One cannot help but sympathize with her."

The elder Barante was enchanted with the chatelaine of Coppet. The younger immediately fell under her spell.

Prosper de Barante was overwhelmed by his illustrious hostess. Her animated face, her flashing eyes, her enthusiasm, now edged with a touch of sadness, all were irresistible to the impressionable young man. He had never before been in the company of a more learned, knowledgeable woman. He needed no urging to revisit. Prosper appeared at Coppet more often than his father.

Germaine found it easy to be gracious to the Barantes. They were cultivated, elegant men from a respected noble family. And they worked for Bonaparte.

By the end of the summer, when Prosper had to return to Paris, he was certain that the emotion he felt for Madame de Staël was love, but he did not reveal his passion. He now called her Madame Germaine and agreed to be her secret agent in Bonaparte's court.

It was late October.

The well-groomed grounds of the Chateau of Coppet were deserted. Madame de Staël's guests no longer sauntered along the paths or gathered on the grass in clusters to chat animatedly. They had dispersed to spend the winter at their own homes or other sanctuaries after an exhilarating season with the new mistress of Coppet.

Germaine had finished editing her father's papers. Together with the preface of his life, the manuscript had been sent to her publisher.

"This book is one of your best," Benjamin told her. He sighed in contentment. Now that Madame de Staël's guests had gone, he only had to share her with her children, Augustus Wilhelm Schlegel and a few friends who came for dinner or to spend an evening from time to time. Though they still argued, there was a quiet harmony between them when they were alone.

"I'm pleased you think so," Germaine told Benjamin. "I've drawn on everything I know to present my father's life and works in fair perspective."

"I have never read a more sincere, more perfect expression of filial devotion than what you have written in your introduction," Benjamin added. "Now that it is finished and there are fewer demands on you . . . " He paused. Germaine saw his blue eyes soften behind their tinted spectacles. She sensed that he wished to talk of their personal affairs, a subject she had avoided all summer. She knew she had to face them for she was making plans for the winter. She let him go on.

"Your parents are dead. You have no father for your children. The burdens of a family should be shared. Marry me, Minette. We have spent many good years together. We can have more, working together as we have in the past. I can be father in fact to Albertine, and Auguste and Albert return my affection."

Germaine was not ready to release Benjamin, but she did not want to marry him. She tried to be kind.

"I cannot think of marriage now," she said evasively, "I'm drained and tired. I feel the loss of my father more than ever without the company of my friends."

"We could take a villa outside Lausanne till you are up to returning. We could study, read, research and write in peaceful surroundings. I could concentrate on my book on polytheism, you could resume your work on German romanticism."

Solitary, scholarly study and marital bliss might be what Benjamin sought but they were anathema to Germaine's temperament. There were other reasons she would not marry Benjamin. She would have to relinquish her title and close doors that would otherwise be open to her and her children. And a union would preclude new, interesting liaisons with other men. Young Prosper de Barante had reconfirmed her conviction that a woman must be loved and cherished all her life. Benjamin had rebuffed her too often when she sought tenderness. He was beyond giving her the kind of love she craved.

"It is too soon after my father's death for me to decide on the future. My sorrow surrounds me here. I must get away."

"Where? You cannot return to France."

"I'm well aware of that. My correspondence with Joseph Fouché and reports from Prosper are very clear. Bonaparte will not permit me to live in Paris, at least for now. I shall keep trying . . . "

"Where, then?" Benjamin asked.

"Somewhere in the south, perhaps. My doctor warns me to watch my health. He tells me to take less opium . . . a warm climate would help. I have always wanted to visit Italy. Would you come with me, Benjamin?"

"Italy?" Benjamin stalled. "My father has pressed me to visit him in Brévans and then attend several business matters for him in Paris. I have put him off too long."

"Then we can meet here again late in the spring," Germaine suggested.

Benjamin agreed, and a weight lifted from his shoulders. He had offered marriage and absolved himself of his obligation to Germaine. He had no sincere desire to have her for his wife.

Early in December, Madame de Staël said good-bye to a group of her friends who had assembled at Coppet to see her off.

She stood on the steps of the carriage and turned to wave. With a theatrical gesture toward the Alps, she declared, "I will pass Pope Pius as I make my way to Rome. He has started his journey north to attend Bonaparte's coronation. I go to bear the burdens of life in Italy, where, they say, one forgets existence."

Germaine climbed into the coach, where her three children and Augustus Schlegel awaited her. Schlegel was to be her guide and instructor about painting, sculpture and architecture, an area of her education she felt had been neglected.

For the first time since her father's death, Madame de Staël felt free to seek diversion, material for another novel that would rouse sympathy for her oppression from Bonaparte.

Benjamin Constant had already departed for France. In a pocket over his heart he carried letters from Charlotte von Hardenberg, promising a rendezvous in Paris. He hoped to convince her to marry him. He would ask for a secret union . . . secret from Germaine.

Chapter 14
Juliette Besieged

"Why is it," Germaine said to Juliette, "that men, most men, lose so much of their fire and passion as they grow older? In their twenties, they are unbridled, exciting and responsive in their work and in love. By the time they're fifty they're jaded."

"And women? Are they so different?" Juliette asked with a knowing smile.

It had been two-and-a-half years since the two devoted friends had parted tearfully at Saint Brice. Their sporadic correspondence had satisfied neither of them. Germaine had broken the separation by asking Juliette to make the long journey from Paris to her present residence at the Chateau of Vincelles, outside Auxerre, forty leagues south of the city. She had sent Augustus Wilhelm and her son Albert in her carriage to accompany Madame Récamier on the sixteen-hour ride.

From Germaine's letters, Juliette knew only the highlights of her journey to Germany, the death of Necker and her six months in Italy. She also knew that Madame de Staël had avoided Bonaparte when he was crowned King of Italy in Milan. And Germaine had written of her return to Coppet, where she had spent the last year working on her book *Corinne*.

In return, Juliette had written about her Paris salon and mutual friends who remained in the city. She had told of a disquieting experience that had provoked the Emperor, but avoided revealing what happened later.

Replying to Juliette's question about women's aging, Madame de Staël said "We differ from men most importantly by never ceasing to want love. I have just turned forty, and my interest in love-making, or in politics or literature has not lessened. I am more intense about living."

"But you, my dear Germaine, cannot be judged as all women."

"Perhaps not. Nor am I as attractive as most women," Germaine said with a rueful smile. "Youth has its own beauty, which fades quickly. I have lost whatever early bloom I once had. I regret its passing. My skin grows more sallow, my figure fuller. But I do not lack for young lovers."

On a warm morning in May, Madame de Staël and Madame Récamier strolled arm-in-arm in the gardens of the Chateau of Vincelles. It was a happy surprise for both women to find that they were closer than ever. Their friendship had deepened as though it had been nourished by their separate experiences.

Juliette, at twenty-nine, looked even younger than Germaine had expected. She was more beautiful, more beguilingly innocent, more mysterious and enchanting. She still moved with an air of demure but confident elegance.

"You still attract young lovers because your appeal is not only feminine, but also intellectual, spiritual and ageless," Juliette said thoughtfully. "Your charm prevails over physical beauty. It is seductive, tantalizing, powerful."

"Sweet Juliette, you have always been kind."

"Perhaps. But truthful," she said with transcending assurance. "There is more. Your charm is disarming." Juliette paused. If she were speaking to anyone else she would have stopped and rendered her listener helpless. She went on as Germaine expected her to. Juliette chose to define and explain. "To disarm can be interpreted variously. It enchants, bewitches, unnerves . . . it even possesses."

"Yes, I possess . . . I go further, I demand. And why not? I encourage men to perform beyond their expectations. You may be more docile than I, but you are no less perceptive. How I have missed you!"

"We must never be apart for so long again," Juliette declared. She longed to discuss what troubled her, but would not intrude on her friend's need for a sympathetic hearing. Urging Germaine to go on, she said "You have here, together under the same roof, all your men. You manipulate them guilelessly."

Arriving at Vincelles, Madame Récamier had seen that Germaine's retinue of admirers included not only her old friends but others who were emotionally involved with her. Each was gallantly amiable, suppressing his own degree of jealousy and dislike for the others. The old guard . . . Jean Charles de Sismondi and Augustus Schlegel, who loved her unrequitedly, Mathieu de Montmorency, who cherished her, and the reluctant Benjamin Constant whom Eugene Uginet had tracked down at Les Herbages and retrieved for Germaine when he balked at returning. The two younger men were obviously infatuated with the wealthy and illustrious Lady of Coppet. One was Prosper de Barante, the young French government official who had met her through his father, the Prefect stationed in Geneva. The other was a twenty-four-year old Portuguese noble, Dom Pedro de Sousa, whom she had met in Rome and invited to visit.

Madame de Staël shrugged. "I love them all," she said, "for different reasons. After much introspection, I have decided to marry Prosper. He is serious, calm and reserved. He is also a devoted, ecstatic lover and has sworn there is no other woman for him but me."

Germaine did not know that since his ardent declaration, Prosper had changed his mind about marrying her but lacked the courage to tell her.

"I met him before I left for Italy," Germaine said. "But I was still overcome by my father's death and too depressed to be aware of the depth of his affection. I fled south to restore my health and try to recapture my youth. I hoped for one more chance at love. I found several but was disappointed. None endured beyond my visit.

"Yet, I had a glorious time. My powers to think and to write were reawakened. I conceived the idea for my book *Corinne* while I was in Naples. I combined the characters of three of my young lovers into its hero, Oswald. Prosper is the first."

"Tell me, my dear," said Juliette, anxious for the details. "You must tell me everything."

"Oh! My adventures began in Milan, where I spent three magnificent weeks with Italy's leading poet, Vincenzo Monti, who seduced me by reading sonnets. He was not a model for Oswald, since he is almost fifty and, like Benjamin, has lost much of his verve. After I left, I learned the fool fawned over Bonaparte, who named him Poet Laureate of the country. There are those, sadly, who have no principles.

"It was in Rome that I met my second Oswald. He is Dom Pedro da Souza, a Portuguese noble whose handsome looks, dark skin and pale blue eyes could dissolve any woman. Disillusioned with girls his own age, he gave himself freely to me. We admired the antiquities together . . . the city is sublime. Rome and Dom Pedro are inseparable for me, but a permanent liaison with him would never endure.

"When the weather turned warmer, we moved on to Venice, where I met and spent five superb days with Maurice O'Donnel von Tyrconnel, my third Oswald. Schlegel and Albertine came with me but Dom Pedro stayed behind, as did Albert and Auguste, who wanted to see more of Rome.

Maurice was on sick leave from the Austrian Army. He is a captain in the engineers, an amusing man in his mid-twenties but neither as intelligent nor intriguing as the others.

"Though I hope to see Maurice again, it is Prosper who will be my husband. When I returned to Coppet last summer he was visiting his father, trying to regain his health. I cannot resist noble young men of delicate health. He soon began to spend most of his time with me. I have been a widow for two years. I would retain my baroncy for he is a baron and my children's future would be secure."

"Oh!" said Juliete bemused. "He's so handsome!"

"Yes, and young. I was sorry to see Prosper leave for his Paris post after his recovery and wrote Fouché again, asking when I might return. Bonaparte was gathering his troops to battle the Austrian and Prussian armies and I counted on his being distracted from domestic affairs. But he still reacts to news of me as a bull to red. In his letter to me, Fouché quoted the Emperor 'I am not fool enough to want her anywhere near Paris. If she comes closer than forty leagues she'll be arrested.'

"Forty leagues is closer than banishment beyond the borders of France and far easier traveling for Prosper and for you. I took the first house I could find . . . it is damp and dingy but it is near you both."

Germaine had seen a fleeting twinge of pain on Juliette's face at the mention of Fouché and Bonaparte.

Putting her arm around Juliette, Germaine said "It looks as though it may rain. Let's go in. We'll still be alone . . . it will be an hour before the rest of my guests stir."

Leaving the garden, they walked up a few stone steps to a terrace at the rear of the house. Olive Uginet opened the heavy, carved wooden door as they approached. "I have set out a tray here for you, Madame la Baronne," she said, closing the door behind them. She indicated a pewter coffee service, heavy crockery cups and saucers and a small basket of croissants. The food was set before an upholstered bench beneath a balcony that surrounded the small foyer.

"You are thoughtful. This will help take off the chill," Madame de Staël told Olive as she departed. "Come, Juliette," she said, pouring the coffee, "you are troubled. I sensed it from the moment you arrived. It has to do with Fouché or Bonaparte. Or both. What is it, my dear?"

"I'm terrified of Bonaparte," Juliette admitted.

"I expected as much! What has happened, Juliette?"

Madame Récamier covered her face with her hands and bent her body forward in humiliation. "He covets me!"

"What a fiend!" Germaine murmured with indignation.

Juliette sat up, looking relieved. It was as though she had released her terror by declaring it to Germaine. Straightening herself with dignity, she began to speak of what happened.

"It began after I had attended the trial of our dear friend General Moreau. I was told that Bonaparte considered this a gesture of defiance on my part, and I was certain that he would forbid Joseph Fouché to attend my salon. I soon learned why he did not. The Minister of Police became a regular guest. Knowing he is a friend of yours, I treated him as cordially as I do everyone else, and spoke freely of my feelings, though not directly to him, about Bonaparte's harshness toward the General and his rigid conditions for your exile."

"You were defying the Emperor," Germaine said softly, pointing out her friend's imprudence.

"It was in my home."

"But within earshot of the Emperor's close associates."

"I avoided speaking out in public."

"But you appeared openly at Moreau's trial."

"How else can one protest for one's friends?" Juliette asked, reaching for Germaine's hands and holding them so tightly her knuckles whitened.

"I admire your courage," Germaine said.

"One summer evening in my salon at Clichy, I felt Fouché's eyes follow me wherever I moved. Later, when most of my friends had begun to leave, he asked to speak with me in private.

"'The Emperor,' he said when we were alone, 'is deeply wounded to see traces of opposition growing in your salon. It would be dangerous to annoy him any further.'"

"The Emperor has insidious methods of retaliating," Germaine said indignantly. "There is nothing sacred to Bonaparte, nothing beyond his reach. He controls life within France and far beyond its borders."

"That was just the beginning," Juliette declared nodding. Fouché sought me out again and suggested I present a petition to be a lady of honor at court. 'Your request will be granted in advance,' he said.

"I declined as graciously as I could," Juliette went on, "'My tastes are simple and lack the extravagance of Bonaparte's court. Besides, my friends and my salon take up all of my time,' I told him.

"He would not accept my regrets. 'You don't understand what the Emperor is offering you. He has not yet met the kind of woman who is worthy of him,' Fouché persisted. 'Josephine has grown too old. He has had every kind of woman, from every level of society. How great his love might be, once he declares himself to a woman as pure as you!'"

Germaine, controlled her anger, placed her arm around the younger woman and drew her close.

"He talked on," Juliette said. "'What a great position of power you would have,' he declared. 'What rewards you would reap as the favorite mistress of the Emperor.' Fouché's eyes closed to narrow slits in a wicked smile."

Madame Récamier again covered her face with her hands. Germaine pressed her closer.

"I was revolted by his crudity," Juliette said, "and told him I was certain Bonaparte would find someone far more worthy than I to fill the role. I closed the subject as well as I could, but he would not be put off. During the next month he tried to manipulate my friendship with Napoleon's sisters, asking them to persuade me. When I managed to avoid their well-intentioned attempts to intervene, Fouché circulated rumors in court that I had submitted and would indeed become Napoloen's mistress.

"A few days later, he maneuvered me into a corner and said, 'You can give no more excuses, Madame. It is no longer I, it is the Emperor himself who proposes a place for you as lady of the palace.'

"I tried to be tactful, but again he could not grasp my resolve to resist. Finally, I screamed out, 'I will not submit to Bonaparte!' Fouché went into a rage and reproached my guests and friends, blaming them for having organized an outrage against the Emperor. Then, he burst out of my home and has not returned since. I was devastated and humiliated."

"You have preserved your good name, Juliette, my dear," Germaine said sadly. "I wonder what price *you* will have to pay for *your* act of independence."

"It has been a painful experience," Juliette said, but it can only have been a minor incident in Bonaparte's exalted life."

"He is a man scorned," Germaine replied. "I would not rule out revenge."

Chapter 15
Betrayed

The view from the tall, arched window was bleak. A sudden gust of the cold November air forced its way through the slim crack in the frame. She drew her shawl over her breasts and pressed close to the heavy drapery to protect herself from the draft. She did not step back. She was spellbound, unable to lift her gaze from the barren, deserted garden. An eerie mist rose from the frozen earth, creeping slowly up the trunks of skeletal trees, engulfing them and the surrounding marble statues in suffocating embrace. In the distance, beyond the low, grey hills, the sky seemed infinitely hostile.

Madame de Staël felt a kinship with the forlorn landscape. It echoed her mood of melancholy.

She had extracted permission from Joseph Fouché to shorten the perimeters of her exile but attempts to break her banishment were futile. She had written Talleyrand, imploring him to help, but he ignored her. Claude Ignace de Barante, the kindly Prefect of Geneva, came to visit but criticized her for her persistence. Was his disapproval political, she pondered, or did he object because of his son Prosper's interest in her as a woman? Germaine was spending the winter in a comfortable mansion in Rouen, thirty leagues north of Paris. Dom Pedro was gone, Prosper was vacillating. Still vowing his love for her, he was trying feebly to back out of his promise of marriage. She felt isolated, abandoned, obsessed with what caused Prosper to change his mind. And she was deeply concerned about Juliette. If only she could be with her friend to offer comfort.

Madame de Staël, turning at last from the dismal scene at the window, picked up from her desk the letter she had written. She stood before a warm fire and read it once more before entrusting it to a courier.

Dearest Juliette:

What sorrow I feel at the dreadful news. How I curse the exile that keeps me from being with you and holding you to my heart. I am also writing to your husband to express my respect and concern.

You have lost all the luxuries that afford living in ease and style. If it were possible for me to envy someone I love, I would willingly give all I have and all I am, to be you, with all that you have lost. Your beauty is unequalled in Europe, your reputation pure, your nature proud and generous. What a wealth of happiness still lies ahead for you in this sad, despoiled life.

I would hope that you would choose to spend three months here, in this small circle of mine, where you would be cared for with devotion. Of course, I know you inspire this same feeling among your friends in Paris.

I do not know how to console you, except to say that in your adversity you will be even better loved and regarded than before.

May I see you soon, so I might tell you that I feel a greater love for you than for any woman I have ever known.

Adieu, my dearest Juliette,
Germaine

Germaine was proved right. Bonaparte had retaliated. It had begun months earlier, when England resumed hostilities with France. An economic panic erupted on the heels of the Emperor's defeat at Trafalgar in October, 1805. The public besieged the banks for gold to replace their paper money. Several institutions folded immediately. Jacques-Rose Récamier's bank weathered this first onslaught, but months later, investments he had made failed, drained his bank and created a huge deficit. He needed a million francs to cover his losses and gain time to put his finances in order.

Jacques-Rose petitioned the Bank of France and the Minister of Finance for a loan. Neither would make a decision without consulting Bonaparte, who was enjoying a battlefield victory at Jena.

Récamier appealed to General Junot, one of Bonaparte's most respected officers, to intervene.

"Their holdings will be wiped out," he told the Emperor, "if you do not grant the loan."

Bonaparte was delighted at the prospect of revenge.

"I am not Madame Récamier's lover," he replied crudely. "Understand, Monsieur Junot, the Treasury does not lend to merchants who are on their way to bankruptcy."

His refusal was absolute.

The Récamier financial network was ruined. One word from Bonaparte would have prevented it. Juliette conducted herself with proud dignity, helping her husband liquidate their assets to settle his debts. She gave up her mansion and its furnishings, her porcelain, her silver, her works of art and most of the jewelry she treasured.

Monsieur Récamier salvaged a few thousand francs, borrowed more and established himself in a small enterprise. The couple purchased a modest home on the Rue Basse-du-Rempart in Paris.

Juliette's misfortune distressed Germaine, but her own situation depressed her beyond endurance. She had hoped that her move to Rouen would encourage friends to visit more often and stay longer. But only a few made the arduous trip, which was still a distance of eight or ten hours by coach.

Dom Pedro da Souza had said good-bye for the last time. The concluding break with the sensitive, indolent young man was a blow to Germaine, who would never see him again.

Augustus Wilhelm added to her distress. For weeks, he'd been down with the ague. Even well, Schlegel was sullen and jealous of the other men in her life. Ill, he had periods of delirium, temper and petulance. He stole hours from her writing *Corinne,* which was almost finished but lacked an ending. Until Augustus Wilhelm recovered, it fell to Germaine to tutor Albert and Albertine. Auguste was in Paris studying for entrance to the Polytechnic Institute. She was grateful for her children, who were her consolation and delight. They were good company, traveled happily at their mother's side and looked on each change of residence as an adventure.

Juliette and Prosper. They caused her such pain. If they were not her dearest friends they could not wound her so deeply. Was it her own fault for having encouraged Prosper, who was back at his government post in Paris, to call on Juliette? It was a device to hold Prosper's affection. Juliette had agreed to plead Germaine's cause and keep him from reneging on his promise to marry her. Though they were responsible for her greatest suffering, could she, in fairness, condemn them?

Juliette had made three visits to Rouen but had not returned again, because her mother was gravely ill. The attachment between Germaine and Juliette had grown closer and deeper. If only they could be together, the tension, all the greater now because of Juliette's financial plight, would surely lessen. In each other's company, any problem, all differences, vanished.

When Juliette's and Prosper's separate letters reached her, Madame de Staël had little trouble reading between the lines. Prosper included weak excuses for remaining in Paris, and confirmed her suspicions. He had succumbed to Juliette's beauty and charms. She was disturbed, but could not fault them. What man could resist such an angel? How could she blame the sublime coquette whom she also adored?

Germaine worried because her friendship with Juliette was threatened. She held Prosper responsible for this unconscionable breach.

"I confess my fear that you will let him love you," she finally wrote in desperation. "Don't do it, Juliette. It would be a mortal sorrow for me."

Both denied that Germaine had cause for jealous speculation. Their visits, each wrote, were social and harmless. "We talk only of you and your affairs."

Madame de Staël knew better.

The tension among them grew. By July, the strain became too much for Prosper, who was being badgered by his father to escape Germaine's dominance. He accepted a commission on behalf of the Emperor, a plum for so young a man, which the elder Barante had sought for him, and left for Spain. "My affection for you is as strong as ever," he wrote Germaine, "but we can no longer be more than passionate friends."

Callous, faithless lover! Devastated but not defeated, Madame de Staël had no intention of permitting him to break away. She bombarded him with florid letters to which he felt bound to reply.

In September, he returned to Paris and resumed his calls on Juliette but made no journeys to Rouen. Couriers tore up the road between the two cities, carrying messages that contained gentle accusations and firm evasions and denials. Then Claude-Ignace de Barante manipulated another mission for Prosper who was preparing to leave both women for Germany.

The letter to Juliette slipped from Madame de Staël's fingers and fell to the floor. Picking it up, she walked to the window and found that the mist had lifted. The trees, the foliage and the statues were now bathed in the harsh whiteness of a sun trying to filter through the clouds but failing to penetrate.

Failing as she had failed . . . failing to achieve freedom from exile, failing with lovers, failing even to complete her book. *Corinne* still lacked a moving, dramatic conclusion.

Was she herself not now living the final chapters? Would the ending not be Oswald's ultimate agony of losing Corinne to suicide?

The drawing room door opened behind her. Madame de Staël turned and smiled. A pretty young face in a frame of auburn curls peered pertly into the room.

"Albertine!"

"Mama? Is it all right to disturb you?"

"Come in, sweet one," Germaine said warmly, "I've finished my letter."

My daughter! Lovely, slight. Her bones are small, her face fine and narrow. She holds her head with a proud tilt, a Necker angle. She is already beautiful at nine. It is the Curchod loveliness, which skipped my generation. Only the red highlights of her hair give her paternity away . . . a question no one has ever raised. A heavenly, delightful child. I'll see to it that she marries for love and does not suffer as I have.

Albertine ran to her mother, who gathered her into her arms and held her face up to her own. She kissed the girl's forehead. My joy!

"What is Albert up to this morning?" Madame de Staël asked.

"He's riding."

"And Benjamin? Has he arrived, ma petite?"

"Yes," the girl answered, her eyes twinkling. "We had breakfast together. I'm so happy he's here. We always have such fun together. He is gayer today than ever."

In a gay mood? It usually takes a day or two for him to overcome irritability on his visits with me.

"Albertine," Germaine said, sealing the letter to Juliette. "Please give this to Eugene and ask him to have a courier leave immediately for Paris. He has other letters I wrote yesterday. They can all go in the same packet." One was to Prosper's father, protesting his interference in her liaison with his son.

Madame de Staël climbed the staircase, raising her skirts to make the ascent quickly. She was eager to see Benjamin. Why should he be cheerful enough to cause Albertine to remark about it? A woman? It had been two or three years at least since they had made love. He visited prostitutes but did not noticeably alter his mood.

Germaine opened the door to his chamber without knocking.

Constant was hunched over his desk, deeply absorbed in writing. He looked up, startled. Instinctively, he dropped his pen and put the paper in a drawer.

Germaine ignored his reaction.

"I'm sorry I did not greet you last night," she said. "I was depressed and exhausted yesterday. I took a dose of opium in the afternoon and slept through till late this morning."

Madame de Staël's open manner deceived Benjamin. "I arrived about midnight," he replied, more at ease. "Eugene showed me in, and this morning Albertine looked after me."

Constant was off guard. Germaine could begin her inquisition.

"What have you been writing?" she asked.

He hesitated, surprised. "A letter."

"May I see it?" Germaine extending her hand.

"No!" Benjamin said sharply.

Germaine feigned astonishment. "You have always shown me what you write."

"Yes. But not this time," firmly.

Madame de Staël walked around the desk and pulled open the drawer. Benjamin grabbed the letter, crumpled it, and strode to the fireplace.

"Benjamin!" Germaine screamed as he tossed the paper into the flames.

"What made you do that?" she asked harshly. "What are you trying to hide from me?"

Benjamin closed his eyes and stood motionless.

"Don't be so perversely inflexible!" Madame de Staël's tone was peremptory.

"I am here because you command me to come," Benjamin shouted. "What more do you want of me? I should be in Paris tending to my own affairs."

Germaine's eyes blazed. "When did you begin to have secrets from me?" she fumed.

Benjamin could not support his argument or sustain his anger.

Intimidated, he stepped back. Why do I tolerate this abuse and intrusion into my privacy he wondered, when I can find peace and happiness elsewhere?

Madame de Staël persisted. "To whom were you writing?"

"To the woman I love!" Benjamin blurted out. "Charlotte von Hardenberg du Tertre!"

"Never!"

"Charlotte is a gentle, tender woman who would devote her life to me and my interests."

"You hardly know her!"

"I know her well. She has been waiting for me for thirteen years, till I free myself from you. She has never uttered a word of reproach and is grateful for the time I spend with her."

"You have been seeing her behind my back!"

"I plan to marry her."

Madame de Staël was stunned. "You would not dare!"

"It is decided. Her husband has agreed to free her."

"You cannot!" Germaine shouted. "You have given me your word that you would never marry. If you do, I shall do away with myself. What of that promise?"

"I gave it under duress."

The verbal war between them continued through the afternoon and into the evening. Rooms grew dim as darkness fell. Servants lighted candles and carried away trays of untouched food.

When Benjamin had returned to Paris in October, he had called on Charlotte du Tertre and found her alone. Her husband was away traveling in Germany. Taut from Germaine's nerve racking tempests, he was moved by Charlotte's calm warmth and promised to return later in the evening after an engagement he had with Prosper de Barante. Benjamin and Prosper were drawn together by a bond of sympathetic understanding in their inability to break with the same woman. They dined together, drinking heavily and sharing experiences they had had with women, but avoiding all mention of Germaine.

The conversation roused Benjamin. He reproached himself for being feckless toward Charlotte. In all the years he had known her, he had never demanded proof of her love. Though he had often held her in his arms he had never pressed her further. She trusted him implicitly.

When he left Prosper and drove on to Madame du Tertre's home, Constant was determined to test her love . . . he had waited too long.

Charlotte greeted him happily and drew him down with her on a comfortable sofa before the fire.

"Have you had any word or papers from Germany?" he asked knowing that Charlotte's husband was attempting to have their marriage annulled. Monsieur du Tertre had been convinced by his priest that he was living in sin, since Charlotte was a Protestant and a divorced woman. Benjamin had helped his cause by advancing him a generous cash settlement.

"I expect to hear soon," Charlotte said, nestling closer to Benjamin.

Talking of what the annulment papers would mean to their future, Benjamin fondled her gently and she responded with unsuspecting joy. When he proceeded more boldly to possess her, she submitted in surprise and ecstasy.

Later she drew away from Benjamin with tears streaming down her cheeks. Neither reproaching him nor speaking, Charlotte wept silently.

Benjamin felt shame and repentance, as though he had injured a child entrusted to his care.

"Charlotte, my love, why pull away from me when you gave yourself so willingly?"

Her body shook with sobs.

"What can you think of me now! I should have been able to resist. I have lost all your respect."

"We have expressed our love."

"I have destroyed our future. How could I have been so weak?"

Benjamin was deeply moved. Any other woman would have considered their intimacy a bond that obligated him to her. He tried to convince her that they were now joined together for life in the eyes of God. He spent much of the night trying to comfort her. When at last he saw that he had persuaded her, he said, "I will protect you for the rest of our lives."

Madame du Tertre's belief in him was that of an innocent girl. "From now on, all that you command I shall do. You alone are in charge of my life, and I have no other duties but faithfulness and submission."

Benjamin Constant was elated by this commitment. During the next two weeks, he returned to Charlotte's home every day. On October 25, he celebrated his fortieth birthday with her. Each time they were together they renewed their vows, securing them with binding love-making.

In early November he reminded Charlotte that he had to leave for Rouen, where Madame de Staël expected him. He would prepare Germaine for the coming break with her. Charlotte let him go without question or complaint.

Now that Germaine was assaulting him with threats of suicide, he felt sapped of strength. He feared that in her anger Germaine might carry out her threat. He would have to retreat and forestall her.

"I misled you," Benjamin said, straining to reach her. "It was Charlotte who pressed me to marry her. Monsieur du Tertre had agreed at first but grew jealous and made a scene. He objected to the cost and the scandal a divorce would cause."

Germaine did not challenge his change in tactics.

"I knew you would not leave me," she said. She had weakened his will. She did not concern herself with his sincerity. Though he might not yet be completely convinced, Benjamin would surely change his plans about Charlotte du Tertre. She was not a worthy rival.

The next morning Germaine rose early and was waiting for Benjamin when he walked into the breakfast room.

"Good morning" she said lightly. "Would you spend the morning in the library with me and review an outline I have begun for my book on the German Romantic movement?"

Later, he listened to Germaine in silent amazement as she read to him. Once she had resolved the personal crises in her life to her satisfaction, he reflected, Madame de Staël was in fact the most generous woman in the world to live with. No other woman had a keener, more brilliant mind. The intellectual affinity they shared was *sans pareil*. Benjamin wondered if he should not consider a reconciliation.

Chapter 16
Bonaparte Defied

The Minister of Police was visibly shaken by the visitor in his portico. Letting Madame de Staël in, he frantically bolted the door behind her.

Joseph Fouché ushered Germaine into his ministry chambers, directed her to a chair and then sat imperiously behind a massive desk piled high with official documents.

"My dear Baroness," he said with agitation, "your surreptitious visits to Paris are compromising my position with the Emperor. You are jeopardizing the freedom you have been permitted in the rest of France."

"I've done nothing to provoke Bonaparte," Madame de Staël protested. "There are many who have. As the most efficient law enforcer in Europe, you know better than I who they are. The Emperor's setback by the Russians is convincing his enemies that he is not invincible after all. His troops are being slaughtered by armies dedicated to defending Mother Russia to the last man. His defeat has encouraged conspiracies here in France to increase. If he continues to lose badly, or if he is killed, the entire government will be overthrown. I have had no hand in any of these plots."

"My dear Madame," Fouché said, exasperated, "you don't have to take an overt action against Bonaparte. Your presence in any group is enough to fan the spark of resistance and cause him to explode. You keep alive the spirit of dissension wherever you appear."

Four months earlier, immediately after she learned of the Récamier's financial reversal, Madame de Staël, deep in despair over her own isolation, had packed her bags and left Vincelles with her entourage to take up residence at the Chateau d'Acosta, outside Meulan. Aware that she was moving boldly and too close to Paris (now only fifteen leagues from the city) she made the transfer quietly and with discretion. But she could not resist turning the huge residence into a small Coppet. Direct control of the

Necker fortune made her one of if not the richest woman in Europe, and with the steady flow of royalties from her books, she could afford to live in whatever style she chose. She supplied her guests with horses and carriages to carry them to and from the capital.

Madame de Staël was jubilant in her new location. The chateau and its grounds were well suited to her needs. The pavilions and the small park surrounding the main buildings provided several pleasant, private areas for entertaining. The atmosphere was conducive to writing . . . at last she was inspired with an appropriate ending for *Corinne*. Her house was filled with friends. Though the triangle with Prosper and Juliette was not yet resolved, Madame Récamier, once again, visited regularly and the two women sustained their close friendship while de Barante was in Germany.

But Madame de Staël was not satisfied. Paris was a magnetic attraction for her. Often, under cover of darkness, she drove into the city in her calèche, rode through the familiar streets and called on sympathetic friends who risked censure for receiving her.

It was just after dusk on a balmy spring day in March that the Baroness came to the office of the Minister of Police. She knew Bonaparte was far from the city, on the battlefields in Poland.

"You condemn me without justification," she told Fouché.

"Oh, Madame! You move closer to the capital without permission. You defy the order which commands you to stay out of Paris. Today you dare to come to my office!"

"You are my friend and I need your help," she replied. "All I wish is to obtain permission to buy an estate at Cernay, a few kilometers from here. I've been cautious," she added. "There is no way the Emperor will know I have been here."

Fouché's face flushed as he struggled to control his composure. His skill at straddling opposing factions was being put to a test. Despite Bonaparte's edicts, Germaine de Staël could not be discounted. She had great wealth, a political heritage, ideological authority and burgeoning literary fame. Nor did he disregard Bonaparte's setbacks, which might diminish or destroy the Emperor's power and restore the Baroness to her former level of influence. Fouché admired her fearlessness in defying Napoleon. He also respected and liked her.

But Bonaparte was Emperor of France, making laws, passing sentences. And he had a perverse aversion to, if not hatred for, Madame de Staël.

"You underestimate His Illustriousness," Fouché replied, groping for a way to make Germaine comprehend the seriousness of her actions.

He rummaged through the papers on his desk and located a file labeled "The Baroness Anne Louise Germaine Necker de Staël Holstein."

"Here!" he said, handing her one item from the dossier. "It is a dispatch from Bonaparte dated December 31 of last year. I apologize for his language: 'Don't let that bitch of a Madame de Staël approach Paris. I know she is not far from it.' This is only one of many, as you can see." He held up a thick stack of papers.

"There's no need to report to him that I'm here," Germaine said.

"It is not necessary. He supplements my spy system with one of his own. He intercepts your mail. He has experts who easily break the sealing wax and replace it with such mastery that no one can detect the infringement."

Madame de Staël was stunned.

Fouché drew another letter from his file. "I received this one yesterday," he said. "The Emperor writes: 'If I showed you the detailed evidence of everything she has done at her country place in the last two months you'd be astonished.' He goes on and gives exact dates and people who were your guests and the times and places you visit in Paris. Do you understand why my position is compromised?"

Germaine leaned forward and picked up a quill from the desk. She fingered the soft feathers slowly then pointed the tip at Fouché. "The Emperor has a remarkable preoccupation with my movements," she replied wryly, no longer shocked but amused. "I'm flattered that he takes time from battle strategy to review my daily routine."

The Minister shrugged helplessly.

"All I want to do is reside near Paris," Madame de Staël continued, "to be close to my sons when they attend the Polytechnic Institute here."

"Would you be willing to make a concession to the Emperor?" Fouché countered.

"From me? A concession?"

"Yes. It might be considered a concession to his vanity. He might even permit you to live in Paris."

The Baroness was puzzled. "After all this time? What would he accept from me?"

"The book you are writing? *Corinne?*"

"Yes. It is with my publisher now."

"The Emperor asked me to encourage you to include passages in the novel that laud him and his actions," Fouché submitted cautiously.

Madame de Staël's eyes, opening wide, turned into blazing embers of anger.

"Never!"

Fouché was fawning. "Bonaparte has even offered to return the two million livres your father loaned the government."

"I will not be compromised or bribed. I have included nothing in my book about the Emperor . . . good or bad. Under no circumstances would I insert a word of flattery. Tell him that for me!"

The Baroness de Staël stood up, pulled on her gloves and with the imperiousness of an empress glared squarely into Fouché's eyes. "Adieu, Joseph," she said. "I understand your position and value your friendship. But I can do nothing for the Emperor."

A few days later, in the midst of a dinner party, at the Chateau d'Acosta, Madame de Staël was handed a letter by Olive Uginet. "It is urgent," the servant whispered. "It comes from the Minister of Police."

Germaine excused herself from her guests. She was surprised at what she read. Fouché quoted from an Imperial order: "Then let her go back to Switzerland! Let her stay there! Or, If she wants to go and libel me in foreign parts, the frontiers are open to her. Make sure you keep her out of the country!"

Again, Madame de Staël was exiled from *all* France. To Bonaparte's chagrin, she slipped into Paris and spent four days in the city before hastening to the safety of Switzerland.

Chapter 17
Corinne, the "Conscience of Europe"

Geneva is Europe!" Napoleon Bonaparte railed in another reprimand he dispatched to Joseph Fouché during the summer of 1807. "It is all that vile de Staël woman's doing! She is a carrion crow hovering expectantly, waiting for disaster to overtake me. I obtain fresh proof of the exceeding evil of this woman who is not only the enemy of the government but also of France . . . that France from which she cannot stay away."

Madame de Staël had returned to Coppet late in April. By the middle of May her book *Corinne* was off the press. By June, the ancient chateau which Germaine often decried as her prison was the gala crossroads terminal for the intellectual, political and social elite of the continent and a haven for many of Bonaparte's enemies, among them, his nemesis, the Austrian Ambassador Clemens von Metternich.

Corinne had created a sensation in every capital of Europe.

Bonaparte had had a special courier deliver one of the first copies to him at his camp in East Prussia. "This is rubbish," he declared, proclaiming the book anti-French and ordering it denounced by the official press.

Madame de Staël's latest work was acclaimed with enthusiasm throughout the Empire.

Corinne had sold out several printings within weeks of its first publication. Anyone who could read and most who could not were talking about Madame de Staël's new masterpiece. Her heroine, Corinne, was an idealized Englishwoman with Germaine's dogmatic idealism and the exquisite beauty and gentle nature of Juliette. The fictional heroine's crusade through Italy against a social system that suppressed liberty was taken as Germaine's single-handed defiance of Napoleon. Women readers were alerted and roused to Bonaparte's megalomania and military aggression. They blamed him for their broken homes and the deaths and maiming of husbands, lovers, brothers and sons. An undercurrent of rebellion spread through the continent, championing the Baroness as the "Conscience of Europe" and Coppet as the symbol of liberty. Germaine was called Corinne.

Bonaparte was irate. While his war machine ran roughshod over armies and devastated villages and towns across Europe a pocket of dissidents in Switzerland had turned him into a villain. His luck on the battlefield, which had altered to his favor, did not appease him. He had won a victory over the Russians at Friedland and signed an alliance with Russia's Alexander that declared the friendship between France and Russia as a cherished dream.

But the ideological arsenal in Coppet, for which that "madwoman" de Staël was responsible, had spread her damaging influence throughout the continent. He blamed himself for his leniency . . . by exiling Madame de Staël he had given her freedom to think, expound and write.

Bonaparte's reaction to *Corinne* was frustration and rage.

Prosper de Barante's was petulance.

Germaine's inconstant young lover was overwhelmed with guilt after reading a copy she had sent him in Breslau. In the novel, her heroine dies when Oswald, who vowed to marry her, deserts her for another. Devastated by her death, Oswald blames himself and suffers remorse the rest of his life. Prosper could not help but identify with the novel's protagonist. Though he wanted to break with Germaine, he was not able to cleanly sever the bond between them. Wounded he wrote her:

> *You reproach me cruelly. You have locked me into Oswald in a manner that prevents me from defending myself. His happiness is lost, his youth is destroyed for having known Corinne. But he cannot write for all the world to know about his feelings, which are no less real or painful than hers. If Corinne is intended to be an act of revenge, it has succeeded, for it weighs heavily on my conscience.*

Madame de Staël was distressed by the letter but did not let it interfere with her life at Coppet. Appearing jubilant, she entertained waves of visitors who came to seek out the illustrious "Corinne." It was a glorious season for Madame de Staël . . . frantic, tumultuous, triumphant.

Her international friends enjoyed a variety of settings around the chateau to which the sun lent mutable charm as it rose behind the Alps each morning, progressed across the sky and descended in striking brilliance in the evening. The guests walked the long, elm-lined roadway leading up to the main gate and looked down over the meadows to the azure waters of the lake or sauntered about the walled courtyard at the west wing of the sprawling, two-storied structure enclosed by shimmering walls alive with virginia creeper. Others gathered in the inner court which was protected by the majesty of tall double towers, or around the reflecting pool and trim, colorful gardens in the broad private park. The wide terrace balcony was a favorite in the late afternoon. Mont Blanc, always a snow capped spectacle, was proud and stalwart on clear days, benign though unyielding beneath angry clouds when storms threatened or raged.

The atmosphere within the chateau was one of informal grandeur, over which the Baroness de Staël presided like a queen. There were rarely fewer than thirty around the tables at mealtime. And frequently more for dinner. The chateau was staffed by fifteen servants to prepare the food, and more than twice that number to respond to the requests of the guests and to maintain the interior and grounds.

Daily life was casual. Only meals were served on schedule: breakfast between ten and eleven, dinner at five and supper at eleven. Madame de Staël generally spent her time before dinner on correspondence, administering the estate with Eugene Uginet and sharing in Albertine's instruction. She wrote constantly, carrying her lap desk with her wherever she went.

The Baroness's guests were as free to wander about the castle as they were the grounds. None of the elegant chambers was ever locked. Talk was the order of the day; it was the principal diversion and the chatelaine's passion. Her friends slipped in and out of the rooms till they found a group discussing a subject that interested them.

Each evening, Madame de Staël provided entertainment in the long, wood panelled drawing room. There was music . . . solos, duets, ensembles, and drama in which Germaine and her guests performed to audiences from Geneva and Lausanne. Often, she and Madame Récamier would play a duet on piano and harp, with Juliette singing in a soft, lilting voice. Inevitably, more talk followed. A few insomniacs joined Germaine, who could now sleep only with a dose of opium, and stayed up talking in her boudoir until early morning.

But beneath the gaiety and excitement at Coppet there was tension and anxiety among Germaine and the men she tried to dominate.

She knew Benjamin Constant tarried with Charlotte du Tertre in Paris. She wrote and threatened to expose his neglect of her to their friends if he did not return to her side. He wrote back, refusing. Within a few days Eugene appeared at his apartment in Paris to reveal that the Baroness was ready to leave Coppet and fetch him herself if he did not come immediately. He submitted. Trying to explain his actions to Charlotte, Benjamin patiently suffered her tears and fainting spells with offers to end his relationship with Germaine. Finally, the lovers decided to meet again in a few months. In the meantime, Charlotte would journey to Germany and try to finalize her divorce.

Benjamin traveled as far as Dole, where his father lived, and told Eugene to go on without him. Before the week was out, Constant was deluged with more letters from Germaine and others from her son Auguste, imploring him to reappear at Coppet. Benjamin did not budge.

Desperate in her efforts to retrieve this truant, Madame de Staël enlisted the aid of Augustus Wilhelm Schlegel. His slavish devotion to Germaine outweighed his jealousy of Constant and her other admirers. Mesmerized by the illustrious Baroness, he had deluded himself into believing Germaine would love him and felt betrayed when he realized she would never return his affection. But he never ceased to hope and did her bidding even when she used him as a whipping boy. Thus he was dispatched to persuade Germaine's errant lover to return to Coppet.

In Dole, he told Benjamin, "If you refuse to come back, Madame de Staël will drive here herself, take a dose of laudanum and die at your feet."

"I cannot leave," Benjamin protested. "I have an obligation to my father, who is eighty-two. He's failing and needs me to help put his affairs in order."

Schlegel grew indignant. "How can you weigh an aging parent against the friendship of so divine and supernatural a human being as the Baroness de Staël?"

Each man argued himself into a rage. After a two-hour harangue, when Schlegel talked of Germaine's spirited intelligence, her kindness and generosity . . . and finally, about Albertine, Benjamin broke down.

Madame de Staël met their carriage as it entered the courtyard and took Benjamin off to the park, away from the chateau and her guests.

Upbraiding him as a laggard, calling him a beast, she made Constant wonder why he had returned. But he stayed, of course, and was quickly absorbed into the Coppet mélange.

While Germaine's fear of losing Benjamin was obsessive, she also dreaded being discarded by Prosper de Barante, who made a brief visit to Coppet on his way home from Germany. Her young lover, rather than spend time with Germaine, showered his attention on Juliette. Prosper compounded Germaine's distress with news of Bonaparte's devastation of Europe. He talked of atrocities he had witnessed and described in vivid detail the burned out villages whose homeless victims were forced to wander across the land laid waste by the French armies.

"The Emperor of France is not only a despot," the Baroness de Staël impugned, "he is also a criminal."

Germaine's boundless energy along with her compulsion propelled the furious social scene at Coppet and allowed her to block out the torment of her personal life and the burden of her exile. Her children continued to give her comfort and happiness, but only the long hours she spent with Madame Récamier gave her peace. Juliette, herself, sought and found contentment with her friend. She had not yet recovered from the blow of her husband's bankruptcy, and also was grieved by the recent death of her mother.

The two women were inseparable during the early days of the summer. To be alone together, they often took short excursions away from the hubbub of the chateau. One day after a guided trip to the glacier of Mont Blanc, they returned to find that Prince Augustus of Prussia had arrived at Coppet. Madame de Staël, who had heard rumors of Augustus's interest in Madame Récamier, had invited him as a diversion for Juliette without telling her about it. The twenty-eight-year-old Prince, a dashing military officer and nephew of Frederick the Great, had met Juliette in Paris and been immediately taken by her innocent beauty and timid charm.

That evening in the castle library, Juliette sang to her own accompaniment on the harp before a small group which the Prince had joined. Her pure and harmonious voice sent a thrill through the audience. She wore a simple white gown, a foil for her porcelain skin, and her dark hair, drawn up away from her face was crowned with a diadem of cameos. Though she was thirty, Madame Récamier had never appeared more youthful. Her movements were as supple and graceful as a vestal virgin's.

Prince Augustus was enchanted and profoundly moved. As the

summer progressed, though he pursued Juliette with caution and delicacy, it was soon obvious that the Prince had fallen in love with her.

In her grief and misfortune, Juliette Récamier was vulnerable. She was moved by the Prince's sincere attention and for the first time in her life dropped her defensive wall of coquetry. Every day her feelings toward him softened, and when she was not with him, the Prince never left her thoughts. Juliette began to wonder how long she could resist his courtship without responding and reasoned that returning to Paris was her only option. And so she wrote her husband complaining that the heat at Coppet was stifling and the social life tiring, and that she planned to return to Paris. Not sensing the urgency of his wife's letter, Monsieur Récamier replied with the suggestion that she stay till winter. He was negotiating for financial assistance from the government and wrote indelicately, "Because of your association with Madame de Staël, who is in disgrace, your presence here might be prejudicial to my business."

Juliette felt the sting of rejection. Bewildered, she was drawn more closely to Prince Augustus. Was this perhaps her destiny?

Germaine piqued by the banker's reply, encouraged Juliette's friendship with the Prince more spiritedly. She had a more personal and selfish reason . . . with Juliette diverted, she had greater hopes of recapturing Prosper's affection.

Prince Augustus and Madame Récamier lapsed into a chaste, idyllic romance. They were so devoted to each other that the rest of the guests looked upon them as a loving couple. They were together always, walking in the fields and parks, riding horseback through the trails and in the forest. Most afternoons, when the sky was clear and the sun bright, they secured a boat and rowed on Lake Geneva, Juliette at the tiller, the Prince on the oars. One day they climbed upon the rocks of Meillerie, the rendezvous of Rousseau's lovers in *La Nouvelle Hèloise.* Inspired by the memory of the novel, Augustus proposed to Juliette. She accepted.

Back at the chateau, Juliette wrote her husband again. This time she asked for a divorce or an annulment of their marriage which had never been consummated. She told him of the man she planned to marry.

Before the reply came from Paris, Prince Augustus was called back to Germany. The lovers exchanged vows and rings and the Prince gave Juliette a golden chain with a pendant of brilliant rubies in the shape of a heart. As he placed the talisman around her neck, Juliette promised to follow him as soon as she heard from her husband.

After the Prince's departure, the banker's letter arrived.

I will agree to a divorce if you request it, he wrote. However, would you be happy in a morganistic union in which you would not share the benefits of your husband as would a woman of royal birth? Also, I appeal to all the feelings of your noble heart during these difficult times for me. I regret having respected the aversions you have felt to a closer relationship that might not have allowed the thought of a separation between us surface.

It had distressed Juliette to write him and seek the break. Now, the man who had never made demands on her, who had been kind, gentle and supportive, was asking her to reconsider, knowing she was in love with someone else.

Juliette turned to Germaine. Unequivocally, Madame de Staël suggested she leave her husband and follow the course of her heart. Juliette, torn between love and duty, began to question her true feelings. Uncertain, and hoping to be forthright with her husband, she replied to one of the Prince's daily letters by saying that she would have to wait and confront Monsieur Récamier face to face alone in their home in Paris.

The worried Prince Augustus wrote back anxiously, "Do not postpone your stay beyond the date we planned, for every day you remain, you delay our happiness together."

The Baroness de Staël stood alone on the gleaming, polished parquet floor of the Coppet library. She wore her long, purple travel cloak and matching velvet turban. She looked about the room, remembering the days and nights when it had been filled with friends from all over Europe. An exciting season had just come to a close but the memories were indelible. Germaine could still see her splendid and eminent guests, she heard the hum of voices, the ripples of laughter, the clinking of crystal goblets.

The Chateau of Coppet had never been her favorite residence, but here, during the summer of 1807, it had served as a perfect setting for entertaining. She had been able to make new contacts, secure old friendships and score with a foray into drama.

Madame de Staël walked slowly toward the end of the long chamber where the stage had been erected for the performances. She stood in position to relive the most memorable scene in her repertoire, performing as Hermione to Benjamin Constant's Pyrrhus in Racine's *Andromache*.

"I cannot hide behind false excuses," Benjamin said as Pyrrhus. "I cannot deny the wrong I do you. My conscience accuses me. Its voice is strong. Yes, I shall wed the Trojan woman. It's true. I plan to pledge to her the faith I promised you. We shall rush to the altar and vow eternal union there. You blame me and call me traitor. I am a willing one. Yet, I grieve that I am false to you."

Madame de Staël was incarnate in the role. Fire burned in Hermione's eyes. "You confess and bare your deceit," she said. "At least you are just to yourself. Though you must break this solemn vow, you see your crime and admit your guilt." Germaine's voice rang in unfeigned anger and condemnation as she inflicted her fury, not on Pyrrhus but on Benjamin. He was shocked. During rehearsals, Germaine had read her lines with little conviction, holding back, planning to release her venom before an audience. The guests, aware of the personal dissension between the players, sensed Germaine's intent. They watched in stunned amazement as the parallel between the private lives of the performers melded into the story of the drama's lovers. "Even in your faithlessness, you have a secret charm," Hermione accused in mounting passion. "You come to me to revel in your shame and watch me as I suffer so you can return to your Trojan woman and . . . as you lie in her arms . . . mock my shame."

Constant fought to recover on Pyrrhus's lines. "Let the past be done," he spat out. "I thank heaven that you are stirred and bitter. I was wrong when I felt remorse. How can one who is not loved be faithless? It was out of duty that we were bound. For you never truly loved me."

"For you," Hermione raved, "for you I scorned the princes of my country. Though you have been false to me, I waited patiently for you to come back. I have loved you though you were not constant. Could I have loved you more if you'd been true? And your lips calmly tell me of the death of my hopes. Oh, faithless one, I think I have never ceased loving you. I see you standing here with me, counting the moments you remain, anxious to return to her. Go! Profane the Majesty of Heaven. Marry her. But remember that the gods are just. They know you perjure your heart which you promised me. Beware, for even there, Hermione awaits you!"

When Germaine took her bow, after the conclusion of the play, the guests stood as one and cheered her stunning performance. The chandeliers had swayed to the clamor.

Now, in the quiet of the empty library, Madame de Staël's lips turned up in a wry smile of memory.

She moved on to her boudoir, entering it to echoes of another performance that took place later that same evening. This scene had been impromptu and unrehearsed. Germaine sat in the chair she had been in that night. She had been reading, trying to induce sleep after her guests had departed. She recalled the moment Benjamin broke in on her, his face flushed, his eyes glaring wildly behind the tinted glasses. He was stung by what he had interpreted as a public denouncement.

"Since it is marriage you want," he had shouted, "I demand we marry immediately."

Madame de Staël had been startled and taken off guard. There was tacit agreement between them that he would be loyal to their friendship but marriage was not part of the bargain. She resented the intrusion on her right to determine the direction of her personal life. If this was a challenge to force her hand, he should have planned more wisely.

Germaine rang the bell to summon Olive Uginet.

"Bring my children here," she commanded. "All of them."

Albert, Auguste and Albertine straggled into the boudoir in their night clothes.

"Behold," Madame de Staël cried out, pointing at Benjamin with a hair brush that she wielded like a sword. "Behold this monster who wants to ruin your mother and destroy your future. He threatens me by demanding that I marry him."

Benjamin placed his hand on Auguste's shoulder and retorted, "Regard me as the vilest of men if I ever marry your mother." He achieved what he sought.

Germaine grew livid. For months she had been pondering the scene that took place years before at Mèzery, when Benjamin had feigned suicide in the middle of the night. Against her better judgment, he had gained her sympathy, weakened her will and seduced her. Madame de Staël launched her second performance of the evening by carrying out what she had threatened to do, or at least act out a reasonable facsimile of it. Germaine swept up a brilliant scarlet scarf from the top of her commode, twisted it around her neck, threw herself on the bed with dramatic gusto and went about strangling herself.

Her sons and daughter watched in weary astonishment. Benjamin rushed to the bed, pulled away the scarf and cradled the distraught Germaine in his arms.

"Minette! Forgive me," he cried.

"Promise me," she said, claiming victory, "that you will stay with me two more months. After that you may have your freedom."

A repentant Benjamin agreed. He plunged into his work of transforming Fredrich von Schiller's three-part trilogy on Albrecht Wallenstein, the powerful general of the Thirty Year War, into a five-act tragedy in verse. Germaine guided and counselled him. They worked together as though no differences existed between them, collaborating in perfect harmony, with intellectual accord.

Peace descended on Coppet. Summer waned. Many of the visitors began to leave for the winter.

Constant marvelled at the ease with which he wrote and how quickly the play progressed. Just before his two months were up, he completed his work. By then, the guests had dispersed to their homes in countries east of the Rhine. Juliette was back in Paris.

In early November, as Germaine promised, she let Benjamin go.

Constant departed sadly. "You have been necessary to me," he told Madame de Staël with complete honesty. "I could not have written my Wallenstein without you."

That parting had taken place a month earlier. Germaine closed the door to her bed chamber and returned to the library, savoring this memory of her conquest over Benjamin.

"Mama! Mama! We are all waiting for you. Everyone is in the carriage ready to leave."

Albertine ran across the room to her mother.

"Here, my sweet," Madame de Staël replied taking her daughter by the hand. "I can go now."

A swift December wind swept through the portico as they walked out of the chateau.

"Good-bye, Mama," her eldest, Auguste, said, embracing his mother. He was a young man, grown tall and slender. "I'll follow you as soon as I have completed the task you have given me."

"I hope you will bring me good news," Madame de Staël replied.

She and her daughter boarded the coach with Eugene Uginet's assistance and took their places beside Albert and Schlegel. Uginet climbed on the perch next to the driver and gave the signal for the journey to start.

Madame de Staël's entourage, comprising her yellow berline and a second coach-and-four, rolled forward in regimented unison toward the road to Lausanne.

The Baroness de Staël's destination was Vienna, where she had arranged to meet Maurice O'Donnell, an Austrian military officer with whom she had once spent several days. She expected him to fill the role of escort and lover during a winter sojourn in the gaiety of Viennese society. She had asked Joseph Fouché to intercede with Bonaparte for permission to travel. The Emperor did not stand in her way. He wanted her as far from France as possible.

Madame de Staël had ambitious plans.

Up to this time, Germaine had confined her opposition to Bonaparte to private attacks against him among friends she could trust and by oblique criticism through analogy in her books. By stirring sentiment against Bonaparte, she had created a role for herself as the Conscience of Europe, but that was not enough. She still could not live in France and she had failed to influence any coalition of power to resist his aggression.

She could no longer mollify her determination to curb Bonaparte's ruthless ambition. She would go beyond the borders of Switzerland and seek out those who shared her antagonism for the tyrant and prod them to take action against him.

Madame de Staël revealed her intentions to no one.

PART IV

CONFRONTATION

Chapter 1
Sojourn in Vienna

It was your grandfather who caused the saturnalia that devastated France!"

Young Auguste de Staël stood alone in the middle of a vast hall, while at a long table against a windowed wall the Emperor of France breakfasted with his staff. Eager aides hovered attentively, refilling cups and plates.

"Jacques Necker was a senile maniac," Bonaparte railed, brandishing a fork at the youth. "Economists are not fit to be tax collectors in the most remote hamlet of my Empire. It was Necker who overthrew the monarchy and led Louis XVI to the scaffold. All the blood shed in the Revolution is on his hands."

Madame de Staël's seventeen-year-old son did not flinch. Like his father, the Count de Narbonne, he was handsome and seemingly imperturbable. He had been waiting for an audience with the Emperor almost a month after his mother left for Vienna. Knowing that Napoleon would pass near Geneva on his way from Italy to Paris, Auguste requested an interview. He would make yet another appeal for his mother's return to France.

"Sire," Auguste said respectfully, "allow me to hope that posterity will judge my grandfather more favorably than does Your Majesty."

Bonaparte looked around the table at his advisors. "Perhaps I should not speak ill of the Revolution," he said smugly, "since it afforded me the throne." He turned again to Auguste, "The era of ideological troublemakers like Necker and your intellectual mother is over."

Bonaparte had aged, though he would not reach forty for another year. The burden of absolute power and a debilitating peptic ulcer were taking their toll on the Corsican tyrant. His once trim figure was now full, his face had rounded, his hair was thin.

The Emperor turned avuncular. "You must respect authority. You are young and well brought up. Follow a better road, get yourself accustomed to subordination. Don't be led by evil principles which compromise the very existence of society."

"I am fortunate," Auguste responded, "that Your Majesty does me the honor of finding me well brought up. Since you approve of me, Sire, Your Majesty must not condemn the ideals of my grandfather and my mother. It was with their principles that I was raised."

Not waiting for a reply, the young man hastened on to the purpose of his audience. "I am here," he explained with a clear, steady voice, "to request that you end the Baroness de Staël's exile."

As Auguste spoke, the Emperor rose from the table and strode toward him. He demonstrated a gesture of imperial favor by pulling the lobe of Auguste's ear.

"If you were my age and had my experience," Bonaparte said, "you would be a better judge of men. But your directness pleases me. Your mother has sent you on a difficult mission and you are acquitting yourself well.

"But," he went on, "my will is unshaken. If your mother were in Paris she would attract too many people away from me. No, she cannot return—Paris is the place where *I* live. I don't want anybody there who is against me. Your mother would promise a miracle but she wouldn't be able to keep from talking politics."

"My mother, Sire," Auguste ventured, "wants only to be with her friends and discuss literature."

"Literature! So that's what it's called! You can make politics by talking literature, the arts, morality . . . anything. Women should stick to their knitting. No, she cannot return. If your mother were in prison, I might grant her a pardon. But she is in exile and nothing will make me call her back!"

"Your Majesty! Exile from one's country and friends is more painful than prison!"

"That is a romantic notion your mother invented. Except for Paris, all Europe is her prison. Why is she so eager to place herself within reach of my 'tyranny.' Can she not go to Rome, Berlin, Vienna, Milan or London?"

Resourceful, Auguste tried another tack. "My brother Albert and I would like to make our home in France, but cannot do so in good conscience if our mother is not allowed to live there too."

"I do not want any of you there!" Bonaparte flailed an arm in emphasis. "Can't you understand! I do not advise you to settle in France! Go to England! The British love the Genevese, the quibblers and the drawing room politicians. Go to England!"

Irritated by the youth's persistence and now bored by the incident, Bonaparte turned away abruptly. With bombastic flourish, he signalled to his staff to follow him as he left the building. The Emperor's mercurial change of mood deflated Auguste's hopes.

When her son's letter about his interview reached Madame de Staël, she was enjoying celebrity in the midst of one of Vienna's gayest seasons. She had rented a spacious house on Plankengasse, in the center of the city, and was grandly entertaining the nobility of the Austrian Empire, from the Fürstenbergs to the Esterhazys.

The snobbish, provincial Viennese aristocracy had been appalled by the daring, the openness and the unaffected manner of this matronly Frenchwoman who made her social calls on the arm of a young Austrian Count and often brought her children along. Their eyes widened at her outlandish, revealing low-cut gowns and her curious turbans, often, in clashing colors. They criticized her for being too intellectual and addressing herself primarily to men. But they could not resist her. They admired her vitality and respected her opinions, which they knew from her books long before her visit. They now sought her out. She had caused a stir at every affair she attended and during the wedding of Emperor Franz II, she diverted attention even from the bride.

Germaine's personal life had been launched as she planned, when Count Maurice O'Donnell von Tyrconnel greeted her ardently on arrival at the Austrian capital. Impressed by her fame and flattered by her interest, he eagerly assumed the role of guide and escort. It was he who was at her side when she made the rounds at parties. The friendship quickly became intimate and the young captain began to spend his evenings at the Baroness's residence, remaining till dawn more often than not. By midsummer, the smitten suitor had proposed marriage. Germaine weighed the offer seriously, since a union with the Count would permit her to retain her wealth and assume a title equal to her own.

The news from Auguste was a bitter blow to Madame de Staël. It was a signal to fulfill her vow to garner support against Bonaparte. She ignored the harsh message and gloried in her popularity among the

Viennese.

The Baroness was constantly reminded of the Emperor's animosity by the lurking presence of the agents keeping surveillance on her, but she was unprepared for and distressed by Bonaparte's directive forbidding her sons from studying in France and launching their careers there.

As she became more and more the center of Viennese life, Madame de Staël began to speak openly against Bonaparte's tyranny. At first the Austrians listened cautiously, fearing the military might of France as its armies moved closer to their nation's borders. But, fuelled by Germaine's attacks on Bonaparte, and disturbing news of the French occupation troops' harassment of the people in nearby German states, Austrian hostility mounted and soon matched Madame de Staël's.

Germaine's personal life was as frenetic as ever. She pressed her suit with the twenty-seven-year-old Maurice and forced their relationship into the same perverse course all her love affairs followed. Her fame, the adulation she spawned and her perpetual activity embarrassed and offended Maurice.

He reproached her. "You encourage men to pay court to you."

"If you accuse me of discussing subjects that interest them then yes, I encourage them."

"And you insist there is nothing between you and Constant yet you correspond with him regularly," the Count complained further.

"Of course we exchange letters! We have been friends for years."

"You say you love me, but I must share you with others. Wherever we go you surround yourself with admirers. I find myself off alone . . . abandoned."

"You object now, to the very qualities in me that attracted you in the first place," Germaine was indignant. "I have a reputation and a following. You cannot expect me to adjust to your provincial attitudes about love and marriage and subordinate myself to you. I am not like most women. You must accept me for what I am."

They argued. It was Benjamin all over again, minus the intellectual stimulation. Finally Maurice withdrew his offer of marriage but continued as her lover.

As the affair deteriorated, Madame de Staël grew restless. It was time to leave Vienna. She bade Maurice a dramatic, emotional farewell. The officer was so touched he weakened and almost asked for forgiveness, but instead promised to visit Coppet in the summer.

The Baroness enrolled Albert (now fifteen and still showing no signs of maturing or of overcoming impetuosity) in the Viennese military academy, hoping the discipline would curb him.

In May, after a five-month sojourn in the Austrian capital, Madame de Staël set out for Germany in her yellow berline with Albertine, Auguste, faithful Augustus Wilhelm Schlegel, her entourage of servants and her usual profusion of boxes, valises and trunks.

When they reached the checkpoint at the border of Saxony, the official on duty questioned Eugene Uginet intently in the guardhouse, making a careful check of Madame de Staël's papers. For several torturous minutes the Baroness worried that Bonaparte's spies had orders to detain her.

At last the official, with Eugene at his heels, walked out of the building and approached the coach. The man was flushed . . . obviously agitated.

"Madame la Baronne de Staël!" he cried out. "It *is* you! I could not believe it might be true. I have read all your books. You are a friend to Germany . . . we have been so moved by your brave attacks on Napoleon's tyranny. I have hoped that one day I might see you in person. Now, I can die happy!"

Madame de Staël handed the Saxon her own copy of *Corinne* and thanked him. She leaned back against the soft, velvet-upholstered seat in the coach and sighed. The incident reassured her and confirmed the wisdom of her decision.

Chapter 2
The Baron von Gentz

The room was large, a little shabby and clearly the lodgings of a man with expensive tastes who lacked the consistent means to afford them. Scattered among the undistinguished but comfortable furnishings were a handsome Louis XV chair upholstered in rich burgundy velvet, a Sèvres vase on a delicate marquetry table, an elegant pair of gold andirons and a few other fine pieces. Off to one corner, the shelves of books and the broad desk, with piles of papers held down by bronze paperweights and the clutter of quills revealed the lodger as a man of letters.

"I admire your courage, my dear Madame de Staël," Baron Friederich von Gentz told Germaine as he offered her another serving of roast pheasant. "Meeting here with me could have serious consequences for you."

Before leaving Vienna, Madame de Staël had arranged to meet the Prussian in the resort town of Toeplitz, in Bohemia, where many European aristocrats spent their summers. Gentz, feeling bountiful at having just received a large purse from the British government for services as propaganda agent on the continent, had insisted on having Germaine brought from her hotel to his residence in his own equipage. And, he had instructed his chef to prepare an elaborate meal for their evening together.

Baron Gentz was a dapper man, not handsome but with regular, distinctive feature. He was sensitive to the point of delicacy. Germaine knew of him beyond his international reputation as a skilled political manipulator and writer. Augustus Wilhelm Schlegel had prepared her. In their early years, the two men had frequented the same intellectual salons in Germany. They were among the aspiring young aesthetes who were writers, artists, philosophers and poets sharing the same living quarters and women. Gentz, Schlegel told Germaine, was one of the most hedonistic of the group. As his political acumen developed, his appetite, as keen for gambling, liquor and pretty women, regardless of their station, as for food, increased. His excesses never interfered with his talent for wielding tremendous influence among the leaders of Europe though this self-indulgence regularly stripped him of the high fees he commanded.

"I'm tired of constraining my actions while Bonaparte runs rampant across the continent," the Baroness de Staël said. "He stands gloating before his gigantic map of Europe. One by one he impales the states and countries he has suppressed with colored stick pins, like a naturalist displaying his collection of butterflies."

Madame de Staël and the forty-four-year-old Baron had a mutual respect for each other's dedication to European peace and stability. They talked for hours . . . his penchant for night long discussions challenging hers. Gentz was an arch conservative, so they argued over liberty, equality and the concepts of sovereignty of the people. But they shared the same profound, abiding hatred for Bonaparte.

"I refuse to permit the limits of my exile," Germaine added heatedly, "to extend to curbing my choice of friends . . . or when and where I meet them."

"Through your writing you have rallied not only legions of Frenchmen and women to your principles, you have also united the people of the continent. The English esteem the support you give their cause . . . "

"England is not my cause! France is!" Germaine asserted. "Bonaparte has defiled our nation. He has bribed Frenchmen with a sense of economic security and convinced them to fight his life-and-death struggle for the leadership of Europe by promising them glory and the spoils of war. He oppresses the people of all countries . . . he is obsessed with the belief that England is his greatest enemy . . . and uses the French to fortify his megalomania and spread his Empire."

"The situation has grown to unendurable proportions," Gentz agreed. "Yet, I have not lost hope. The experience of the ages teaches us that all human acts and endeavors, especially the unjust and the violent, prosper only up to a measured level . . . just as excruciating pain forces man to lose consciousness and relieves his misery."

"Your observation is valid," Germaine replied. "But how long are we to wait for the tide to be stemmed? The leaders of the continent should have joined long ago to challenge this self-indulgent supremacy. I've come to appeal to you . . . to affirm that efforts are being made to unify such opposition . . . and to offer my assistance."

"The time will . . . must . . . come. It is not far off. I am certain you will be among those called on to help."

The two met once more a few days later at Pyrna. Gentz repeated his promise.

Reports of Madame de Staël's meetings with the British agent spread through the capitals of Europe like flames blown by the mistral across the dry grass of Provence meadows. Though Bonaparte was immersed in trying to put out the insurrection in Spain, he withdrew from the conference table long enough to place more rigid restrictions on the Baroness. In her golden chariot, which was a gleaming beacon streaking across the countryside, Germaine was easy prey for the Emperor's surveillance teams. Authorities in every town and hamlet on her route spotted her quickly and, under strict orders of severe penalties to their own positions, they stopped and cross-examined her party.

Madame de Staël tolerated the personal harassment. But she was anguished at the evidence she saw of Bonaparte's tyranny as she crossed Germany on her way back to Switzerland. She saw for herself what Prosper de Barante had reported to her earlier . . . the devastation of the lands and the suffering of the people in Thuringia and neighboring German states where thousands of families were destitute after plunder and destruction by French armies.

When she reached the shores of Lake Geneva in July and returned to Coppet, Germaine found a letter from Joseph Fouché. She was not surprised. He quoted Bonaparte:

> *Madame de Staël has become mixed up with the clique of German plotters and with the gamblers of London, particularly with a man named Gentz. Place this female under police supervision at Coppet and give orders accordingly to the Prefect of Geneva and the Commander of the Gendarmes. In the past, I have looked upon her as an irritant; now, I want you to understand, I count her a menace. I've instructed my Foreign Minister to inform all my agents at foreign courts about this change of attitude . . . .*

Chapter 3
Two Friends in Deep Despair

The roses on the table beside Madame Récamier's narrow bed in the chamber reserved for her at Coppet were a delicate pink. They reminded Madame de Staël of Juliette's complexion, almost white with a faint blush of color, just enough to assure the beholder that life flowed happily and vitally beneath flawless skin.

Germaine insisted that these flowers be replaced with fresh ones everyday. It had been ten months since her dearest friend had been in this room which opened onto her own. No matter how crowded the mansion, she permitted no one else to occupy this haven in Juliette's absence. Though alone, now, Madame de Staël sensed Juliette's presence.

Careful to avoid disturbing the rest of the bouquet, the Baroness withdrew one rose whose blossom was ready to unfold. She sat on the bed, sinking deep into the soft quilt over which a pale green coverlet was spread.

Your safety would be threatened if you were here with me, Germaine mused, fingering the bloom, but I wish, sister of my choice, that you were here beside me. So often my life seems no more than a vague noise around me, entering neither my mind nor my soul. Conjuring your spirit is a kind of opium I take which helps me escape my suffering. I dazzle myself with a household of friends, but nobody comes within miles of my soul. I must speak with you, within the sanctuary of my heart, where everything is decided. I have reduced my company to the quiet and passionless elite of a few essential friends. There are no longer the hordes of last summer . . . and little entertainment. Without you, I find it impossible to think of amusements. My theatre is quite deserted.

I have but one sorrow and it is a cruel one . . . it is the fear of not being loved. There are times when I wonder if I should replace this love with a belief in God.

Much of my time is spent on my work on Germany. I write and I read in order to write . . . this is the foundation of my days.

For this summer of 1808, Germaine added two new permanent guests, Madame Julie de Krüdener and Zacharias Werner, proselytizing mystics, who roused her interest in religion. Germaine was fascinated but cautious, distrusting Madame de Krüdener's zealousness and Werner's tendency to combine literary and moral obeisance.

Julie de Krüdener had visited Coppet when the Neckers were still alive and she had been a striking young blonde. She was notorious for attracting well-known men as lovers over whom she cast a spell of despairing gloom . . . two died under mysterious circumstances. Julie lost both her beauty and lustrous hair early, then turned to wearing a wig and preaching. Germaine listened but was not wholly convinced.

She found Zacharias, a brilliant writer, more irresistible. Though he was frenzied and unstable and had a sunken, cadaverous build, Werner had a sensual appeal. She rated him the third greatest German dramatist, after Goethe and Schlegel. Intrigued by his hostess's agonized soul and colossal heart, he called her "Notre Dame de Coppet" and wrote sonnets to her. He described her as "a queen who is the image of grace."

Foreign princes, diplomats and ministers from Holland, Prussia, Austria, Bavaria and other countries filled the chateau for short visits. It was through one of these guests, her friend Clemens Metternich, the Austrian Ambassador, that Madame de Staël's fears were confirmed about the danger to which Juliette would be subject if she made the journey to Switzerland.

The Ambassador called on Germaine to discuss her meetings and continuing correspondence with Baron von Gentz. He also brought word about Madame Récamier.

"Bonaparte is irate with the reports he has on Juliette's salon," Metternich related. "He resents her popularity and the sway she has over the members of his court. His own ministers and other government officials escape the rigors of their duties and mingle with foreign dignitaries in the relaxed atmosphere of Madame Récamier's unpretentious receptions. One evening during an imperial party, aware that many of his staff were missing, Bonaparte turned petulant. 'Since when,' he asked acidly, 'have the Council meetings been held at Madame Récamier's?' The Emperor considers your friend's salon the Paris branch of Coppet. He has published a decree declaring every foreigner who frequents her residence a personal enemy. It deters only the most timid."

Learning this, Madame de Staël, who had been imploring Juliette to make the journey to Coppet, ceased pressing her. The risk would be too great. Germaine ached, knowing that a visit would ease the rift that was widening between the two of them since Juliette had renewed her encouragement of Prosper de Barante's attention . . . and help her face the suffering which those she loved were causing.

The major antagonist in her private world continued to be Benjamin Constant. He persisted in refusing to adjust to a lasting, intellectually compatible relationship for which she insisted on writing the rules. Instead, Germaine lamented, he prefers to pursue the whimpering Charlotte von Hardenberg du Tertre. She considered even the contemplation of sharing the rest of his life with this ignorant, vapid woman an insult to their long association.

Madame de Staël plucked a petal from the rose for Constant, another for Charlotte. Then a third, for Maurice O'Donnell. They lay in her lap on her blue chiffon gown. Germaine pulled four more petals which fell into place around the first three.

The four comprised a labyrinth all their own . . . Juliette, her husband Jacques-Rose Récamier, Prince Augustus of Prussia and Prosper de Barante.

The Prince wrote often to Germaine asking her to intervene with Juliette who held him in suspense by postponing the commitment of her vows to him. "She binds herself by proprieties that resemble duties," he complained. "She makes cruel sport of what is more to me than life. She mocks the oath she took on her soul's salvation."

Madame de Staël encouraged the despairing lover and suggested he be patient. She did not press Juliette, on the other hand, for she knew she was tormented by Jacques-Rose's gentle but firm urging that she decide in favor of duty to her husband over love for a prince.

Germaine could understand that her friend was torn between loyalties . . . but why did Juliette have to turn for consolation to Prosper, whom she herself still hoped to marry! Of course he'd comply . . . he saw Madame Récamier everyday and no man could resist this lovely creature. Madame de Staël was distressed, knowing that, like Juliette, Prosper also vacillated. He was a sensitive young man unable to shake his commitment to Germaine while being helplessly infatuated with Juliette.

Madame de Staël drew out one more petal . . . as she did the rose fell apart. This last was for Augustus Schlegel, her adoring slave and indispensable personal scholar who often sulked with unrequitable love. The rest were for those who no longer mattered.

Germaine stood up. The petals fell languidly down her skirt to the floor.

The day had darkened as the afternoon slipped into evening. The soft, lustrous greens on the ceiling and wood panels which complemented the color of the silks on the furniture struggled to sustain the remaining daylight. The airy scene of birds of paradise in flight among willowy branches on the Oriental wallpaper behind the Louis XV bed vibrated magically in the dimness.

Madame de Staël left Juliette's room for her own and sat at her desk where lighted tapers flickered in a candelabra. She began a letter to her friend. "I am moved by your letters," she wrote. "When you start to write to me, tell yourself that each additional line is a pleasure for me in my wretched loneliness."

She paused. Before she went on, Madame de Staël walked to the window. "Coppet is strangely beautiful tonight. I looked at the moon which is reflected like a column of fire on the lake. Ah, if only you were here!"

In Paris, the modest Récamier residence on Rue Basse-du-Rempart was strangely mute. No guests had been invited for the evening and Jacques-Rose was out of the city seeking to rebuild his financial resources. The mistress of the town house had dismissed her small staff of servants and was alone as dusk encroached.

Juliette Récamier stood motionless, with the bearing of a goddess. She was dressed in white . . . all white . . . a long, simple gossamer gown, flat satin slippers, a narrow ribbon holding back black curls, releasing a halo of ringlets that fell softly about her pale face. The only color was in the deep pink of her lips and the violet of her luminous eyes. When Juliette moved, she floated from room to room like a celestial being worshipping at altars in a temple. The slender candle she carried in a bronze holder cast shimmering shadows and lighted the way for this ethereal maiden who paused briefly before a painting, a small sculpture, a porcelain epergne and the few other treasures she had retained from her precious collection.

At the entrance to her bed chamber, Madame Récamier hesitated, turned, glanced back at the dimming hallway behind her, then reluctantly, as if fearing what lay behind the door, pushed it open and entered. She glided past the ivory carved wood bed, the one superb concession to luxury in the room . . . it stood on a carpeted dais, one step up from the polished floor. Her body slipped compliantly into the chair at the bureau plat on which Juliette placed the candle. She drew out a phial from the drawer, removed the stopper and emptied the contents . . . a profusion of opium pills . . . onto the lace handkerchief she spread on the writing pad. She started to count, stopping at thirty, there were at least as many more. She scooped them up, cupping the fatal dose in her palm as she raised them to her lips.

Not yet, she murmured. She held the capsules over the opening of the bottle, let them trickle back, one by one, then returned the cap.

The candle sputtered, startling her. She sighed, relieved that no one had interfered with her ritual, took a quill from the stand, dipped it in the ink well and began to write:

> *My Dear Jacques:*
> *I am determined to leave this life and wish to tell you that till my last heartbeat, I shall keep the memory of your kindness and the regret that I have not been all to you that I should have been. I count upon your friendship, of which you have given me so many proofs, to carry out my last wishes. I wish that my death should not break the ties which unite you to my family and that you will be as generous and helpful to them as you have always been.*
>
> *I have contributed with some of my friends to an orphanage. I desire that you should do as much as you can for this establishment. I commend to you those who are fond of me.*
>
> *I leave to you the consoling thought that I owe you all the happiness that I have found in this life.*
>
> *Juliette*

Madame Récamier placed the letter in an envelope, took another sheet of ivory vellum from the neat stack at her elbow and began again.

Dearest Germaine . . .

Juliette stared at the blank page. Words would not come. How could she explain to her friend that she chose to take her life rather than face making a decision between two men to whom she felt equally and intractably bound? She gazed into the flame of the candle seeking an answer in its clarifying brilliance. Her head began to pound. Her heart beat so rapidly that Juliette placed her hand on her bosom to subdue the throbbing.

Why should the resolution to this dilemma be more difficult than her decision to reject the advances of Bonaparte? Then, there had been much at stake . . . the possibility of financial ruin. The alternative . . . mistress to the Emperor . . . had been unthinkable. There had been no choice . . . doubt as to her course had never entered her mind. She had gambled and lost . . . lost her material possessions. Though she had lost, she had won. Together with her husband, she had maintained their social position and friends . . . and she had preserved her dignity.

Now, alas! This impasse was her own fault . . . her own doing . . . her own weakness.

She had betrayed two kind, tender, forbearing men. Her husband, who for years had surrounded her with luxury, respected her privacy and tolerated her innocent flirtations without question. And Prince Augustus, who, in good faith, offered her his love and an exalted position at his side through marriage into the imperial family of Prussia.

Neither man deserved to suffer the humiliation and injury she would inflict on him if she chose the other. Only through death could she free them . . . because for them, sorrow would be easier to bear than rejection.

But Germaine . . . for her, Juliette's death would be more than rejection. Dear God! How could she impose more grief on the woman whom she loved so dearly!

The struggle for decision seemed greater now than Madame Récamier first determined to take her life. She reached out, fumbling for the phial of opium and knocked it over . . . the bottle rolled off the edge and fell to the floor.

Madame Récamier gripped the desk, pushed herself away and sank to the floor crawling about in search of the container. Finding it, she clutched it tightly and threw herself across the bed.

Juliette lay back, at first unable to control her trembling. Her mind went blank. Then the pain lifted, somehow, and she slipped into a deep, peaceful sleep.

When she awakened, the chamber was dark. The taper had burned itself out. She felt strangely relieved and refreshed. Her mind was clear. The decision made. She felt absolute confidence and contentment in what she had to do. She *knew* she had to live!

The overwhelming vision of Germaine de Staël in anguished mourning over her death had granted Juliette the determination to live . . . to restore the weakened bonds of their friendship and savor its joy.

Germaine had kept Juliette from suicide by the power of her passion and her intellect. There was no need for her presence in making the other decision. She would have stayed Juliette's hand, of course, but she would have interfered with her decision between the men. This was a choice Juliette had to make herself . . . as the kind of woman that Germaine had inspired her to become . . . a woman with her own identity.

Juliette Récamier chose Jacques-Rose Récamier . . . not the man . . . nor the husband. She chose life as she lived it with him . . . not the wealth which they no longer enjoyed nor the possibility of a renewed fortune. Nor was it for love, though her affection for him was deep. Jacques-Rose created an atmosphere . . . free of stress, demands and dissension . . . in which she could flourish. He was indulgent to the point of being permissive. He was helpful, supportive, understanding and paternal. Even his request which put her under the greatest stress of her life by forcing her to reconsider her wish to leave him . . . was no more unfair to her than her own petition for a divorce was to him.

Life with Jacques-Rose meant the freedom to think and act by the principles Germaine had taught her.

Rejecting Prince Augustus tore at her soul. She would have to live with this agony. She loved him as she had never before loved anyone. He possessed her heart. Her hope was that he would realize that as a commoner she would have stood in the way of his obligations. The formalities of court life would have made demands that competed with her need for privacy and independence . . . the duties thrust upon a royal princess required a submissive nature, not the free spirit of an unrestrained Frenchwoman.

The Coppet idyl had separated both the Prince and Juliette from reality. Together, they had been dazzled . . . by the brilliant sun against the snow-covered Alps, by the sparkling waters of Lac Léman and by the ghosts from romantic interludes in history.

Bittersweet memories! If only it had been another time, earlier in their lives before they had built bonds with others . . . and if only it had been another less enchanting place.

Juliette accepted the guilt for having succumbed to Augustus's tender persistence and hoped he would bear the injury of rejection without malice.

In her introspection, Madame Récamier went further. She accepted the blame and responsibility for the rift in her friendship with Madame de Staël. She had the will to face the girlish delight she enjoyed in her coquetry. She vowed she would no longer toy with Prosper's affection which could destroy the cherished closeness she had with Germaine. Though she would not refrain completely from indulging her whims, she would modify her pleasures . . . but never again would she yield to the temptation of Prosper.

Nor would she reveal this crisis nor its outcome to Germaine. Madame de Staël would know of the change from the restraint in Juliette's actions toward the young man and by the visits she would make to Coppet in spite of Bonaparte's restrictions. There would never again be a question of the depth of Madame Récamier's devotion to her dearest and only true friend.

Juliette returned to her desk. Instead of composing a letter to Germaine, she wrote to Prince Augustus. She promised to see him again during the following summer in Switzerland and closed by saying, "After profound thought, I have decided to free you from your oath. Your rank requires a wife of royal blood, of which, sadly I have none. I would only expose you to dangers for which one day you would not forgive yourself. My heart is heavy. But there is no other way."

Prince Augustus was devastated and sent a letter by return post. "You have destroyed all my illusions and made me the unhappiest of men. You do not even grant me the courtesy of an explanation . . . not even a lie to account for this sudden change. I beg of you, dear Juliette, do not reduce me to despair. You do not know what I am capable of doing. I place my destiny in your hands. I know you will not abuse it."

Her reply was gentle. "I did not wish to plunge you into despair. I would like to see you again and wish only to replace our love with a deep friendship."

The exchange of letters which followed vacillated from all degrees of anger to extremes of tenderness and continued for several months. The strain became too much for the Prince. He finally wrote:

"I feel, unfortunately too late, that we were not meant to be happy together. I beg you not to write to me again. Your letters give me too much pain. Adieu, ma chérie, for the last time."

When Juliette received this message, she was back at Coppet with Madame de Staël. "At last he acknowledges the futility of trying to continue our relationship on the same basis it was when we parted," she told Germaine. "But I do not read this without sadness."

The Prince wrote to the mistress of Coppet in an effort to justify his wish to make the break complete with Madame Récamier. "I have recovered from the illusions of love ever since Juliette misled me. However, I forgive her all the suffering she caused me."

The book on the great love of Juliette Récamier's early life was closed.

Chapter 4
Talleyrand "Punished"

Y
ou are a thief, an ingrate, a traitor, a liar, an atheist and a coward!'"
Jean-Baptiste Bernadotte, Marshal of the Grand Army of France,
paced with long, deliberate strides across the highly polished floor
of Madame de Staël's library, mimicking Napoleon's rage with fiendish
delight. Germaine listened in bemused silence.

"The Emperor," he told her, "flung these words and many others at
Charles Talleyrand before a special meeting of the Council . . . in the
presence of all the ministers."

"At last, there is a subject on which I agree with Bonaparte,"
Germaine conceded with a wry smile.

Jean-Baptiste, the handsome, strong-willed Gascon who had plotted
against Bonaparte years before in Madame de Staël's Paris residence, was
visiting the Baroness at Coppet on his way to the battlefront in Austria.

"While Napoleon was in Spain," he explained, "he received a letter
from his mother revealing collusion against him by his two top advisors,
Talleyrand and Fouché. With evidence from so unimpeachable a source, he
was compelled to depart, leaving the Spanish uprising unresolved."

Bernadotte's first-hand report helped lift the desolation Germaine
suffered . . . like a trapped fugitive . . . in her small corner of Switzerland.

Six months before Bernadotte's visit, Napoleon's military
invulnerability had begun to seem founded on myth. His armies were
meeting assault on all fronts. He began racing across the continent from one
front of his empire to the other, trying to put out pockets of flame in a
spreading fire.

The British had gained control of the seas. Under the leadership of
the Duke of Wellington, they had landed in Portugal and were marching into
Spain to assist the Spaniards against the French.

In Erfurt, Bonaparte organized a spectacular congress to extract a promise for military assistance from Czar Alexander to shore up his eastern defenses if the Austrians attacked. The Czar vacillated, and Napoleon was forced to leave without a commitment to quell the Spanish insurrection, which slaughtered three hundred thousand French troops.

At the time Austria did declare war on France, the French Emperor heard that Talleyrand and Fouché were conspiring against him. He rushed back to a Paris festering with open criticism of his setbacks and with plots to overthrow him. Opportunistic friends were taking advantage of his beleaguered position.

Within hours of his arrival in the capital, Bonaparte had given Fouché a bitter tongue lashing . . . in private. He then summoned the Council and launched the tirade against Talleyrand openly before an embarrassed assemblage of officials.

"Napoleon," Bernadotte chuckled as he continued his account, "whipped himself into a fury at Talleyrand. 'Nothing is sacred to you! You would sell your own father,' he declared in a flood of revilement that lasted a full hour. He blamed Talleyrand for the murder of the Duc d'Enghien . . . for the Spanish war . . . for all the opposition he has been encountering."

Madame de Staël smiled disdainfully. "But Talleyrand did not move a muscle nor change his expression," she said.

Jean-Baptiste nodded. "He demonstrated supreme control," he replied, "even when Bonaparte ridiculed his lameness and taunted him about his wife's stupidity and infidelity. 'I have the power to break you into a thousand pieces,' he shouted, 'but you are too contemptible for me to bother.'

"The Emperor stopped as though he had exhausted his vocabulary of invectives. 'You,' he hissed finally, 'on whom I have bestowed the title of His Most Serene Highness, the Prince of Benevento, are dung in a silk stocking!'"

"And what infamous sentence did Bonaparte impose on the great Talleyrand?" Madame de Staël asked acidly. "Did he banish the traitor to the West Indies?"

"I have learned not to try to anticipate the workings of the Emperor's mind," Bernadotte replied. "A few days after the public reproof, the two met at a reception that gave Talleyrand the opportunity to make the first move toward a reconciliation. The Emperor may consider naked disgrace sufficient reprimand. Talleyrand is no longer Grand Chamberlain, but he continues as the Vice-Grand Consul."

"Bonaparte has no human compassion," Germaine observed. "He would rather have Talleyrand on his side than against him."

She paused reflectively, fingering the gold letter opener that Talleyrand had given her. "Napoleon's advisors, who would betray him as Brutus did Caesar, go free, while I remain in exile."

"One of his commandants asked him how he excused Talleyrand's deceit," Bernadotte said. "The Emperor replied offhandedly. 'I can't be rid of him. He is the only person with whom I can carry on an intelligent conversation!'"

Remembering the profound, spirited discussions in which she had indulged with the faithless Charles, Madame de Staël felt only a twinge of regret.

"When Juliette Récamier learned of Bonaparte's remarks," Jean-Baptiste added, "she was amused and remarked, 'If he had used his genius wisely, Bonaparte could have enjoyed the constant company of the most eloquent conversationalist in all Europe . . . the Baroness de Staël!'"

"Bonaparte deserves the infidel," Germaine said with a shrug.

Chapter 5
Madame Constant

The Baroness de Staël pushed open the heavy door to one of the plush chambers in the luxurious Hotel de l'Angleterre in Sécheron and burst into the room, startling a small pretty woman in a pale green nightgown who sat on a low stool bathing her feet in a porcelain basin.

"I have come," Germaine announced in the commanding tones of Hermione, "because you are a Hardenberg!"

The woman to whom this assertion was addressed recognized the intruder and recovered instantly from her surprise.

"Excuse me," she said politely. "It is late . . . after ten o'clock: I hardly expected you tonight." She drew a towel from the couch on which Germaine had settled herself, wiped one foot and then the other with careful deliberation and pulled on embroidered satin slippers that matched her gown.

With haughty reserve, Madame de Staël followed the final stages of the pediluve out of the corner of her eye. What an imposition it was, she reflected, to interrupt the absorbing evening she was having with her children when she had left to travel the few kilometers from Coppet to Sécheron.

Germaine treasured the time she shared with her daughter and sons when she left her guests to fend for themselves. These rare evenings were spent in the small, second floor drawing room and were devoted to discussing family affairs or pursuing individual interests in quiet contentment. Auguste, almost nineteen, played the harpsichord. Fifteen-year-old Albert had developed a talent for sketching and drew likenesses of his mother as she worked on her manuscript of *De l'Allemagne*. Albertine, now twelve, read from a growing collection of books.

This evening they had been involved in a discussion of their ambivalent feelings about the war between France and Austria. They wanted Bonaparte to lose but they also wanted victory for their friend Marshal Bernadotte. Madame de Staël had begun to lay out plans to leave Europe when Olive Uginet brought her a letter sealed with the Hardenberg crest.

Germaine scanned the short message, which was signed "The Countess Charlotte von Hardenberg." The writer implied that she had a communication from Benjamin Constant that would be of interest to Madame de Staël and extended an invitation for Germaine to meet with her at the hotel in Sécheron. No time was specified for the interview.

The Baroness's curiosity was aroused. She sent no reply. Instead, she ordered her calèche and set out for Sécheron as soon as she finished dining with her children.

Madame de Staël mulled over every rumor, every detail she had heard of Benjamin's friendship with Charlotte. Could the reason for this meeting be that Benjamin sought Germaine's permission to marry Charlotte? Should she disapprove? Why should she? She did have one objection, which was more a condition . . . that they wait until she herself had remarried. The thought of losing Benjamin while she had no firm prospect for a husband was too humiliating to face.

Now, after sitting in the same room with this child-woman, Germaine could not imagine that Benjamin Constant would be attracted to someone so prosaic, so shallow, so cloying.

After removing the bowl of water, Charlotte returned, approaching Germaine with an air of confidence that was out of character.

"I am now Madame Constant," she announced calmly. "My husband is Benjamin Henri Constant de Rebecque."

Madame de Staël was stunned. "Madame Constant! Husband!" That the union had already taken place was reprehensible, beyond belief.

"When did it happen?" she screamed.

"Almost a year ago," Charlotte said bluntly.

Germaine was outraged. "Where *is* he?" she demanded.

"He's not here." Charlotte was unruffled.

"You mean he has left you to tell me . . . he could not face me himself!"

Charlotte did not reply.

"He is a coward," Germaine said, irritated by the new Madame Constant's control. "Where is he hiding?"

Germaine despised betrayal only slightly more than defeat. More than just anger, she felt disgraced, cornered. Trying to match her rival's outward restraint, she began obliquely: "Since Benjamin won't speak for himself I will do it for him. What do you know about him?" she asked not expecting a reply.

"He's a good man," Charlotte replied softly.

"What has he told you of the years we spent together? How we met? How he pursued me? How I respected his brilliant mind and his eloquence but rejected him as a lover?" She told how Benjamin had feigned suicide in order to seduce her, talked of his initial eagerness to comply in every way to her demands, told of their happiness together, their intellectual compatibility, their intimacies. How hard she worked to help and advise him, how she introduced him into powerful circles to advance his career, loaned him money that he never repaid. And then, how he changed and their violent arguments began. How he vacillated, rejecting her but always returning, professing that his happiness was with her and that he could not exist away from her. Germaine told Charlotte everything except that Benjamin was Albertine's father.

Toward the end of her confessional, Germaine saw that Charlotte's faith was beginning to falter. She had remained silent except to murmur unsteadily, "He is a good man," when Germaine hesitated to catch her breath.

"Benjamin has *no* sensitivity to the needs of a woman," Madame de Staël said. "He's vain and self-centered. He rarely considers others. He imposes himself on his friends. He attaches himself to a woman and takes from her. I am not the first nor will I be the last victim to suffer from his selfishness. Among them all, it is I who have done the most for him. Without me he would not have achieved the social acceptance and the political success he enjoys in France. He owes everything to me."

Charlotte's advantage as Benjamin's wife did not sustain her through Germaine's torrent. She could neither match nor tolerate the hours of persistent ranting. Her head throbbed, her heart ached. Was Benjamin truly the insensitive monster Germaine so dramatically described? He had vowed to Charlotte as he had to Germaine, that he could not live without her. To whom was he sincere? Charlotte was reminded of the years of broken promises and the neglect she suffered each time Benjamin left her to return to Madame de Staël.

The Baroness walked to a window and drew back the drapery as she planned her next move. Dawn was breaking . . . it was four o'clock in the morning.

"Since you are already married to Benjamin," she said quietly, "there is nothing I can do to alter your position." All the rancor was gone from her voice.

Charlotte, worn down by the lengthy recital, felt a measure of compassion for her visitor.

Quick to exploit any seeming weakness, Germaine said, "There is something that you might do for me."

"What would that be? I'll do what you ask and bind Benjamin to the same terms," Charlotte replied meekly.

"You must vow to keep your marriage a secret for as long as I wish. It should not be difficult since you have already done so for almost a year. I plan to leave for America soon . . . you can announce your union when I've left. In the meantime, you must return to Germany and Benjamin must come back with me to Coppet till the end of the summer."

The exhausted Charlotte submitted. "I agree. I will do it for my future happiness with Benjamin." But she had little confidence in the security of her role as Madame Constant.

Later that day, Benjamin Constant returned to the hotel, eager to hear the outcome of the meeting between the two women in his life. He found Charlotte in a state of unrestrained agitation. She had been reviewing every facet of the interview with growing frustration, concluding finally that Germaine had successfully manipulated her.

"Madame de Staël," she said, "overwhelmed me. She is humiliated at having lost you, and reacted with an outpouring that makes me doubt the wisdom of our marriage . . . and I made promises I now regret."

Charlotte broke down and wept bitterly.

Between sobs she revealed the conditions Germaine had demanded. Benjamin tried to comfort his wife, saying he would also have to accept Germaine's terms.

"But don't you see," she protested. "We have been duped. Madame de Staël controls the path to our happiness . . . she could delay her departure as long as she wishes . . . or worse, she might never leave the country and might never lift our bonds of secrecy."

"You have accepted the conditions," Benjamin replied with irritation and disbelief. "We have no choice but to comply."

He suggested that Charlotte leave immediately for Germany, but she reminded him that Bonaparte was waging war in the area of her family estate. Benjamin decided then that Charlotte should stay with his father at Brèvans while Benjamin went on to Coppet.

The elder Constant was furious with his son for agreeing to separate from his wife. Benjamin had been at Coppet for barely two weeks when, in an effort to appease Captain Constant, he slipped away to stay with Charlotte at a small auberge in the hamlet of Arbois at the foot of the Alps. He was certain he had escaped from Germaine who was involved with plans for a journey to Lyons to attend the theatre where the famous actor Talma would be performing.

On Benjamin's second day with his wife, Auguste de Staël arrived at Arbois and convinced Constant to uphold his part of the bargain with his mother. To avoid further agonizing scenes, Benjamin complied and went on with Auguste back to the den of the lioness in Lyons.

On the eighth of June, the Baroness de Staël was hosting a grand reception in her suite at the splendid Hotel du Parc in Lyons after the premier performance of the theatre season. The drawing rooms were crowded with most of the actors and many of her friends who had come down from Paris.

At the height of the party, Charlotte suddenly appeared, uninvited and unannounced. Benjamin was chagrined. With Madame de Staël at his side he abruptly escorted his wife to the lobby.

He fought to suppress his anger. "What are you doing here?" he asked Charlotte.

"It is the eighth of June," she whimpered. "Today is our wedding anniversary."

"Must I remind you of the promises you have made to Madame de Staël," Benjamin replied without a trace of acknowledgment or sentimentality in his voice. "I suggest you leave, immediately."

Benjamin walked his wife out to her carriage, chiding her for a lack of good taste. Germaine watched the exit in triumph.

At midnight, while the party was still in progress, Benjamin was delivered a message from Charlotte who had taken a room in a small hotel down the street. "I've just taken a dose of opium," she wrote. "You have abandoned me but I do not blame you for perhaps your heart is broken too. Before leaving this life, I pray to God to pardon me and to forgive you. I have no ill will for anyone, not even for the woman who destroys me. But can I not see you just once more? Please make haste."

Germaine and Benjamin rushed away from the guests to Charlotte's side. They found her lying limp on a couch with an opened bottle of laudanum in her hand. She was pale and weak as a victim of the plague. Yet, Charlotte was conscious and lucid for she had not taken a fatal dose. Holding her in his arms Benjamin told her he still loved her. Germaine looked down on the poor women with pity and disdain and assured her that though the conditions she set forth for the marriage would not be lifted, Charlotte and Benjamin would soon be permitted to live together openly as man and wife.

Madame Constant smiled listlessly wondering whether she should have emptied the vial and died in peace.

Chapter 6
Destination America

The summer of 1809 at the Chateau of Coppet was no less stimulating or rewarding than it had been in earlier years. But when news reached Madame de Staël of Napoleon's victory over the Austrians at Wagram, where Jean-Baptiste Bernadotte had been in command, she gathered her children in the privacy of her boudoir and told them that she feared remaining within the boundaries of a Europe in which Bonaparte was all powerful. Together they made plans to leave for America.

Germaine wrote first to Thomas Jefferson, whom she had befriended during his stay in Paris in 1789 and who was now President of the United States. "When shall we see each other again?" she asked. "If this Old World is to be nothing but a single man, what is the purpose of staying here?"

Jefferson was cautious in his reply, avoiding a direct invitation to Germaine by offering his hospitality to her son in order to preserve the delicate international ties he maintained with France.

> *My dear Baroness:*
> *The grandson of Monsieur Necker cannot fail to receive a hearty welcome in our country, which has held your father in such high esteem. I, myself, have loved the virtues and honored the great talents of the grandfather, the attention I received in his natal home and particular esteem for yourself are additional titles to whatever service I can render him. Auguste will find a sincerely warm welcome at Monticello, where I shall be, at the time of his arrival, in the bosom of my family.*
> *Most cordially,*
> *Thomas Jefferson*

Gouverneur Morris, who handled most of Germaine's American investments including large parcels of land he secured for her along the St. Lawrence River in New York State, was free to write without inhibition.

> *My dear Baroness de Staël:*
> *After you and your son arrive in New York, you will come here to Morrisania to drink milk and rest. Early in July you will visit your lands. By mid-September you will come back to rest from your efforts, pick peaches, go for walks, write poetry, novels, anything you like. When my retreat has lost its charms, you will settle in town, where with the help of a good cook you will dine very well. The amusements of New Yorkers are, as elsewhere, to digest, to say witty things, to speak ill of your neighbors and the rest. We look forward to your arrival.*
> *May you have a good crossing,*
> *Gouverneur Morris*

While Madame de Staël waited for replies, Bonaparte shocked his commanders by deposing the Pope, who had dared to issue a bill of excommunication against him. The people of the Empire, predominantly Catholic, were terrified that Bonaparte had challenged God by making the head of the Church a prisoner within the walls of the Vatican.

Bonaparte was as unmoved by revolts as he was by attempts on his life. With his mastery of publicity and instinct for timing, he capitalized on the momentum of seething opposition by stunning his enemies with a startling declaration.

The Emperor of France announced that he would divorce his wife Josephine and marry a royal princess who would produce an heir and thus establish an hereditary empire. This woman was Marie-Louise, Archduchess of Austria, daughter of Emperor Francis II, and niece of Marie Antoinette, the guillotined Queen of France!

Simultaneously, Germaine de Staël, whose eagerness to flee Europe had softened, set about her own plans for marriage. She ached to even the score with Benjamin and puncture his vanity. She wrote her dear friend Mathieu de Montmorency in Paris and asked him to approach Prosper de

Barante to remind him of his proposal and to urge him now to carry out his vow.

Prosper replied with a long, passionate letter sent directly to Germaine. He explained that he had anguished long over his decision between faithful friendship and love and had decided on the former. "Though I cannot take you as my wife, you will always be for me the dearest of sisters," he wrote, "and yours the heart with which mine has had the greatest harmony. It has been a difficult choice . . . a moment of despair. But I hope you have sensed, as I have, that two people have never been granted such deep understanding of one another as we have . . . even to the most fleeting nuances we have enjoyed."

To escape the reality of this rejection and resolve her vacillation about a trip to America, Madame de Staël turned to working on her book, *De l'Allemagne*. She worked with such concentration that she was amazed at her own absorption. Everything is stormy in and around me, she reflected, and, amidst it all I carry out an intellectual assignment as if the mind could be separated from the heart.

Chapter 7
Bonaparte Is Distracted from the Baroness

Madame de Staël smiled but spoke firmly to Uginet, who stood at flawless attention across from her in the library.

"Do sit down, Eugene," she urged. "Must I address you as 'Monsieur Uginet' to have you realize that you deserve more than the station of an ordinary servant in our household? Come, join me. We have matters to review which have vital bearing on my . . . on our future."

"As you wish, Madame la Baronne," Uginet said, sliding his broad frame onto a stiff, high back chair near the doorway.

"No. Over here, near us, close to the fire," Germaine insisted. "You must be chilled through after your long journey back from Paris in this frigid February weather."

With the warmth of the blazing logs penetrating his dark, bulky jacket and coarsely woven breeches, the stocky emissary mumbled his appreciation. He sat across the front of the fireplace from Madame de Staël who had Auguste at her side.

Eugene had no quarrel with the structured, titled society he served. He performed as he was asked, took pride in his work and was confident in his execution of assignments. His employer treated her staff with geniality but this familiarity surprised him.

Anxious to pursue the details of Uginet's mission, Madame de Staël circuited his unease.

"So," she said skimming the legal document Eugene had given her on his arrival. "Monsieur Nicolle has accepted my manuscript." Gabrielle-Henri Nicolle, a Paris bookseller, was the leading publisher in France.

"He is enthusiastic and is willing to publish your book under the terms we negotiated," Uginet responded.

"With only one third of the manuscript complete?"

"Yes."

"I'm relieved not to have to accept an offer from a German publisher," Germaine said with satisfaction. "I have worked six years on *De l'Allemagne*, which I consider will be my masterwork and I want it to appear first in France."

Auguste de Staël was following the conversation with interest. "But what about censorship?" he asked. Madame de Staël had come to rely more and more on this poised, intelligent young man now approaching twenty. "The latest decree requires that a complete work be submitted for the censor's approval before it is published."

"Monsieur Nicolle is confident that Madame la Baronne will finish the book in time to meet the censor's demands," Uginet responded quickly. He adjusted readily to the informality of the meeting. He adapted to the amiability but would not overstep the line of propriety.

"Your concern is well taken, Auguste," Madame de Staël told her son. "But I trust Nicolle's judgment. I don't need encouragement to go on, but his confidence will be a spur."

"There are other restrictions on books that do not apply to other written matter," Auguste went on. "Even after the censors have approved the manuscript, both the Director of Publications and the Minister of Police have the power to block the work."

Germaine scoffed at this possibility. "Do you believe that my friend Joseph Fouché would stand in my way?"

"I doubt he would. But what if he were replaced by a man who doesn't know or respect you and wants to impress Bonaparte?"

"That will never happen. Even when he plotted against the Emperor, Fouché was severely reprimanded but not dismissed. As for Bonaparte, his upcoming marriage has put him in an ebullient frame of mind. There is speculation that at the time of the wedding, in early April, he will relax several restraining regulations."

Uginet waited thoughtfully while mother and son thrashed out the censorship issue, then he gestured toward the papers Germaine held on her lap. "Monsieur Nicolle has made arrangements outlined in the agreement to have type set immediately on the pages I left with him. The galleys will be sent to you for correction and then, go to the censors. Meanwhile, you will work on the balance of the manuscript. This procedure is slightly irregular but it is not a violation."

Madame de Staël read the document as Eugene spoke. "Which

printer has Monsieur Nicolle selected?" she asked.

"He decided that Mame will be most cooperative."

"Yes. Here it is! Mame . . . in Tours!" Madame de Staël's eyes danced with delight. Eugene and Auguste were puzzled as she relished this bit of information: "An ideal location!"

"But Mama," Auguste queried. "Tours is hundreds of kilometers from Coppet!"

"It is only forty kilometers from the Chateau of Chaumont!"

"Chaumont?" Auguste was still perplexed.

"I have been corresponding with Monsieur James Le Ray who owns the chateau," the Baroness explained. "He has offered it to us while he is visiting America."

"Will your exile permit us to travel so far into France?" Auguste asked.

"Chaumont is on the edge of the forty-league limit of my exile from Paris . . ."

" . . . and on the route to Nantes, one of the ports of embarkation for the United States." Auguste had grasped the reason for his mother's excitement.

"These arrangements will please Monsieur Nicolle," Uginet said. "While you continue your writing at Chaumont, the galleys can travel quickly to and from Mame's shop."

"We shall have a glorious summer!" Madame de Staël exulted. "I shall convert Chaumont into another Coppet for all my friends who have not been able to make the long journey here." Germaine looked into the embers of the fire and envisioned herself among the crowds in the drawing rooms of Le Ray's ancient castle overlooking the Loire Valley. There will be Juliette, she smiled, Prosper, Mathieu and, perhaps even Benjamin, who must be ready to escape from his simpering wife.

"If my book is the success I anticipate," she announced, "we shall never have to leave France!"

The Emperor of France was an impatient, lovesick bridegroom-elect. For weeks, he prepared for his wedding to the Archduchess of Austria. Working with dressmakers to select silks, satins, chiffons and laces from hundreds of bolts of fabrics and trimmings, Bonaparte ordered an extravagant trousseau as a gift for the bride he had never seen. He presided with meticulous attention over the details for the grandiose ceremony and lavish nuptial fetes.

On the day Marie-Louise was due to arrive in Paris, a heavy thunderstorm raged. When word reached Napoleon that her entourage was delayed outside the city, he set out on horseback to find the travelers himself. By the time he encountered the carriages, the Emperor was soaked through. Unheralded, he bounded into Marie-Louise's coach, startled the poor young woman and ordered her ladies-in-waiting into another carriage. Later, at court, he announced suggestively that he and his bride-to-be suited one another "exceedingly well."

The royal wedding, a triumph for Bonaparte, took place on the first of April. A festive mood spread out from Paris to help dispel the Empire's sense of gloom and threat of war.

At Coppet, the day came and went without a ripple of acknowledgment.

On April 15, the Baroness de Staël and her caravan set out for Chaumont-sur-Loire, traveling by way of Lyons, where she received a letter from Juliette. "I promise, ma chérie, to spend the summer with you," she wrote. "And, I'll encourage our friends who are not afraid of solitude to do the same."

There was also a brief note from Prosper de Barante. This errant lover, now twenty-three, met Germaine at Chaumont before the arrival of her children and guests. They spent an idyllic week alone. During this tryst they drank a toast to celebrate Germaine's forty-fourth birthday. Madame de Staël was no longer blind to the role Prosper played in her life. She regarded him as a foolish fancy with whom she might spend an occasional sensual interlude.

With Prosper gone, Germaine swept through the chateau guiding the refurbishing of its chambers in anticipation of a deluge of friends from Paris. She also reviewed the work she still had to complete on *De l'Allemagne*. She was confident she would produce a manuscript that would force the Emperor of France to his knees.

Chapter 8
Chaumont

D
o you consider me a woman of torment or a woman of desire?"

"You are a divine woman, a little disguised to make you more charming."

"Do you love me?"

"If I dare."

"In answer to your dare: I do not wish to compromise myself in writing, but if you will come talk with me this evening I will tell you what I think."

The woman engaged in this written dialogue was the beauteous Juliette Récamier, the eternal coquette.

Her respondent was Augustus Wilhelm Schlegel, still Germaine de Staël's devoted slave, but willing enough to engage in a harmless flirtation.

The two of them were seated at a large round table with Madame de Staël and several other guests in the grand banquet hall at the Chateau of Chaumont. They were playing a game Germaine had devised as a substitute for theatrical productions. Conducted in complete silence, "petite poste" added sparkle and a touch of intrigue to an otherwise quiet life-style. All conversation was replaced by written notes, folded accordion style, that were passed from hand to hand to the addressee, who in turn replied on the same sheet. The rules called for complete privacy and no show of emotion by recipients as they read messages.

Madame de Staël invited to Chaumont only friends with whom she could find quiet diversion . . . those who would not distract her from completing *De l'Allemagne*. Besides her three children, Schlegel and Juliette, there were two new members in her intimate circle: Pertosa, an Italian music teacher and guitarist, and Fanny Randall, a penniless English spinster. Miss Randall was a starchy, disapproving woman, angular and long-faced, a pathetic figure, perhaps, but solid and trustworthy. She had developed a fanatical attachment for both Germaine and Albertine and served them superbly as companion and confidante.

Miss Randall frowned on the frivolity of "petite poste" but stood by, fascinated by the silent excitement.

Scores of notes . . . cryptic, erudite, humorous, accusing, challenging . . . shot back and forth around the table.

Germaine opened one from Juliette that read, "You have not spoken to me today."

"Dear angel," Madame de Staël wrote back, "do not blaspheme even in fun. I have been working on my manuscript till I am almost ill. But it seemed to me that I was talking to you because I was writing to the sound of your voice."

As players tired, the game ended and guests dispersed.

Later, Auguste, Schlegel and Prosper who was down for a brief visit gathered with Juliette in Germaine's apartment. While Pertosa plucked the strings of his guitar, Juliette danced for them, moving lightly and quickly across the tile floor. Her white chiffon gown, hung loosely from the shoulders, swayed in rhythm with her movements, suggesting the suppleness and grace of the firm, virginal body beneath it. As the Italian musician increased the tempo of the music on his guitar, Juliette's slender legs kept pace until at last a crescendo approached. Juliette raised her arms and with a flick of her fingers loosened the pin that kept the hair piled on top her head. The long, dark, glistening waves cascaded down her body in rich, thick clusters. She stopped, spent, her gown slipping to the floor as she sank at Germaine's feet.

Quietly, Pertosa, Auguste, Prosper and Schlegel walked out, leaving the room to Germaine and Juliette.

It was a glorious day. Madame de Staël, leaning back against the stone balustrade of the courtyard, chatted animatedly with some of her guests. Behind her, and below the cliff on which the chateau was built, the verdant plains of the Loire valley stretched far into the distance to meet an unblemished sky.

Looking beyond the vast U-shaped castle, Germaine's eye picked out a couple . . . the woman in white, the man in black . . . who strolled toward the archway that would lead them to the cultivated grounds of the estate. It was Mathieu de Montmorency, tall and slender in the somber garb he had recently adopted, black boots, frockcoat and breeches, with Juliette Récamier, carrying a white parasol to protect her from the sun. Together, they crossed the moat to walk toward the stables.

Out of sight, Madame Récamier's face showed deep concern. "Is there a chance that what you tell me is not true?"

"It is not a rumor," Mathieu replied. "The announcement was made in *Le Moniteur*, the official voice of the government . . . Joseph Fouché has been dismissed as Minister of Police."

"But Germaine was counting on Fouché to ease her book through the censors!" Juliette said with distress. "She will be devastated."

"I know," Mathieu replied. "I need your help to prepare her."

"What of his replacement?" Juliette asked. "Is he someone we know, someone at all sympathetic?"

"We know him all right," Mathieu said. "The new Minister of Police is the most ruthless, single-minded, uncompromising man in France. Beside him Bonaparte is benevolent. He is the Duke of Rovigo . . . Anne-Jean-Marie-René Savary!"

Juliette covered her lips with her hand. "Oh no! He assisted in carrying out Napoleon's orders to execute the Duc d'Enghien!"

The Duke of Rovigo had served Bonaparte all too well in a number of posts. "When he appointed Savary Police Chief," Mathieu went on, "he told friends that the Duke was the best man for the job. 'He can be moved by no man's tears,' Napoleon said. 'If I ordered him to eliminate his wife and children, he would not hesitate for a second.'"

"What a monster to control the fate of Germaine's manuscript," Juliette deplored.

Over the past three months Madame de Staël had put herself under tremendous pressure to complete her book. She stayed up through the night and stole daylight hours as well to meet the contract with Nicolle. She had finished the first two sections of *De l'Allemagne*, which examined the literature and the arts of Germany, and corrected them in galleys. They had been approved by the censors with only minor deletions. The final and most profound part of the book, a probe of the recondite areas of German philosophy, religion and ethics, was still in outline.

"Germaine could fall into a deep depression, take more opium and slip into a lethargy that will prevent her from writing," Juliette said. "Should we wait till she finished her book before we tell her?"

"How much time does she need?" Mathieu asked.

"At least a month."

"Someone else might tell her."

Juliette shook her head. "That's doubtful as long as she stays here at Chaumont. She deliberately invites no new visitors from Paris."

Madame de Staël's self-imposed regimen to complete her book was almost thwarted by the early return from America of Chaumont's owner. Monsieur Le Ray urged his illustrious tenant to take her time in making a move but he had appeared with his own entourage of children, servants and baggage. Feeling obliged to leave at once, Germaine spent most of early August, packing, unpacking and establishing her household in a comfortable country residence at nearby Fossé.

More than a month had passed since Fouché's dismissal and Juliette and Mathieu began to worry that Germaine would learn of it from an itinerant guest.

One day, after a frenzied session of writing, Madame de Staël went for a walk with her two friends. Mathieu guided the conversation, casually mentioning that Fouché was no longer in office.

Germaine showed concern for the man who had been her buffer against the Emperor. "Losing a government post he has held for years," she said, "will be a disgrace for Joseph and his family." But when she learned that Savary would replace Fouché Germaine was shocked.

Juliette tried to reassure her. "The first two volumes passed the censors with only slight objections," she reminded Germaine. "They even survived Bonaparte's scrutiny."

Germaine was too shaken to be convinced.

"The Emperor approved the manuscript only to hasten my departure for America," she said, disheartened. "My only weapon against Bonaparte is my book."

Madame de Staël buried herself in her library. By mid-September, she breathed more easily. She had a complete proof copy of *De l'Allemagne* in her hands and the Paris authorities appeared to have forgotten about her. The only news that filtered down from Paris was that the Emperor of France was overjoyed about the pregnancy of Empress Marie-Louise.

Relieved and confident, Madame de Staël called a family conference in the cheerful yellow drawing room of her latest household. Her three children, Schlegel, Juliette, Mathieu, Eugene and Miss Randall gathered to discuss how best to get the censors' approval of her book.

After much discussion, it fell to Madame Récamier, who had a good friend on the Board of Censorship, to deliver the manuscript to Paris. Her contact was a regular guest at her salon...a fervent, longtime admirer, the poet, Esménard. Besides serving as liaison between the two departments involved, the Ministries of Police and Publications, Esménard, more importantly, had the respect and ear of the new Police Director.

The next morning, the twenty-fifth of September, was crisp and breezy. Several grooms gave last-minute attention to horses, harnesses and two waiting carriages. The polished black finish of the coaches glistened in the sunlight.

Juliette and Germaine walked slowly, almost reluctantly, along the short path from the house. Beneath her ivory velvet cloak, close to her heart, Madame Récamier clutched tightly the precious package.

Germaine embraced her. "There is no one else to whom I could entrust this task with such confidence," she whispered.

Juliette, glowing with the urgency and gravity of her mission, ascended one coach. The wheels of the carriage ground deep as they rolled forward to the strain of the horses and sprayed pebbles onto the lawn. From the rear window Juliette threw a kiss to her friends.

With Mathieu, Germaine mounted the second carriage and began a leisurely drive to the Montmorency estate, La Forêt, five leagues away.

Chapter 9
The Fate of "De l'Allemagne" in Balance

I am afraid we are lost, Madame la Baronne," the driver called down from his perch through the talk box to Germaine and Mathieu. "In this darkness, I cannot see nor recognize any landmarks."

"I should have insisted we leave earlier," Mathieu said apologetically.

"Not at all," the Baroness replied. "These two days at your family chateau have been enchanting. Just what I needed. I've felt miles away from the pressures of deadlines, and I wanted to stretch out the hours at La Forêt forever. It was my fault we started so late."

Germaine was in no hurry to return to Fossé. It would be days before she expected to hear from Juliette.

"Perhaps we should wait in the carriage till dawn breaks," Mathieu suggested.

"That would be best," the driver said. "I am sure of the way in the daylight."

Not long after their agreement to wait, the trio heard the sound of an approaching horseman. Within moments, the rider reached the stranded party and drew his horse to a halt.

"I was attracted by your lights," he said. "May I help? I am Jacques Chevalier. I live down there," he pointed, "with my parents at the Chateau de Conan."

"I know of your family," Mathieu said and introduced himself and Germaine, explaining their predicament.

"You are headed toward Fossé," the genial young man offered. "It is about an hour's drive beyond our home. But there are several twists and turns that you might miss in the dark."

"Could you direct us?" Madame de Staël asked.

"It would be my pleasure. But I am sure my parents would be

pleased to accommodate you for the night. Follow me now and then leave in the morning."

Germaine accepted the invitation and soon, she and Mathieu were welcomed into the lavish interiors of the Chateau de Conan.

In the morning, Mathieu appeared drawn and ill-at-ease and showed no interest in polite breakfast conversation with their hosts, the Chevaliers.

Finally drawing Germaine aside, he said, "I have a note for you, my dear, from Auguste."

"My son?" How did it get here?"

"He was on his way to meet us," Mathieu replied slowly, "In the breaking light of morning he saw our carriage in the courtyard as he rode by, he stopped. Not wanting to waken you, he asked the servants to rouse me. He wrote this note and went back immediately." Mathieu held out the folded letter to Germaine.

She skimmed the brief message, which suggested she leave at once for Fossé since her book was "experiencing difficulties with the censors." Madame de Staël shrugged. "It's too early for news about my completed manuscript," she told Mathieu. "Auguste must be referring to the changes I made on the first two parts of *De l'Allemagne*."

The Baroness saw no need to leave in haste.

"For now," Mathieu said, "you must accept my word for the urgency of your return. Auguste had no choice but to find us. I will tell you all I know once we have started back."

Mathieu was not ready to reveal what Auguste had told him till they were safe. He feared Germaine might break down once she learned the full truth. Finally, trusting Mathieu's judgment, she agreed to leave immediately.

Within twenty minutes, the de Staël carriage was wending its way swiftly through the forests of the Vendômois plains. "Don't spare the horses," de Montmorency called up to the driver.

"The publication of all of *De l'Allemagne* is in jeopardy," Mathieu explained, his countenance grim. "Yesterday, your friend, the Prefect de Corbigny called at your house at Fossé. He was agitated and embarrassed when he asked Auguste where you were. He apologized for the intrusion. Auguste, expecting us last night, told the prefect we would return late today to allow us time to prepare. When we did not arrive, Auguste grew anxious and set out to look for us. Before de Corbigny took his leave he informed your son that he would be back and waiting for you on your return. He also handed him this letter from Police Director Savary."

Madame de Staël opened the envelope and was jolted.

"This is dated 'September 24, 1810' . . . the day *before* Juliette left for Paris!" Then she read on:

> *This is to instruct you, Madame, that you are under orders to leave for a western port within forty-eight hours. There you will be under proper supervision to await embarkation for America. Or, if you prefer, you may return to Coppet subject to the same time limit.*
>
> *Furthermore, I hereby now demand for confiscation the manuscript of your book on Germany, together with all the proofs still in your possession.*

Madame de Staël was stunned. She winced. Her face turned white. "This cannot be true!" she decried in disbelief.

"There's more," Mathieu said gently. "Savary has seized the five thousand copies of your first two volumes and the proofs of the third. All the type is under seal at the printer's establishment in Tours."

Germaine sat back motionless.

"Savary made his moves before Juliette started for Paris," Mathieu went on. "He has preempted the censors and assumed the prerogative of absolute arbiter. I wonder if he acted on his own or on the orders of Bonaparte."

Madame de Staël wept. Her body quivered.

Tender and caring, Mathieu held her close as they were jostled about in the speeding carriage. From the gentle pressure of Mathieu's arms Madame de Staël drew an uplifting strength she had elicited only from her father. She knew there was no time to indulge in a scene.

"I shall have to conquer myself once more," she said displaying cool, Necker control. She knew she had to prepare for an uncertain reception at Fossé. Would Albertine, Albert and Auguste be waiting for her in fear? Would de Corbigny be alone, or had Savary sent several agents to make sure his orders were carried out? And her manuscript . . . was her house being searched, her papers seized?

Freeing herself from Mathieu's hold, she leaned forward picked up her lap desk, which had fallen to the floor. It held vital notes on her book.

By the time her house came into view, Madame de Staël had ceased trembling, but she was totally unprepared to see her courtyard swarming with gendarmes.

Her driver straining at the reins skillfully maneuvered the horses into the compound through the waiting cordon of officers. As the horses slowed, there was a heavy pounding on the window. Germaine, terrified, held fast to her writing case as the door, opposite from the police suddenly flew open. A young man, all long arms and legs sprawling about fell in and pulled the door to a crashing close behind him.

The intruder was Albert, her seventeen year old son.

"Don't worry, Mama," he whispered with husky bravado. "Auguste gathered together all your important papers and your original manuscript and gave them to Miss Randall . . . she has hidden them where no one will find them."

"I must go, Mama," Albert said, pulling away from her embrace. "I'll take care of this." He wrenched away her writing case, slipped out of the coach, eluded the gendarmes, vaulted over the garden wall like a graceful sprinter gliding over a hurdle and escaped from sight.

Once she assured herself that Albertine, Auguste and the rest of her entourage were in no danger, Madame de Staël breathed freely. She could do nothing but wait for de Corbigny to arrive and face a confrontation.

In the early afternoon, the Baroness herself as formidable as a prison guard, opened the door to the prefect.

De Corbigny made a cursory search of the house and came up empty handed. Then, timorously, he repeated Savary's order for Madame de Staël to leave France.

Germaine responded with imperious indignation. "My dear Monsieur de Corbigny, you know very well the size and scope of my household. It is an imposition to expect me to gather my belongings in forty-eight hours."

"I realize your situation, Madame. It is not by my choice that I serve you with this notice. It is out of my hands." De Corbigny, though he knew the Baroness was stalling, conceded. "I shall send to Paris for further instructions."

Madame de Staël smiled graciously and asked the prefect to stay for dinner. He bowed deeply and declined.

Germaine gained the time she wanted.

Albert and Auguste were dispatched to Paris to alert Juliette to Savary's interference and to deliver two letters pleading their mother's case to members of the imperial circle . . . Michel Regnault, the Councillor of State, and Hortense, one of Bonaparte's favorites, the daughter of his former wife Josephine.

Within forty-eight hours of the time Albert and Auguste left Fossé Madame de Staël learned her fate. The two young men had barely time to get to Paris, deliver the letters and return.

Minutes after her sons dismounted from their horses to announce the outcome of their mission, a messenger delivered indisputable orders from the Minister of Police.

"Both Michel Regnault and Hortense approached the Emperor at the same time," Auguste explained. "They simultaneously requested a decision on your book."

An infuriated Bonaparte exploded: "My entire court is petitioning me on behalf of this contemptible woman!"

The Emperor picked up his proof copy of *De l'Allemagne* and threw it into the fire. Summoning Savary, he pronounced judgment on the spot. "Send her away," he raved.

The directive from the Minister of Police was clear:

I regret, Madame, that you have obliged me to begin my correspondence with you by an act of severity. I should have preferred to offer you only my high esteem.

Your exile is the natural consequence of the course you have followed for years.

Your last work is un-French. I am the one who stopped the printing. I cannot permit its publication.

We allowed you to leave Coppet only because you expressed the desire to go to America. If my predecessor Fouché allowed you to reside in the department of Loire-et-Cher, this was no reason to regard that act of tolerance as a revocation of the measures taken with regard to you.

I am forced to see their strict execution.

I am instructing Monsieur de Corbigny to

carry out the order I have given him as soon
as the delay I granted expires.
Your most humble and obedient servant,
The Duke of Rovigo

With her children, Mathieu and Miss Randall, Madame de Staël reviewed their alternatives. A departure for America was out of the question. A winter crossing of the Atlantic was far too hazardous. England was her first choice but when Miss Randall made inquiries about passage she learned that Bonaparte had blockaded all ports to the country.

There was no place else to go but Coppet.

Shortly after her arrival in Switzerland at the end of October, the Baroness de Staël learned that Savary had ordered a detachment of gendarmes to the printing plant in Tours. While sentries stood guard at the exits making certain not a single copy was removed from the contraband, the type and forms for *De l'Allemagne* were smashed with sledge hammers. The books were carefully counted, carted away, crushed into pulp and sold for five hundred francs.

Searching relentlessly for every outstanding copy, the Minister of Police demanded that publisher Nicolle furnish a complete record of distribution, including each proof copy. Savary went further and ordered the Director of Publications to surrender the censors' copies.

At the final reconciliation of his recall, the Duke of Rovigo found four copies still missing. He turned blue with rage. He knew the Baroness de Staël still had them in her possession!

Chapter 10
Isolated

T he Baroness de Staël smiled sympathetically at her friend's uneasiness. "Is this an official visit, Claude?" she asked.

Germaine walked beside the grim Baron Claude-Ignace de Barante across the marble floor of the foyer toward Coppet's cheerful, sunlit library. The elder Barante, despite objections to his son Prosper's continuing, though inconstant, romantic attraction to the Baroness, respected this formidable woman. He approached the call he was making in his capacity as Prefect of Geneva with repugnance.

"I have orders from Paris," he said ruefully. "From Savary."

"Please Claude, don't stand on ceremony. We *are* friends. Do have a cup of coffee with me," Madame de Staël offered. "Olive has just brought a fresh potful."

The prefect forced a smile and accepted.

"What oppression does the Duke of Rovigo wish to impose upon me this time?" she asked.

Barante balanced his saucer precariously on his knee and sipped the hot beverage. "Your book, *De l'Allemagne . . .*"

"What about it? That vulture has destroyed six long years of intense intellectual labor."

"But you still have the original manuscript and several copies, Madame?" he queried tremulously.

"No! I do not! If I did, I would not admit to it!"

"You must surrender them."

"Surrender what I do not have? They are out of the country."

"Very well," Barante sighed helplessly. "I have other orders for you, Madame la Baronne. *All* France is now forbidden to you," he said gravely. "You are confined to Coppet, Geneva and the road between them. If you go beyond these boundaries, you will be incarcerated."

"Except for an occasional excursion," Madame de Staël replied sardonically, "I am already a prisoner."

"There's more," the prefect faltered, "Another restriction. You are forbidden to write. You can publish nothing . . . not a pamphlet, a paper, a book. Not so much as a single line in any newspaper or periodical."

The Baroness stood speechless, unable to reply. If she complied she would lose all reason for living.

Barante felt the sting of his own words, "I'm sorry," he said and left.

The winter of 1810 and 1811 was severe in Switzerland. The snow fell steadily and temperatures hovered close to zero for weeks at a time. When the skies opened between storms, the winds whistled eerily around the chateau and whipped mountains of snow into crazy drifts across the roads in the barren parks and open fields.

Germaine's spirits matched the desolate intensity of the weather. All her friends were in France . . . Mathieu, Juliette, everyone. Her children, Schlegel and her attentive servants could not fill the void.

She detested the emptiness and lamented the isolation. How sad life is when one's hopes for emotional fulfillment are denied. I am a woman with and without whom no one can live. Everyone sees me as an oddity . . . I can no longer deceive myself about Benjamin and Prosper. They are lost to me. There is nothing I can expect from them but I cannot rid my mind and heart of them. There is only Juliette . . . sweet Juliette . . . on whom I can rely with complete and unwavering certainty.

To keep sorrow and depression at bay, Madame de Staël set out on a course of whirlwind activity. During the season's most bitter months, she took a palatial apartment on the Grand Rue in Geneva. After an introduction to the winter's social whirl at a dinner party held in her honor by her cousin Albertine Necker de Saussure, Germaine swept along the steep, snow-covered streets attending parties, concerts and balls as the most sought-after guest of the Genevese elite.

But as the year wore on, it became more difficult for Germaine to maintain the facade of sociability because her recent actions were taking a toll on her friends in official positions who had tried to help her. She felt responsible for their reversals and suffered deep remorse.

The Prefect of Geneva, Père de Barante, had been relieved of his duties for failing to extract the missing copies of *De l'Allemagne* from the Baroness. Declared incompetent to perform surveillance on Madame de Staël, he was ordered to leave the area and retire to his estate in Auvergne.

Jean de Corbigny was also discharged as Prefect of Blois. He was charged with neglecting his duties in handling the offenses of the Baroness de Staël. A broken man, he died shortly thereafter.

Gabrielle-Henri Nicolle, the publisher, was forced to declare bankruptcy after the pulping of *De l'Allemagne*. The thirteen-thousand franc advance that Germaine returned to him was not enough to save him from ruin.

Contemplating the future, Madame de Staël was often stricken with terror. At other times she was unexpectedly calm and dared to hope that Juliette might join her. But such joy, she knew, was impossible. Germaine did not ask her dearest friend to Coppet, knowing that Juliette's coming could elicit reprisals against her for consorting with an exile from France. Juliette, too, could be forbidden to return to Paris.

Chapter 11
John Rocca

"Mama! Come look into the courtyard with me!" Albertine de Staël called out bursting in on her mother who was writing in the library of their apartment on Geneva's Grand Rue. "You must see what Monsieur Rocca is doing. It's for you!" Albertine put her arms around her mother's neck and nestled close. "Do come with me. Please Mama!"

The Baroness de Staël could not resist the urging of this pretty child, who at fourteen, was maturing into a true beauty. She put down her quill and hugged Albertine affectionately.

I am blessed, she reflected as she admired her daughter's auburn curls falling forward to frame her heart-shaped face.

Germaine rose and followed her daughter into the foyer. Opening the shutters wider to afford a better view of the snow-covered courtyard, Albertine shivered like a wayward waif, her flimsy pink muslin dress with embroidered sleeves was no protection from the frigid air. Madame de Staël draped her own paisley scarf over the child's shoulders.

Below them was a dashing young horseman in a lustrous Hussar uniform astride a sleek Andalusian mount. When he saw the Baroness and Albertine, the handsome soldier pulled the reins and began putting his horse through the restraining paces of dressage. John Rocca was a superb horseman. For thirty minutes, he and his magnificent animal, Sultan, moved together fluidly in each maneuver, without error despite the crusted snow. For the finale, Rocca drew his horse to a halt and sat motionless facing the watching women. On instruction, Sultan curved his neck, slowly bent his knees and bowed in a graceful pantomime of gallantry toward Germaine.

Albertine was enchanted. Madame de Staël was indifferent. That foolish boy, she speculated, will kill himself. She knew that Rocca had to manipulate his nimble-footed steed up a precipitous climb along the winding, icy roads of Geneva to reach her home.

As Rocca rode off, Albertine turned to her mother. "Why do you discourage Monsieur Rocca?" she asked thoughtfully. "He is devoted to you."

"Dearest Albertine . . . would you understand if I explained?"

"I'll try, Mama. But I shall also try to persuade you to show more interest in him."

Madame de Staël wondered how much her daughter could understand about her liaisons with men so much younger than she. Only twenty-three, John Rocca showed the same symptoms as the vacillating Prosper de Barante, Maurice O'Donnell and other youthful admirers. Germaine had been introduced to Rocco by his aunt soon after she started her rounds of the social circles in Geneva in the fall. After this first meeting he began to appear at every function she attended, watching her from a distance. He was shy and rarely mingled. His eyes never left her but he never approached her.

To be kind, Madame de Staël had invited him to receptions at her apartment, but he was intimidated by the intellectual repartee and withdrew. At the edge of the circle, he would resume his watch.

The de Staël brothers, pleased to find someone more their own age at their mother's parties, befriended the officer and pried from him stories of his military adventures. Sentimental Albertine, touched by his passion for their mother, hoped Germaine would acknowledge his interest.

Albert-Jean-Michel Rocca was the youngest of a patrician family whose antecedents had emigrated to Switzerland several generations earlier from Piedmont. He had superb manners and, as a bachelor, was welcome in the noblest homes of Geneva by parents of marriageable daughters. His father was a state councillor and a member of the Senate . . . his mother had died when John was born. A lonely child, he grew up a romantic and passionate sportsman. At seventeen, he defied his father's wishes that he pursue a formal university education and ran away from home to enlist in the Hussars of the French Army.

Young Rocca displayed extraordinary daring and courage that earned him rapid advancement and a promotion to the rank of lieutenant. After four years of training and field experience in Germany, he was assigned to Spain to support Bonaparte's campaign during the height of the French offensive. On an early morning patrol with his captain and forty men, Rocca's contingent was trapped by the enemy. Deliberately, John rode Sultan away from the others to draw fire to himself. Both he and his mount were wounded. Sultan's injuries were slight but Rocca's left leg was shattered. Forced to return home for medical attention, he had been recuperating when Germaine moved to Geneva. Though he had to walk with a cane his ability to ride was unimpaired.

Madame de Staël was hesitant to tell Albertine about her feelings for this new young admirer.

"John is very young," she began cautiously when they returned to the comfortable, wood-panelled library. The room, like the rest of the apartment, reflected the Napoleonic decor that was the fashion in most of the distinguished homes in Geneva. The woods were no longer finished in the gold leaf prevalent during the reigns of Louis's, but stained to show beautiful grains. The fabrics were rich and patterns bold, no longer delicate and muted. The furniture was large and angular, with a strong Egyptian influence.

"He is not much older than Auguste," Germaine said carefully, "and still too young to unravel the threads of his emotions. I am sure he admires and respects me . . . as have other young men. But they change their minds and break their promises. They start with an infatuation that is often deep and stirring. They are in awe of my reputation and are carried away by my intellect and fame. In their minds they create a portrait of me as an ideal woman, which I am not. They all believe they are in love, and they are. But they are in love with the _concept_ of love . . . not with me. They court me frantically . . . till I succumb."

"You are talking about other men, Mama," Albertine protested. "John is not like that, I can tell."

"He may be convinced he is in love with me . . . " Germaine began, then stopped abruptly. She would not reveal the pain and frustration she endured at the whims of impetuous young acolytes. She was weary of immature suitors who hastily offered constancy . . . who became possessive or disenchanted, or both . . . who did not honor their commitments and drove her to seek solace in opium. But it was not in her to reveal more to Albertine, and thereby destroy the young girl's romantic fantasies.

Lieutenant Rocca reappeared in the courtyard every afternoon at the same hour. It took two weeks to crack the armor of Madame de Staël's resistance. She did not admit to Albertine that she was moved by the officer's resolve and eagerness, but offhandedly said she was afraid the Hussar's horse would lose his footing, fall and harm them both. In truth, she was curious to know what made Rocca persevere in such punishing weather.

On the most bitter afternoon yet of the winter, Madame de Staël sent a servant to invite Rocca in from the cold.

During their first meeting alone, Germaine was surprised to find that away from the superficiality of a crowded drawing room the lieutenant was a different man. He was still quiet and withdrawn but he was no longer the diffident, distant admirer. He seemed a confident suitor. Accepting her offer of tea and brandy, John warmed himself before the blazing fire, leaning against the arm of a massive chair to relieve the weight on his crippled leg.

Madame de Staël was amused and admiring. She could not take her eyes from his splendid, sinewy figure, his fine features, his clear olive skin, his black wavy hair, his handsome sideburns and trim Hussar's mustache. But despite his manliness, there was an air about him of irresistible fragility.

Germaine probed lightly, trying to draw him out like an attorney with a reluctant client. "You spent much of your army career in Germany," she said, giving him an opening to boast of his experiences.

"Yes," he said.

She waited. "Or did you prefer Spain?"

"No."

"Then Germany?"

"No. Neither." Rocca faltered. "I'm sorry. I find it difficult to talk about my service in the army."

"Then . . ."

Rocca struggled. He did not want to offend Germaine. "But I will try. I will tell you whatever you wish . . ."

"It is not important," Madame de Staël said, knowing she had struck a sensitive chord. She respected John's reticence and talked about her own travels in Germany. He listened raptly.

After the first visit, Rocca returned to spend an hour or two each day with Germaine. Without pressing him, she found that his military service had matured him beyond his years and instilled within him an acute perception of the pointlessness of war. His courage was confirmed . . . he had no fear of death or physical pain, but he deplored the horrors of combat, the maiming and killing, the devastation of towns and villages and the suffering of the homeless, the widows and orphans. He had come to despise the barbaric militarism of Bonaparte and his maniacal drive to conquer Europe.

Rocca was neither an intellectual nor a conversationalist. He was unimpressed by Germaine's celebrity and her famous and erudite friends.

Often, during their visits, a word did not pass between them. Madame de Staël worked at her desk while Rocca, happy to be alone with her, watched patiently and undemandingly. She sensed the depth of his feelings for her and tried to comprehend his overwhelming obsession. Did he seek in her to escape the painful memories of the grisly realities of battle . . . to forget the loneliness of his childhood . . . to find the mother's tenderness of which he had been deprived? She knew she helped to fill the abyss of his loneliness and ease his despair. But what was there to share with him?

One afternoon John became unusually pensive. He began to pace the floor behind her, walking back and forth from her chair to the window. After several minutes he stopped, dropped his cane, placed his hands firmly on the desk in front of Germaine and leaned forward, his eyes shining directly into hers with intensity.

"I love you, Germaine," he said with solemn simplicity. "I love you more than my own life. I shall continue to love you with such persistence that in the end you will have no choice but to marry me."

Germaine smiled compassionately. His attraction to her was blind and unreserved. It was a depth of devotion she had longed for all her life. It had come too late. At forty-five, she was beyond returning such a love.

Though she did not encourage him, Rocca's admiration had a buoyant influence on Madame de Staël. She had a surge of vitality. Her health improved. She needed less opium and her skin took on a youthful glow she thought she had lost forever. She insisted they stop spending time alone together and surprised her friends by drifting in and out of their presence on Rocca's arm, displaying radiant vivacity.

Deflecting John's advances, Germaine tried to interest him in women his own age. She invited eligible daughters of wealthy Swiss families to her receptions. The girls were enchanted. The young war hero was unstirred.

John chided Germaine. "You are wasting your time if you believe there is another woman for me. You can never change my heart."

By midwinter, Genevese society began to cool toward the Baroness de Staël. After the dismissal of Claude de Barante, the Prefect of Geneva, Germaine's movements were placed under surveillance. Those who once coveted her as a guest feared for their own safety. She received fewer social invitations and attendance in her own drawing rooms dropped. Those who did come frowned on her relationship with the handsome Hussar who was so much younger than she.

John Rocca took the hovering police and the malicious gossip in stride. When a meddling matron confronted him with the tasteless remark that Madame de Staël was old enough to be his mother rather than his mistress, he replied with disconcerting grace, "I am pleased, Madame, that you have pointed out yet another reason for me to love the Baroness."

The young lieutenant's zeal and gallantry in love equaled his wartime valor. He was tireless. And by springtime, he had won. When Madame de Staël moved back to Coppet John Rocca went along as a member of the diminished family circle with her children, Augustus Schlegel and Miss Fanny Randall.

Chapter 12
Benjamin Challenged

L ife at the Chateau of Coppet was bridled.
Its chatelaine bemoaned the fact that most of her Swiss friends had been frightened away. And the international consorts who seasoned her summer with zest were prevented from traveling to the shores of Lake Geneva by the Emperor's warring armies as they swarmed over Europe.

Madame de Staël did not lack visitors, however, her cousin, Albertine Necker de Saussure, her childhood companion, Catherine Huber Rilliet, and others came to see her regularly. Benjamin Constant, who was in Lausanne with his wife tending to pressing business affairs for his father, also dropped by occasionally. Though he loved the obliging Charlotte, Benjamin was bored and came alone. At dinner, he and Germaine monopolized the conversation with easy wit and sharp ripostes. Rocca heard them in sullen silence.

Chafing at confinement, bored by the tame life at Coppet, Germaine made plans to escape. Since she required sanction to leave, of course, she sent her son Auguste to Paris to apply for passports to England. If that failed he was to submit alternate applications for Italy, and then for Vienna. The twenty-year-old, still smitten by Madame Récamier, was thrilled by the mission that would give him the chance to call on the beauteous Juliette.

Young de Staël did not wait long for the processing of his mother's petitions. Each application was promptly reviewed and denied.

Madame de Staël was crestfallen.

One evening, as she wrote at the desk in her bedchamber, she looked up over the shelves of books before her to the oval oil painting of Juliette in its ornate, gilded frame, hung against a satin-striped wall-covering of ochre and ivory.

"There is little to lift my spirits, dear Juliette," she wrote. "Schlegel has faults that often conceal his virtues. Though I love my son Auguste very much, he has no closeness nor empathy with anyone except you. Albert is imprudent and hotheaded. Albertine is still too young. I spend most of my time contemplating death. I can see that my friends and my children would be better off if I were dead."

But then Madame de Staël sought to channel her shackled energy into a project she had been considering for several years. She started to write a book titled *Ten Years in Exile* in which she planned to chronicle the oppression she suffered at the hands of Napoleon Bonaparte.

And she found solace in John Rocca who followed her about like an adoring pet. Patient, tender and understanding, he agonized with her in her melancholy. He became more than her lover, he was her friend. As she continued to draw him out, Madame de Staël learned that he had a receptive mind and an intuitive cultural awareness. Surprised and pleased, she prepared a program of reading for him in the classics, history and philosophy and arranged for instructions with Albert and Auguste. When she found Rocca had a flair for words she encouraged him to use this talent in recording his army exploits. John responded dutifully and diligently, often working at a table near her.

Rocca got on well with the de Staël children who considered him another brother, a happy addition to the family. Albertine was delighted to see Germaine and John content in each other's company.

Fanny Randall, patterning her sympathies on those of her mistress, developed a motherly disposition toward the romantic lieutenant.

Augustus Schlegel sulked. He resented the intrusion of this young upstart, but did not voice his dissent. He observed Rocca's quick mind but gloried when the Hussar sat silent during any profound political or literary discussion.

It was almost midnight at Coppet.

Madame de Staël's bedchamber shimmered in the flickering shadows cast by tapers on the commode beside her large canopied bed.

From his post by the fireplace, John Rocca, regal in his black dressing jacket, watched Germaine remove her dark green silk peignoir and drop it on a marquise. She took a step toward the bed and leaned over the candelabra.

"Don't Germaine!" Rocca said, his voice muted. "Don't blow out the candles. You know I like to see you when we make love."

The slender Hussar moved quickly to the woman he adored. He slipped the straps of her pale green gown from her shoulders and let it drop to the carpet. With his hands caressing each curve of her body, John kissed her neck softly and then drew her down beside him on the bed.

"I vow," he said covering Germaine's body with his, "that I shall possess you completely. Now that we share the same roof I want you to bear my name. But more important, I want you to bear a child . . . a child that we will call '*petit nous.*'"

On the first day of May, 1811, Germaine rewarded Rocca with a unique premarital arrangement. In a secret ceremony conducted in the presence of her minister, Madame de Staël and John Rocca entered into a contract that confirmed their intentions of marrying "as soon as circumstances permitted." The agreement was kept from everyone, even Germaine's children. The only witness at the ritual was the discreet and devoted Fanny Randall.

Rocca, believing that in the eyes of God he and Germaine were married, became protective and possessive.

Strangely, for the first time in such a liaison, Germaine did not cringe at this attitude but found it appealing and comforting.

When John asked her to break her ties with Prosper de Barante, she willingly wrote to tell her one-time lover that she released him of all the vows he made to her.

But John's jealousy toward Benjamin Constant was deeper and close to violent. One evening, a few days after the premarital agreement had been signed, Benjamin came again for supper and slipped into intimate familiarity with Germaine. Rocca, incensed, interpreted Benjamin's actions as an affront, and still careful to conceal his claim on Germaine, proceeded to assert his secret rights by challenging Benjamin to a duel.

Stunned, Benjamin had no choice but to accept the gauntlet.

The following day, Auguste de Staël intervened. He convinced Rocca to withdraw and asked Benjamin to do the same. Benjamin who had no experience with pistols or swords complied.

John, who had grudgingly agreed to the truce, was not satisfied. In a fit of anger, he mounted his black stallion and galloped off to Benjamin's hotel. He repeated the challenge.

When Auguste told his mother of the second encounter, she screamed in horror, "He'll kill Benjamin! Don't let him do it!" She took only a few moments to decide on a course of action.

First she summoned John and spoke to him.

The next day, on the morning of May 11, she ordered a calèche and drove alone to Lausanne.

Germaine's affection for Rocca had deepened. In her loneliness she needed him. She was not prepared to disrupt the harmony and accord of her household . . . however dull. Though she was not ready to marry Rocca, the day might come when she would consider formalizing their agreement.

Though the Baroness still craved intellectual interchange with Benjamin Constant, she knew she lacked the stamina she once had for a continuing battle with him. The pace she had sustained through the years, her uncontrolled outbursts, the increasing doses of opium . . . were sapping her energy and affecting her health. Nor was she still a young woman. She had her family's safety and future to consider, careers for her sons and a dowry for Albertine.

Madame de Staël was already subject to heavy surveillance by the police. Word of a duel between men close to her . . . and a death . . . would reach Bonaparte's ears and precipitate even further restrictions on her movements.

The Baroness's calèche drew up in the courtyard of the Hotel Couronne d'Or where Constant and his wife had temporary lodgings.

Germaine climbed the long, broad stone stairway which led to the hotel's vast portico. Halfway up, she hesitated and stopped on a narrow landing.

Benjamin emerged from the entrance to the foyer and crossed the portico. He showed no surprise when he saw Germaine and quickly walked down to where she stood.

"I've come to apologize for John," she told him. "I'm sorry he has caused you anxiety."

"I don't hold you responsible for your young barbarian's savagery," Benjamin replied.

At another time or with someone else, Madame de Staël might have defended her lover with angry remonstrances. Today, she was calm, controlled. She knew that John Rocca was smoldering for satisfaction. Only she could prevent him from killing Benjamin. She had extracted a promise of restraint from him.

"It is I, this time, and not my son, who has come to assure you that John will not carry out his threat. I have his word. There is no need to fear him."

"I'm ready to die," Benjamin said with weary resignation. "I've prepared my will and arranged for my second."

"There will be no duel," Germaine said dispassionately. "I told John that I would inform you that you must not call on me again."

"If that is what you wish," he replied.

For the first time since their relationship had begun to flounder Germaine de Staël spoke with unwavering conviction and sincerity about their separation. She commanded. Benjamin felt the chains that had bound them loosen and fall at his feet. There was a finality in Germaine's voice that he had never perceived before.

Germaine released him. He was free.

"I sense," Madame de Staël said sadly, "that we are destined never to meet again in this lifetime."

"That is as it should be," Benjamin replied.

She offered her hand. Benjamin held it for just a moment.

Germaine turned and walked down the stairway. She felt she had closed a heavy door on an important chamber of her life. Behind her she heard Benjamin murmur faintly, "Alas, dear Albertine."

Germaine ascended her waiting carriage.

Chapter 13
Capelle's Revenge

It is my privilege, Madame, to assure you that your exile will end. The Emperor of France wishes to solicit a small levy from you which is easily within your command to grant. For this, most, if not all the restrictions which confine you, will be lifted."

The Baroness de Staël suppressed her surprise at this promise of freedom. She neither replied nor acknowledged the offer that Bonaparte's swaggering sycophant proffered.

Baron Guillaume-Antoine de Capelle, was a handsome, foppish dandy of thirty-five who had succeeded Germaine's mild-mannered friend Claude de Barante as Prefect of Geneva. The handpicked favorite of French Police Director Savary, Capelle had been a lover the lecherous Elisa Bacciochi, whom Napoleon banished when her debauchery reached scandalous proportions. The young prefect, however, had qualities that were too useful to discard. Since he was callous, ambitious and subservient, he was granted an opportunity to eradicate his transgressions by reaffirming his loyalty and fitness in an assignment in Geneva.

The zealous prefect rallied to the challenge and presented himself at Coppet with imperious arrogance.

"For an authoress as eminent and prolific as you," he declared, strutting back and forth before Madame de Staël in his tight-fitting prefectural uniform, "the task is a simple one that can be executed quickly."

Germaine, revolted by his unrestrained pretension, adjusted her turban, smiled coolly and remained silent.

"All I ask," Capelle declared, "is that you write a poem or a tribute to Bonaparte's heir, the King of Rome."

Madame de Staël bristled. All Europe had reverberated to the news of the birth of Bonaparte's son, Napoleon II, an event heralded in Paris with a 22-gun salute.

"Such a gesture would be ludicrous," she said contemptuously. "The Emperor has continually rejected and banished me."

Capelle abruptly stopped his pacing. He was wide-eyed at this unexpected rejection.

"But Madame, it is for the Emperor of France!"

The Baroness stood firm.

Capelle was insistent.

Angry words spattered about the room like molten metal from a blacksmith's anvil.

Finally, the floundering prefect knew that Madame de Staël would not budge. In desperation, he pleaded with her. "What, Madame, shall I tell the Emperor's minister?" he implored.

She shrugged.

"Won't you at least express your good wishes for the health of the King of Rome?"

"Very well," Madame de Staël retorted, her eyes gleaming with spite, "tell him, if you like, that I wish him a good wet nurse!"

The startled Capelle was incredulous.

"Madame! A single page, a simple paean to the Emperor and his victories!"

"Not so much as a line!" the Baroness declared, escorting her dazed caller to the door.

Germaine de Staël paid dearly for her candor.

Capelle, chaffing at the failure of the assignment that would have restored him to Bonaparte's favor, set out to avenge the affront. With absolute precision, he executed the instructions from Paris to harass the Baroness de Staël.

His first move was to inform Madame de Staël that her travel was now confined to a radius of two leagues from Coppet. He then assigned gendarmes to trail her wherever she went. Even within the boundaries of the chateau's park, Germaine, Schlegel, Rocca and her children sensed that agents lurked behind shrubbery to keep watch like wild animals stalking prey. Intimate details of her daily life, exacted from a bribed servant, were reported by the Geneva prefect to the Duke of Rovigo and then funneled to Bonaparte.

The harassment was continuous. The Baroness received daily messages reminding her of her restrictions. "You cannot set foot on French soil." "You cannot go to any country adjacent to France." "You cannot travel more than ten kilometers from your residence." "Your sons are not permitted to resume their studies in Paris." "Any visitors you receive may be questioned and subject to punishment similar to your own."

Germaine moved about with an air of carefree defiance. Her friends admired her courage, the police her restraint.

But Madame de Staël was in fact frightened by every gendarme she encountered, certain that each one was assigned to arrest her and take her to prison. She was convinced that once he decided to incarcerate her, Bonaparte would ignore all pleas from her friends and leave her to disintegrate in a dungeon.

Toward the end of May, shortly after she had taken her final leave of Benjamin Constant, Madame de Staël was shattered by what she read in the day's dispatch from Prefect de Capelle. It prescribed Augustus Wilhelm Schlegel's immediate departure from the country.

Germaine ordered a carriage, drove to Geneva (the city was still in her sphere) and stormed into police headquarters. Demanding to see Capelle, she brushed past the intimidated clerks and forced her way into his office.

"By what jurisdiction," she fumed, "do you issue orders in a foreign country?" Though Geneva was in French domain, nearby Coppet was within the borders of Switzerland.

The prefect looked up only briefly and then continued writing. With a flick of his forefinger, he spun a globe on his desk, then, patronizingly, he turned his head in the direction of his visitor.

His face wore an insipid grin. "Ah! Madame de Staël! I see you have received the order of the day."

Germaine crossed her arms and stretched her heavy, weary body to its full short height. Her eyes blazed.

"As a citizen of France," she declared, "*I* must tolerate your harassment. But Herr Schlegel is a German visiting in a Swiss village."

"My dear Madame," Capelle said priggishly, "it is in your own interest that we have undertaken such a rigorous act. Herr Schlegel is transforming you into a woman who is anti-French. The proof is in his literary opinions opposing the glory of French writers."

"I am touched by the French government's paternalistic concern for my welfare," Madame de Staël replied equably, "and for its wish to protect me from poisonous influences."

Capelle had the advantage. "If you prefer, I will transmit my orders to the Swiss authorities through the French Ambassador. Either way, the German must go."

The diplomatic route would not prevent Schlegel's ouster . . . at best it would only delay it for a few days. To avoid a confrontation, the scholar prepared to leave without protest. Before he departed, he and Germaine conceived a plan they hoped would permit her to flee to Berne, where the salvaged copies of *De l'Allemagne* were stashed and where he would wait for her.

Though Schlegel's absence left a void in her life, Madame de Staël's newly kindled interest in religion and prayer . . . encouraged by her pious friends Julie de Krudener and Zacharias Werner . . . helped her cope with the separation.

Since travel in France and across Germany was forbidden to her, the Baroness had planned with Schlegel to take the near-impossible, two-thousand-league route by way of Eastern Europe, Sweden and the North Sea to reach England. As the wife of a former Swedish diplomat, she could count on a warm welcome in Stockholm. An old friend, the Gascon, Jean-Baptiste Bernadotte, would be there to greet her. Bernadotte, who had once conspired against Bonaparte with her blessing, had been adopted as son by the ailing, childless King Charles XIII and elected Crown Prince of Sweden.

Dreaming of escape, Germaine wanted once more to see Mathieu de Montmorency and Juliette Récamier . . . she feared she might never return to France.

Madame de Staël sent her son Auguste to Paris to convey this request to her friends. Mathieu responded without hesitation and set out immediately for Coppet. Juliette, who had promised to visit Germaine later in the year, changed her plans and arranged to follow in a week.

On the fourth day of his stay, de Montmorency was delivered a *lettre de cachet* from Prefect de Capelle exiling him to a forty-league limit of Paris.

His banishment was more painful to Germaine than her own. She bore the burden of guilt heavily, finding no solace in religion for the calamity she brought down on Mathieu. Mathieu accepted the blow stoically and tried to calm Germaine who refused to be comforted.

Seeking to prevent further grief, Germaine sent Auguste to meet

Juliette and convince her now to bypass Coppet. When they met at the border of Switzerland, Juliette would not be swayed. "I secured permission from the ministry of police to visit the baths at Aix," she insisted. "Coppet is a village along the way."

Juliette and Germaine had little time together.

Madame Récamier's nephew, a French official in Geneva, learned of his aunt's brash visit, appeared the day after her arrival and finally convinced her that she should leave with him.

The precaution was too late. Capelle had been informed of the route Juliette had taken and sent word to Savary in Paris. The Minister of Police sent an agent to serve her with papers of banishment. Like Mathieu, she was ordered to remain forty-leagues from Paris.

The proscription was issued by Emperor Bonaparte himself to the woman he had once coveted as his mistress and had called the "beautiful Juliette." Now, he labelled her that "dangerous Récamier woman."

Madame de Staël's remorse over Juliette's fate was oppressive. "I beseech you not to hate me," she wrote her friend at Châlons, where Madame Récamier was living out her exile. "In God's name, take care of yourself and try to extricate yourself from this evil that I may live. Alas, I hardly retain my reason and I shall have no rest till you are delivered from your exile. At times I suffer such profound melancholy that I would accept death. A kind of despair and morbid fatality devours me. I turn to prayer but I often feel that even the Savior wearies of me. I stand in the way of my children and friends and believe that the best service I can do you and Mathieu . . . and everyone around me . . . is to flee."

Prefect de Capelle increased his hounding and called again at Coppet. He repeated his request for a tribute to Bonaparte's son. Again, Germaine refused. He persisted. She would not comply.

De Capelle appeared regularly to remind the Baroness of restrictions against her. When he did not call in person, he alternately sent agents to interrogate her.

The harassment took its toll on Madame de Staël's health. She took larger doses of opium and was often reduced to long periods of depression and apathy. Her features were drawn, her skin took on a yellow hue, her weight increased, her waist thickened.

At first, Madame de Staël blamed these symptoms on the narcotic and the boredom of house arrest. In the early months of the winter, she came to realize the cause of her declining health. Despondently, she knew she had to delay or forgo completely her plans to escape.

At forty-five, the Baroness de Staël, again, was pregnant.

Chapter 14
Plans for Escape

Germaine de Staël tried desperately to conceal her pregnancy from her family and friends. Her greatest fear was having the news reach Prefect de Capelle.

As a young married woman, the Baroness had few misgivings about having a child by a lover and ascribing its paternity to her husband. She considered such actions acceptable if handled with discretion. But in her present circumstances, as a husbandless woman of celebrity with grown children she was vulnerable to attack by police and journalists who would delight in painting her as a promiscuous tart. Revelation and gossip could destroy her reputation and ruin her children's chances for successful careers and good marriages.

Madame de Staël's sympathetic physician, Louis Jurine, a professor at the Academy of Geneva, relieved her anxiety by letting it be known that she had a debilitating illness that would require prolonged confinement to her home. Throughout the winter months, Madame de Staël, with John Rocca constantly at her side, stayed in her bedchamber. Miss Randall hovered protectively, permitted no visitors other than Auguste, Albert and Albertine and held even them at arms length to keep the secret from them.

Germaine suffered also from dropsy and the debilitating effects of opium. Though she was ill, uncomfortable, subject to lapses of mental anguish and had to spend most of her time in bed, the Baroness's mind remained lucid. Hours on end, she sat propped up against several pillows, writing with dogged perseverance. She worked on her book, *Ten Years in Exile,* completed a long essay on suicide and did research for a poem about Richard the Lion-Hearted.

The cold, dreary winter dragged.

In early March, Madame de Staël's mood was uplifted by signs of spring. On warmer days, Rocca helped her to the parapet where, for short periods, she soaked up the sun and admired the magnificence of Mont Blanc. Melting snow trickled down the hillside from the chateau in small streams to Lac Léman.

Germaine's spirits were further bolstered by an unexpected letter from Moscow:

> *My dear Baroness de Staël:*
> *I have taken great precautions to assure that this letter reaches you without falling into the hands of the French authorities. It is my understanding that you hope to make a journey to England. With most all routes closed to you, I would like to suggest that you consider traveling by way of my country.*
>
> *I also urge that you start your trip as soon as possible. You will find that a visit to our court may be of great benefit to you and your family and perhaps to all of Europe.*
> *The Czarina and I look forward to your arrival.*
>
> *Alexander*
> *Czar of Russia*

Madame de Staël knew Alexander could not reveal his reasons for writing. But the implications were clear to her. He was eager to discuss the rumblings of dissension among the Eastern powers against Bonaparte's unbridled aggression. The Baroness had kept close watch on the escalation of the political struggle between the East and the West. Neither the Russian Czar nor the French Emperor were honoring the provisions of the Treaty of Tilsit that they had signed in 1807.

Germaine knew Alexander no longer maintained watch over the Prussians and Austrians as he had agreed in order to forestall and restrain their armies if they moved against France . . . and that Napoleon, distrusting the Czar, was eager to demonstrate his strength to the Russians. In a megalomaniacal move to assume the crown of both East and West, Bonaparte was mobilizing his troops in Dresden to prepare an assault on Moscow in the summer.

Madame de Staël placed her hands on her swollen body as she lay in her canopied bed, felt the stirring of her child and prayed it would be born soon so she could start her flight before the Grand Army of France launched its march.

On April 17, her prayers were answered: Madame de Staël gave easy birth to another son, Louis Alphonse.

Only Dr. Jurine, Rocca, and Miss Randall knew of the birth. For five days, on the pretext of doctor's orders, they managed to exclude her children from her bedchamber.

On the sixth day, Germaine and Rocca smuggled the infant out of the chateau and drove to the nearby village of Longirod where the baby was baptized by the local pastor. Arrangements were made with the minister and his wife to care for the child until the parents were free to acknowledge him.

The following week, attempting to discount rumors of pregnancy, the Baroness de Staël, on the arm of her Hussar, attended several social events in Geneva. She looked so wan that neither friends nor detractors doubted her doctor's diagnosis and never guessed she had given birth.

Prefect de Capelle's contacts with Madame de Staël's household revealed that she was converting a large portion of her assets into cash for a trip to England. But he could not extract details or confirm the reports.

For five weeks, Germaine endured the regimen of her doctor's orders. She rested, refrained from taking opium and gradually regained her health.

She set May 22 as the date for escape.

On the twenty-first, her courage faltered, her determination waned. The two-thousand league trek across ravaged and desolate lands to an unknown future loomed as a threatening specter.

She had always considered Coppet a kind of prison. But now, as she sensed she might never again enjoy its reassuring splendor, she was uncertain, agitated.

Covering her shoulders with a lightweight scarf to protect her from the chill of the gray day, she wandered out to the park. She sat on benches and chairs where she had rested with her father and observed pale green sprouts in the flower beds, blue and pink hyacinths crowding through blades of grass, trees bursting into leaf.

Germaine left the gardens and walked to the glen where the stone mausoleum held the remains of her parents. Leaning against the iron door, she invoked the memory of her father. For more than an hour she prayed for assurance and strength, knowing now that she had to leave Coppet.

Strolling slowly, Madame de Staël crossed the courtyard and

returned to the chateau. She entered her father's study where she had kept the furnishings and his papers as he had left them. She sat in his armchair, her hand on his desk. One by one she fingered the pens, the inkstand, the bibelots he had collected. When she walked out of the room, Germaine picked up Necker's cloak which lay on the back of the chair . . . to wrap around her for comfort in moments of despair she knew lay ahead of her.

Early the next afternoon, Albert de Staël rode around the village, checking carefully all the grounds and the roads leading to the chateau. Only a few peasants trudged the cobblestones.

"All is clear," he reported to his mother.

At two o'clock, Madame de Staël told her servants she was going for an airing and gave them instructions to serve the evening meal at the customary hour on her return. She and Albertine dressed lightly, for the air was warm. They carried only their fans and parasols. Auguste and Rocca, their pockets filled with cash, joined them in the coach.

As they drove off, Madame de Staël, with mingled emotions of nostalgia, regret and uncertainty turned and looked back at the castle.

After several kilometers, the Baroness sent one of her footmen back to Coppet to tell her servants that they would not return till the next day. Then, the fugitives drove on for one-hundred-and-fifty kilometers till they reached the farm outside Berne where Augustus Wilhelm Schlegel awaited them.

The next day, Auguste rode back to Coppet to thwart any attempt the authorities might make to confiscate the family estate. In anticipation of her flight, the Baroness had transferred the ownership of the property to the young Baron Auguste de Staël. He helped Albert and Eugene Uginet load Germaine's yellow berline with baggage and servants and set them on their way to join her.

The Baroness de Staël had outwitted her guards.

Not until ten days later, did the red-faced, disbelieving Baron Guillaume-Antoine de Capelle discover that she and her family had fled the country. By that time, Madame de Staël was on her way to Austria, completing the first leg of her journey to Russia . . . and England.

PART V

THE RACE AND THE VICTOR

Chapter 1
Salzburg

An eerie wailing reverberated through the Tyrolean Alps, caressing the moonlit stillness of the night with what seemed a single voice. Savage wolves, alone and in packs along the lofty range, howled a mournful serenade under the star-studded sky.

Germaine lay awake listening, comfortable in a rustic hostelry nestled within a mountainside village.

The wolves' cry was a chilling reminder of the hazardous roads she and her small party had taken in the last two days . . . a plaintive prelude to the long, implausible journey that lay ahead.

Though Schlegel and Albertine were with her, Madame de Staël felt forsaken and frightened. She had spent several disquieting days in Berne where John Rocca had reluctantly left for Geneva on personal business. That he promised to rendezvous with Germaine along the route in Austria did little to relieve her anxiety. Since the French military was demanding his arrest, she feared he would be apprehended and imprisoned.

With forged passports that Schlegel had obtained in Berne, he, Albertine and Madame de Staël slipped furtively out of the old Swiss capital. Albert and Eugene Uginet were behind them with luggage.

Their driver had handily maneuvered the de Staël coach along familiar routes through the Swiss Alps and its gentle valleys into Innsbruck. After that, conditions changed. The carriage lurched and lunged as the horses strained to climb the narrow, precipitous roads up and around the glistening Arlberg mountains of the Tyrol. Often the team misstepped, and the coach would dangle perilously over bottomless gorges. Germaine was petrified not only of the ascent but at the possibility that Bonaparte's gendarmes could be in pursuit of them.

Madame de Staël was all but oblivious to the stunning beauty of nature which surrounded them . . . shimmering, ice blue peaks and glaciers dominated the broad stretches of valley.

As night fell, the party made an easy descent and stopped for the night at an inn. Through the dimness of the chamber, Germaine looked at the figure of her sleeping daughter on a cot next to her. She was reassured. Before long, Albertine would turn fifteen.

In the pale gray of dawn, the journey resumed. Madame de Staël opened the carriage windows and breathed cool Alpine air scented with the fragrance of pine and spruce. Soon, the entourage was racing through valleys and low, undulating hills which were dotted with multibuilding compounds of stone and stucco. Farmers tilled the rich brown soil . . . cattle grazed in greening fields. Occasionally, the coach was rocked by the föhm, the winds that blew up warm, dry and strong from the south to melt snow and muddy roads and nourish corn crops in the lowlands.

Lulled by the steady whir of carriage wheels, Germaine brooded about the future. To distract her, Albertine pointed out birds that fluttered among the trees, a buzzard gliding overhead, squirrels and rabbits that scampered into the brush to escape steadily pounding hooves. Madame de Staël responded listlessly to her daughter's patter.

"Over there . . . in the distance," Albertine called out. "What are those vast buildings, Herr Schlegel?"

"The castle of upper Salzburg."

Roused, Germaine turned to look. Silhouetted against a cloudless sky the majestic eleventh-century fortress, Festung Hohensalzburg, rose out from the top of the mountain, an imposing structure flaunting ramparts and turrets. From this bastion, Germaine derived a sense of security she had not felt since leaving Coppet. The medieval stronghold towered intrepidly above the town. Though built on part of the Monchsberg ridge, the castle appeared from the distance to stand alone on its own gigantic peak.

The travelers entered the Austrian city of Salzburg through long narrow alleys that appeared to be ceilingless tunnels. The houses, with common walls, were even narrower, and boasted dates carved on their stone facades in the thirteenth-century. There were miniature shops, quaint inns and cafés on the first level. Balconies and portico galleries jutted out over the walkways from the second and third-floor living quarters.

When the carriage drew up to the hotel in the center of the city, Schlegel disembarked and mounted the steps of the building while footmen helped Germaine and Albertine from the coach.

A craggy old man in Austrian garb approached Schlegel at the top of the stairway. He eyed the Baroness and her daughter as they approached and then, in thick dialect, addressed the scholar. "A French official in uniform stopped here this morning," he said, "to inquire about a carriage that would arrive from Innsbruck. He was looking for a woman and a young girl who are traveling together. He will return later today to see if they have arrived."

Madame de Staël understood every word. She turned pale.

The stranger explained that the Frenchman had questioned the hotel staff and left for the Austrian border to continue his search.

Schlegel and the Baroness concealed their alarm until they closed the door of their sparsely furnished second-floor apartment.

Remembering how she had harbored fugitives in her home in Paris during the revolution, she said, "I will go into the streets and walk from house to house . . . there is certain to be a sympathetic Austrian family who will give us asylum."

Schlegel's face clouded. Suddenly holding a finger to his lips, he signalled Germaine to be silent. "There are footsteps in the hallway," he whispered, "coming this way."

All three froze where they stood.

A knock sounded heavily on the door. No one moved. At the second knock, Schlegel reluctantly responded, turning the key slowly. A slender young man in a French courier's uniform pushed open the door and entered.

Madame de Staël drew Albertine close and turned toward the intruder.

"Jean!" she cried in surprise. "It's you!"

Germaine and Rocca embraced. Schlegel quickly locked the door as they listened to the Hussar's explanation.

"I disguised myself as a courier to escape detection and to enable me to command a quick change of horses. When I found that you had not yet arrived here, I took the route from Munich to the Austrian frontier to learn if the officials have been notified of your escape. They do not know yet . . . but I am sure they soon will."

The fugitives did not stay to find out. In the oncoming darkness, they fled the city. They did not stop on the east bank of the Salzach River to view one of the most beautiful sights in the world . . . a medieval town pierced by the spires of a dozen baroque churches resting peacefully in the shadow of an ancient fortress.

Madame de Staël turned her back on the city that only a few hours earlier she had approached with a promise of refuge.

Chapter 2
A Burdensome Bureaucracy

"How deliciously refreshing!" Albertine de Staël announced happily as she pulled on a dress of lilac cotton gauze. It was more than two weeks since she and her mother had a complete change of clothes.

Stepping gingerly between two maids who were emptying the tubs in which the travelers had just bathed, the girl joined Madame de Staël beside a glistening white porcelain stove that filled a corner of the dressing room. They relished the warmth that radiated from the wood fire, for though it was late spring there was still a chill in the air.

"It is a small miracle," Germaine said, pushing back a soft auburn curl from her daughter's forehead, "that we've reached Vienna so soon."

Albert and Eugene Uginet, with most of the baggage, had caught up with them in Melk, where they had stayed at a sprawling Benedictine Abbey overlooking the Danube. Madame de Staël and her family transferred to the yellow berline, heavy under its load of familiar possessions, while the servants mounted the coach that had brought her from Coppet. The two-carriage entourage entered the capital of Austria on the sixth day of June.

John Rocca was dropped off at a small boarding house where he would stay alone, safe, they hoped, from the scrutiny of the French Military Police. A few blocks farther, in the fashionable district that skirted the Burg Ring, with its vast complex of palaces and government buildings, Germaine had engaged a large suite of rooms in the splendid Hotel Zum Römischer Kaiser.

When the maids departed, Madame de Staël approached the handsomely draped windows and looked beyond the small balcony to the stately buildings that lined the street and down to the cobblestone paving two stories below.

The day was dampened by a steady drizzle but Germaine was in good spirits, relieved to have been able to put so great a distance between herself and France, even though she was far from being out of the range of her oppressor. She had been shocked to see how the long arm of Bonaparte was crushing the spirit of Austria. Though not a part of the French Empire, it was bound to France by alliances that were plunging its economy into disaster. During stops at larger towns and commercial centers along the way, the Baroness had been appalled by the changes that had taken place since her last visit. Paper money had replaced gold and silver. The Austrian people, once industrious and carefree, were now demoralized, sinking under the weight of enforced subjugation and taxation.

One of the maids returned. "Madame la Baronne," she said, handing her mistress a card, "there is a gentleman here from the Russian Embassy."

Germaine's face brightened. "Come, ma petite," she said, holding out her hand to Albertine, "let us see what news he has for us."

Together they entered the suite's drawing room, a small version of the grand chambers at the Schönbrunn Palace. Painted soft yellow and gold, it had royal magenta damask on the wall panels and upholstery. They crossed the Aubusson rug to greet their guest.

"How good of you to come, Count de Stackelberg," Madame de Staël said. "And so soon . . . we have been here only two hours."

"We have been expecting you," the Russian Ambassador replied. "I am here on behalf of Czar Alexander to offer you any assistance you may need."

The Baroness expressed her appreciation, introduced her daughter with maternal pride and inquired about Alexander.

"He is at Vilna with his family," de Stackelberg said. "He is anxious to learn your plans."

"We hope first to rest for a few days," Madame de Staël said, and then recounted the story of the escape and the rigors of the journey, and of her joy on reaching Vienna.

A footman approached with a tray of coffee and pastries. Albertine filled the demitasses and helped the Count to a rich chocolate confection.

De Stackelberg cautioned Germaine not to expect the city to glow with the brilliance and gaiety it had in the past. Her friend Clemens Metternich, the Austrian Foreign Minister, and many other members of the court were in Dresden, conferring with Bonaparte.

"The reins of government," the Ambassador explained, "have been left in the hands of lesser, unsophisticated functionaries who do not understand politics nor foresee the cataclysm that lies ahead. They know, however, of Bonaparte's antipathy toward you and though they may not harass you they will not make your stay easy. They respond only to the glory and glitter of the Emperor's charismatic authority. Even the aristocrats who are still here in Vienna, those who treated you cordially before, may avoid you. They fear jeopardizing their own positions."

Madame de Staël instinctively reached out toward Albertine who sat beside her.

"I hastened here," de Stackelberg went on, "to assure you that the Czar is most eager to have you reach Russia. We are prepared to expedite the papers you need . . . and would have done so sooner but we did not know how many were in your party or the route you would take."

Together they studied maps and filled out visa applications for Schlegel, Rocca, Albertine, Albert, Madame de Staël and Auguste, who would follow later.

"When do you think we will be able to leave?" the Baroness asked.

"The documents should be prepared within three weeks," the Count replied.

Germaine concealed her disappointment and dread of a delay.

The first ten days were quietly pleasant. With her children and Schlegel, she strolled Vienna's narrow streets and boulevards and took rides into the country. Rocca spent most of each day with them but returned always to his own lodgings. Several of the Baroness's friends . . . Friederich von Gentz, the Prince de Ligne, Wilhelm von Humboldt . . . came to call and entertained her in their homes.

On the morning of the eleventh day, Madame de Staël and Albert went to shop along the fashionable Kärntnerstrasse. As they looked in the window of a pastry shop, Albert tightened his hold on his mother's arm.

"Mama," he whispered, "don't be frightened and don't turn around. We are being followed . . . and have been for some time by a plainclothes agent."

They made a small purchase in the bakery and returned to the hotel. To confirm his suspicion, Albert summoned the de Staël coachman to drive them in their carriage along the tree-lined roads of Praeter Park. A sleek cabriolet, with the same dark-suited man at the reins, kept pace close behind, never losing sight of them.

The Baroness was not surprised on the following morning when Eugene reported that a uniformed official was in the lobby requesting an interview. The caller was the Director of the Vienna Police Department. He approached with cold formality, stopped abruptly and stood with ramrod stiffness.

"You are no longer welcome here in Austria," he announced. "I suggest you make plans to leave as soon as possible." He brushed off all gestures of cordiality, refusing even the chair Madame de Staël offered.

"You may be sure," she replied haughtily, "that I have no intention of remaining in your country. I shall leave the moment our visas for Russia are delivered."

"Russia!" The director allowed himself a chortle. "I would not count on a quick response from them. It could take months. You must pursue other avenues of departure, Madame."

"Thank you, Herr Director, for your solicitude. I have already started such inquiries. Austria no longer holds any charm for me."

"What's more," the Police Director said with menace, "you are harboring a fugitive by the name of John Rocca."

"I harbor no one!"

Ignoring this retort, the official declared, "The Emperor Bonaparte orders that Rocca, as a French officer, be handed over to the military."

"That's preposterous!" The Baroness would not be hectored. "Monsieur Rocca has been declared physically unfit to return to active duty and has been properly separated from the Army."

"This is a serious matter, Madame la Baronne."

"I agree. You have no authority over this man."

The Police Director flushed, stunned that the brass-studded uniform of his office had failed to daunt or constrain this inflexible Frenchwoman.

"Madame," he responded unsteadily. "Would you have us declare war on France on his account?"

"And why not?" Germaine replied, moving quickly with the momentum she had gained to usher her visitor to the door. "You see, Herr Director, Monsieur Rocca is not only my good friend . . . but very soon he will be my husband."

The Police Director increased the surveillance by assigning an agent to the entrance of the Zum Römischer Kaiser and a team to pursue their prey. Though they did not attempt to detain the Baroness, the guards were tenacious watching and recording all her movements.

Madame de Staël turned cautious. She rarely left her apartment and warned Rocca to go out only in darkness and to wear Austrian clothes.

Fearing that anyone who visited her would be compromised, she advised her friends to stay away. Most of them ignored the warning and continued to call at her hotel.

Since the passports had not arrived from the Czar, Germaine turned again to Count de Stackelberg for help. She also made inquiries on her own. She learned that travel through Europe, once open and encouraged by heads of state, was in a huge net of Bonaparte's creation, entangled by restraints and shackles . . . handled by an inept, cowed bureaucracy.

In an effort to explore other routes out of Austria, Madame de Staël sent Eugene Uginet to foreign embassies located in Vienna for information. Soon, her suite was overrun with agents dressed in colorful, exotic costumes chattering rapidly in foreign tongues through interpreters. They represented Riga, Malta, Greece, Turkey, Cadiz, Sicily, Serbia, Portugal . . . all eager to strike a bargain.

Madame de Staël was confused by the alternatives.

Those who guarded her were bewildered by the chaos.

Twice everyday, the Director of Police called and pushed his way through the pandemonium in Germaine's drawing room.

"You must leave Vienna!" he would order raising his voice above the clamor.

Each time, Madame de Staël would sigh helplessly. "That is my objective, Herr Director."

Chapter 3
Poland

It was June 23, 1812, one month after Madame de Staël had slipped away from Coppet. Now, with Albert and Albertine, she set out in her golden equipage from Vienna for Russia.

On the same day, the Emperor of France declared war on that desolate nation of the Czars.

The Baroness did not know that her adversary, mounted on his white stallion, was leading five-hundred-thousand troops in the same easterly direction out of Dresden.

Under the pressure of the Vienna police, Germaine had departed without the passports from Vilna. Leaving Wilhelm Schlegel behind to await them, she left hastily after receiving an invitation to stop over at the palace of the noble family of Lubomirski in Lanzut, the capital of Galicia, once part of Poland and now under Austrian domination. She had sent John ahead in disguise to avoid detection. Eugene Uginet returned to Switzerland to confer with Auguste about where to meet his mother.

As she sped along rough dirt highways, Madame de Staël again encountered somber, forlorn Austrians bent under Bonaparte's yoke. When news of his advancing armies reached her, Germaine panicked, though the Emperor of France was hundreds of kilometers behind her. Physical evidence of his vigilance haunted her . . . printed placards with her name and description were posted outside all police bureaus. Jittery officials stopped her carriage and disputed the documents she carried that allowed her movement within the borders of Austria.

After a week of discomforting jostling, Madame de Staël's weary and bedraggled party reached Brunn, in Moravia. The yellow berline, now a dingy ochre, was beginning to show signs of buffeting and neglect.

As they registered in a small inn, the rumpled travelers were confronted by a local agent who informed them they would be detained in

Brunn indefinitely. There was no explanation.

Germaine was incensed. She called on the governor of the province, who proved as obdurate and unsympathetic as his lackeys. Shrugging, he told the Baroness, "I have my instructions," and showed her the dispatches that carried Bonaparte's own seal.

After three days, there were new orders from Napoleon.

"You must depart Brunn at once," the Governor told Madame de Staël, "and vacate Austrian territory posthaste."

"But I do not yet have the papers to permit me to cross the border into Russia," she protested. There was still a long distance her party had to cover . . . most of the province of Moravia and all of Galicia before reaching the frontier.

"That is not my concern," the Governor replied inflexibly.

Resuming the journey with her children, the Baroness urged her driver to proceed slowly, hoping Schlegel was not far behind.

Within a week, Madame de Staël stopped in the university town of Olmütz, where she was cheered by a letter from Juliette Récamier with news that Auguste had visited her regularly in exile in Châlons. Germaine worried about her son's unrelenting devotion to the beautiful woman and wrote her friend commending him to her care. She asked Juliette to encourage Auguste to leave Switzerland and meet her in St. Petersburg.

Crawling over the last kilometers of Moravia, the Baroness's carriage finally rolled into the province of Galicia. Here the people were even more oppressed than those to the west. Germaine was grieved by the wretchedness and deprivation of the once proud, freedom-loving Poles. The countryside was as dull as the people were downcast. Outside each posthouse, her party was ogled by groups of men standing listlessly . . . always the same . . . hawking Jewish merchants who traded throughout the provinces . . . pitiful Polish beggars with long beards wearing musty old Sarmatian costumes . . . frightening, hulking German spies.

A sullen agent or clerk, sometimes both, would emerge from the posthouse, walk slowly about the entourage, stick a burly head inside the coach, draw deeply on a pipe, blow acrid puffs of smoke around the occupants and stalk off without a word. But not without a nasty grunt at the driver to move on and a cuff at the horses to try to bolt the carriage.

Finally, just as Germaine began to despair of ever seeing Schlegel again, he appeared with the passports. The de Staël's had stopped outside the city limits of Lanzut before proceeding to the Lubomirski Palace, where they planned to spend two days resting for the journey across Russia.

It was a happy reunion. While Germaine and Albertine shared their experiences with Wilhelm, Albert left the coach to attend the frustrating routine of the police inspection in the posthouse.

"Soon, I will be able to leave behind me the oppression of Bonaparte," Madame de Staël sighed, relieved. "I shall never return to a nation that is his ally or under his jurisdiction."

"You have thwarted your tormentor," Schlegel replied.

"I am not yet beyond his shadow."

Wilhelm shook his head. "You need not fear him. He dreads the challenge of intellectuals and you are the inspiration of an ideological cult that opposes him."

"Perhaps. Yet, there have been times when Bonaparte could have destroyed me as he did the Duc d'Enghien. I suffer intolerable anguish because of him, but I sense that I dominate his will . . . preventing him from ordering me to prison or to my death."

Schlegel nodded thoughtfully. "Does he spare you because you are the daughter of Jacques Necker? Or . . . is it you? Does the challenge of stalking a brilliant woman excite him . . . like a hunter who is obsessed by the hunt but is disenchanted by the kill? He is a man of action . . . incited by the deception and fascination of battle but unable to cope with the idleness of peace."

Albertine interrupted. "Pardon me, Herr Schlegel," she said and turned to her mother. "Mama, why do you suppose Albert is taking so long?"

"I don't know, my dear," Madame de Staël replied. "The agent should have finished checking our papers by now. Wilhelm, will you go . . . " she asked.

In minutes, Albert, irritated and agitated, emerged from the posthouse with Schlegel. A surly, lumpish guard was close on their heels.

"The Captain has assigned this repulsive subaltern to accompany us as far as the Russian border," Albert explained to his mother. "My protest did no good. He has been briefed about John Rocca and every member of our family. He is to watch over you every moment. We also have been ordered to limit our stopover at Lanzut to only eight hours."

The guard gave the Baroness a vacuous smile and bowed obsequiously. Then, stretched to his full stocky height, he forced his way into her coach.

Madame de Staël recoiled. Schlegel helped her into the carriage, where Albert abrogated the center of the seat to separate his mother from the agent. Schlegel sat opposite, beside Albertine.

As the cortege drew up to the palace at Lanzut, Germaine saw Prince Henry Lubomirski waiting with John Rocca in the courtyard. Startled, she signalled before the guard recognized the lieutenant. The prince responded instinctively and warned Rocca who disappeared into the widespread chateau.

The nobleman maintained his composure and welcomed his visitors with casual grace. He treated the Austrian guard with respect, persuading him to allow his guests to remain the two days Germaine had hoped for. Meanwhile, Rocca kept to a remote wing of the complex.

The agent attached himself to Madame de Staël like a stray dog, wandering along behind her wherever she went in the palace. He stood at her side when she lounged in the drawing room, behind her chair at dinner. Germaine was humiliated by the inconvenience she caused her host and hostess.

When she prepared to retire to her chamber for the night, her guard announced that he would sleep in her room.

Albert de Staël was infuriated.

The Austrian was insensitive. "I must not let her out of my sight," he insisted boorishly.

"If you place one foot inside my mother's chamber," Albert bellowed, "I will pitch you out the window!"

"Ja Woll, Herr Baron!" the agent replied, bowing abjectly. Then he squatted on the floor outside Germaine's door and settled down for the night.

The next morning, Madame de Staël rose early. She had not slept. She thanked the prince and princess for their patience and hospitality and apologized once more for the loutish guard.

She departed Lanzut long before the expiration of her leave and set out for the Russian border determined to be rid of her jailer before the day ended.

Chapter 4
The Southern Plains of Russia

E h bien! I have always wanted to see the gilded minarets of Moscow," Germaine de Staël said with a wistful smile when she learned she would have to alter her course to St. Petersburg.

Her carriage had crossed the frontier into central Russia on July 14, the anniversary of the storming of the Bastille, the first day of the French Revolution. At the same time, the Grand Army of France had also moved in . . . its soldiers were occupying the direct roads to St. Petersburg. The Baroness had to divert more than three-hundred leagues, rerouting eastward by way of Moscow.

Across the border, John Rocca had rejoined the party.

They sensed something notably different about Russian Poland. The poverty and desolation were the same, but there was less oppression. And the people were not the barbarians they had expected. They were friendly, fearless, gentle, moving about with an air of coarse elegance . . . a Russian peasant nodding to every woman, regardless of her age, as he passed her on the road, and she responding with a bow. Though none in Germaine's party knew Russian, speaking only the language of the invading armies, they were treated cordially.

With an ukase issued by Czar Alexander which granted her unrestricted passage, Madame de Staël felt welcome on the vast plains of Russia

"We are happy to have you stay here at my chateau," her host, a Polish nobleman, told her when she made her first stop in Russia at Gitomir, the principal town of Volhynia. "But the French armies will enter our province within eight days."

The de Staël carriage hastened on. The Russian driver, pressing his horses at a gallop, encouraged them with a melodic chant, "Forward, my friends. We understand each other. Fly! Forward!"

But not even their lightning pace across the Ukraine countryside, with no sign of dwellings or inhabitants, relaxed Germaine's alarm of being overtaken by the Emperor of France. As her entourage raced through endless fields of wheat, she concentrated on composing her poem about Richard the Lion-Hearted to ease her fears.

On an afternoon late in July, the travelers approached Kiev, capital of Ukraine, with hundreds of small weather-beaten houses on its outskirts.

"Look," Albertine exclaimed, "from here the homes look like tents so the city resembles a moveable camp of nomads on a desert."

Rising in the midst of these fragile, humble huts . . . often swept away by raging fires and rebuilt again within days . . . were sturdy, towering palaces and beautiful churches boasting lustrous green and gilt cupolas. These were permanent structures that endured the elements. The bright rays of the afternoon sun danced with dazzling brilliance on the shiny domes, illuminating them as if for a holiday festival.

Kiev, like all Russian cities, bore no resemblance to any in Western Europe. Once inside its limits, Germaine found the city's arcane feudal atmosphere fascinating and deserving a visit. But, still fearful, she insisted they press on.

"We are well out of reach of the troops," Schlegel assured her. "Our entourage moves much more quickly than battalions of cavalry, infantry and artillery. We can stop here for two or three days and still be safe as we go north to Odessa."

Albert and John Rocca agreed. Together they convinced Germaine to make a stopover.

The party was greeted by the Governor of the province, Mikhail Miloradovich, and his wife and given the hospitality of the official residence for their brief stay.

Miloradovich, a vigorous, confident man of boundless good will, accompanied his guests on a tour of the city. When Madame de Staël expressed her anxiety over the impending battle, he reassured her that the might of the Russian Army would prevail over the invading French.

Within Kiev's urban environment, the Baroness felt she was at the gate of another world, closer to the East than she had ever expected to be.

The Russian men grew long beards and wore capacious, bright blue robes with broad scarlet bands tied about their waists. The women's costumes, in many vivid colors, reflected strong Oriental influences.

The Russians were devout, Madame de Staël observed. They never failed to make the sign of the cross when they walked by one of the many houses of worship in the city. Germaine marvelled at the regal majesty of the Greek Orthodox service, the idolatry of the ancient Grecian ritual, the splendor of the churches whose architecture drew heavily from the Turkish and the Arabic, and the heady fragrance of incense that clouded the air of the naves. The tunnels beneath the structures reminded her of the catacombs of Rome and she was moved by the masses of peasants who made pilgrimages on foot to visit these burial vaults from as far as the borders of China.

Back on the road to complete the nine-hundred versts to Moscow, Germaine feared she may have lingered too long in Kiev. There were signs that the battlefields were nearby . . . military couriers traveled in both directions in rough-hewn two-horse carts; the vehicles were so crude that when they struck a rut the riders were catapulted into the air from the loose wooden planks that served as seats. The Reserve Corps of Cossacks making their way slowly to join the regular Russian Army trudged along carrying lances and wearing coarsely woven, ill-fitting garments with large hoods. Their outfits were dull and colorless. There was no order to their march. But there was a transcendental aura about these untrained soldiers. They knew their country was being invaded and were inspired by a dedication to duty, discipline and a love of the motherland.

The monotony of the endless landscape brought crushing boredom to the de Staël party. "It's like walking on into infinity," Schlegel remarked. "We keep moving but never seem to advance."

At the halfway point between Kiev and Moscow, with fewer horses available because of military commandeering, Madame de Staël's concern that they might not escape from the battle area was renewed. The travelers had already experienced long waits of an hour or two for fresh horses at earlier stops. Now, as the time stretched to four, five and more hours, they languished at the height of the Russian summer, hot and uncomfortable, in the coach since there were no public shelters at the lonely posthouses.

And, they found little relief at the hostelries where they spent the nights. "Even the meanest French peasant has less wretched food and accommodations," Germaine noted.

After several grueling days, the de Staël party pulled away from the threatened regions and began to breathe more freely as they reached the town of Orel, and then Toula.

Here, deep in the heartlands of Russia, Madame de Staël was

surprised to find expressions of refinement and erudition among the people. Scholars called on her at her small suite in the local inn and amazed her with their knowledge of Western culture and philosophy. She was flattered when they commended her on her writings which they had read, studied and discussed. The aristocrats received her in luxurious apartments appointed with tasteful furnishings, handsome paintings and musical instruments that evoked memories of French pavilions and chateaux.

But she could not stay.

Drawing closer to Moscow, there was nothing to indicate that the country's largest city lay ahead. The wooden villages were as far apart as they had been in the South. Everything appeared lost in the openness . . . a farmer in the fields, a herd of cattle, a large noble residence. The terrain continued empty, as though abandoned by inhabitants. There was an eeriness in the silence . . . no birds fluttered or warbled to stir the stillness.

Late one afternoon, to escape the unbearable heat of their stuffy coach, Madame de Staël suggested they stop when she saw several women peasants returning home from work in the fields. They were dressed in flowing regional costumes in a kaleidoscope of bright reds, blues, yellows and greens. As the woman shuffled along through the tall grass by the side of the road, they sang melancholy Ukrainian airs extolling love and liberty.

Using the few words of Russian she had learned, the Baroness asked them to perform one of their native dances. They obligingly agreed, laughing and talking, their voices echoing a metallic quality, like striking bells, when they spoke certain sounds of their language. Germaine had not heard any like them in the dialects of the West.

The women danced with natural grace and modest voluptuousness. In their movements there was a mixture of traits . . . indolence and vivacity, reverie and vigor, and a kind of mild gaiety that civilization had not inhibited. As the tempo of the dance increased the de Staël party sensed the passion of these women . . . in their peasant ignorance they might be provoked, rousing themselves and their men to heights of violence and savagery and not easily curbed.

On the first day of August, Madame de Staël's carriage, crusted with the dust of road and field, sagging heavily under the weight of baggage, rolled drearily along behind a four-horse team like a lonely desert caravan.

Lusty sheaves of amber wheat, heavy with morning dew and nodding sleepily in the sunlight of dawn, extended into an infinite haze in the distance till the earth met the heavens without definition. There was no relief. No break. No horizon.

Except to the North.

There, against a blue-white sky, the gilded cupolas of Moscow slowly emerged through a misty expanse.

Chapter 5
Moscow

A warm breeze whipped briskly through the belfry in the steeple of the cathedral of Ivan Veliki, the highest point in the Kremlin. From below, muted voices of a choir and the full, sonorous tones of an organ wafted up the spiral stone stairway.

The Baroness de Staël and her daughter Albertine held fast the ribbons under their chins to secure their bonnets as they strolled around the bell tower. Walking close behind them, Albert de Staël tried without success to subdue his windblown, sandy hair.

It was a glorious day. The sun seemed to take delight in splashing its rays on the thousands of gleaming cupolas. The sky was a clear and liquid blue. The purity performed an absolution for Germaine, freeing her of her fears.

"It does not seem possible," she said, sweeping her arm over the vast panorama below, "that any human power could disturb the sanctity of this place."

But the Baroness could not deny that all Russia was in danger. The Emperor of France was amassing troops for a battle at Smolensk, less than one hundred kilometers to the west. Soon Bonaparte, himself, might stand there and view the entire city of Moscow just as the de Staël's were admiring it now.

They gazed down on the splendid palace of the Czars . . . other beautiful edifices in greens, yellows and pinks, sculpted ornately, like gigantic baked confections . . . the crenellated walls of the Kremlin flanked by towers of eccentric shapes . . . many of the city's fifteen-hundred churches with their glittering gold-and-mosaic minarets . . . the rushing silt-laden currents of the meandering Moscova River . . . and beyond, to the flimsy wooden homes of the populous in crammed, colorless masses.

The de Staël cortege had reached Moscow the day after Czar

Alexander had left for St. Petersburg. It was during the height of the summer season when most of the aristocracy deserted the city for their country villas. On hearing of her arrival, the nobles and their ladies scurried back to catch a glimpse of the celebrated Frenchwoman or, if they were lucky, to entertain her.

Madame de Staël was besieged by social invitations throughout her six-day visit and was taken on elaborate guided tours of the sprawling metropolis and the Kremlin.

The party was escorted through the interiors of the buildings of the vast complex . . . the ancient arsenals, the apartments of the Czars and the chamber dominated by the divided throne of Peter I who was responsible for introducing Western European culture to Russia, and his brother Ivan.

In the public buildings, open to all Russians, Germaine de Staël was struck by the evidence of wealth, generosity and charity which the nobility shared with the populace. Anyone could pray within the awesome opulence of the churches where walls and artifacts were heavily laden with gold and silver and inlaid with precious stones as startlingly colorful as peacock plumes. The hospitals were beneficently endowed with comfortable but spare accommodations and treatment facilities for both poor and rich.

Though here all Russians benefitted from the philanthropy of the aristocrats, Madame de Staël came to learn that a broad abyss separated the very wealthy from the peasant in their daily life and work. There were only two levels of Russian society. No middle class bridged the gap as in France.

Along the streets of the commercial district through which the party strolled, where the atmosphere was flavored by the Far East, the shops were filled with tantalizing merchandise of luxury that only the nobility could afford. Merchants wearing bright turbans and every manner of Oriental costume exhibited rare furs from Siberia, fabric and trinkets from India, porcelains from China, gems and carpets from Persia.

The Baroness observed more of this lavish exotica in the homes of her hosts. The garden and palace of the Razoumovskis contained the most extraordinary collection of plants and minerals she had ever seen. In Count Boutourlin's extensive library, which he had spent more than thirty years assembling, were countless volumes of priceless value, among them several books with notes in the handwriting of Peter I.

The de Staël party dined at the isolated estate of the Count and Countess Rostopchin at the edge of the city, accessible only by boat across a placid lake and then by coach through a forest. The gardens surrounding the elegant country house rivalled those designed by the most sought-after landscape architects in France.

Madame de Staël was fascinated. With Schlegel, she visited the university intelligentsia and learned that most of the professorships in the sciences and letters were held by Germans. "They are making a mistake," she told Schlegel when she realized that the Russians were imitating French writers. "They should develop a literature of their own and call on the writings of the Greeks rather than the Latins, since their alphabet is similar to Greek and their history is linked to the Byzantine Empire."

Wherever she visited the aristocracy, the conversation centered on the sacrifices that were being made for the war. The noble families donated large portions of their income to the government and turned over many of the peasants from their landed estates to the army. Some gave one or two hundred while one nobleman offered over a thousand for military service. "How does one *give* men to a government?" Madame de Staël posed to John Rocca not expecting a reply.

Most of the Moscovites who encountered the Baroness de Staël at the public events and private parties she attended were jolted by her appearance and disregard of decorum. Instead of the ambassadress of French style, taste and refinement they expected, they saw a heavyset, aggressive woman in bizarre clothes who preferred the company of men to women, took delight in dominating conversations and had a distracting habit of fingering a quill, a twig or a narrow reed. Russian noblewomen who had never been to France were far more graceful than she.

Nonetheless, Moscow was overwhelmed.

On her last evening in the city, the Baroness and her daughter entered the royal box at the ballet with Governor Milordovich and his wife. The eyes of the entire audience, from the farthest corner in the orchestra to the highest tier in the opera house, focused on Madame de Staël.

A patronizing Russian Countess leaned toward her husband and, in a hoarse whisper that carried far into the hushed assembly, said, "The Baroness de Staël is wearing another of her ridiculous turbans. She looks so old, she must be at least fifty. How can a matron so fat and ugly have the audacity to wear a gown meant for a woman half her age!"

The Count, continuing to watch Germaine, did not turn. "My dear," he replied to his wife with cutting sang-froid, "with her reputation and intellect, Madame de Staël would intimidate the entire court of the Czar if she made an entrance looking like a chambermaid!"

Chapter 6
The Conscience of Europe

The Union Jack waved from the mast of an English ship docked in the transparent waters of the Neva River.

"It is a favorable omen!" Madame de Staël observed as her carriage entered St. Petersburg late in the afternoon of August 10. She was encouraged by the sight of the flag, her first view of the port capital of Russia, and acknowledged it as a symbol of power and a portent of the future.

The Baroness's party had left Moscow sadly to resume the journey northward in order to avoid encountering French troops. On the outskirts, Germaine had asked the driver to stop briefly so she could watch the peasants on holiday basking in the sun. Women and children sat on the grass with hair drawn back and faces tilted skyward to take full benefit of the sun, which in this part of Russia penetrated grey skies only a few minutes at a time.

Madame de Staël envied these Russians their carefree innocence.

Her berline continued on over sandy ground and through rainstorms that washed away roads and turned the earth black. Farther north, the land turned marshy. The terrain was forever desolate and the mitigating groves of birch trees grew scarcer.

Though it was summer, the travelers sensed the shortness of the season and the threatening winter lurking behind clouds that continually blocked out the sun. Only the small villages with their dreary clusters of wooden huts broke the monotony. Here in the north, the houses showed signs of modest influence and the ingenuity of their residents. The windows were trimmed with arabesque carvings, the doorways, here and there, were flanked with columns and some of the facades were painted with Russian symbols.

Germaine's first view of St. Petersburg was a magical vision created by an enchanted hand to reveal all the wonders of western Europe and Asia flowering in the midst of a desert . . . one of the most beautiful cities in the world.

Built more than a hundred years earlier, the city was a marvel of engineering, a monument to Peter the Great who directed its construction with Paris and Versailles as his models. The Russian spirit conquered the forces of nature. Its people constructed St. Petersburg resting its foundations on a bottomless marsh in a relatively short period of time.

Upon their arrival in the capital, Germaine and her party moved into a suite in a building near the Neva River overlooking a small park where a massive statue of Peter the Great on horseback presided with regal dignity.

The city bristled with activity and excitement. It was the center of political intrigue for all Europe. Germans, Spaniards, Englishmen and even French émigrés, sharing a common hatred, rallied here to plot resistence against the scourge of the continent, Napoleon Bonaparte.

By nightfall, the foyer of the Baroness's residence bustled with foreign agents eager to call on her.

Among her visitors were the Prussian statesman, Baron Karl vom Stein, the English General, Sir Robert Wilson, the former French diplomat, Count Alexis de Noailles, and a Genevese author, J. A. Galiffe, who handled foreign correspondence for the banker of the Russian court, Baron de Rall.

"You are the conscience of an outraged Europe," Baron vom Stein told her. "I speak for all who come to welcome you."

"It is not I," Germaine replied, her dark eyes gleaming with pride and satisfaction. "It is the Emperor of Russia, Czar Alexander who has become the Chief Hope of Mankind, of the French as well as of their enemies."

"You are an inspiration," Stein asserted. "By your presence and with your encouragement, our young ruler will strengthen his resistance and confirm his faith."

Madame de Staël felt a sense of vindication. For ten years she had been hounded by the diminutive Corsican who restricted her travel, ridiculed her ideas and suppressed her writings. Here, she was embraced as a member and collaborator of the burgeoning movement to destroy him.

Her spirit was rekindled, her health appeared restored. She showed no signs of fatigue from the arduous two-thousand-league trek from Switzerland. In no time, she became the hub of the social and political life of St. Petersburg. Galiffe became her escort, interpreter and secretary. Accommodating and devoted, he squired her on rounds of the embassies and court functions handing her a flower or a piece of paper which she unconsciously manipulated as she spoke.

Meanwhile, the Emperor of France moved closer to Moscow. He had defeated the Russian Army at Smolensk and was mobilizing for a definitive battle at Borodino, only eight leagues from Moscow.

Madame de Staël held her tongue, fearing she would reveal her shock and chagrin.

"He came to me with an appeal from Bonaparte," Czar Alexander confided. "I was still in Vilna at the time and felt obliged to honor his request for a hearing."

Madame de Staël listened with uncustomary restraint to details of the mission her former lover had carried out for Napoleon. To avoid bursting out with the resentment she harbored, she forced herself to observe the thirty-four year old Czar . . . his appearance, his manner . . . anything to calm her. His clear blue eyes were alert and expressive. He had a distracting physical beauty with regular, almost delicate features. Despite the receding line of his blond hair, his head and profile were like those of a Greek God. His figure, tending toward fullness, was majestic.

"Count Narbonne wanted to persuade me to return Russia to the Continental System," he was saying. "He was eloquent and knowledgeable. His movements and style reflected his Bourbon heredity and the traits of his unfortunate cousin, Louis XVI."

Germaine did not want to be reminded, but how could she forget? The Czar knows Louis Narbonne and I were friends, she reflected. He may even suspect our intimacy. I cannot allow his actions to unnerve me into disclosing that he is the father of my sons. I have been aware of Louis' sympathy toward the Imperial Court of France. That, as well as his abandonment of me, I can rebuff, if not without pain. Now, however, he has defected to my enemy, serving my oppressor as a messenger and a lackey. He has betrayed me, my principles and ideals . . . the ones we shared that could have brought him honor.

Alexander, in a dark blue uniform with wide gold epaulets that gave needed breadth to his shoulders, stood with the slightly stooped air of a finely sculpted statue. "I was surprised when I was delivered the Count's message," he went on. "I received him almost immediately after he arrived in the city. He spoke confidently and expansively of the strength of the Grand Army but showed no hint of a threat. He implied that all we had to do was close our ports to British trade and the imminence of war would end.

"I told him that, as Czar, I have worked to uphold a political system which might lead to universal peace. I am prepared to risk an appeal to arms rather than besmirch the honor of the nation over which I rule. If the Emperor Napoleon is determined on war, and if fortune does not smile on our just cause, I informed Narbonne, Bonaparte's hunt for peace will take him to the uttermost ends of the world."

Alexander spoke with feeling and persuasive charm. Germaine was moved. Rather than interrupt, she encouraged him to go on.

"I realized the Count had not anticipated the power of my resolve," he said. "He had hopes of trying to persuade me. He gave me a letter from Napoleon that emphasized his desire for peace and assured me that even if our two Empires found themselves at war, his personal regard for me would remain undiminished."

Madame de Staël tensed, alarmed that the Czar might have vacillated, or worse, submitted.

"I did not alter my position," Alexander said. "I know he expected to stay several days to wait for my ministers to influence me and change my mind. I invited Narbonne to review with me two of my regiments on the next day and to join me at dinner. Of course, he accepted. That was the extent of my hospitality.

"The following morning after our day together, I sent three members of my retinue to call on him. They gave him a letter for Napoleon . . . a brief, coldly polite refusal to capitulate . . . and told Narbonne that his horses would be ready that evening for him to return to Dresden."

Germaine sighed deeply, freed of the weight of doubt. Her betrayer had lost. Narbonne had been forced to report a failed mission to Bonaparte.

"I had no choice," Alexander said, obviously anguished by the ordeal of his decision which assured war. "I rely on the loyalty of my subjects. I cannot subjugate them to the yoke of an invader. I cannot forsake even the serfs."

"Your people have a remarkable spirit," the Baroness said, impressed with the dignity and sincerity of this troubled man. "They have a reputation for invincibility that has brought your country many successes.

Your nobility have a natural pride and all Russians have an inherent inclination toward devotion and a deep religious fervor. They are an energetic people . . . it is rooted in their blood. All this together with their hatred of foreigners will rouse them to rally behind you."

Alexander responded with studied enthusiasm. "We are capable of achieving greatness. If a single man no longer dispenses evil in the world, I shall devote myself solely to improving my country. I will seek to establish laws guaranteeing for Russia the happiness which only I can assure. I have a deep desire to improve the lot of the peasants who are still subject to slavery."

"Sire," Germaine said with empathy, "your character is a constitution for your empire and your conscience is its guarantee."

"One of my deepest regrets, is that I have not been a great captain," the Czar replied.

"A sovereign is much more rare than a general. By sustaining your nation's spirit with your own example you achieve the greatest triumph."

"You are generous," Alexander said. "I must return Russia to its people. But it will be a long struggle. It is only a matter of time before Bonaparte enters Moscow. The thought saddens me. His conquest will be an empty one, for as they leave, my subjects will set fire to the city they love. Napoleon's victory will cool among the ashes of their homes and their churches."

Germaine was horrified. She envisioned the conflagration that was destined to envelope the beautiful city she left only a few days earlier. She shuddered at the passion of the Russians which would provoke them to defend their freedom with self-destructive violence.

"If Bonaparte takes St. Petersburg as well," the Czar pursued, "we shall go to Siberia. There we will resume the ancient customs of our ancestors . . . grow beards to our waists, eat potatoes and return to win back our land."

Alexander walked from the center of the room where he had been standing and moved toward a large window framed by heavily fringed draperies. He turned slowly and again faced his guest.

"Sweden is the key to our strategy. It has not yet declared its intentions and can play a decisive role in the political future of Europe. Sweden can tip the scale . . . either in favor of the French or to the Allied forces which we lead."

It was as Madame de Staël had deduced . . . her relationship to the

Swedes through her deceased husband, and her long friendship with Jean-Baptiste Bernadotte, who was now Prince Royal, could be valuable. Without thought, she leaned toward the large desk beside her and selected a jeweled letter opener which she fingered, unaware, waiting for the Czar's petition.

"It is here that we need your help. Within a few days I plan to leave for Abo to confer with your good friend Bernadotte. Though by rank and title he is heir to the throne of Sweden, he is much more than Crown Prince. With the declining health of the king, he is making all policy decisions."

"You have a difficult task ahead of you," the Baroness replied. "The balance is heavily weighted in Bonaparte's favor. First, Jean-Baptiste is a Frenchman." Germaine knew the dilemma Bernadotte would face. Her own loyalties had been tested severely since her arrival in St. Petersburg where allied diplomats condemned all Frenchmen along with Bonaparte. She was repelled by their vindictiveness. "He has served as comrade-in-arms with Napoleon and they share a mutual respect for each other's military sagacity. There is also a personal bond between them, a family tie. Bernadotte is married to Désirée Clary, sister of Joseph Bonaparte's wife."

"There are other hurdles," Alexander offered reluctantly. "As you will remember, four years ago we marched against Sweden and seized their territory of Finland. We still maintain a force of 20,000 troops on that frontier, which has strained relations between us and aggravated an unfortunate animosity." He hesitated. "On the other hand, the Swedes should be open to concession since Bonaparte's offensive threatens us both." Again, he paused, "I have hoped you might give me an insight into Bernadotte to help me understand him . . . his character, his principles, his candor, his sense of justice . . . before we meet. I do not expect to convert the Prince to the Russian and Allied cause . . . all I want is to convince him to continue to maintain Sweden's neutrality."

Though the Baroness deplored the idea of taking an active role in the battle against Frenchmen, she felt an excitement well up within her as she realized she could contribute to the downfall of the self-proclaimed Emperor of France.

"Bernadotte is a man of honor," she explained to the Czar. "He is a proud, stubborn Gascon with a strong sense of allegiance and a dedication to constitutional authority. He has committed himself to lead Sweden and would feel a deep obligation to uphold its interests. But if he were forced to make a choice, he would not hesitate to go to war against his former comrade. For his principles and his honor, he will act with unbridled passion."

Alexander listened intently. He tilted his head slightly toward Germaine to compensate for the hearing loss he had suffered as a child when he was quartered close to the Admiralty where he had to endure cannon fire for ceremonial salutes.

"You must understand the undercurrent of animosity that exists between the two men," Madame de Staël said. "Napoleon has never forgiven Jean-Baptiste for marrying Désirée Clary, Bonaparte's first fiancée. With fierce arrogance and in his unconstrained pursuit for power he broke their engagement to marry Josephine. Désirée was heartbroken but it is widely thought that Napoleon still loved her.

"And Bernadotte has pride." Germaine went on. "He controls his ambition for self-aggrandizement with elegant reserve. After all, in 1799, Bernadotte was a strong contender, along with Napoleon, in the race for the leadership of France. I am sure he still harbors a bitterness for having lost. So, you see, he may be convinced to take part in the coalition against Napoleon if he were made an appealing offer. I doubt he would refuse the Regency of France or its throne after Bonaparte's fall!"

A flash of hopeful surprise brightened the Czar's face.

Czar Alexander returned from Finland on September 3. On the following morning he met again with the Baroness de Staël.

"The Prince Royal of Sweden has given me a firm promise of neutrality," he informed her, without showing the enthusiasm Germaine had expected the commitment would have evoked. "He advised me about Bonaparte's military tactics, encouraging me that a retreat in depth by our forces would exhaust the Grand Army and rattle Bonaparte."

"A neutral position does not relieve the pressure on your battalions," Germaine said, sensing the disappointment he tried to conceal.

"I am fully satisfied with his zeal and his generous and loyal principles," the Czar replied, deflecting the remark. He had not expected more from the Crown Prince. However, with both the French and Russian armies poised for battle at Borodino and the people of St. Petersburg taut in the expectation of defeat, Alexander regretted that he had not pressed for military support from Bernadotte.

Madame de Staël anticipated Alexander. "You fear he may be coerced into changing his mind and his policy."

"Unfortunately, yes. The Swedish people are not sympathetic to my country or any of the allied nations. Their king's advisers are pressing to declare war on Russia and regain Finland. I could not hold Bernadotte responsible if he submitted. Should that happen while you are in Stockholm, please convey this sentiment to him."

The Baroness accepted this as an invitation, a request and a directive that she represent the Czar in further talks with Sweden's Crown Prince.

"Jean-Baptiste is expecting me," she told Alexander. "Since my sons bear the distinguished name of the noble Swedish family of de Staël, he has expressed an interest in discussing their careers with me for appointments in the Military or the Diplomatic Corps." She assured the Czar that she would install herself within the royal community and work for more than just fortifying the Crown Prince in his position of neutrality. She would urge him to ally himself with the enemies of Napoleon.

Madame de Staël prepared to leave for Stockholm at once. She had hoped that before she departed her eldest son, Auguste, would have joined her party. Instead, on her last evening in St. Petersburg, as she dressed to attend a farewell reception given in her honor by the foreign diplomats and Russian aristocrats, a letter was delivered to her from Switzerland.

The young Baron wrote that he had no intention of following his mother to Russia. Juliette Récamier, with whom he was still passionately in love, had refused to accompany him so he planned to stay in Lyons, where the Récamiers now lived. Though she did not encourage his ardor, Madame Récamier welcomed his company, for in her exile she had no other friends. Germaine was sympathetic but was concerned that her son was abandoning his family and the direction Jacques Necker had set forth for him. Yet, she knew that if she wrote a letter of gentle entreaty to Juliette she could persuade her friend to release him. There would be time for that when she reached Stockholm.

Madame de Staël made a grand entrance at her farewell party on the arm of her son Albert. There was no sign at the gala affair that indicated the fate of Europe was hanging in balance.

Chapter 7
Caught in a Storm at Sea

This looks like nothing more than a fishing boat," Madame de Staël fretted, eyeing askance at the vessel she was waiting to board for her journey to Stockholm.

The sky was overcast with heavy, dark clouds. The water of the harbor, reflecting the heavens, stretched out ominously cold, grey and choppy.

"My dear Baroness," Jacques Galiffe, her obliging escort, said sympathetically, "I am afraid it *is* a fishing boat."

The Swiss writer stood with Germaine and Albertine on the dock in Abo, the capital of Finland, where Czar Alexander and Jean-Baptiste Bernadotte had met just a week earlier. Nearby, the men of her party were overseeing the loading of the luggage into the ship's hull. Galiffe, who had accompanied the travelers, had offered to help them embark.

The Baroness was indignant. "You must find another ship . . . book us on anything else. This one would not withstand a strong gust of wind, let alone survive the rigors of a long sea voyage."

Galiffe was apologetic. "I am sorry, Madame la Baronne. All the vessels are about the same . . . the next might be smaller than this."

"The boats on Lake Geneva are bigger," she complained, envisioning catastrophes on the open waters of the Baltic Sea. Her imagination was fired by her fear of the sea and the unrelenting anxiety over her flight from Bonaparte and his armies. Germaine was insecure about spending days on a boat. Her only experience at sea had been in crossings of a calm English Channel.

The Baroness turned and with nostalgic longing looked back at the faded, travel-worn berline she was now leaving behind.

"Would you prefer, Madame," Galiffe asked, trying to be helpful, "to return to St. Petersburg?"

"Never," she retorted. Madame de Staël anticipated her mission in Sweden with the intensity of a poised fighting cock. And, she had come too far to turn back. The journey through Finland had been enlightening but she had no desire to repeat it.

Crossing the border from Russia into Finland, the travelers immediately knew that they had entered another country. Instead of marshes and plains, there were rocks, low mountains and forests. In the vast woodlands, the trees were the same pines and birches. Open fields along the roads were scattered with enormous blocks of granite that gave the land a stark vigor, emphasizing its barrenness since the vegetation grew scarcer as they traveled northward. The towns and villages were infrequent and thinly populated. The people in no way resembled the Russians in appearance or temperament. They had Germanic features, fair complexions and blond hair, and were gentle, practicing the sober ethics of Protestants.

Germaine had found lodgings along the way with pastors who welcomed visitors out of Christian duty. Since there were few Finnish lords or castles, these religious men were the leaders of the communities in which they lived and preached.

Madame de Staël viewed Finland as a dreary land. Short summers bestowed only brief intervals of sunlight. In winters that lasted eight months, the Finns were confined by heavy snowfalls and plagued by prowling bears and howling wolves. The physical struggle to survive against the rigors of nature contributed to the strength of the Finnish character but held nothing to attract Germaine. She longed for the purifying rays of the southern sun.

Even in the capital of Abo, in which a diligent faculty strove to encourage university study, the primary task was to maintain a tolerable physical existence.

Galiffe tried again to reassure the Baroness. "Everyone makes this crossing in these boats," he said. "They all have made the voyage safely."

Albertine also tried to brace her mother. "There is nothing to fear, Mama."

Hearing Germaine's protests, Augustus Schlegel approached her, placed his arm about her shoulder and pointed to a complex of buildings in the distance.

"Over there," he said, "is a prison in which Eric XIV, the most unfortunate of the kings of Sweden, was confined for months. Later he was transferred to another dungeon near Gripsholm, where he died. If he were there now, he would long for the crossing that terrifies you."

At last, the Baroness de Staël conceded. "I have little choice. I will take to the sea to avoid the prison cell to which Bonaparte would condemn me."

As she and her party boarded the ship, the other passengers ogled the bizarre company . . . the stout, turbaned French matron, the handsome, lame and adoring Rocca, the dapper, scholarly Schlegel, the jaunty, high-strung Albert and pretty, self-assured Albertine.

The boat disclosed no happy surprises. The vessel's cargo smelled heavily of fish, the stairways were steep, the corridors hardly wide enough to manipulate and the cabins cramped.

Yet, during the first days of the voyage, Madame de Staël admitted she had been unreasonably anxious, for she enjoyed the sailing. Though the sun never broke through the gloomy haze of the heavens, the days were clear and the sea gentle. As the ship made its way along the mainland and then among the islands, Germaine felt secure . . . she was still in sight of land. Later, when the water seemed to touch the sky on the horizon without interruption in whatever direction she looked, her apprehensions resurfaced.

Early one morning, Albert bounded into his mother's cabin with cheering news. "We can see the Aaland Islands!" he announced. "Tomorrow, we will be docking at Stockholm!"

Madame de Staël was relieved.

In mid-afternoon, the de Staël party now feeling sanguine strolled the narrow deck with other travelers, observing the islands in the distance.

Suddenly, without warning, daylight turned to darkness and a violent wind churned up the ocean. As strong gales buffeted the fishing craft, it bobbed precipitously on forty-foot waves.

Caught off guard, terror-stricken passengers stampeded to doorways as water washed across the deck. Albert de Staël held up his mother who was disconcerted and struggling to stand. Schlegel gripped a teetering Albertine tightly. Slowly, they made it safely to their cabin and huddled together as valises and other loose objects slid wildly about the floor.

As the ship tilted from side to side the captain gripped the wheel firmly and kept the craft from capsizing. Finally, after battling the storm for more than an hour, he managed to change course and veered the vessel toward one of the Aaland islands. Relieved, the travelers scrambled to disembark and waited for the storm to abate.

On solid ground and still shaken, Madame de Staël's courage began to return. Her party, with members of another as eccentric as her own, whom she had befriended on shipboard, ambled among the huge boulders and low trees inland from the shore. The woman of this group was the flamboyant Henriette Hendel, a famous German actress who was making the crossing with her two young daughters, her fourth husband, an historian scholar and her newborn infant in her arms.

Germaine and Henriette put together an impromptu theatrical performance to entertain the crew and the rest of the passengers.

On the broad sandy beach, a startled but appreciative audience applauded skits, dances, poetry recitals and pantomimes in which the plucky acting members of both families including the infant, took part.

Madame de Staël challenged the tempest into submission with a blusterous delivery of monologues from her role of Hermione.

The sea calmed.

The assembly gave the Baroness a roaring ovation.

Chapter 8
The Tide Begins to Turn

The clamor was deafening.

In the bleak great hall of the Swedish legislature, scores of agitated nobles and foreign diplomats milled about like frightened cattle, pushing, shoving, expostulating. The growing din bounced off the rafters of the cathedral-high ceiling and penetrated the thick blue and silver tapestries . . . depicting momentous events in Sweden's history . . . to reverberate against the stone walls.

The crowd was too nettled to observe the opening of the heavy carved oak doors and the two who entered, passing under the marble archway. Unnoticed, Crown Prince Charles-Jean, strikingly handsome in military uniform, escorted Madame de Staël to an empty seat at the front of the vast chamber.

Ignoring the uproar, he smiled down at Germaine. "Wait for me here," he said, leaning close to make sure she heard him above the dissonance.

The Baroness gave no indication of her astonishment. She was overwhelmed . . . impressed by her friend's unruffled comportment. Just seconds earlier, before they entered the hall, the Crown Prince strained to conceal his distress. He had been calm and in control but was obviously shaken. Now, completely composed, he showed no sign of fear or doubt.

It was September 24, 1812. The de Staël party had disembarked from their craft early in the afternoon, startled by the urgent cant of street hawkers:

"Bonaparte defeats the Russians at Borodino!"

"Thousands slaughtered in bloody battle!"

"The French occupy Moscow!"

Madame de Staël reacted swiftly to the disturbing news. She instructed Albert to engage a carriage immediately. Then, while the rest of her entourage stayed behind to wait for the unloading of luggage, she and her son drove directly to the gigantic, six hundred-room castle where they sought out the royal apartments. Jean-Baptiste, the Crown Prince, received them warmly. After briefly reviewing the reports on the Russian disaster with her, he invited the Baroness to accompany him to the legislative chambers.

Bernadotte and Madame de Staël walked through the eighteenth century structure along corridors overlooking the enclosed courtyard and at last reached the grand hall. From her vantage point, Germaine watched the Crown Prince mount the dais. At forty-seven, she observed, her friend revealed a mature prudence. He had subdued much of his youthful impulsiveness without losing his dash. His eyes were no less piercing. His height, his jet-black, curly hair and his aquiline nose lent an air of majesty to the future king.

Charles-Jean raised his hand . . . an aide rapped for order. Instantly the Prince gained the attention of the assembly as though a stroke of lightning had flashed to spread silence through the hall. He spoke with elegant and commanding ease. He confirmed the facts of Bonaparte's victory and the burning of Moscow. He was firm, precise and dispassionate, leading his audience slowly and deliberately to a daring, climatic prediction.

"I have served with the Emperor of France," he intoned. "I was one of his closest counselors before his latest wanton aggression against mankind. I have worked beside him, observing his moods, his mental processes, his military techniques and his fits of temper. I understand the patterns of his strategy and I know his vulnerabilities. He is a formidable adversary, but he is human. He, too, can err. One major mistake 'was to undertake the Spanish campaign. He has just made another . . . the invasion of Russia. This is his final and fatal, mistake. Though he will attempt to recoup his losses, retrench and rearm, he will *never* recover!"

There were murmurs of hope and pockets of cheering.

Prince Charles-Jean of Sweden had risen to the crisis and he acquitted himself with dignity and authority. For the moment, he had rallied the assembly and dispelled the sense of doom from the chamber.

Madame de Staël pondered the conviction of what she had heard. Were those hollow words? Were they meant only to allay the fears of the assembly and delay the impact of the Russian defeat? She was eager to believe Bernadotte. Yet, Bonaparte's occupation of Moscow confirmed his supremacy. Only a superhuman effort, she reasoned, fortified and sustained by the allied powers, could bring about the downfall of this ruthless despot.

The Baroness de Staël rented a spacious apartment on the Arsenalgatan, across from the opera house and near the Swedish royal palace, where she installed herself with Albertine, Albert, John Rocca and Augustus Wilhelm Schlegel. She unpacked most of her trunks and hired a steward and a staff of footmen and maids.

Germaine was entrenching for a long stay.

She was determined to persuade Bernadotte that he was the only man who could successfully oppose Bonaparte and to influence the leaders of the allied nations to rally behind him. Within four days, she had transferred the center of international intrigue from St. Petersburg to the capital of Sweden, and established her home as the headquarters of opposition against the Emperor of France.

Madame de Staël ignored the debilitating signs of illness that persisted in sapping her strength since giving birth to her last son, Louis Alphonse. The sea crossing aggravated her condition and the Swedish climate did not help. The weather was already cold and dreary and the anemic sun rarely broke through the murky skies. She turned regularly to opium for relief.

Yet her mind was as taut and as lucid as a steel spring. She was in an expansive mood. The Crown Prince, in consulting with her, let loose her infinite reserve of energy and her redoubtable Curchod spirit.

The Baroness took Stockholm by storm, entertaining on a scale unprecedented even for the Lady of Coppet. Her drawing room swarmed with foreign dignitaries. She talked, she intrigued, she prevailed. No one refused her invitation. First, the Swedes were curious, then they were impressed and finally overwhelmed, they were calling her receptions "conversational dances." When not hosting in her own suite, the Baroness de Staël went from embassy to embassy, from diplomat to diplomat. She had no time to visit the sights as she had in other cities. During her rounds, when she passed a museum, a theatre, a cathedral or some other tourist attraction in Stockholm, she would say to Schlegel, who often accompanied her, "Remind me to come back here before we leave Sweden!"

Germaine also resumed her writing at a furious pace. In the preface of an essay on suicide which she completed and published she extolled

Charles-Jean. She got Schlegel to write a pamphlet. *The Continental System in Its Relation to Sweden,* which was published anonymously and influenced public opinion in favor of the Crown Prince throughout Europe. John Rocca, always adoring but silently aching from neglect by the preoccupied Germaine, finished his *Memoirs of the Spanish War,* which condemned Napoleonic military tactics.

Madame de Staël conducted a steady flow of correspondence with agents in Berlin and Vienna and with Galiffe and Czar Alexander in St. Petersburg. Seeking support for the cause of Europe, she even wrote to President Thomas Jefferson in the United States. In reply, he recalled pleasant memories of Paris, when he had visited Germaine and her father. He condemned Napoleon: "It is by millions that Bonaparte destroys the poor, and he is eulogized and deified by the sycophants even of science," he wrote. "These merit more than the mere oblivion to which they will be consigned; and the day will come when a just posterity will give to their hero the only preeminence he has earned . . . that of having been the greatest destroyer of the human race."

The Baroness had deliberately selected her residence on the Arsenalgatan so she could be within easy reach of Bernadotte. They met at least once a day, either at the palace or her apartment. She encouraged him to discuss every issue and every problem that confronted him. He welcomed her understanding and often sought her advice. When not conferring in person, Germaine and the Crown Prince were in touch every hour by messenger.

Charles-Jean assigned Albert de Staël a commission as a second lieutenant in the Hussars of the Swedish Royal Guard, which the young man accepted with eager pride. He took to his duties zealously, dashing into receptions like a conquering hero, in the full trappings of his uniform, his plumed military hat under his arm and his sword, spurs and cartridge belt swaying at his side.

The Crown Prince was impressed by Schlegel's knowledge and his ability to assess and summarize critical, complex issues. With Germaine's blessing, Bernadotte asked the scholar to serve as his private secretary. She looked on, bemused, as the ivory-tower professor tackled the everyday business of politics and war. Schlegel at last had found himself. He was flattered when Charles-Jean, sharing his views, asked him to research and document methods of organizing a revolt in Germany.

During her collaboration with Bernadotte, Germaine was constantly reminded of the extremes and contrasts in his character. In private, her old friend revealed traits he masked well in public. His charm was irresistible, but if he were cornered or trapped he would react with sudden anger, exploding in a torrent of argument.

There were days when he brimmed with confidence and conviction, firm in the decision he had made, never doubting the ultimate collapse of Bonaparte's Empire. At other times he faltered, weakening under the pressure of advisers and ministers who wanted him to break his agreement with the Czar and declare war on Russia.

On these days, Madame de Staël bolstered and sustained him. "You are the only man in all Europe with the courage, the knowledge and the military perception to challenge Napoleon's offensive," she exhorted. She read dispatches to him that she received from her foreign correspondents confirming their support of her urging that he take the helm of France after Bonaparte's surrender.

She praised, cajoled and flattered him. "You are the union of genius and virtue, the savior of Europe and the hope of humanity."

The Prince did not protest or disagree.

Charles-Jean was grateful for Germaine's reassurance and counsel and slowly began to respond to her prodding. Cautious to avoid jeopardizing the security of Sweden and his own position as heir to the throne, he weighed the possibility of changing his neutral stand to a more active role in the Allied cause. It was not all beneficence, valor and sound advice that convinced him. Germaine had piqued his ambition for personal glory and his desire to even the score with Bonaparte.

Bernadotte in turn supported Germaine in her intrigue. When letters from Czar Alexander indicated the Russian ruler was wavering in his opposition to Bonaparte and might submit to a meeting to discuss the end of hostilities with the French Emperor, the Prince reviewed her drafts to Alexander, strengthening her arguments. "Bonaparte's position is declining," he wrote adamantly. "Morale among the French soldiers is low. It is only a matter of time before he acknowledges defeat."

The beleaguered Czar was finally braced. Reinforced by the barrage of letters from Stockholm, he stood his ground and returned Bonaparte's dispatches unopened.

In Moscow, the Emperor of France paced the floor in his Kremlin headquarters. Pausing impatiently at a window, he looked out on the blackened city that reeked with the stench of smoldering ruins.

"Incredible," he grumbled under his breath. "A stupendous decision! The people destroyed it themselves! And so many beautiful palaces!"

Bonaparte had entered the city on September 15, and was stunned to find the city in flames and the streets empty. The populous had fled.

On the first night he had been forced to vacate the Italian-styled palace he chose as his residence to escape the sudden blaze that was engulfing nearby buildings. Hundreds of Russian convicts had been freed to set fire to whatever structures were still standing. In all, eighty percent of the city had been destroyed.

But Napoleon found the area of the Kremlin still intact, with ample housing for his army in the ornately decorated residences of the aristocrats. Their well-stocked cellars held a supply of food and drink that would last the entire winter.

Buoyed, Bonaparte decided to press the Czar for a treaty, stay till spring and then continue on to conquer Persia and India. He sent a courier to Alexander in St. Petersburg with a dispatch suggesting a meeting to negotiate the peace.

Two weeks passed without a reply. He sent another message.

Napoleon grew restless. He studied records of Russian weather of previous years and learned that the first frost came to Moscow in mid-November.

Days passed in tedious monotony. Still no word from the Czar. The inactivity oppressed him. His impatience mounted. He became obsessed with the passing of time and the approaching winter.

Early in October, growing uneasy, Bonaparte decided to return to France. Without offering a reason to his commanders, he alerted them to prepare for the march. Then he delayed, vacillating, hoping to hear from the Czar. On October 15, the graying ashes of the city were covered by a clean blanket of snow. Three days later, in a surprise attack by the Russians, twenty-five hundred men in one of Bonaparte's cavalry units were killed.

He no longer hesitated. The next day, barely a month after its triumphal entry into Moscow, the Grand Army of France began its retreat.

The troops were well prepared for their trek. They had sacked the wardrobes and the larders of their Russian hosts. Most protected themselves against the elements in fur-lined boots and fur caps and coats they plundered. They carried enough food to last them twenty days, but only one week's fodder for their horses.

On the sixth day of the march, five thousand bloodthirsty Cossacks swooped down on horseback, scattering and killing many of the French and pillaging their supply wagons. Bonaparte barely escaped with his own life. Then the snows fell. Despite the forecasts, the frost came early. By the first of November, freezing temperatures, high drifts and the harassing Russian Army, assisted by vengeful peasants, took a devastating toll on the retreating Grand Army. During the last days of the month, the ice of the Berezina River, which Bonaparte had expected to cross easily, had been melted by an unexpected thaw into a torrent of rising rapids almost a thousand feet wide. While crossing a hastily constructed bridge over a narrow ford, the French troops panicked as the Russians became visible on the distant hills. The soldiers broke rank, crushing to death thousands of their comrades who fell in the stampede.

On December 5, unnerved by his routed army and with news from Paris of a plot against him, Bonaparte abandoned his pathetic stragglers. With General Caulaincourt next to him in one sleigh and his bodyguard, two aides, three valets and a Polish interpreter in two others, Napoleon took flight toward France.

Two weeks later, grizzled, bedraggled, unrecognizable in a matted great coat and hat, he skulked into Paris. Until he forcibly announced himself, his servants denied him entry into his own palace.

The next day, Bonaparte set about recruiting another army. Of the original half-million troops that had marched into Russia only twenty thousand survived the French Emperor's blunder.

Chapter 9
The Three Great Powers of Europe

It had been almost a year since she had last seen her son Auguste. He looked older than his twenty-three years and much more like his father, Louis Narbonne, than the endearing, mercurial Albert. He was taller . . . or had he grown? He stood erect, moving with effortless grace in a meticulous dark suit and high white cravat. His good looks had a distracting serenity, a quiet sadness.

Madame de Staël was relieved that Auguste had reached Stockholm showing no other ill effects of his separation from Madame Récamier.

The young Baron crossed the drawing room where the family gathered. Extending his hands to his sister Albertine, he drew her up from the sofa on which she had been sitting next to John Rocca. Holding her at arms length, he looked admiringly at her from head to toe.

"You have become quite the young lady," he said. "Your freckles have disappeared."

"Look harder," Albertine giggled.

"I don't see any."

"Silly," she replied disarmingly. "I still have them. Oh, they are paler . . . I cover them with powder."

"You are a radiantly lovely girl," Auguste said, letting his sister go. As she sat down, John Rocca adjusted the collar of her dress which had slipped from her shoulders and tucked back an errant auburn curl of her hair.

"Do you have any message for me from Juliette?" Germaine asked her son as he settled comfortably in a cushioned armchair beside her. She wondered if it were too soon to ask. Auguste had arrived late the night before and was still weary from the long journey. She had deliberately avoided any discussion of his activities during the last months fearing he might voice the bitterness his letters revealed when she wrote and asked him to join her.

Auguste stiffened. "No!" he replied flatly. "Madame Récamier left abruptly for Italy. I had no choice but to do as she suggested and follow you here."

Madame de Staël dropped the subject. So that is how Juliette resolved the problem, she reflected. In January, when her political manipulations were beginning to show results, Germaine had written her friend saying, "Send me my son in March." It was now May. Aside from the delay, Madame Récamier had done precisely what Germaine had requested.

"Miss Randall?" she asked. "And the Uginets . . . how are they managing at Coppet?"

"Fortunately, they have little interference from the authorities. Perhaps it is Miss Randall's inflexibility . . . she frightens them away." Auguste was no longer put out by the reminder of Juliette. "Everyone looks forward to the day you return."

"And so do I . . . if ever it comes. You said you saw Albert and Herr Schlegel?"

"Yes," Auguste responded readily. "As I traveled closer to Sweden I learned that Bernadotte was amassing troops at Hälsingborg. I altered my itinerary hoping our paths would cross. Luckily they did. I was overjoyed to find Albert and Schlegel with the Prince. Albert wanted me to tell you not to worry about him. He is trying to avoid trouble so you won't have to write to reprimand him."

"Dear Albert!"

"He approaches military life with gusto," young de Staël said. "Prince Charles-Jean treats him as a son . . . and greeted me in the same way. He has arranged for me to meet with the Minister of Foreign Affairs here so I can prepare for a diplomatic assignment."

"Bernadotte has taken us in as his family," Germaine said. "He is a generous human being and a great friend."

"He speaks of you with great admiration," Auguste replied. "He credits you for Sweden's decision to join the war on the side of the allies . . . and he explained how you helped create the Allied Coalition."

Rocca who had been silent, now leaned forward eagerly, his pale cheeks flushed with color. "Your mother mounted an international campaign of diplomacy worthy of a French military commandant," he enthused. "There was never a quiet moment . . . our suite buzzed with intrigue. The tempo built with such momentum that when Bonaparte returned to Paris in January every thing exploded. Europe's leaders at last realized that

Germaine was right . . . they had to unite to stop him. After that her plans fell into place."

Madame de Staël, with bemused satisfaction, watched these two men who meant so much to her. How rare it was to see Rocca so completely engrossed, gesturing and explaining. Her son Auguste alert, listening intently.

The ailing French lieutenant spoke animatedly of the private talks Germaine had held with the British Minister and others later that included Bernadotte, the two turbulent months of negotiations and the culmination . . . a treaty between Sweden and England.

"It was a joyous occasion for your mother when the Prince Royal announced Sweden as an enemy of Bonaparte," Rocca told Auguste. "Bernadotte was executing his part of the bargain when you met him at Hälsingborg. He was mobilizing thirty thousand troops to be transported to Stralsund in Prussia."

"Prussia's declaration of war against France was a crucial maneuver," Germaine interjected.

" . . . a result of meetings you, my dear, arranged between the Prince and the Prussian Minister von Tarach. It surprises me, Auguste, that your mother shows such modesty," Rocca said smiling. "Bernadotte fortified the minister who went on to convince his king, Frederich Wilhelm, to act."

"Oh, Mama . . . all this explains what I hear is circulating in the courts of Europe," Auguste said.

"What talk?" Albertine perked up.

"They are saying that three great powers have unified to destroy Bonaparte . . . England, Russia and the Baroness de Staël!"

The Baroness smiled ruefully. Her salon was strangely empty and quiet. She missed Bernadotte and Schlegel. She deplored the depressing Swedish climate.

"I have done all I can during the eight months we have been here," she said. "It is time to move on to England. We will wait there for the outcome of battles now being fought on the continent."

Chapter 10
Albert, the Impetuous One

The smell of fish, wet rope and salty sea air was no longer offensive to Madame de Staël. Instead, it seemed to lend a bracing quality to the atmosphere of the thriving port of Harwich which teamed with weathered sailors, bustling dock men and shuffling travelers. On shipboard everything about the sea intimidated Germaine. On firm land, she lost her dread of the ocean. She also felt secure, now that she had landed on England's east coast.

Though John Rocca did not complain, he was suffering from the arduous journey. Auguste and Albertine helped him board a hired landau where he sank down beside Germaine and rested his head on her shoulder. Wan, thin and weak, he held a handkerchief over his mouth to suppress his coughing.

"We'll arrange for you to stay in Bath till you recover," Madame de Staël suggested as they drove over the narrow cobbled streets of the medieval harbor town.

The carriage passed busy custom houses, the fine residences of prosperous merchants and the tread-wheel crane on the village green. The vehicle continued on along marshy plains where wild geese honked in formation overhead and sea gulls dipped crazily down to the water while others scurried briskly on spindly legs over the beaches.

Farther inland, Madame de Staël felt relief at last from the barren wastes and the piercing cold of Sweden. Here, the countryside was tranquil and freshly verdant. There were low-lying hills, rolling heathlands, villages perched on hummocks or nestled along rivers and ponds. Best of all, there was the June sun . . . long hours of dazzling brilliance and warmth. And a glorious sunset across the shimmering fens.

In Colchester, England's oldest town, the de Staël landau mounted the great Roman highway that extended more than a hundred kilometers southward to the capital. The road bridged several languid streams and skirted flourishing villages in which neatly dressed women tended tidy stone and thatched-roofed cottages and their men worked the rich, brown freshly ploughed outlying fields. Here and there large manor houses of stucco and timber stood proudly among ornamental gardens and high hedges.

After more stretches of meadowlands and market towns basking confidently under gentle skies, the travelers entered Epping Forest, the former hunting grounds of Saxon, Norman and Tudor kings, just north of London. The de Staël carriage and its four-horse team scattered herds of deer and flushed out flocks of birds seeking sanctuary among the thousands of acres of leafy sunlit glades, rough heaths and great hornbeam trees.

London itself was a surprise to the Baroness. It had changed since her visit twenty years earlier. Despite Bonaparte's boycott of British trade and the floundering currency, England showed healthy signs of unexpected economic growth. New housing spread out to the countryside from the city proper. Commercial and industrial establishments prospered. A sense of freedom prevailed . . . people's rights were protected under the law.

The wandering exile's entrance into English society was expectedly triumphant.

Madame de Staël selected a large Georgian mansion in Berkeley Square as her residence, and set about establishing a salon. She quickly wrested away the leadership of London social life from the distinguished, and stunned Edgeworth family.

Auguste de Staël, who worked at the Swedish Legation in London, and the poised, confident Albertine were charming adornments at the de Staël receptions. John Rocca had left reluctantly, packed off to Bath to take the curing waters at the fashionable resort.

Germaine found English aristocracy less restrained and discriminating than the French. At the affairs she attended in the great houses of Britain . . . and she was invited to them all . . . she was almost suffocated by the curious throngs. Otherwise dignified women, fashionably clad, climbed on chairs and tables to peer over the heads of other gawkers eager to get a glimpse of the female literary genius who had challenged Bonaparte and then barely escaped him in a flight across Europe. Elbowing her way among the crowds, Madame de Staël thwarted, at first, was unable to carry on a conversation or enjoy an interchange of ideas. A houseful of a thousand guests at a party was not uncommon.

But once this initial curiosity was met, Germaine was able to develop friendships with many of the country's leading political, intellectual and literary leaders. Intimate dinner parties were given her by eminent nobles . . . Lords Holland, Grey, Scott, Harrowby, Erskine, Lansdowne and Sir James Mackintosh and many more. She was delighted when the Prince Regent arranged to meet her privately at the home of Lady Heathcote, since protocol demanded that they be introduced before she could be invited to royal functions.

Even Lord Byron, who was contemptuous of any woman who aspired to write, succumbed to Madame de Staël's conversational charm. They became fast friends, and he was soon forced to admit that she was "a fine creature with great talent and many noble qualities immeasurably superior to other women authors."

The Baroness followed closely the tumultuous, changing scene on the continent and was kept well informed by the steady flow of letters from Bernadotte and Schlegel. The scholar continued to amaze and amuse her with his sense of importance . . . his latest was a command that he be addressed as Chevalier Schlegel, since he had been granted the order of Gustavus Vava by the Crown Prince.

Germaine encouraged discussion of the war in her salon and observed the reactions of her guests. When an armistice was declared between Bonaparte and the Allies, her drawing rooms were in an uproar. Austria's Foreign Minister Clemens Metternich was named moderator, since Austria remained neutral. Earlier in the spring Napoleon had won two significant victories at Lutzen and Bautzen in Germany with the three-hundred-thousand troops he had miraculously recruited and trained in less than four months. He was in no rush to negotiate. "I cannot make peace because I'm winning," he quipped. Then, word came from Spain that the French had suffered a numbing defeat at Vitoria at the hands of Britain's Duke of Wellington. Bonaparte continued to stall. Metternich grew impatient but agreed to a deadline for a reply to the proposed peace terms. The day passed with no word from Napoleon. The Allies denounced the armistice. Austria declared war on France and on August 17 the nations of the Coalition began to prepare for an all-out war against Bonaparte.

One evening before the armistice had been aborted, Madame de Staël was delivered a pouch from Schlegel that was heavier than usual. She was eager for news, having learned from Augustus Wilhelm that Bernadotte was nursing wounded pride for having been given a lesser command than he expected and for having graciously declined a cool invitation to the talks at Prague.

Germaine impatiently tore open the seal and drew out the thirty-page epistle. As she began to read she let out a piercing scream.

Albertine, who had just left her mother, burst back into the bedchamber.

"Mama! Mama! What's wrong?" she asked, seeing the pages of the letter on the floor.

"Albert is dead!"

Albertine was stunned. She stopped where she stood, petrified, looking like a pretty mannequin. But just for a moment. She rushed to the stricken woman and held her in her arms.

Madame de Staël grew suddenly and strangely calm.

"What I have feared for him for so long has happened," she said. Her voice was toneless. "He was not yet twenty."

She bent to the rug to gather the scattered papers.

Schlegel had done his best to break the news gently. But he knew the Baroness would want to be given all the details. He had gone to the town where Albert had died and interviewed everyone who had last seen him.

Germaine's grief became more acute as she read that her headstrong son had not been killed in battle but had fallen ignobly in a duel.

During his few brief weeks of military service, Albert had displayed a fierce penchant for bravery and astonished the more experienced, courageous men in his corps. He acted with reckless ardor, seeming at ease only when his life was threatened, volunteering for duty where he would be exposed to danger. Madame de Staël recalled that when he had left with the Crown Prince, Albert had said to her, "I will cover myself with glory or return no more." War had been what he lived for.

While on leave he had drunk, gambled and debauched in excess . . . but always with transcendent panache that made him a favorite among his companions. His mother had written him to control his indulgences and refused to pay his debts unless he complied. Bernadotte reprimanded the exuberant youth and had him confined for a week on the Swedish island of Rugen . . . punishment which he levied out of deep concern and affection for the son of his friend.

When young de Staël returned to duty, the Crown Prince relented and granted him leave at Doberan, a small resort with a gambling casino on the coast of the Baltic Sea. Charles-Jean had extracted a vow from Albert that he would not gamble, but the carefree aide-de-camp could not resist temptation. He led the fast playing and the heavy betting at the gambling tables. Toward dawn a quarrel erupted among the soldiers in the casino. A Prussian cavalryman challenged Albert to settle the matter with swords.

"The encounter took place," Schlegel wrote, "in a clearing on top of a wooded knoll in a lovely grove." The devoted scholar had tried to learn more when he heard rumors that Albert had not put up a defense. There was no duel. The first thrust of his opponent's long, formidable sabre severed Albert's head from his body.

Madame de Staël wept silently for the son who had so tenaciously shielded her during a torturous journey across Europe.

Chapter 11
Dilemma

I delight in it. I like it prodigiously. I read it again and again," Lord Byron told Germaine.

"The voice of Europe has already applauded the genius of the author of *Corinne,*" Sir James Mackintosh wrote in the *Edinburgh Review* of Madame de Staël's latest published work. "Her current book is the most vigorous effort of her genius and probably the most elaborate and masculine production of the faculties of woman. Her chapter on taste is exquisite. The part on metaphysical systems is a novelty in the history of the human mind and the conclusion is most eloquent. In its entirety, the work, for its variety of knowledge, flexibility of power, elevation of view and comprehension of mind is unequalled among the writings of women and not surpassed by many among those of men."

The critics outdid one another as they heaped accolades on Madame de Staël's *De l'Allemagne.*

Soon after she arrived in London, the Baroness had contracted with the English firm of John Murray to publish her manuscript on the people, the manners, the philosophy and the arts of Germany. In the preface she related the incident of Bonaparte's confiscation and pulping of the original printing in France and how she had concealed a single copy in her luggage through her year-long flight from Switzerland. The British, accustomed to freedom of thought, speech and the press, were shocked by the Emperor's petty, preemptory actions. They clamored for the book. Within three days after copies appeared on the shelves in bookstores in early October, the first printing was sold out.

Madame de Staël was already sought after, feted and toasted as London's social and political luminary. Now, as the literary lioness of the season, she was in even greater demand. She made command appearances with élan. To all English society and even to her close friends, Germaine appeared exuberant, energetic, sparkling and witty. She was caught up in a torrent of activity. She corresponded prodigiously with statesmen on the continent and started another book, *Reflections on the French Revolution.*

When she paused, she would slip into deep depression, grieving for Albert and worrying about her health and that of John Rocca, who had moved into London. To avoid offending the proper English, Madame de Staël arranged for John to stay in a small hotel nearby. He had contracted tuberculosis and his leg injury, aggravated by the hazards of travel, pained him.

Only her son and daughter could understand their mother's suffering and were able to comfort her. "I don't know what I would do without Auguste and Albertine," she wrote in reply to a message of condolence from Juliette Récamier. In a letter to Schlegel, she said, "My book is a howling success. But nothing lifts the weight from my heart. Since our separation and Albert's death, I feel isolated. My health is destroyed. In short, it hurts me to live and I know of no other remedy than the sight of you."

The turn of events on the continent added to Germaine's distress. She endured the torment of conflicting emotions and loyalties. The English papers reported the catastrophic defeat of the Grand Army of France after the Battle of Nations at Leipzig and the retreat of Napoleon. The Baroness de Staël had pangs of guilt about riding the crest of celebrity in London while the fate of France and Europe was being decided on the battlefields in Germany.

As early as her first encounters with British ministers in the spring, Germaine had sensed a shift in strategy for the political future of France after Bonaparte's defeat. The English government was devising its own blueprint for a new France that did not include Crown Prince Charles-Jean of Sweden. England was determined to push back French borders to old frontiers, eliminate many of the freedoms it had won during the Revolution and restore the Bourbon dynasty. With a subdued France and a handpicked king, Louis XVIII, on the throne, England's leadership of the world could not be challenged.

Madame de Staël felt tainted. She had hobnobbed with many members of the Bourbon family who were in exile in England. The Duke Pierre de Blacas, Louis's prime minister, sent Count Edouard Dillon to call on her. When he asked her to lend her pen and her voice to their design for restoring Louis to the throne, she knew Bernadotte's acceptance as leader of France was waning.

"My opinion would carry no weight," she demurred.

Dillon pressed. "But surely, you have great influence. You are considered the first woman of Europe."

The Baroness parried and made no commitment.

While Bonaparte had scourged the continent, his demise had seemed remote. Now, with his defeat imminent, Germaine was forced to acknowledge reality. The fate of Napoleon could not be divorced from that of France. The downfall of the Emperor would bring about a broken France.

On December 31, 1813, the Allied forces crossed the Rhine.

Madame de Staël recoiled from the truth. France was being invaded!

Her English friends could not fully comprehend her dilemma. They had watched her survive the terrors of the Revolution and escape the persecution of the Imperial Bonaparte while others . . . statesmen, writers, philosophers . . . succumbed to compromise and bribery. She had been faithful to her principles, invincible in her conscience. A solitary opponent . . . a formidable woman!

Surely she had reason to celebrate.

"You must be delighted by the Allied victories," a British cabinet minister said to her. "What direction will France take now?"

"I hope Bonaparte will win and be killed," she replied. "France should have two armies . . . one to destroy the enemy, the other to overthrow tyranny."

Tormented, she wrote to her son Auguste, who had left to join Bernadotte in battle. "This blow is cruel. All London is intoxicated with joy and I alone in this great city suffer from the events. They congratulate me. What for? My despair?"

Madame de Staël had to accept the outcome. She had contributed to it.

Paris fell to the Allies on March 30, 1814.

Even in defeat, Bonaparte was ennobled by an aura of grandeur. His officers parted in sadness from the man with whom they had shared so much glory. Their leader was the military genius of all time. The honor he had brought France would remain a vivid memory.

On May 4, Napoleon Bonaparte, former Emperor of France, arrived at the Island of Elba, an exile from the world.

A few days later, Germaine de Staël, no longer an exile, left England for her homeland.

Chapter 12
Paris Restored

A lbertine de Staël held tight to the railing on the deck of the ferry as it skimmed the silvery, deep blue waters of the English Channel. The surface was as calm and sleek as a mirror. On the horizon to the south, through a chilly fog that was fast disappearing, the outline of buildings in the port of Calais were becoming discernible.

A sudden gust of cool, clear air caught the young woman off guard and tilted her high, small-brimmed velvet hat askew. As she turned to adjust it, she saw her mother approach on the arm of Augustus Wilhelm Schlegel. The scholar had rejoined the de Staël family in London after the Allies occupied France.

"Isn't John coming up?" Albertine asked.

"He's resting until we disembark," Schlegel replied.

"Then he will miss our first wondrous view of France," Albertine said, disappointed. "Look . . . there!"

Madame de Staël was distracted from the sight of her country by the lovely vision of her daughter in an ensemble just acquired in London. Albertine wore a fashionable azure spencer in the same velvet as her bonnet, trimmed in red, a crisp, narrow white ruff around her neck, a full white skirt embroidered at the hem with tiny pink flowers. An edging of petticoat lace peeked out just above her velvet slippers. She is almost seventeen, Germaine reflected, and ready to marry . . . it must be to someone she loves.

Then the Baroness looked toward France.

Albertine revelled in the view. "Over there," she bubbled. "The beaches are so beautiful . . . they stretch out so far and are so flat. And the sand . . . glistening in the sunlight!"

The thrill of landing on French soil was marred for Madame de Staël as she walked down the gangplank at Calais. Soldiers in the intimidating uniform of the Prussian Army, shouldering rifles, paced the dock. More were stationed at street corners, at public buildings and at the base of the imposing belfry tower of the fifteenth-century town hall. The Prussians were certainly in command of the city.

Rocca tried to make light of the troops. "It is to be expected," he explained. "We are close to the border."

But with every soldier she saw, Germaine grew more distressed. "I'll not stay here any longer than we have to," she said. "Wilhelm, instruct the driver to leave for Paris at once!"

Even as the coach-and-four sped along the popular-lined roads across terrain where canals meandered through fertile low-lying farmlands and windmills dotted the landscape, they were forced to slow to permit Prussian cavalry and small patrols to pass.

As the travelers reached Picardy, the countryside was more familiar and marching troops were fewer. The highway was bordered by rich, damp pastures with contented, grazing cows. Fields were beginning to green with crops of chicory, cauliflower and leeks. The land was flat and waterways and marshes formed oddly shaped islets crowned with small stucco houses and gardens. In the distance, willow trees and majestic elms stretched up to vivid cerulean skies.

The steeples of the imposing Gothic cathedrals at Amiens, then Beauvais and the domed turrets of the romantic chateau of Chantilly moved Madame de Staël to impatience for the splendor of the capital of France.

At last, the gates of Paris!

Foreign guards permitted them to pass without incident or inspection.

Germaine remained silent during the ride through the city until the carriage wheels and horses' hooves clanked loudly on the stone of the boulevards along the Seine.

"I feel I am having a painful dream," she said. "Are we in Germany? Or is this Russia? I see styles of architecture in the houses, churches and palaces that declare we are in France. But everywhere there are Russians or Germans!"

In the Bois de Boulogne and along the Champs Elysées, burly, bearded Russian foot soldiers in baggy pantaloons cooked meals in large iron pots suspended over wood fires. The odor of burning logs, boiling meat, and garbage, mingled with clouds of smoke and drifted into the de Staël coach. Within the city, uniformed soldiers crowded shoulder to shoulder with street vendors; cocoa makers dispensed their steaming brew from large leather barrels strapped to their backs; sausage sellers sold roasted meat from small charcoal stoves on trays suspended from their shoulders by broad hide straps.

Madame de Staël was offended. Foreigners were violating the spirit of Paris.

At night, the lighted streets took on a carnival atmosphere. Officers, in full regalia and with weapons in their belts, strutted through the galleries of the Palais Royale to gamble and bargain for the favors of willing ladies of the evening.

Seeking escape from the occupying forces at the Opera House and the Théâtre Français, Madame de Staël was disappointed there, too. Russian sentinels guarded staircases and the audience wore the uniforms of the invaders. The music, the dance, the sets, the performances . . . all were the same. French perfection and style were being set before sabres and flowing mustaches. Actors and artists bowed obsequiously to amuse the conquerors. Not a single French officer in familiar tri-color uniform graced the assembly.

So, the Baroness de Staël spent her time either in her manor house on the rue Royale or in the drawing rooms of friends.

In these settings, she began to experience a quiet contentment in her personal life. She was reunited with those who meant most to her. Olive and Eugene Uginet put her house in order and maintained it with meticulous care. Fanny Randall took charge of her mistress and John Rocca, chiding them both for neglecting their health. Juliette Récamier, who at thirty-seven had lost none of her beauty, was again her constant companion. Her son Auguste, who had either conquered his passion for Juliette or chose to conceal it, was assigned to the Swedish embassy.

Though she was often in physical pain, Madame de Staël refused to acknowledge failing health and fought off depression by setting out, indefatigably as always, to reopen her salon.

Her drawing rooms took on a flamboyance that had emblazoned them during the Directory.

The political, intellectual and military leaders of Europe came, as before, to pay their respects, to renew friendships and enjoy the de Staël hospitality. They left inspired, again, by her enthusiasm and vitality. Among them were Alexander of Russia, Metternich and General Schwartzenberg of Austria, England's Duke of Wellington, Freiderich von Gentz, the Bonapartes who had defected, Mathieu de Montmorency . . . they all came.

Everyone but the Prince Royal of Sweden. Germaine was disappointed that Bernadotte had stayed in the city only two weeks after the Allied entry. He left when he discovered that Charles Talleyrand had, once again, artfully straddled the change in governments. The tergiversating former bishop had influenced Czar Alexander to restore Louis XVIII and manipulated for himself the post of Foreign Minister. To his credit, Talleyrand was recovering much of its dignity for the defeated France. Jean Baptiste, accepting the outcome with grudging yet good grace, wrote to Germaine, "I would rather be wise than brilliant" and returned to Sweden with honor, assured of a strong position within the European community.

Her reentry into the center of Paris's elite society after ten long years in exile was the Baroness de Staël's greatest personal triumph.

Her book *De l'Allemagne*, printed in Paris, Geneva and Milan, came in for fresh praise with each edition. In Germany, Goethe hailed the work as a wedge breaching the wall that had barricaded German literature from the rest of Europe.

Germaine's celebrity was reconfirmed.

"He bears his glory as if it were of no consequence," the Baroness Anne Louise Germaine Necker de Staël-Holstein said to Juliette Récamier as they descended the wide marble staircase of the mansion on the rue St. Florentin, that was the home of the Prince de Benevento, Charles Talleyrand, Foreign Minister of France.

The Baroness referred to the Duke of Wellington, the hero of Vitoria, who looked up at them from the base of the stairs among a glittering gathering of international personalities. The flames from the hundreds of tapers in the crystal chandeliers cast dancing shadows on the damask walls of the huge reception hall. The military uniforms dazzled . . . royal blue, yellow, red, hunter green, maroon . . . sporting gold, steel and silver buttons, buckles, swords and medals of blinding polish. Women were in fashions that reflected a return to the monarchy. They wore gowns lavishly ornamented with lace, embroidery and ribbons. Most were white but some were in pink, pale blue or soft green gauze and silk tulle. Skirts were bell-shaped, many tier-on-tier with hems stopping just above dainty, heelless slippers.

Juliette flushed and held her fan up to her eyes, clear and radiant, that only now began to evidence slight lines creeping out from the corners.

Her skin was still a translucent alabaster above the white she always wore, her lithe figure concealed under the full folds of her gown. She had never stopped playing the coquette. The Duke of Wellington, bewitched at their first meeting, enlisted Germaine's help in his pursuit of her.

Madame de Staël moved quickly down the steps, holding the banister as she went. Her gown hung loosely about her almost sunken body, less full than it had ever been. But no one observed how she had changed. Her spirit was still expressed through her dark amethyst eyes.

As the two friends reached the last step, they breathed the quiet fragrance of flowers and French perfumes that pervaded the mansion.

The event was another extravagant affair arranged by Charles Talleyrand, this time to honor the Baroness de Staël, his longtime friend, his unflinching adversary.

Moments before she reached Wellington, Germaine whispered to Juliette, "Never did nature make a great man at so little expense!"

The Duke bowed slightly, first to Germaine and then to Juliette. He was tall and regally handsome. His uniform was imperial scarlet, with a wide, gold-braided collar that touched his sensually protrusive jaw. He extended his arm to the Baroness, who took it smiling politely. Juliette's white-gloved hand barely touched the Duke's other arm. He escorted them to a thronged drawing room in which guests were assembling.

"I cannot reconcile political liberty," Madame de Staël said to Wellington, "which you English profess, with the servile customs that remain between individuals in your country."

"Words and formalities shock no one in a truly free society," the Duke replied. "We maintain our old traditions to do homage to the past, just as an old monument is sustained when the original object it represents no longer exists."

At the end of the chamber, Wellington guided the Baroness to a throne-like armchair while Juliette remained at his side. Officers, diplomats and their ladies gathered around the honored guest.

"Is it true," Germaine asked, "that your Lord Chancellor kneels when he speaks to the King in Parliament?"

"It is true."

"How is it done?"

"Why, my dear Baroness," he laughed, "as I say, he kneels before the king!"

"But how?" Germaine persisted, her eyes dancing, taunting.

"Shall I show you exactly how?" the Duke of Wellington offered.

"If you would."

The victorious general of Vitoria complied. He kneeled at the feet of the Lady of Coppet.

"What happiness if one could be queen for a day," Madame de Staël murmured as she rested her hand on the kneeling Duke's shoulder. "What wonderful things one could say!"

From far across the room a deep, sonorous voice broke the solemnity of the play-act of ritual.

"All the world should see this!"

The guests turned to see who had spoken. They moved back, opening a narrow corridor to let him pass.

Their host, the Prince of Benevento, Foreign Minister of France, walked slowly, with the familiar trace of a limp, through the crowded drawing room. His suit was black velvet, his face ashen above a high-collared, white ruffled shirt. He bore his ensemble with ardent, meticulous indifference. Leaning heavily on his cane, he advanced toward Germaine, searching out her eyes with a direct, unyielding gaze. She returned his appeal with a cold, steady glare. The meeting-points of their lives flashed through her mind's eye. This man had been friend, lover, mentor, mendicant, deceiver.

There was an awesome aura, an exaltation about him. His dynamism, his grace were unchallenged. His presence was all-encompassing.

The Duke rose and moved standing alongside Juliette Récamier as Talleyrand approached.

"My dear Madame la Baronne de Staël! You are a woman of courage and intellect. Your spirit is indominatable. Through your single-mindedness, your perseverance in opposing Napoleon Bonaparte, you set an example for all the people of Europe." Talleyrand's voice was barely above a whisper, yet it was heard clearly by the hushed assembly. "The former Emperor of France acknowledges you as a formidable antagonist. Despite his confinement at Elba, he hopes he may one day be reconciled with you."

A murmur drenched the chamber.

Germaine did not reply. Only her fingers gripping the arms of her chair indicated that she had heard his remarks.

"Now," Talleyrand resumed, "I speak for myself."

He turned to a footman in his wake and took from him a purple velvet box tied with a golden strand. The Prince de Benevento held the gift out to the Baroness.

She untied the bow and removed the lid.

Inside lay a miniature scepter of gold. She picked it up by the staff and displayed it. The guests exclaimed in wonder. The hilt was a small bust carved in ivory, in the image of Germaine de Staël!

The Baroness smiled, remembering Talleyrand's earlier gift to her of the ivory letter opener with the bust of Hatshepsut, Egypt's most powerful queen.

"Germaine, my dear. You richly deserve the position you hold. You have earned the power you wield! You are the consummate woman . . . your dedication and determination have been largely responsible for the peace and unity we now enjoy.

"In France, in Europe . . . you are rightly Queen!"

Epilogue

Germaine de Staël and Napoleon Bonaparte never again came face to face.

The Baroness did not deliberately avoid her oppressor but neither did she attempt to retaliate for the years of suffering he had caused her. Indeed, on one occasion she was responsible for saving his life.

During the summer of 1814, spending time at Coppet after her glorious, frenetic reception in Paris, she learned from a guest that a group of royalists planned to murder the former Emperor. Summoning a calèche, she rode off to the chateau in nearby Prangins where Napoleon's brother Joseph resided. There she revealed the plot and proposed continuing to Elba herself to warn Bonaparte. Phlegmatic Joseph calmed her and suggested that someone less visible act as courier. Alerted, Napoleon was able to thwart the assassins and sent a message expressing his gratitude to the Baroness.

Germaine withdrew from active participation in the affairs of government but maintained a keen interest in politics, expressing her views in pamphlets, and books she continued to write. She stayed aloof from Bonaparte's aborted one-hundred-day return to France and his final defeat at Waterloo on June 18, 1815 as well as from the reign of Louis XVIII. She considered the restored Bourbon regime reactionary, differing little from the Empire with its press censorship, its limitations on political rights for the masses and its efforts to revive the *ancien regime.*

Her family became Madame de Staël's primary concern. Preoccupied with her finances and her daughter's future, she vigorously petitioned Paris for the repayment of Necker's two-million-livre loan. When the King finally granted her request, she used most of the funds for Albertine's dowry. She was delighted that her daughter made a love-match in her marriage to the Duke Victor de Broglie, whose politics happily agreed with Germaine's.

Though she suffered from the ravages of opium and her own

declining physical condition, Madame de Staël nursed John Rocca who was failing as rapidly as she. Making certain that their union would remain secret until after her death, she married her youthful lover and provided for him and their child in her will.

During her last years, Germaine was surrounded by a coterie of her close friends and was grateful for the unwavering devotion, particularly, of Schlegel, Mathieu de Montmorency and Miss Fanny Randall. She continued her travels, visiting Italy and journeying seasonally to Paris and Coppet, where she continued to entertain extensively. When she was too ill to leave her bed, she often called on Albertine to take her place as hostess in her crowded drawing rooms.

At the age of fifty-one, on July 14, 1817 (the anniversary of the storming of the Bastille), with Miss Randall at her side, the Baroness de Staël died of a stroke from which she collapsed while attending a ball in Paris. John Rocca died six months later. Her body was returned to Coppet and placed in a casket in the family tomb at the foot of the black marble basin where her parents lay. The mausoleum was sealed forever. To this day it has never been opened.

Madame de Staël's dream of a French constitutional monarchy was fulfilled in 1830, when King Louis-Philippe mounted the throne and ruled for eighteen peaceful, progressive, prosperous years. She would have rejoiced had she lived to know that her son-in-law was Minister of Foreign Affairs during that period.

Both the Baroness's sons, Auguste and Alphonse, married but left no heirs. Her line continues through her daughter. Her descendants include historians, scientists and distinguished statesmen. Many serve France today.

Bonaparte outlived his exasperatingly persistent adversary by less than four years. He died in exile on St. Helena on May 5, 1821. He was also fifty-one years of age. He had devoted his time in lonely isolation to writing his memoirs, which contain several references to the Baroness de Staël. A significant passage concerns his persecution of the authoress during the *De l'Allemagne* incident. "I read her last work while on the Island of Elba," he wrote, "but I found not a single idea in it which should make it prohibited." Yet, at the time, he had banished the author from France.

Napoleon's only legitimate heir, his son, Napoleon II, died without issue in Vienna at the age of 21. Bonaparte's nephew, son of his brother Louis and grandson of his wife Josephine through her first marriage, was King of France from 1848 to 1852 and Emperor Napoleon III for eighteen years thereafter. Eventually, in 1873, he too lost the throne and died in exile.

It is fascinating to contemplate what the destiny of the world might have been if these two strong-willed personalities . . . the visionary ideologue, Germaine de Staël, and the reactionary, charismatic opportunist, Napoleon Bonaparte . . . had blended their genius to rule Europe!